THE STORY OF ALL OF US

MANKIND™

MANKIND THE STORY OF ALL OF US ™ Volume Two, November 2012. First Printing. Published under license by Silver Dragon Books, Inc., 433 Caredean Drive, Ste. C, Horsham, Pennsylvania 19044. Silver Dragon Books and its logos are ® and © 2012 Silver Dragon Books, Inc. All Rights Reserved. Printed in Canada.

THE STORY OF ALL OF US

MANKIND

FOR SILVER DRAGON BOOKS

EXECUTIVE EDITOR
JOAN HILTY

TRADE EDITED BY
HANNAH GORFINKEL

ART DIRECTION BY
ANTHONY SPAY

PRODUCTION BY
CHRISTOPHER COTE
KATIE HIDALGO

**DIRECTOR, LICENSING
& BUSINESS DEVELOPMENT**
JENNIFER BERMEL

PRESIDENT & PUBLISHER
JOE BRUSHA

COVER BY
MICHAEL GOLDEN

FOR HISTORY˚

EXECUTIVE EDITOR
SHAWN BROCK

HISTORICAL CONSULTANT
DR. KIMBERLY GILMORE, PhD

HISTORY.

silver
dragon
books

THE STORY OF ALL OF US

MANKIND

TABLE OF CONTENTS

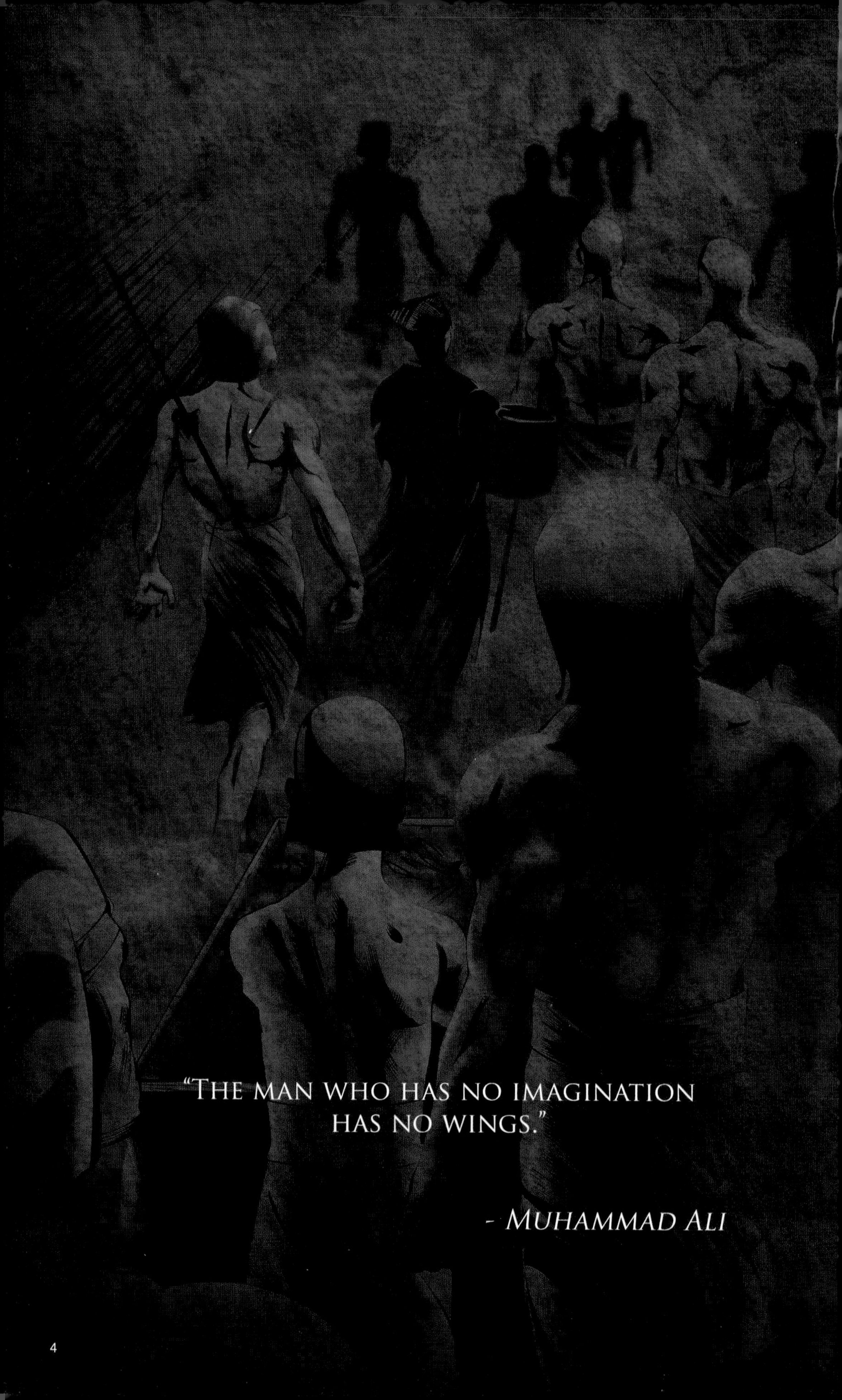
"THE MAN WHO HAS NO IMAGINATION HAS NO WINGS."
- MUHAMMAD ALI

INTRODUCTION

You are about to begin an epic journey, one with a most unlikely hero: us. It is a gripping tale that is stranger than fiction: how one species rises against all odds to dominate a planet. In the great science fiction film *2001: A Space Odyssey*, an ape hurls an animal bone to the heavens, which metamorphoses into a space ship. This striking image captures mankind's story. Bound by the earthly forces from which we are birthed, we reach for the heavens.

Mankind arrives incomplete. Our fate is a riddle and a race: can we decode the keys hidden within our hostile environment in time to ensure our survival? Ninety-nine percent of all species on earth have gone extinct. What armed homo sapiens with the tools to prosper? Powered by our brain, the most complex structure known in the universe, we are hard-wired with the ability to transform the world through thought. It is this power of imagination that is a game-changer. Thinking bigger gives mankind a unique edge. It fuels our ability to harness the powers embedded in the universe to enhance our own strength.

The story of mankind's ingenuity and ambition is told again and again across many cultures through the use of myths. Take the ancient Greek mythological tale of Prometheus. It begins with a mind game (imagination!). Prometheus, a mortal, tricks Zeus, ruler of the gods, into eating the bones of a slain bull, thus preserving the meat for man. For this transgression, Zeus withholds the element of fire (no way to cook the meat!). Going undercover, Prometheus enters the realm of the gods, stealing fire and bringing it back to empower the mortals. Prometheus's bold act unleashes the powers of the universe in the service of man: writing; agriculture; the domestication of animals; the ability to track the seasons by the star; engineering; the power to make medicines; to sail the seas; to unearth the secrets of mining. Myth rubs up against history in this story. *MANKIND THE STORY OF ALL OF US* ™ is the real story of those who dared to change the world, to unlock the keys that would transform our destiny.

We share a common destiny. Adventure is in our DNA, we seek new powers, we innovate and thus transform our world and our fate. The graphic novel you hold in your hands is based upon the television series produced by Nutopia for HISTORY® called *MANKIND THE STORY OF ALL OF US*. It presents history's greatest adventure, the biography of who we are. We mortals start here. Mankind takes flight.

Julian P. Hobbs

Executive Producer, *MANKIND THE STORY OF ALL OF US*

THE MONGOL WORLD

WRITTEN BY
KEVIN BAKER

ART BY
DENNIS CALERO

LETTERS BY
JIM CAMPBELL

AS BARBARIANS STORM THE GATES, A CHINESE PRINCESS RESOLVES
TO CONQUER THEM FROM WITHIN

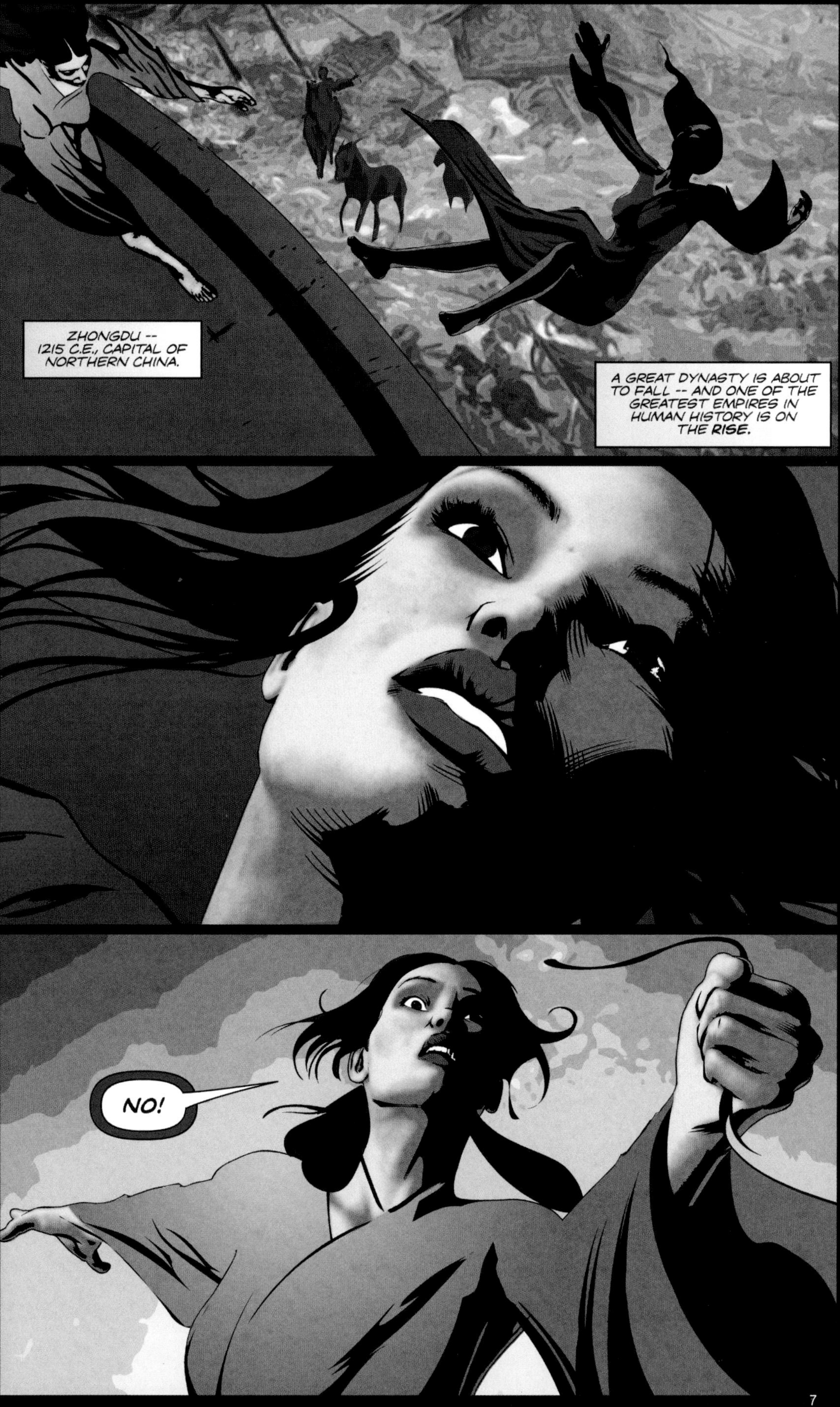
ZHONGDU -- 1215 C.E., CAPITAL OF NORTHERN CHINA.
A GREAT DYNASTY IS ABOUT TO FALL -- AND ONE OF THE GREATEST EMPIRES IN HUMAN HISTORY IS ON THE RISE.
NO!

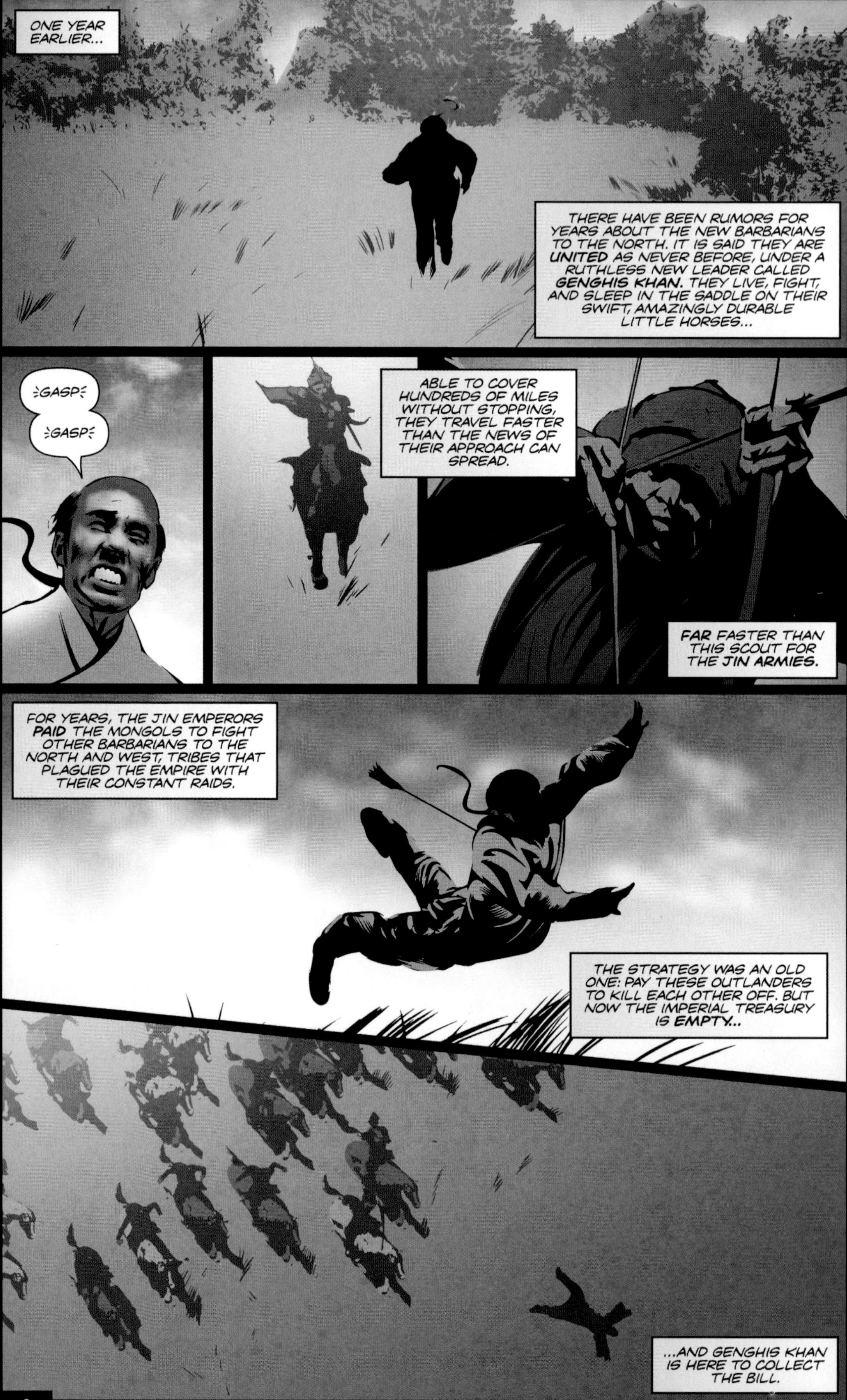
ONE YEAR EARLIER...
THERE HAVE BEEN RUMORS FOR YEARS ABOUT THE NEW BARBARIANS TO THE NORTH. IT IS SAID THEY ARE UNITED AS NEVER BEFORE, UNDER A RUTHLESS NEW LEADER CALLED GENGHIS KHAN. THEY LIVE, FIGHT, AND SLEEP IN THE SADDLE ON THEIR SWIFT, AMAZINGLY DURABLE LITTLE HORSES...
GASP
GASP
ABLE TO COVER HUNDREDS OF MILES WITHOUT STOPPING, THEY TRAVEL FASTER THAN THE NEWS OF THEIR APPROACH CAN SPREAD.
FAR FASTER THAN THIS SCOUT FOR THE JIN ARMIES.
FOR YEARS, THE JIN EMPERORS PAID THE MONGOLS TO FIGHT OTHER BARBARIANS TO THE NORTH AND WEST, TRIBES THAT PLAGUED THE EMPIRE WITH THEIR CONSTANT RAIDS.
THE STRATEGY WAS AN OLD ONE: PAY THESE OUTLANDERS TO KILL EACH OTHER OFF. BUT NOW THE IMPERIAL TREASURY IS EMPTY...
...AND GENGHIS KHAN IS HERE TO COLLECT THE BILL.

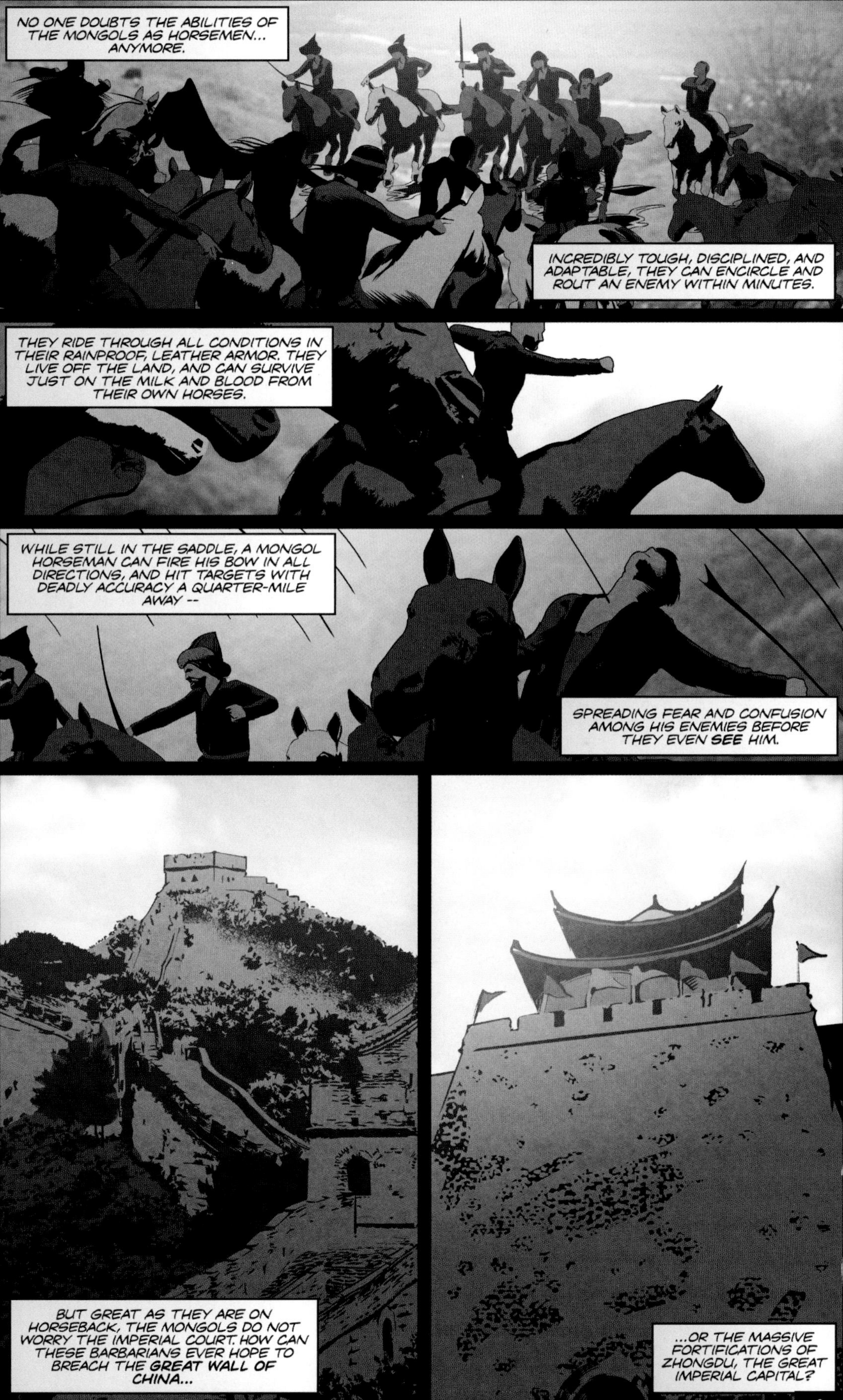
NO ONE DOUBTS THE ABILITIES OF THE MONGOLS AS HORSEMEN... ANYMORE.
INCREDIBLY TOUGH, DISCIPLINED, AND ADAPTABLE, THEY CAN ENCIRCLE AND ROUT AN ENEMY WITHIN MINUTES.
THEY RIDE THROUGH ALL CONDITIONS IN THEIR RAINPROOF, LEATHER ARMOR. THEY LIVE OFF THE LAND, AND CAN SURVIVE JUST ON THE MILK AND BLOOD FROM THEIR OWN HORSES.
WHILE STILL IN THE SADDLE, A MONGOL HORSEMAN CAN FIRE HIS BOW IN ALL DIRECTIONS, AND HIT TARGETS WITH DEADLY ACCURACY A QUARTER-MILE AWAY --
SPREADING FEAR AND CONFUSION AMONG HIS ENEMIES BEFORE THEY EVEN **SEE** HIM.
BUT GREAT AS THEY ARE ON HORSEBACK, THE MONGOLS DO NOT WORRY THE IMPERIAL COURT. HOW CAN THESE BARBARIANS EVER HOPE TO BREACH THE **GREAT WALL OF CHINA...**
...OR THE MASSIVE FORTIFICATIONS OF ZHONGDU, THE GREAT IMPERIAL CAPITAL?

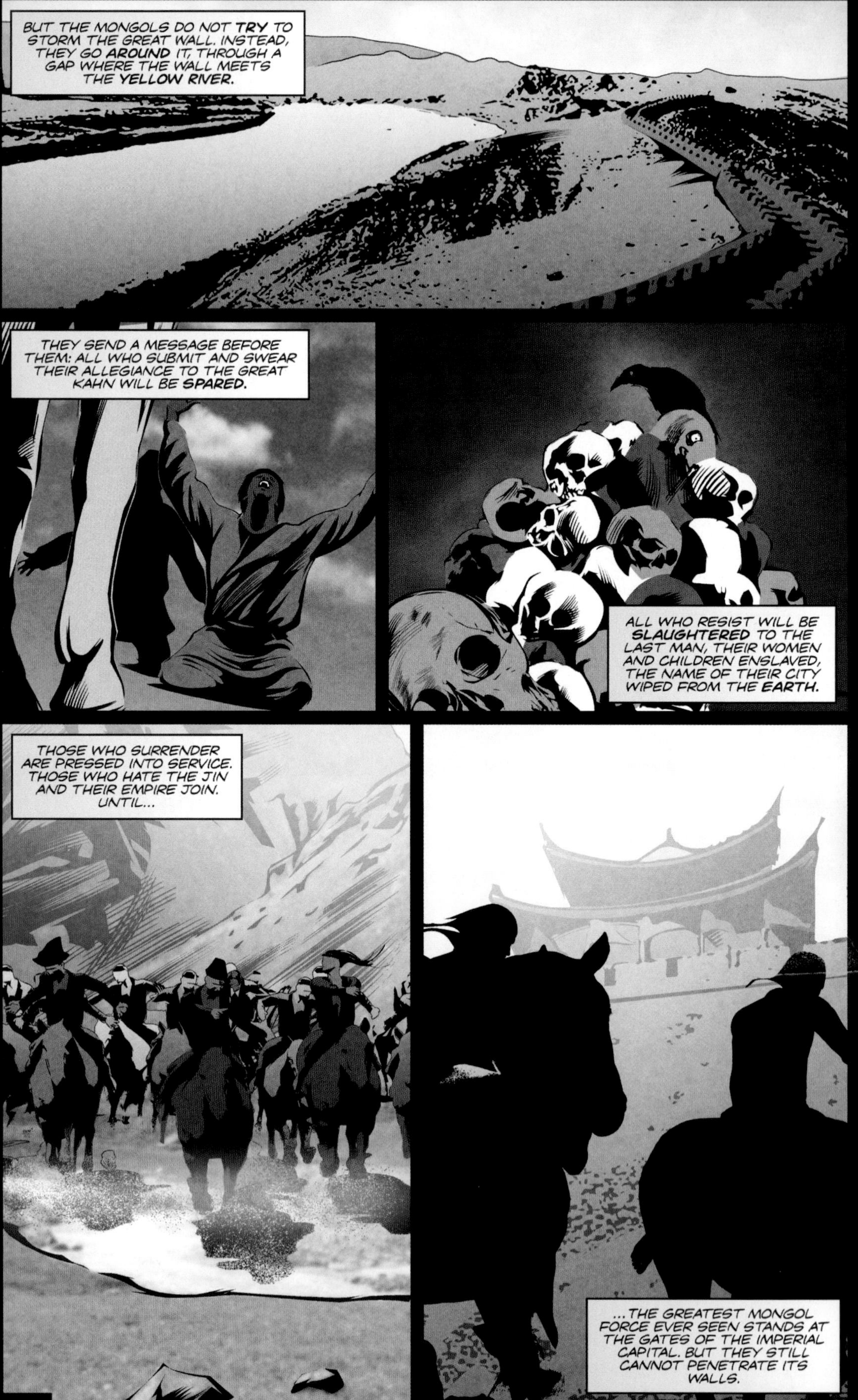
BUT THE MONGOLS DO NOT TRY TO STORM THE GREAT WALL. INSTEAD, THEY GO AROUND IT, THROUGH A GAP WHERE THE WALL MEETS THE YELLOW RIVER.
THEY SEND A MESSAGE BEFORE THEM: ALL WHO SUBMIT AND SWEAR THEIR ALLEGIANCE TO THE GREAT KAHN WILL BE SPARED.
ALL WHO RESIST WILL BE SLAUGHTERED TO THE LAST MAN, THEIR WOMEN AND CHILDREN ENSLAVED, THE NAME OF THEIR CITY WIPED FROM THE EARTH.
THOSE WHO SURRENDER ARE PRESSED INTO SERVICE. THOSE WHO HATE THE JIN AND THEIR EMPIRE JOIN. UNTIL...
...THE GREATEST MONGOL FORCE EVER SEEN STANDS AT THE GATES OF THE IMPERIAL CAPITAL. BUT THEY STILL CANNOT PENETRATE ITS WALLS.

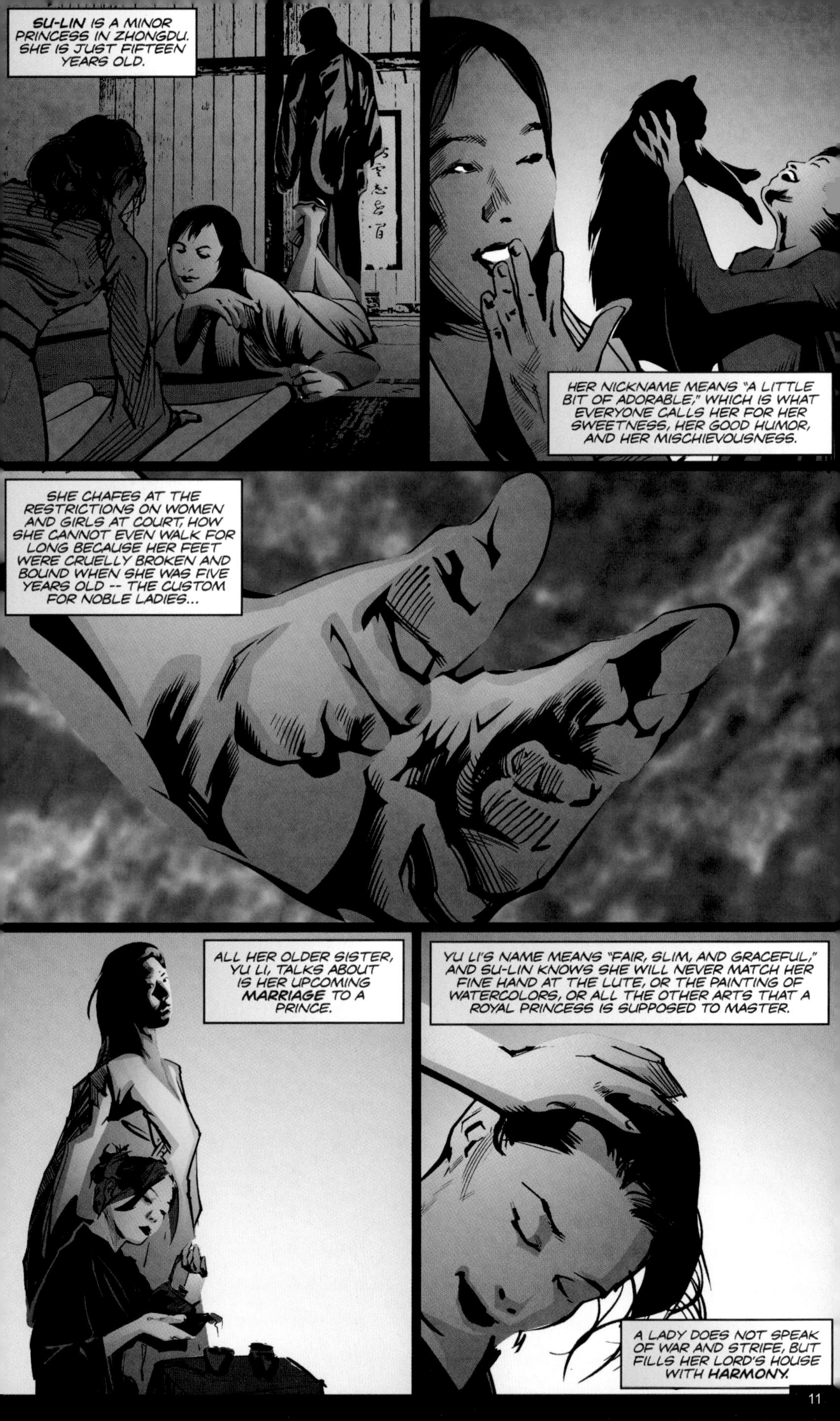
SU-LIN IS A MINOR PRINCESS IN ZHONGDU. SHE IS JUST FIFTEEN YEARS OLD.
HER NICKNAME MEANS "A LITTLE BIT OF ADORABLE," WHICH IS WHAT EVERYONE CALLS HER FOR HER SWEETNESS, HER GOOD HUMOR, AND HER MISCHIEVOUSNESS.
SHE CHAFES AT THE RESTRICTIONS ON WOMEN AND GIRLS AT COURT, HOW SHE CANNOT EVEN WALK FOR LONG BECAUSE HER FEET WERE CRUELLY BROKEN AND BOUND WHEN SHE WAS FIVE YEARS OLD -- THE CUSTOM FOR NOBLE LADIES...
ALL HER OLDER SISTER, YU LI, TALKS ABOUT IS HER UPCOMING MARRIAGE TO A PRINCE.
YU LI'S NAME MEANS "FAIR, SLIM, AND GRACEFUL," AND SU-LIN KNOWS SHE WILL NEVER MATCH HER FINE HAND AT THE LUTE, OR THE PAINTING OF WATERCOLORS, OR ALL THE OTHER ARTS THAT A ROYAL PRINCESS IS SUPPOSED TO MASTER.
A LADY DOES NOT SPEAK OF WAR AND STRIFE, BUT FILLS HER LORD'S HOUSE WITH HARMONY.

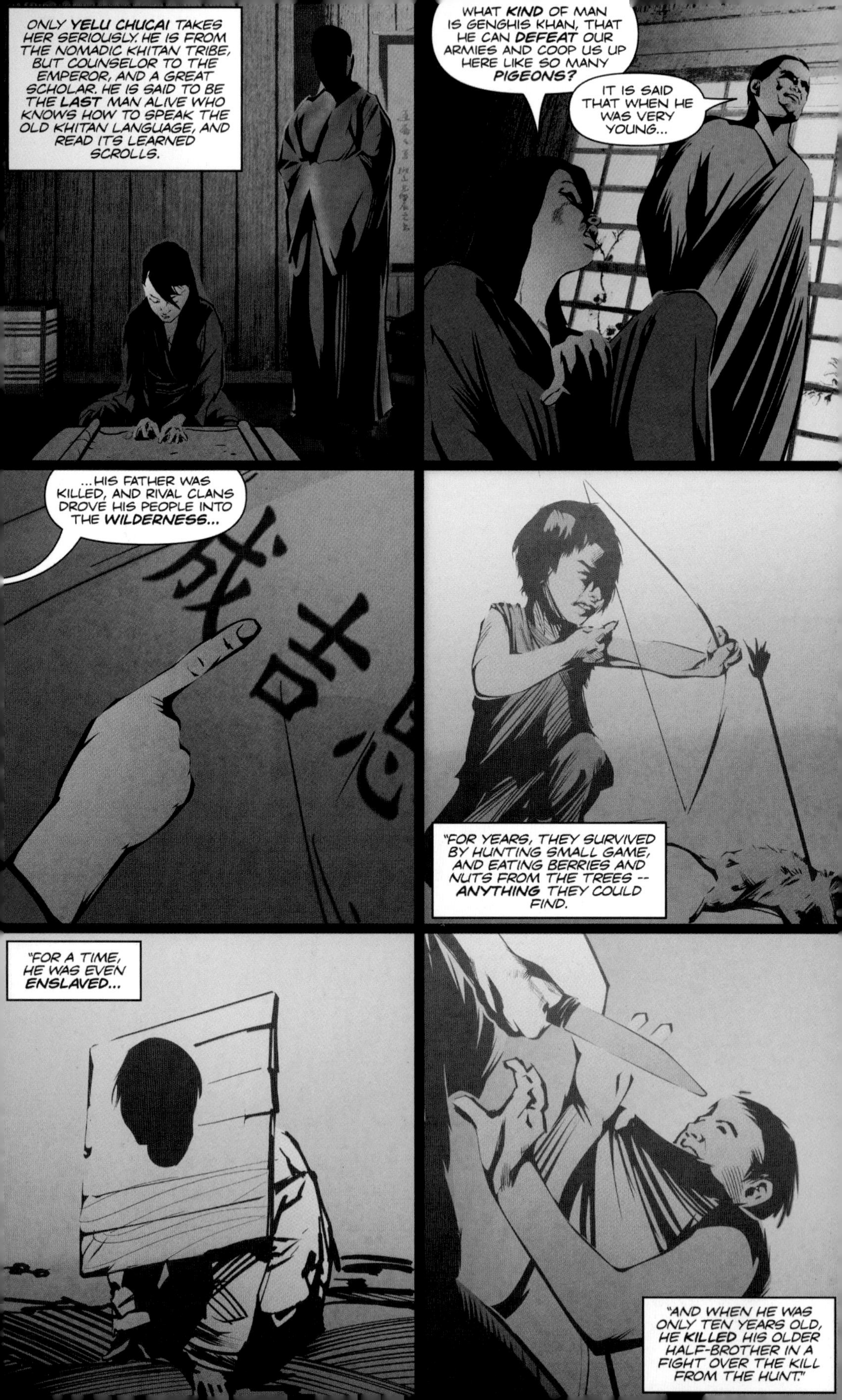
ONLY **YELU CHUCAI** TAKES HER SERIOUSLY. HE IS FROM THE NOMADIC KHITAN TRIBE, BUT COUNSELOR TO THE EMPEROR, AND A GREAT SCHOLAR. HE IS SAID TO BE THE **LAST** MAN ALIVE WHO KNOWS HOW TO SPEAK THE OLD KHITAN LANGUAGE, AND READ ITS LEARNED SCROLLS.
WHAT **KIND** OF MAN IS GENGHIS KHAN, THAT HE CAN **DEFEAT** OUR ARMIES AND COOP US UP HERE LIKE SO MANY **PIGEONS?**
IT IS SAID THAT WHEN HE WAS VERY YOUNG...
...HIS FATHER WAS KILLED, AND RIVAL CLANS DROVE HIS PEOPLE INTO THE **WILDERNESS...**
"FOR YEARS, THEY SURVIVED BY HUNTING SMALL GAME, AND EATING BERRIES AND NUTS FROM THE TREES -- **ANYTHING** THEY COULD FIND.
"FOR A TIME, HE WAS EVEN **ENSLAVED...**
"AND WHEN HE WAS ONLY TEN YEARS OLD, HE **KILLED** HIS OLDER HALF-BROTHER IN A FIGHT OVER THE KILL FROM THE HUNT."

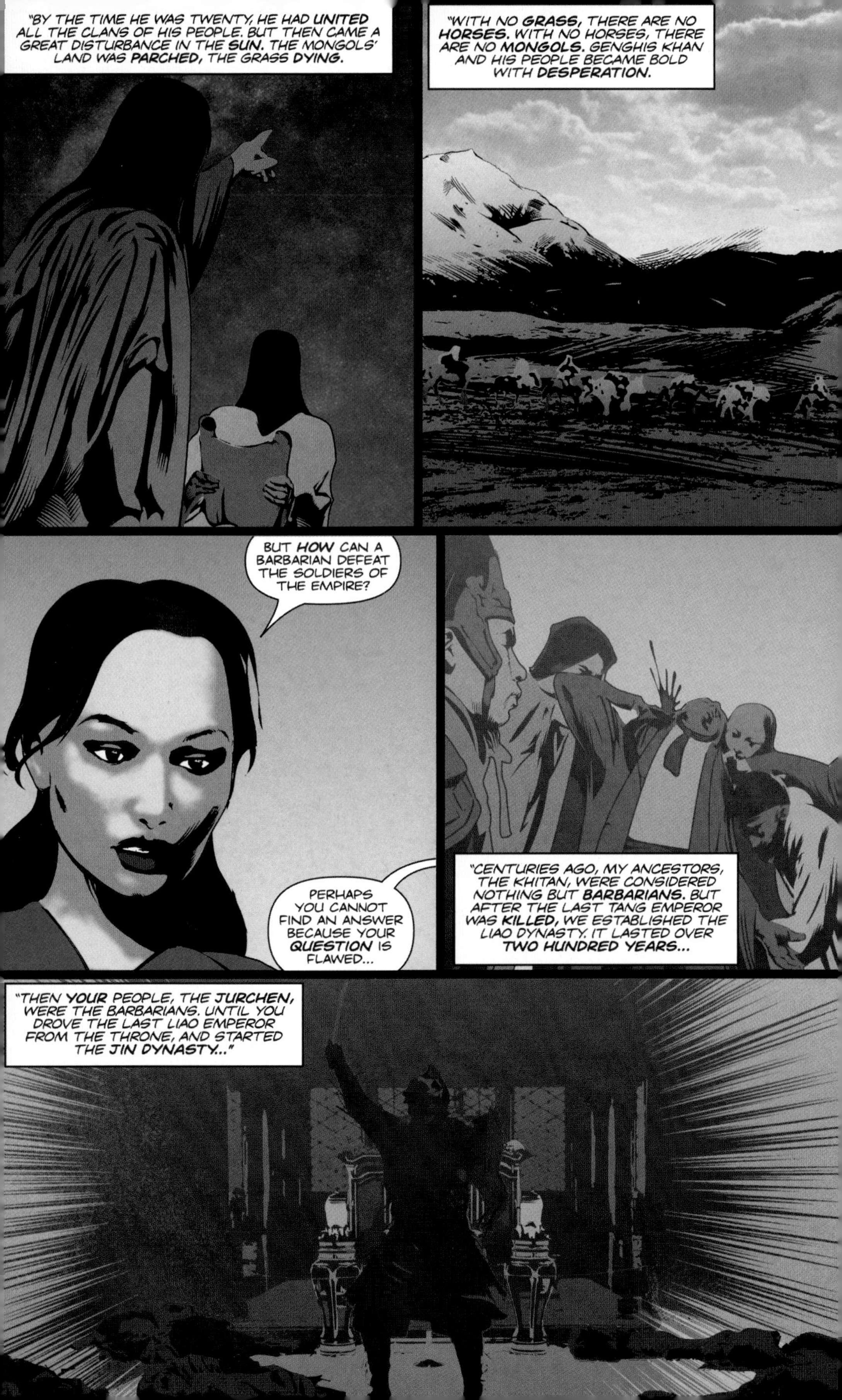
"BY THE TIME HE WAS TWENTY, HE HAD UNITED ALL THE CLANS OF HIS PEOPLE. BUT THEN CAME A GREAT DISTURBANCE IN THE SUN. THE MONGOLS' LAND WAS PARCHED, THE GRASS DYING.
"WITH NO GRASS, THERE ARE NO HORSES. WITH NO HORSES, THERE ARE NO MONGOLS. GENGHIS KHAN AND HIS PEOPLE BECAME BOLD WITH DESPERATION.
BUT HOW CAN A BARBARIAN DEFEAT THE SOLDIERS OF THE EMPIRE?
PERHAPS YOU CANNOT FIND AN ANSWER BECAUSE YOUR QUESTION IS FLAWED...
"CENTURIES AGO, MY ANCESTORS, THE KHITAN, WERE CONSIDERED NOTHING BUT BARBARIANS. BUT AFTER THE LAST TANG EMPEROR WAS KILLED, WE ESTABLISHED THE LIAO DYNASTY. IT LASTED OVER TWO HUNDRED YEARS...
"THEN YOUR PEOPLE, THE JURCHEN, WERE THE BARBARIANS. UNTIL YOU DROVE THE LAST LIAO EMPEROR FROM THE THRONE, AND STARTED THE JIN DYNASTY..."

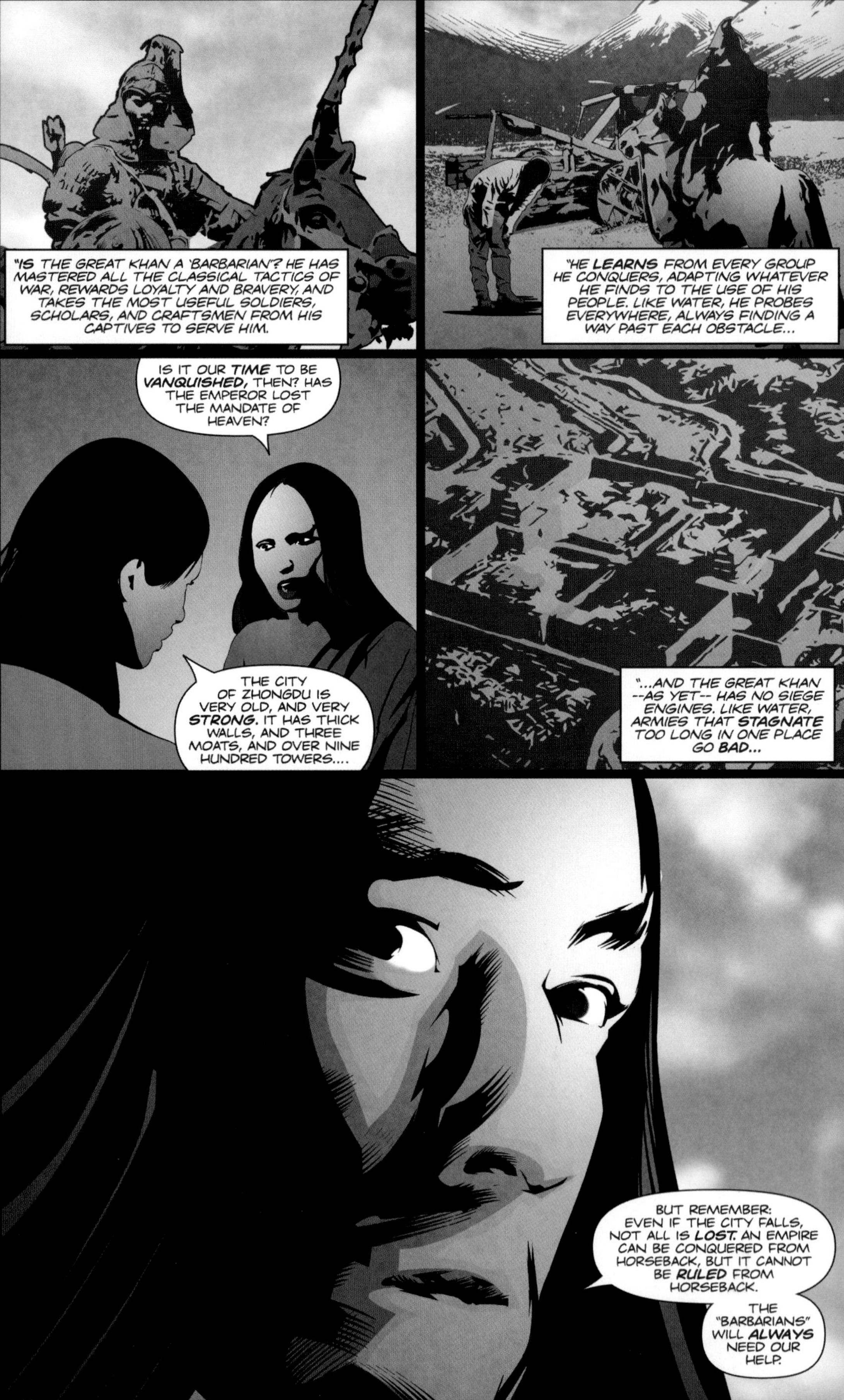
"IS THE GREAT KHAN A 'BARBARIAN'? HE HAS MASTERED ALL THE CLASSICAL TACTICS OF WAR, REWARDS LOYALTY AND BRAVERY, AND TAKES THE MOST USEFUL SOLDIERS, SCHOLARS, AND CRAFTSMEN FROM HIS CAPTIVES TO SERVE HIM.
"HE LEARNS FROM EVERY GROUP HE CONQUERS, ADAPTING WHATEVER HE FINDS TO THE USE OF HIS PEOPLE. LIKE WATER, HE PROBES EVERYWHERE, ALWAYS FINDING A WAY PAST EACH OBSTACLE...
IS IT OUR TIME TO BE VANQUISHED, THEN? HAS THE EMPEROR LOST THE MANDATE OF HEAVEN?
THE CITY OF ZHONGDU IS VERY OLD, AND VERY STRONG. IT HAS THICK WALLS, AND THREE MOATS, AND OVER NINE HUNDRED TOWERS....
"...AND THE GREAT KHAN --AS YET-- HAS NO SIEGE ENGINES. LIKE WATER, ARMIES THAT STAGNATE TOO LONG IN ONE PLACE GO BAD...
BUT REMEMBER: EVEN IF THE CITY FALLS, NOT ALL IS LOST. AN EMPIRE CAN BE CONQUERED FROM HORSEBACK, BUT IT CANNOT BE RULED FROM HORSEBACK.
THE "BARBARIANS" WILL ALWAYS NEED OUR HELP.

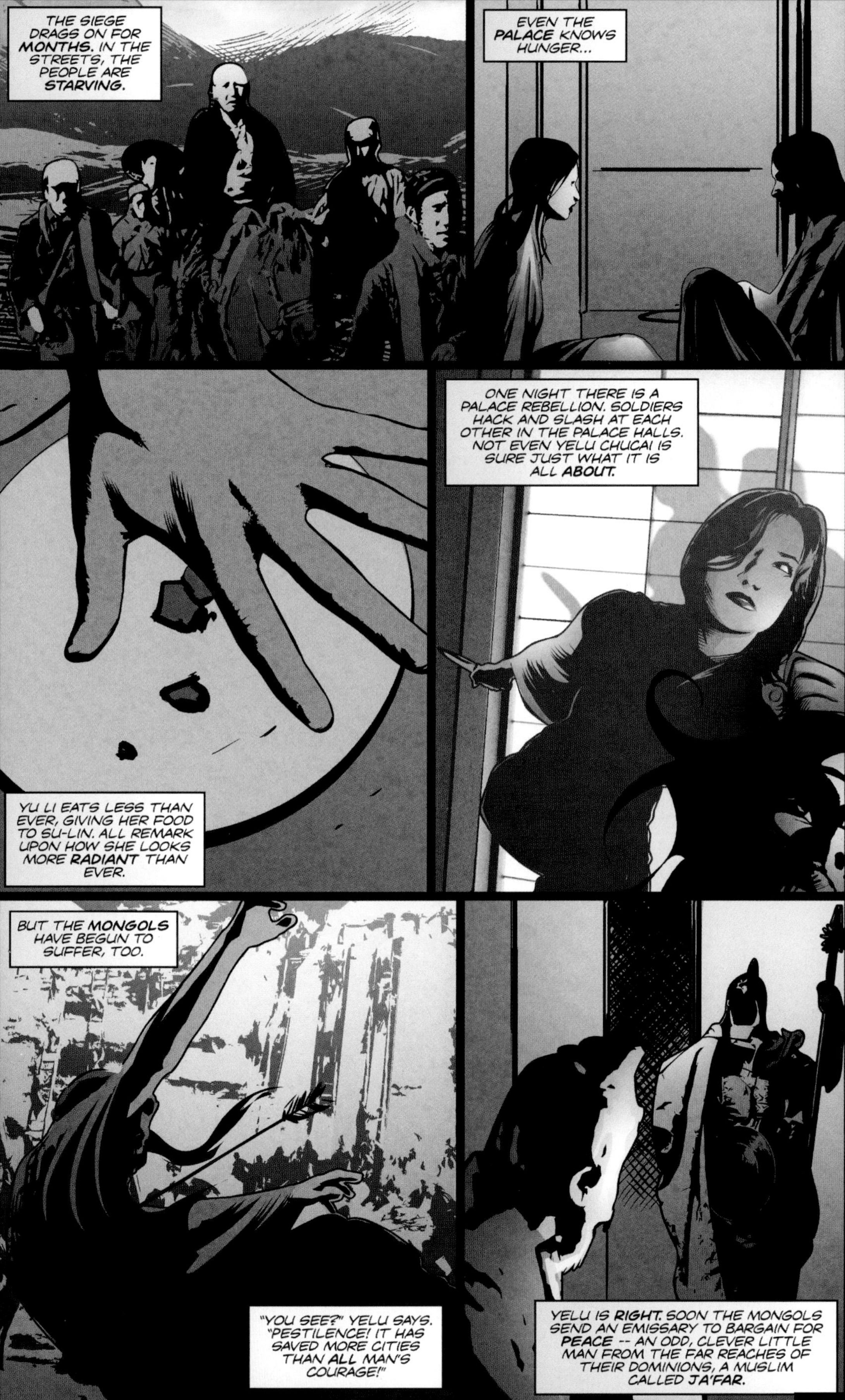
THE SIEGE DRAGS ON FOR MONTHS. IN THE STREETS, THE PEOPLE ARE STARVING.
EVEN THE PALACE KNOWS HUNGER...
YU LI EATS LESS THAN EVER, GIVING HER FOOD TO SU-LIN. ALL REMARK UPON HOW SHE LOOKS MORE RADIANT THAN EVER.
ONE NIGHT THERE IS A PALACE REBELLION. SOLDIERS HACK AND SLASH AT EACH OTHER IN THE PALACE HALLS. NOT EVEN YELU CHUCAI IS SURE JUST WHAT IT IS ALL ABOUT.
BUT THE MONGOLS HAVE BEGUN TO SUFFER, TOO.
"YOU SEE?" YELU SAYS. "PESTILENCE! IT HAS SAVED MORE CITIES THAN ALL MAN'S COURAGE!"
YELU IS RIGHT. SOON THE MONGOLS SEND AN EMISSARY TO BARGAIN FOR PEACE -- AN ODD, CLEVER LITTLE MAN FROM THE FAR REACHES OF THEIR DOMINIONS, A MUSLIM CALLED JA'FAR.

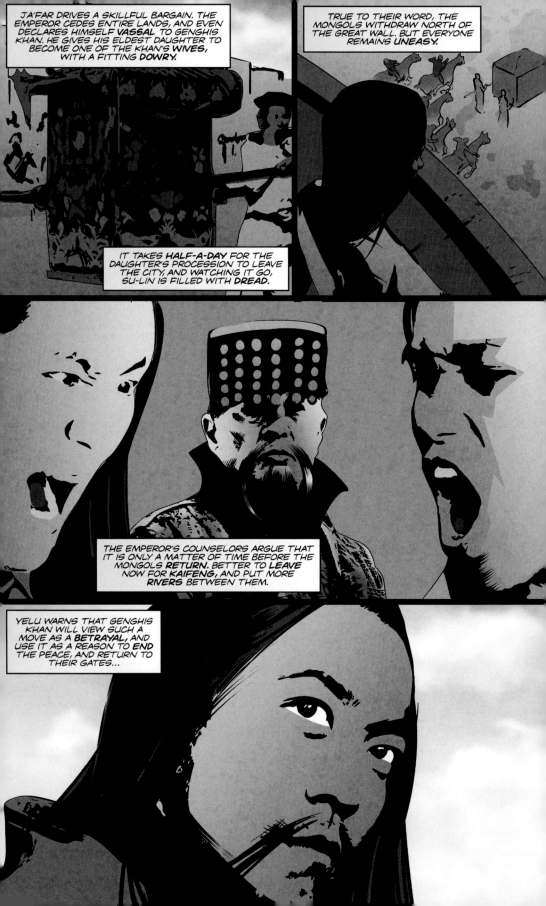

JA'FAR DRIVES A SKILLFUL BARGAIN. THE EMPEROR CEDES ENTIRE LANDS, AND EVEN DECLARES HIMSELF VASSAL TO GENGHIS KHAN. HE GIVES HIS ELDEST DAUGHTER TO BECOME ONE OF THE KHAN'S WIVES, WITH A FITTING DOWRY.

TRUE TO THEIR WORD, THE MONGOLS WITHDRAW NORTH OF THE GREAT WALL. BUT EVERYONE REMAINS UNEASY.

IT TAKES HALF-A-DAY FOR THE DAUGHTER'S PROCESSION TO LEAVE THE CITY, AND WATCHING IT GO, SU-LIN IS FILLED WITH DREAD.

THE EMPEROR'S COUNSELORS ARGUE THAT IT IS ONLY A MATTER OF TIME BEFORE THE MONGOLS RETURN. BETTER TO LEAVE NOW FOR KAIFENG, AND PUT MORE RIVERS BETWEEN THEM.

YELU WARNS THAT GENGHIS KHAN WILL VIEW SUCH A MOVE AS A BETRAYAL, AND USE IT AS A REASON TO END THE PEACE, AND RETURN TO THEIR GATES...

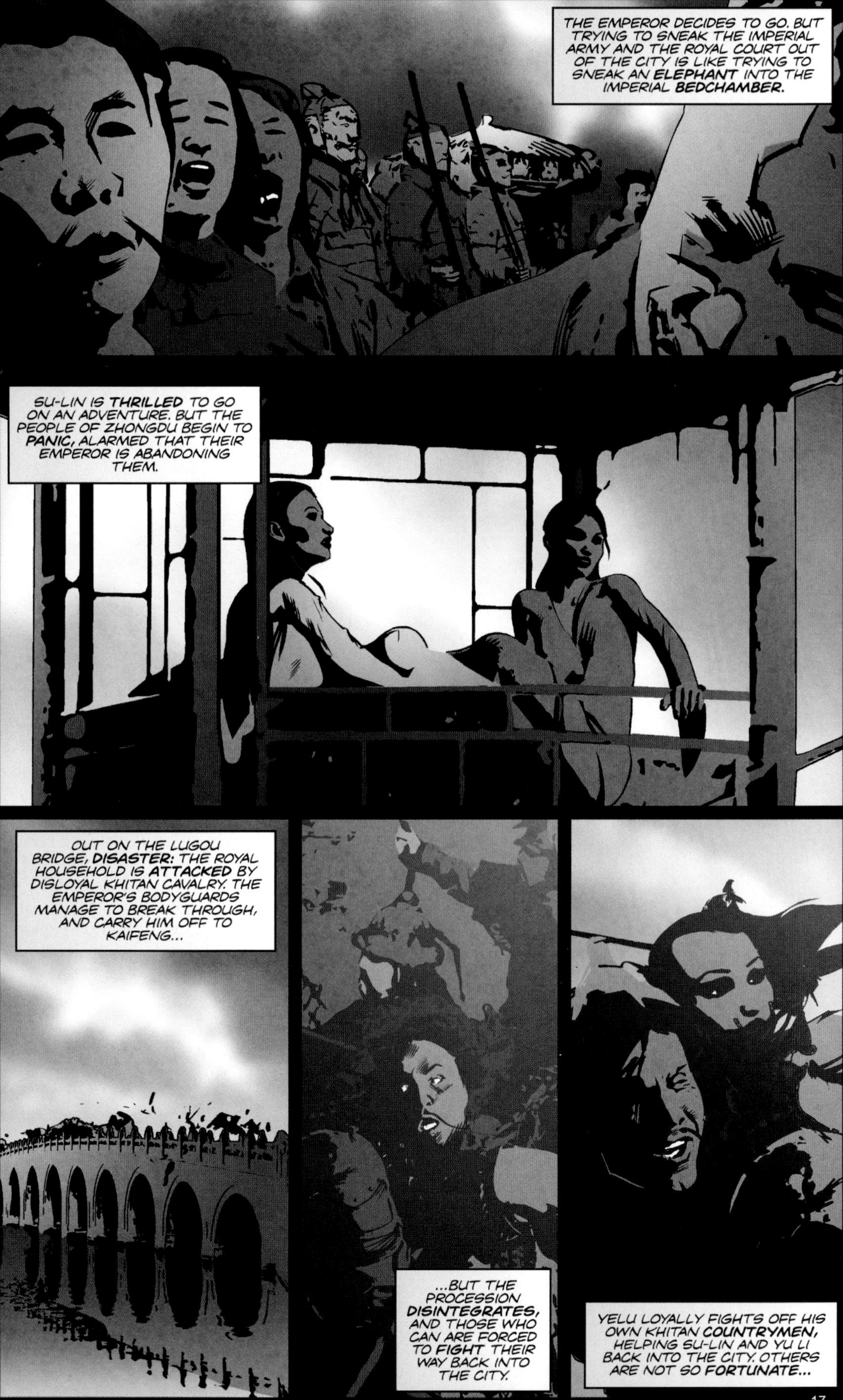
THE EMPEROR DECIDES TO GO. BUT TRYING TO SNEAK THE IMPERIAL ARMY AND THE ROYAL COURT OUT OF THE CITY IS LIKE TRYING TO SNEAK AN ELEPHANT INTO THE IMPERIAL BEDCHAMBER.
SU-LIN IS THRILLED TO GO ON AN ADVENTURE. BUT THE PEOPLE OF ZHONGDU BEGIN TO PANIC, ALARMED THAT THEIR EMPEROR IS ABANDONING THEM.
OUT ON THE LUGOU BRIDGE, DISASTER: THE ROYAL HOUSEHOLD IS ATTACKED BY DISLOYAL KHITAN CAVALRY. THE EMPEROR'S BODYGUARDS MANAGE TO BREAK THROUGH, AND CARRY HIM OFF TO KAIFENG...
...BUT THE PROCESSION DISINTEGRATES, AND THOSE WHO CAN ARE FORCED TO FIGHT THEIR WAY BACK INTO THE CITY.
YELU LOYALLY FIGHTS OFF HIS OWN KHITAN COUNTRYMEN, HELPING SU-LIN AND YU LI BACK INTO THE CITY. OTHERS ARE NOT SO FORTUNATE...

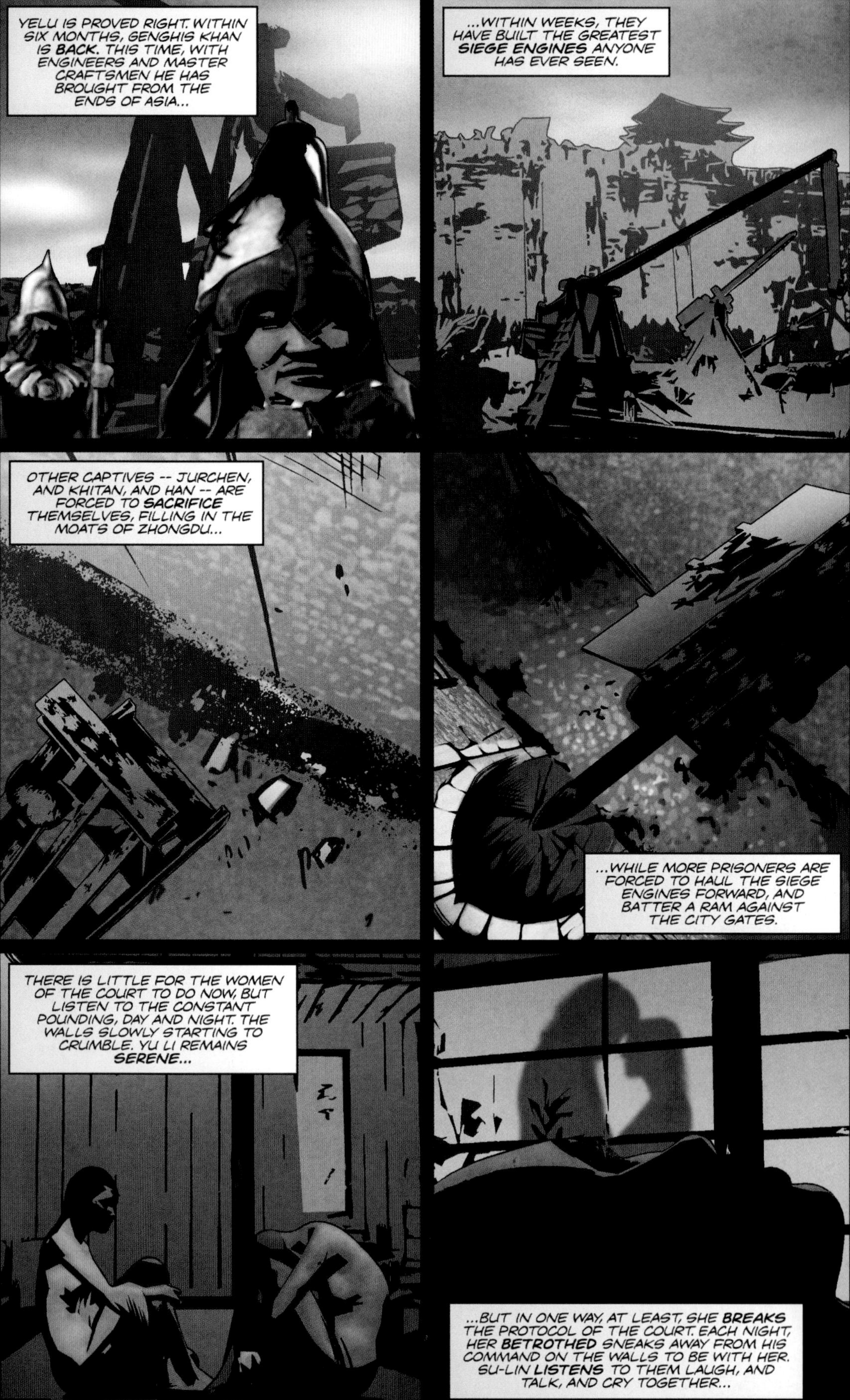

YELU IS PROVED RIGHT. WITHIN SIX MONTHS, GENGHIS KHAN IS BACK. THIS TIME, WITH ENGINEERS AND MASTER CRAFTSMEN HE HAS BROUGHT FROM THE ENDS OF ASIA...
...WITHIN WEEKS, THEY HAVE BUILT THE GREATEST SIEGE ENGINES ANYONE HAS EVER SEEN.
OTHER CAPTIVES -- JURCHEN, AND KHITAN, AND HAN -- ARE FORCED TO SACRIFICE THEMSELVES, FILLING IN THE MOATS OF ZHONGDU...
...WHILE MORE PRISONERS ARE FORCED TO HAUL THE SIEGE ENGINES FORWARD, AND BATTER A RAM AGAINST THE CITY GATES.
THERE IS LITTLE FOR THE WOMEN OF THE COURT TO DO NOW, BUT LISTEN TO THE CONSTANT POUNDING, DAY AND NIGHT. THE WALLS SLOWLY STARTING TO CRUMBLE. YU LI REMAINS SERENE...
...BUT IN ONE WAY, AT LEAST, SHE BREAKS THE PROTOCOL OF THE COURT. EACH NIGHT, HER BETROTHED SNEAKS AWAY FROM HIS COMMAND ON THE WALLS TO BE WITH HER. SU-LIN LISTENS TO THEM LAUGH, AND TALK, AND CRY TOGETHER...

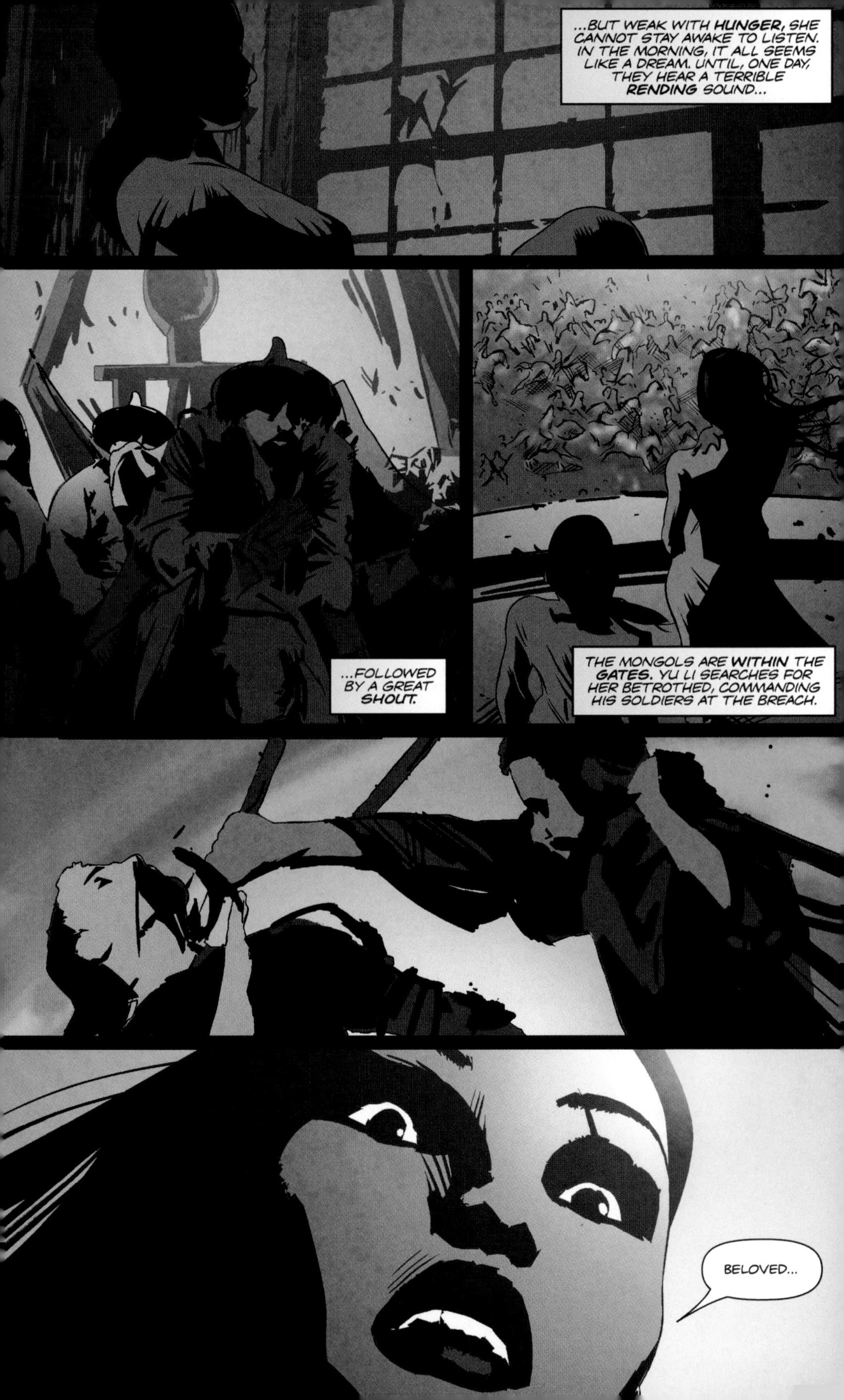
...BUT WEAK WITH HUNGER, SHE CANNOT STAY AWAKE TO LISTEN. IN THE MORNING, IT ALL SEEMS LIKE A DREAM. UNTIL, ONE DAY, THEY HEAR A TERRIBLE RENDING SOUND...
...FOLLOWED BY A GREAT SHOUT.
THE MONGOLS ARE WITHIN THE GATES. YU LI SEARCHES FOR HER BETROTHED, COMMANDING HIS SOLDIERS AT THE BREACH.
BELOVED...

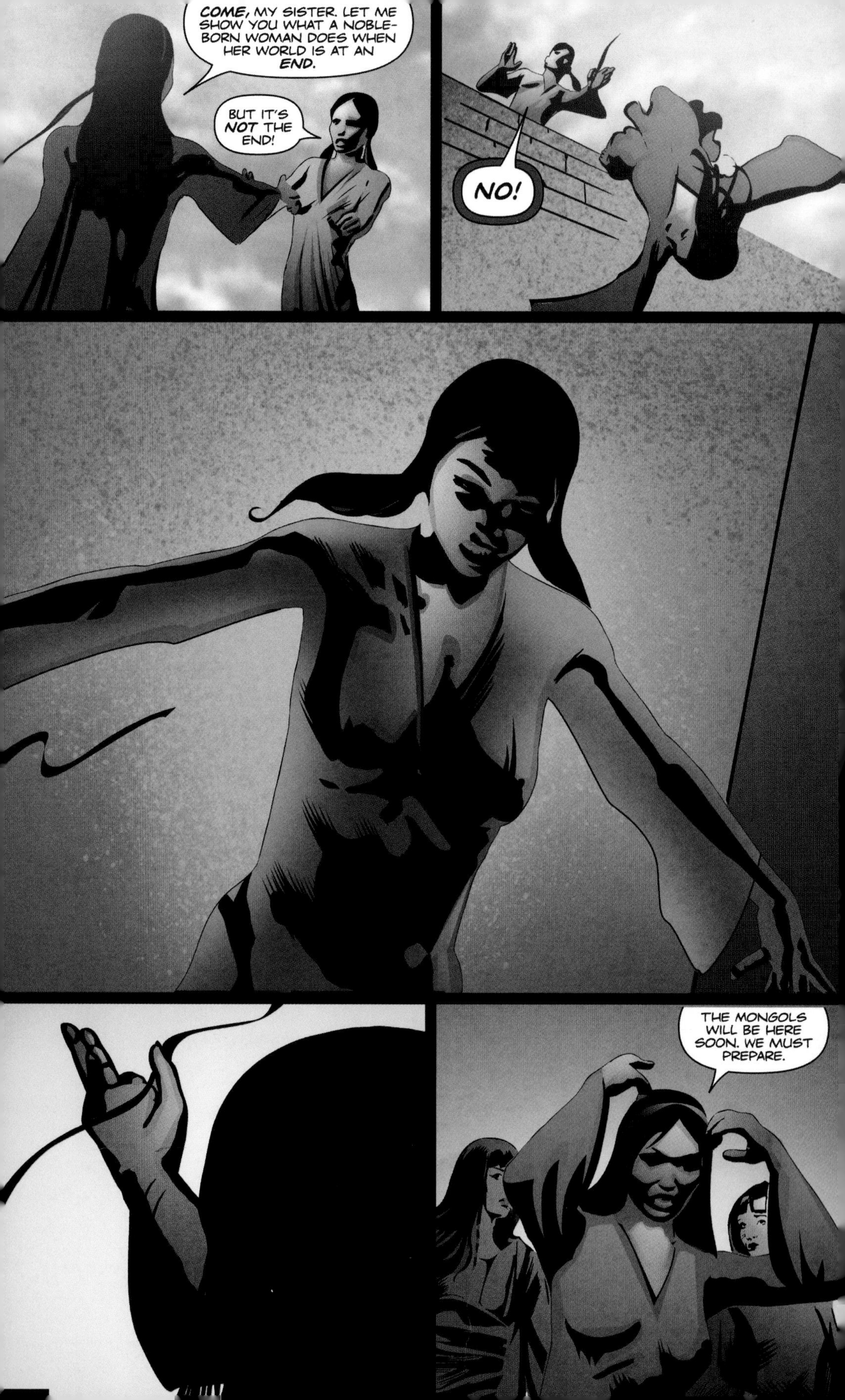
COME, MY SISTER. LET ME SHOW YOU WHAT A NOBLE-BORN WOMAN DOES WHEN HER WORLD IS AT AN END.
BUT IT'S NOT THE END!
NO!
THE MONGOLS WILL BE HERE SOON. WE MUST PREPARE.

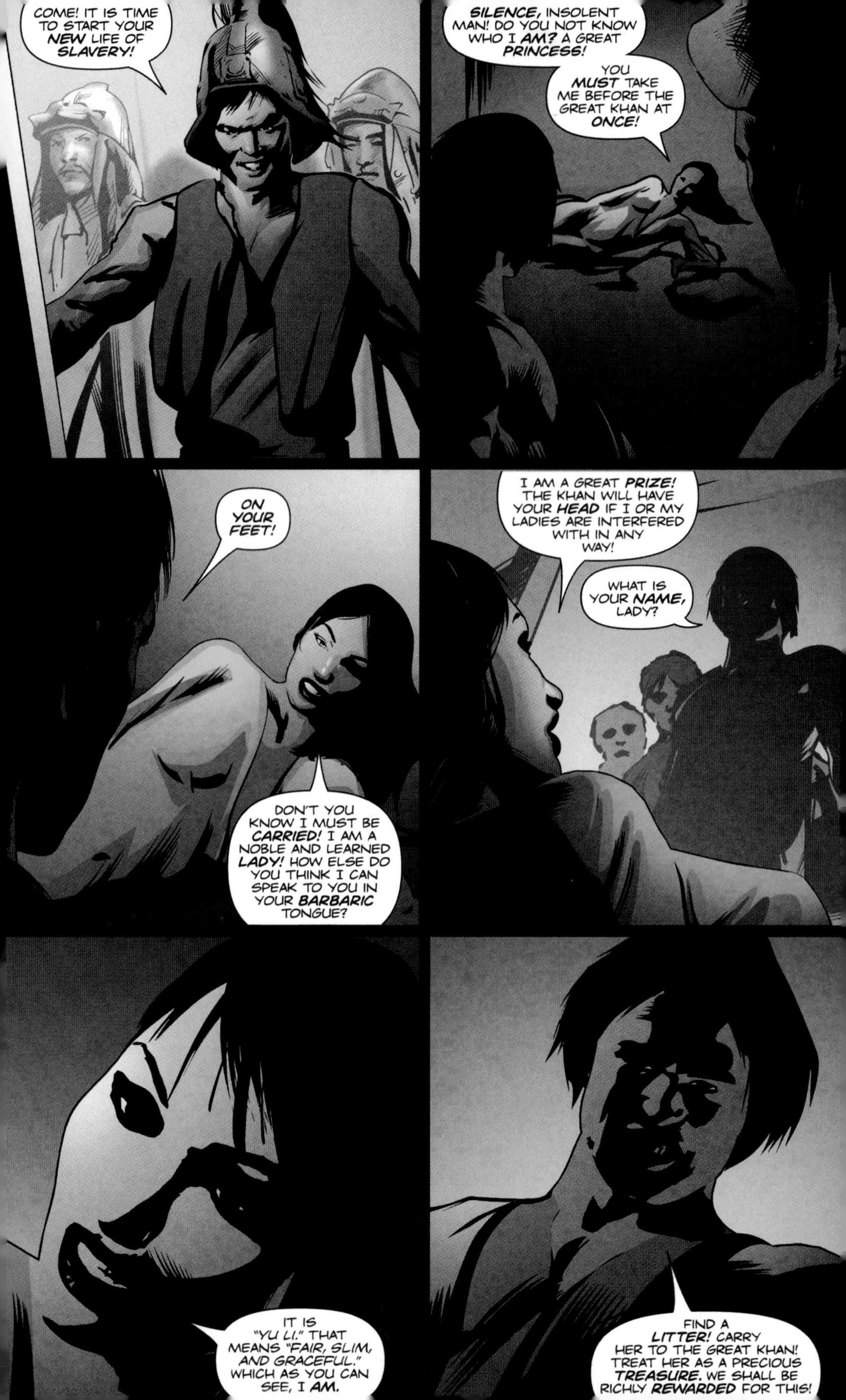
COME! IT IS TIME TO START YOUR NEW LIFE OF SLAVERY!
SILENCE, INSOLENT MAN! DO YOU NOT KNOW WHO I AM? A GREAT PRINCESS!
YOU MUST TAKE ME BEFORE THE GREAT KHAN AT ONCE!
ON YOUR FEET!
DON'T YOU KNOW I MUST BE CARRIED! I AM A NOBLE AND LEARNED LADY! HOW ELSE DO YOU THINK I CAN SPEAK TO YOU IN YOUR BARBARIC TONGUE?
I AM A GREAT PRIZE! THE KHAN WILL HAVE YOUR HEAD IF I OR MY LADIES ARE INTERFERED WITH IN ANY WAY!
WHAT IS YOUR NAME, LADY?
IT IS "YU LI." THAT MEANS "FAIR, SLIM, AND GRACEFUL." WHICH AS YOU CAN SEE, I AM.
FIND A LITTER! CARRY HER TO THE GREAT KHAN! TREAT HER AS A PRECIOUS TREASURE. WE SHALL BE RICHLY REWARDED FOR THIS!

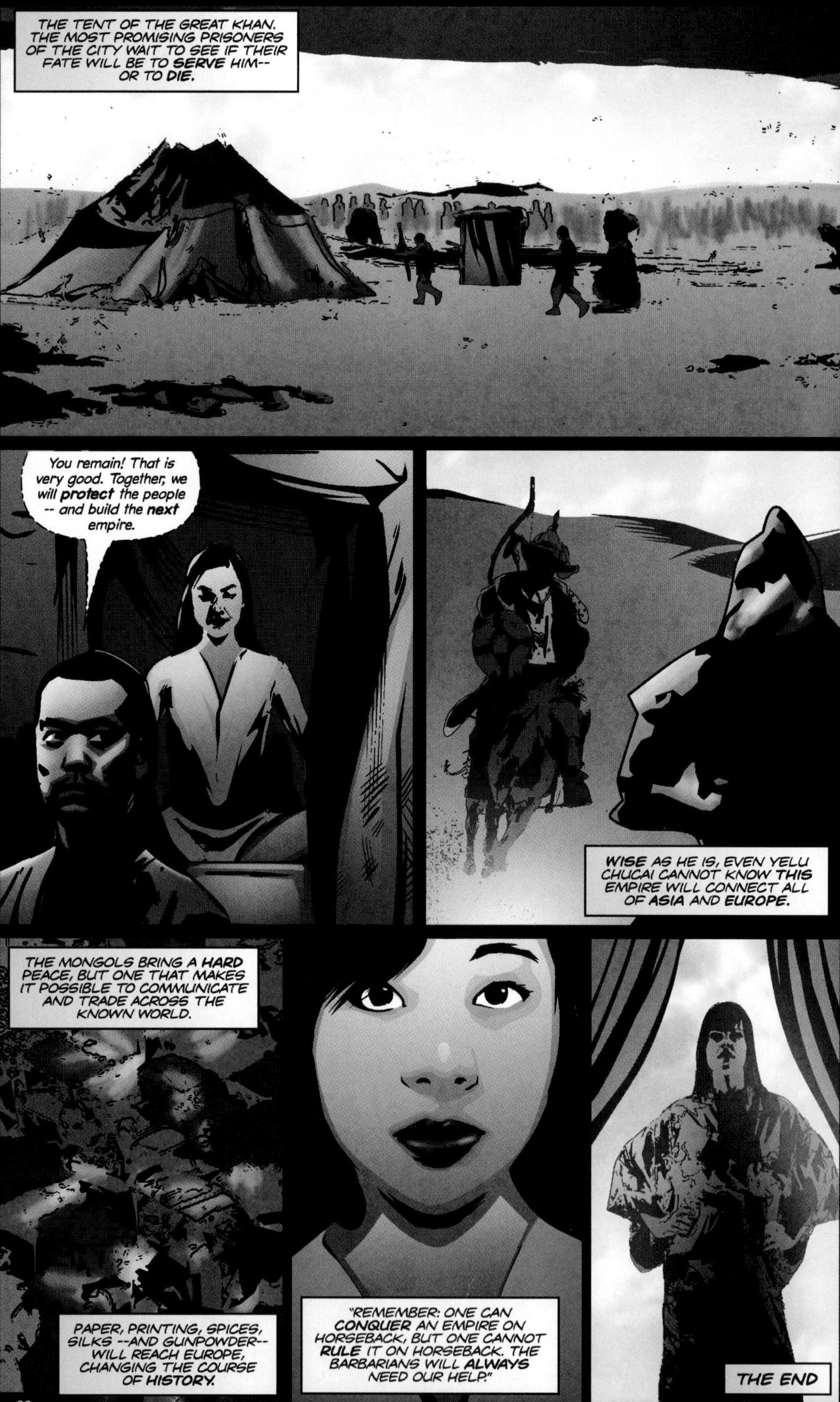
THE TENT OF THE GREAT KHAN. THE MOST PROMISING PRISONERS OF THE CITY WAIT TO SEE IF THEIR FATE WILL BE TO SERVE HIM-- OR TO DIE.
You remain! That is very good. Together, we will protect the people -- and build the next empire.
WISE AS HE IS, EVEN YELU CHUCAI CANNOT KNOW THIS EMPIRE WILL CONNECT ALL OF ASIA AND EUROPE.
THE MONGOLS BRING A HARD PEACE, BUT ONE THAT MAKES IT POSSIBLE TO COMMUNICATE AND TRADE ACROSS THE KNOWN WORLD.
PAPER, PRINTING, SPICES, SILKS --AND GUNPOWDER-- WILL REACH EUROPE, CHANGING THE COURSE OF HISTORY.
"REMEMBER: ONE CAN CONQUER AN EMPIRE ON HORSEBACK, BUT ONE CANNOT RULE IT ON HORSEBACK. THE BARBARIANS WILL ALWAYS NEED OUR HELP."
THE END

THE GUN

WRITTEN BY
CHARLES SOULE

ART BY
UNAI ORTIZ DE ZARATE

COLORS BY
MICHAEL WATKINS

LETTERS BY
JIM CAMPBELL

A NEW WEAPON HAS THE POWER TO CHANGE THE WORLD AND
TAKE ONE MAN FROM PEASANT TO EMPEROR

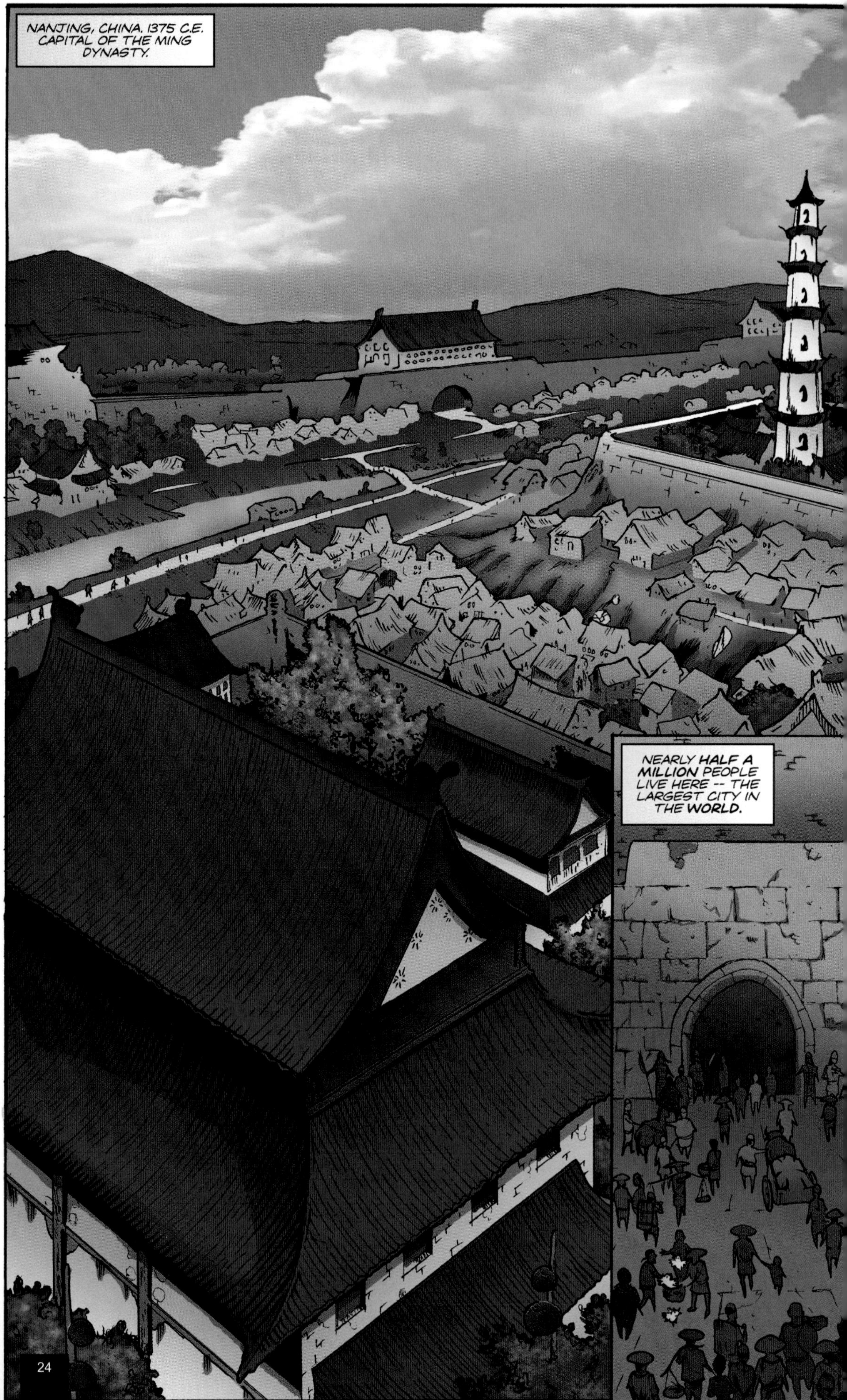
NANJING, CHINA. 1375 C.E. CAPITAL OF THE MING DYNASTY.
NEARLY HALF A MILLION PEOPLE LIVE HERE -- THE LARGEST CITY IN THE WORLD.

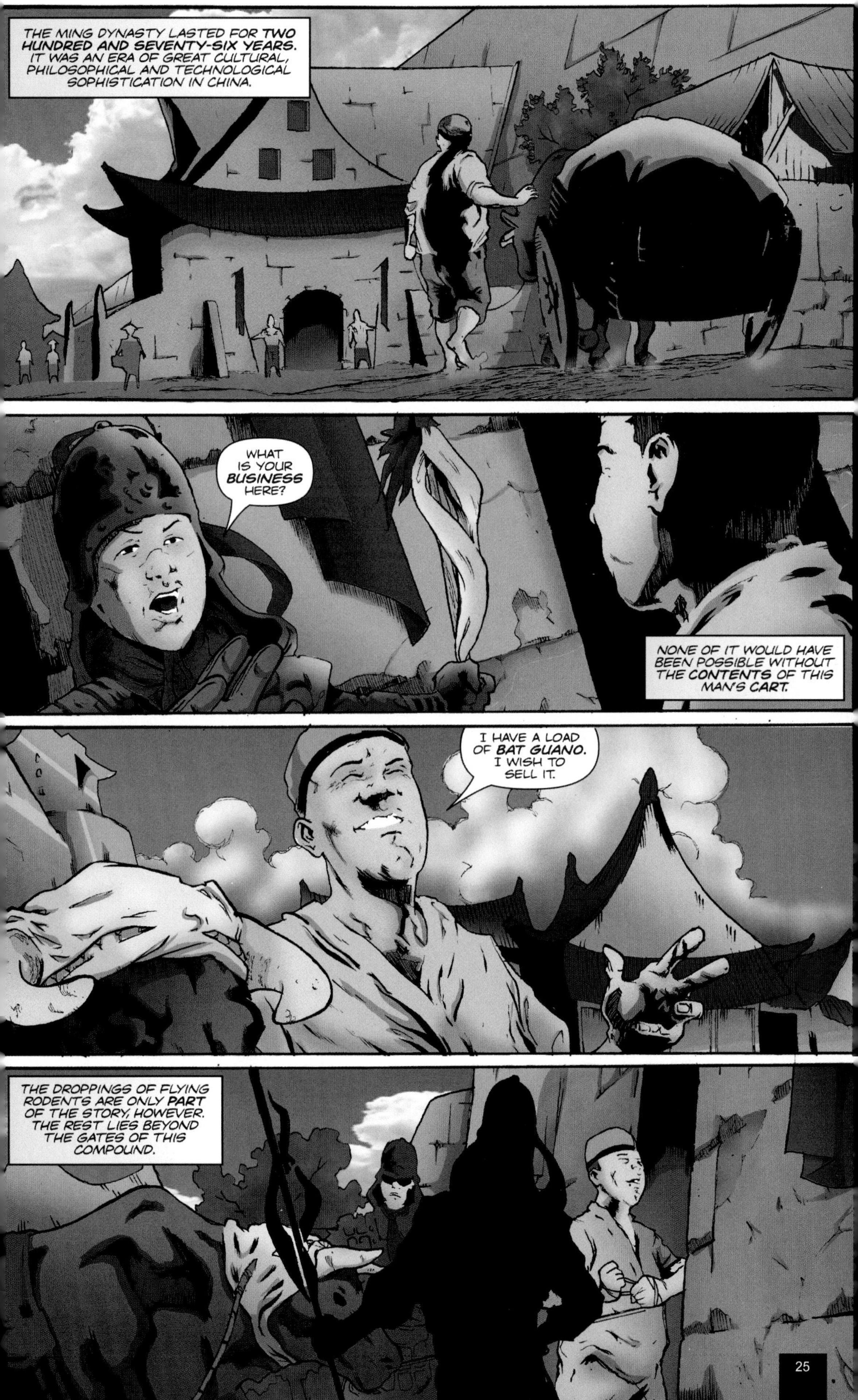
THE MING DYNASTY LASTED FOR TWO HUNDRED AND SEVENTY-SIX YEARS. IT WAS AN ERA OF GREAT CULTURAL, PHILOSOPHICAL AND TECHNOLOGICAL SOPHISTICATION IN CHINA.
WHAT IS YOUR BUSINESS HERE?
NONE OF IT WOULD HAVE BEEN POSSIBLE WITHOUT THE CONTENTS OF THIS MAN'S CART.
I HAVE A LOAD OF BAT GUANO. I WISH TO SELL IT.
THE DROPPINGS OF FLYING RODENTS ARE ONLY PART OF THE STORY, HOWEVER. THE REST LIES BEYOND THE GATES OF THIS COMPOUND.

MANY WHO LIVE IN NANJING WISH THIS PLACE WERE LOCATED FAR OUTSIDE THE CITY WALLS, BUT ITS SECRETS ARE TOO *PRECIOUS* TO BE LEFT UNPROTECTED.

THE GUANO WILL BE TREATED WITH TECHNIQUES DEVISED BY **ALCHEMIST MONKS** HUNDREDS OF YEARS EARLIER, WHO EXPERIMENTED WITH SUBSTANCES OF ALL KINDS IN THEIR SEARCH FOR AN ELIXIR OF **IMMORTALITY**.

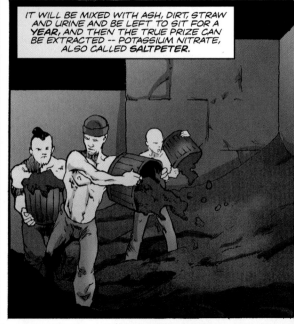

IT WILL BE MIXED WITH ASH, DIRT, STRAW AND URINE AND BE LEFT TO SIT FOR A *YEAR*, AND THEN THE TRUE PRIZE CAN BE EXTRACTED -- POTASSIUM NITRATE, ALSO CALLED **SALTPETER**.

WHEN MIXED WITH SULFUR AND ORDINARY CHARCOAL IN THE PROPER PROPORTIONS, YOU HAVE A SUBSTANCE THAT HAS HAD MORE **IMPACT** ON THE HISTORY OF MANKIND THAN ALMOST **ANY OTHER**...

...GUNPOWDER.

WHOOMP

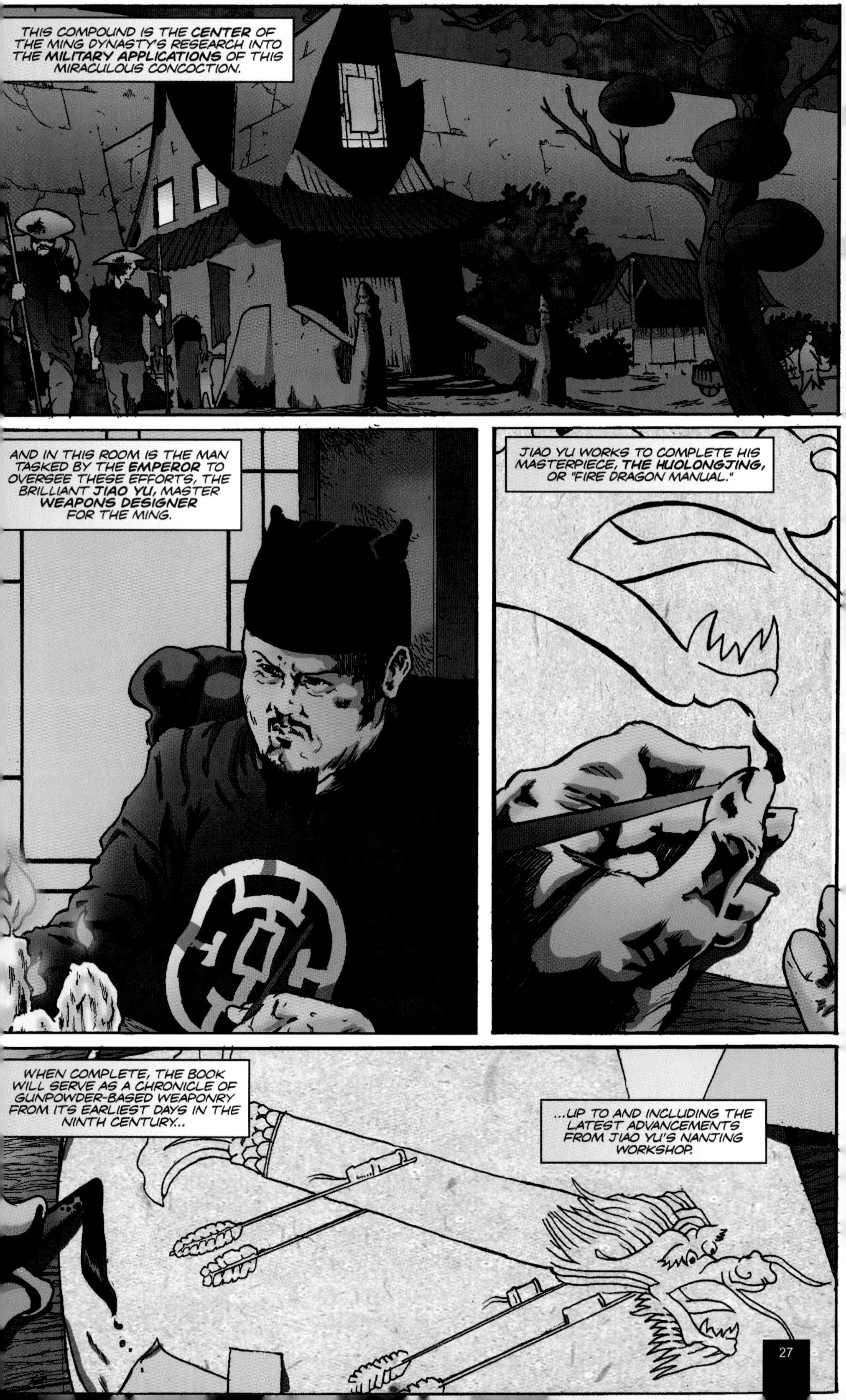
THIS COMPOUND IS THE CENTER OF THE MING DYNASTY'S RESEARCH INTO THE MILITARY APPLICATIONS OF THIS MIRACULOUS CONCOCTION.
AND IN THIS ROOM IS THE MAN TASKED BY THE EMPEROR TO OVERSEE THESE EFFORTS, THE BRILLIANT JIAO YU, MASTER WEAPONS DESIGNER FOR THE MING.
JIAO YU WORKS TO COMPLETE HIS MASTERPIECE, THE HUOLONGJING, OR "FIRE DRAGON MANUAL."
WHEN COMPLETE, THE BOOK WILL SERVE AS A CHRONICLE OF GUNPOWDER-BASED WEAPONRY FROM ITS EARLIEST DAYS IN THE NINTH CENTURY...
...UP TO AND INCLUDING THE LATEST ADVANCEMENTS FROM JIAO YU'S NANJING WORKSHOP.

BRILLIANT, TERRIFYING DEVICES SUCH AS THE 'FLYING CLOUD THUNDERCLAP ERUPTOR.'

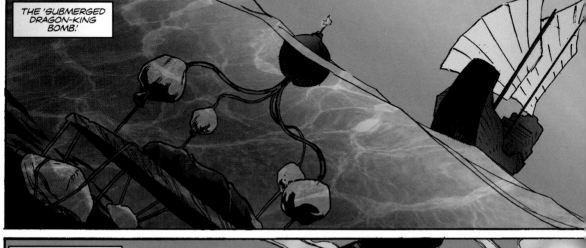

THE 'SUBMERGED DRAGON-KING BOMB.'

THE 'FLYING CROW WITH ROCKET BOMB.'

AND THE 'PHALANX-CHARGING FIRE GOURD.'

BUT OF ALL THE MANY DEVICES DEPICTED IN THE HUOLONGJING...

...THERE IS **ONE**, MORE THAN ANY OTHER, THAT IS RESPONSIBLE FOR THE MING DYNASTY'S RISE TO POWER.

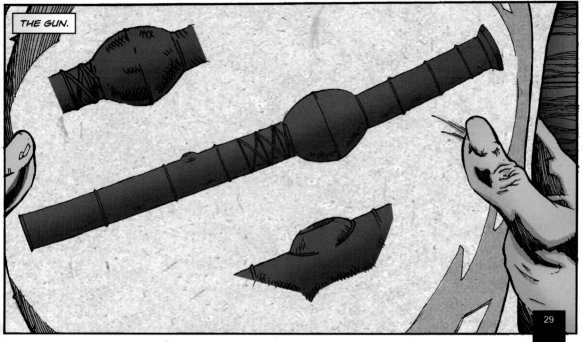

THE GUN.

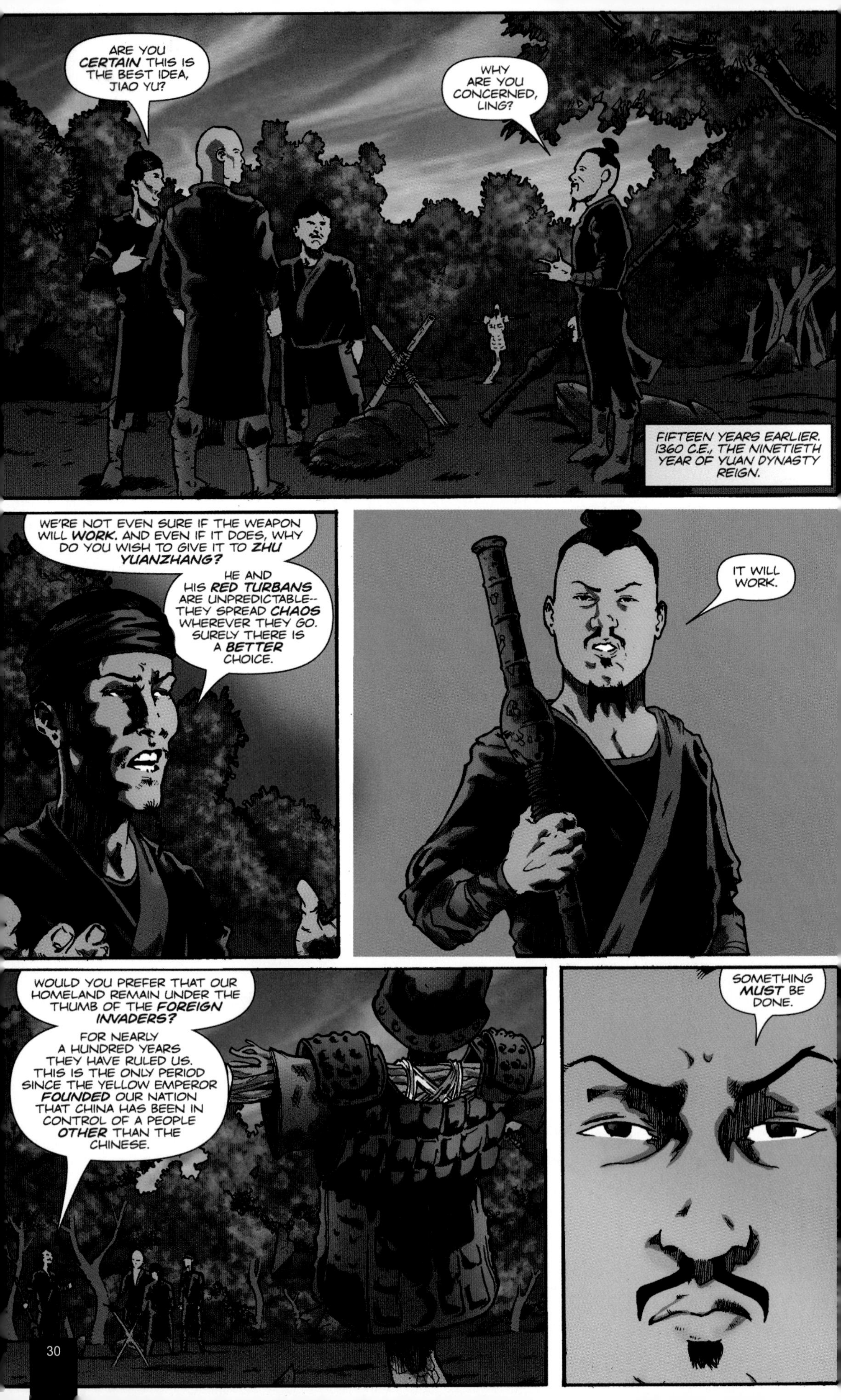
ARE YOU CERTAIN THIS IS THE BEST IDEA, JIAO YU?
WHY ARE YOU CONCERNED, LING?
FIFTEEN YEARS EARLIER. 1360 C.E., THE NINETIETH YEAR OF YUAN DYNASTY REIGN.
WE'RE NOT EVEN SURE IF THE WEAPON WILL WORK. AND EVEN IF IT DOES, WHY DO YOU WISH TO GIVE IT TO ZHU YUANZHANG?
HE AND HIS RED TURBANS ARE UNPREDICTABLE-- THEY SPREAD CHAOS WHEREVER THEY GO. SURELY THERE IS A BETTER CHOICE.
IT WILL WORK.
WOULD YOU PREFER THAT OUR HOMELAND REMAIN UNDER THE THUMB OF THE FOREIGN INVADERS?
FOR NEARLY A HUNDRED YEARS THEY HAVE RULED US. THIS IS THE ONLY PERIOD SINCE THE YELLOW EMPEROR FOUNDED OUR NATION THAT CHINA HAS BEEN IN CONTROL OF A PEOPLE OTHER THAN THE CHINESE.
SOMETHING MUST BE DONE.

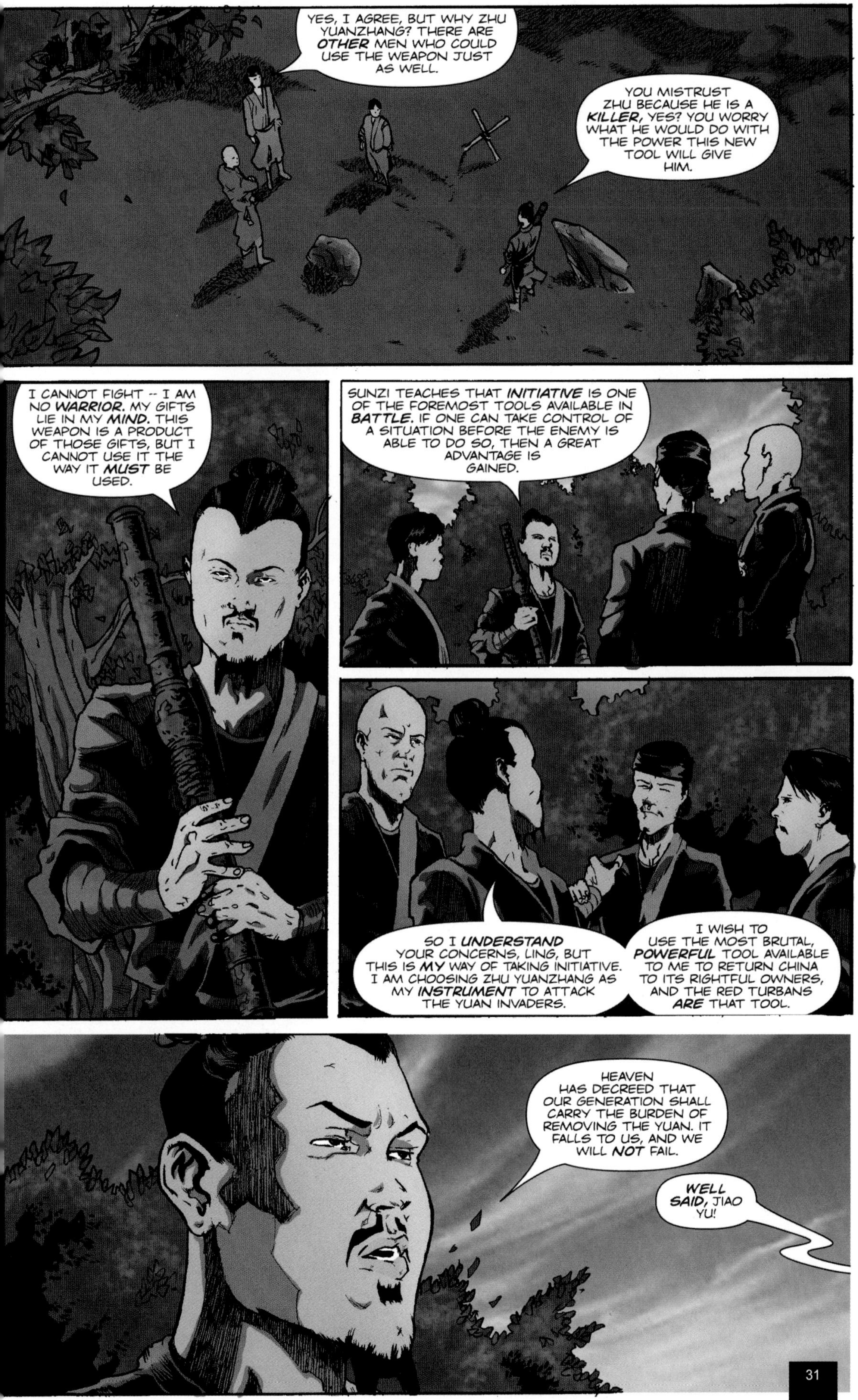
YES, I AGREE, BUT WHY ZHU YUANZHANG? THERE ARE OTHER MEN WHO COULD USE THE WEAPON JUST AS WELL.
YOU MISTRUST ZHU BECAUSE HE IS A KILLER, YES? YOU WORRY WHAT HE WOULD DO WITH THE POWER THIS NEW TOOL WILL GIVE HIM.
I CANNOT FIGHT -- I AM NO WARRIOR. MY GIFTS LIE IN MY MIND. THIS WEAPON IS A PRODUCT OF THOSE GIFTS, BUT I CANNOT USE IT THE WAY IT MUST BE USED.
SUNZI TEACHES THAT INITIATIVE IS ONE OF THE FOREMOST TOOLS AVAILABLE IN BATTLE. IF ONE CAN TAKE CONTROL OF A SITUATION BEFORE THE ENEMY IS ABLE TO DO SO, THEN A GREAT ADVANTAGE IS GAINED.
SO I UNDERSTAND YOUR CONCERNS, LING, BUT THIS IS MY WAY OF TAKING INITIATIVE. I AM CHOOSING ZHU YUANZHANG AS MY INSTRUMENT TO ATTACK THE YUAN INVADERS.
I WISH TO USE THE MOST BRUTAL, POWERFUL TOOL AVAILABLE TO ME TO RETURN CHINA TO ITS RIGHTFUL OWNERS, AND THE RED TURBANS ARE THAT TOOL.
HEAVEN HAS DECREED THAT OUR GENERATION SHALL CARRY THE BURDEN OF REMOVING THE YUAN. IT FALLS TO US, AND WE WILL NOT FAIL.
WELL SAID, JIAO YU!

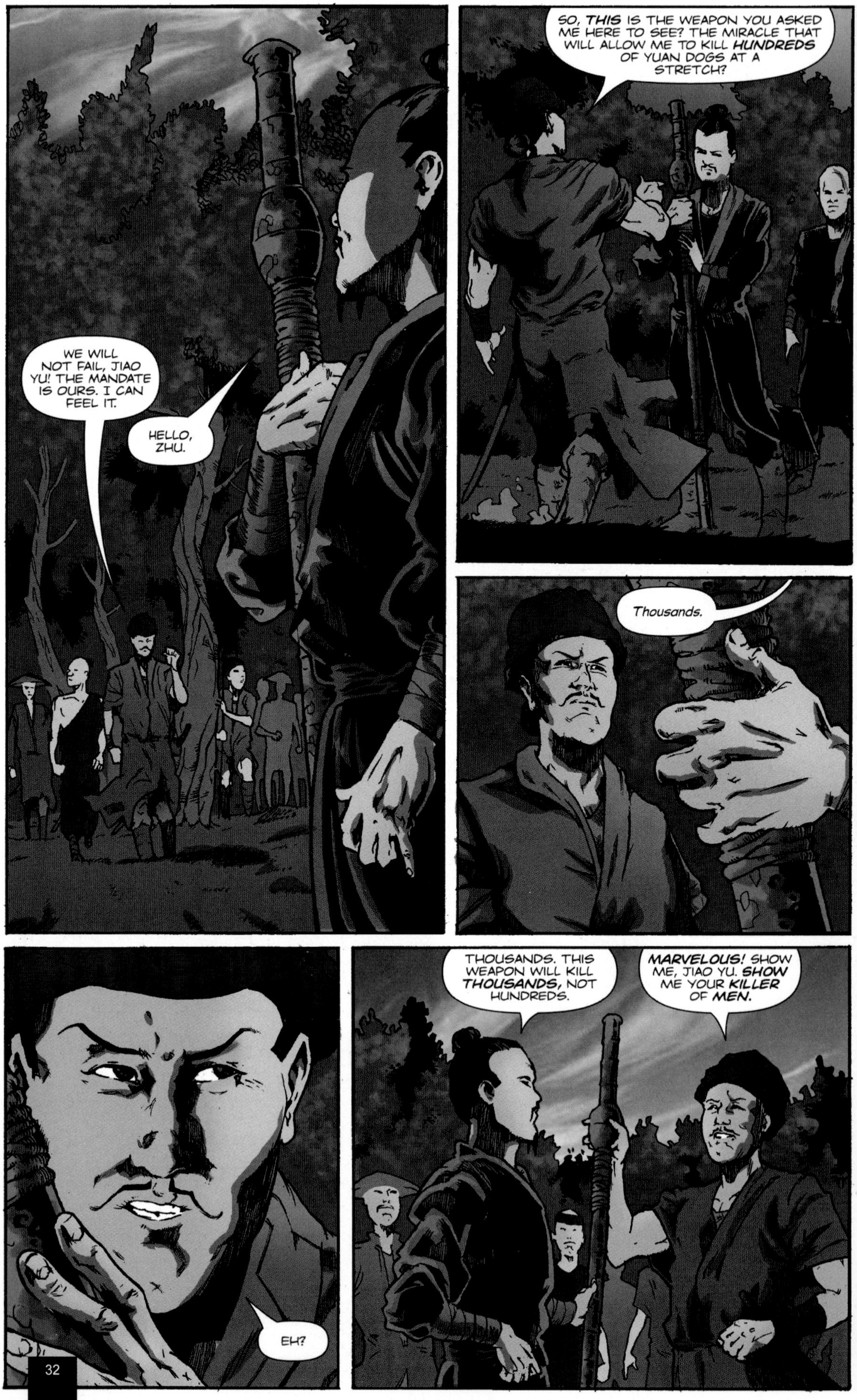
WE WILL NOT FAIL, JIAO YU! THE MANDATE IS OURS. I CAN FEEL IT.
HELLO, ZHU.
SO, THIS IS THE WEAPON YOU ASKED ME HERE TO SEE? THE MIRACLE THAT WILL ALLOW ME TO KILL HUNDREDS OF YUAN DOGS AT A STRETCH?
Thousands.
EH?
THOUSANDS. THIS WEAPON WILL KILL THOUSANDS, NOT HUNDREDS.
MARVELOUS! SHOW ME, JIAO YU. SHOW ME YOUR KILLER OF MEN.

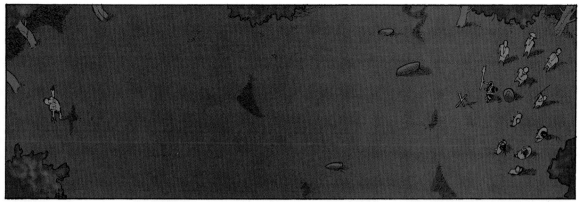

FIRE IT!

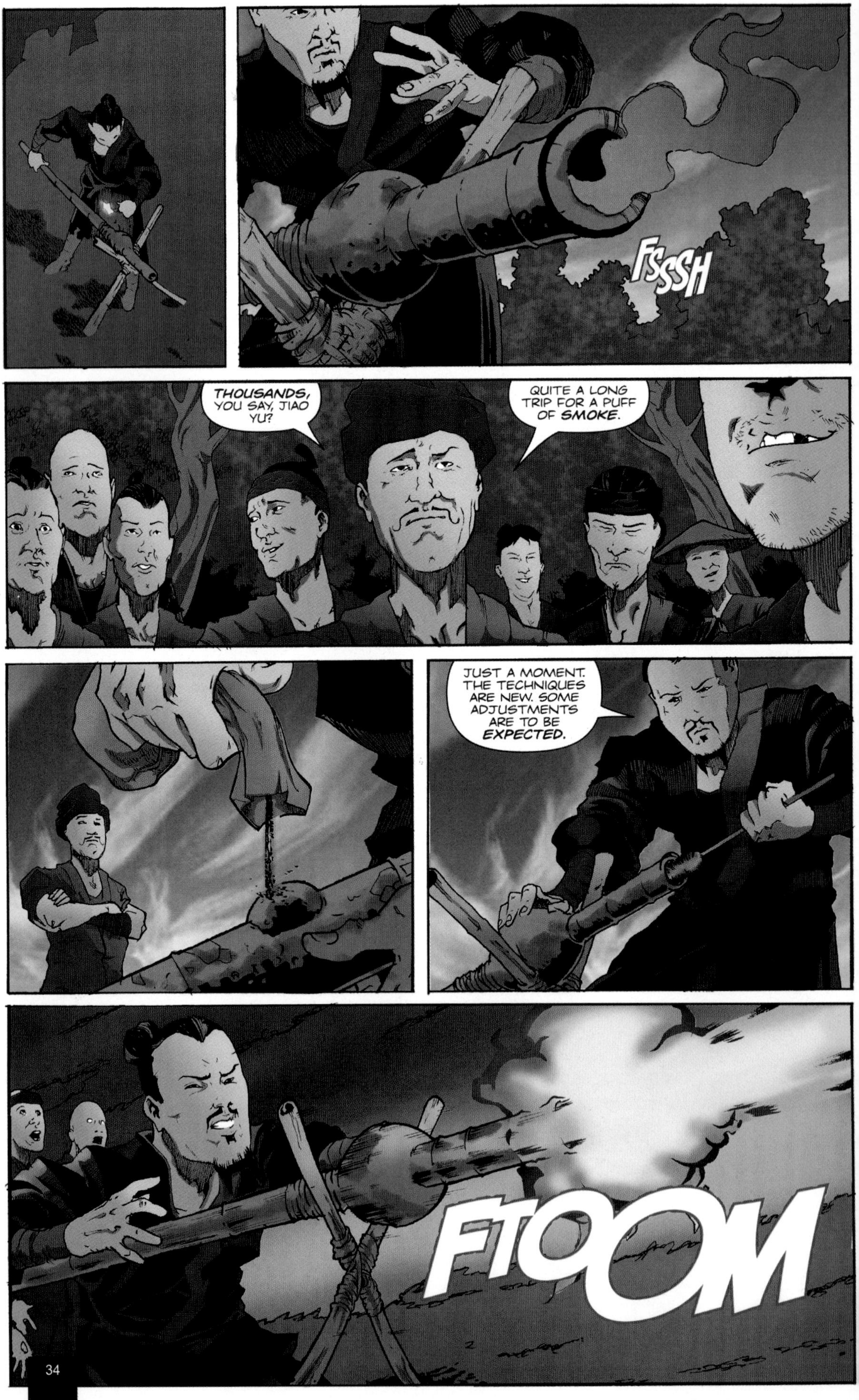
FSSSH
THOUSANDS, YOU SAY, JIAO YU?
QUITE A LONG TRIP FOR A PUFF OF SMOKE.
JUST A MOMENT. THE TECHNIQUES ARE NEW. SOME ADJUSTMENTS ARE TO BE EXPECTED.
FTOOOM

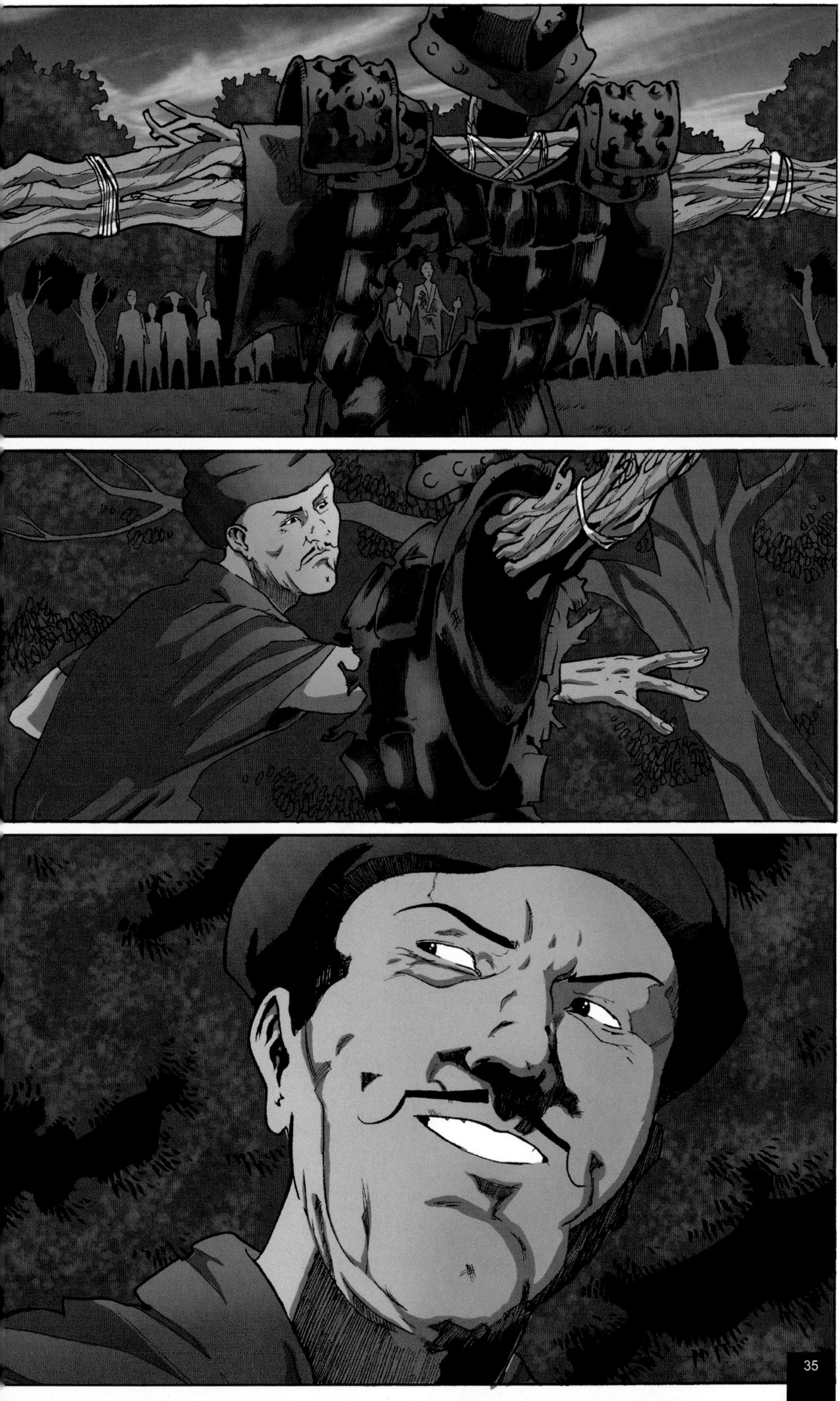

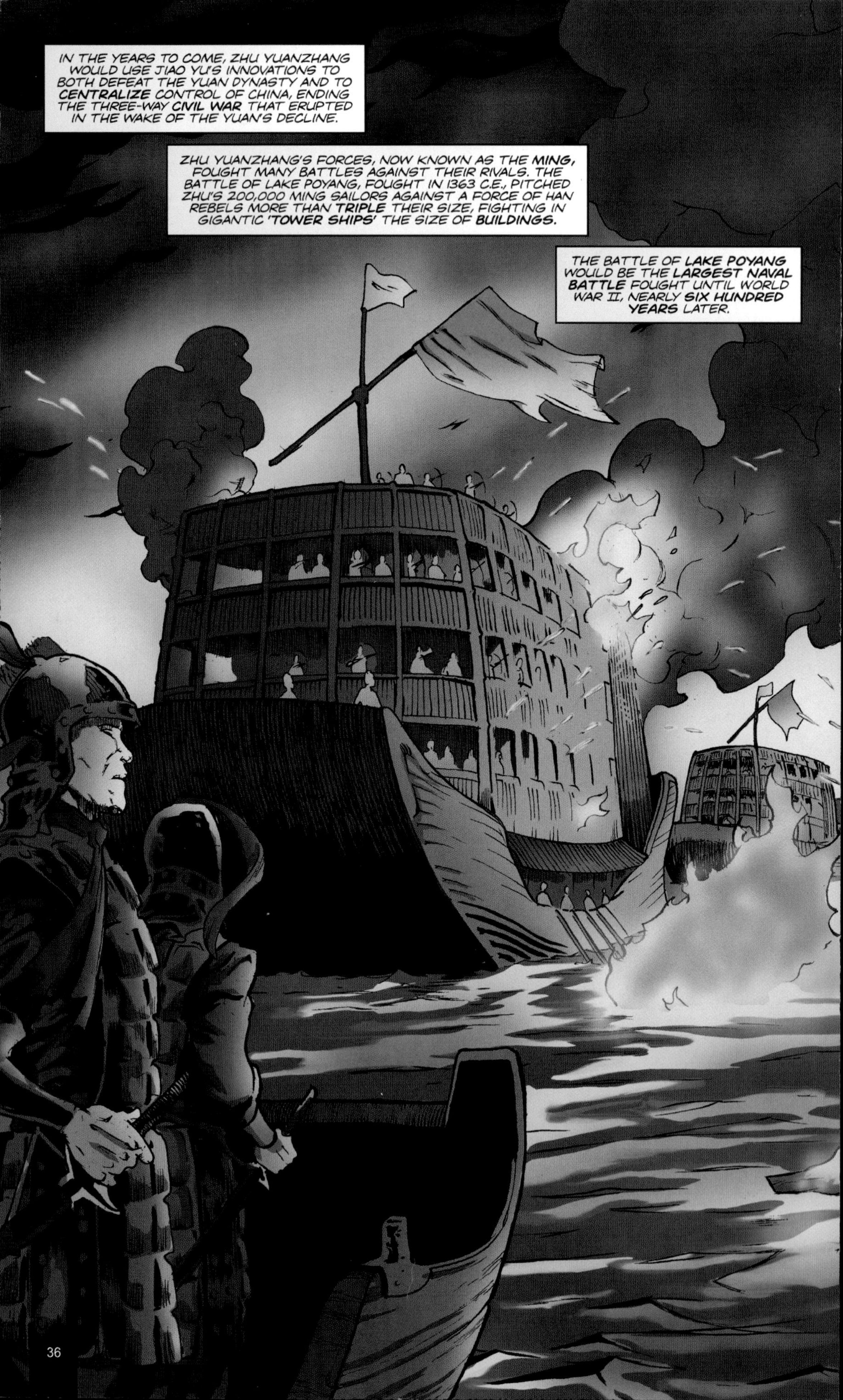
IN THE YEARS TO COME, ZHU YUANZHANG WOULD USE JIAO YU'S INNOVATIONS TO BOTH DEFEAT THE YUAN DYNASTY AND TO CENTRALIZE CONTROL OF CHINA, ENDING THE THREE-WAY CIVIL WAR THAT ERUPTED IN THE WAKE OF THE YUAN'S DECLINE.
ZHU YUANZHANG'S FORCES, NOW KNOWN AS THE MING, FOUGHT MANY BATTLES AGAINST THEIR RIVALS. THE BATTLE OF LAKE POYANG, FOUGHT IN 1363 C.E., PITCHED ZHU'S 200,000 MING SAILORS AGAINST A FORCE OF HAN REBELS MORE THAN TRIPLE THEIR SIZE, FIGHTING IN GIGANTIC 'TOWER SHIPS' THE SIZE OF BUILDINGS.
THE BATTLE OF LAKE POYANG WOULD BE THE LARGEST NAVAL BATTLE FOUGHT UNTIL WORLD WAR II, NEARLY SIX HUNDRED YEARS LATER.

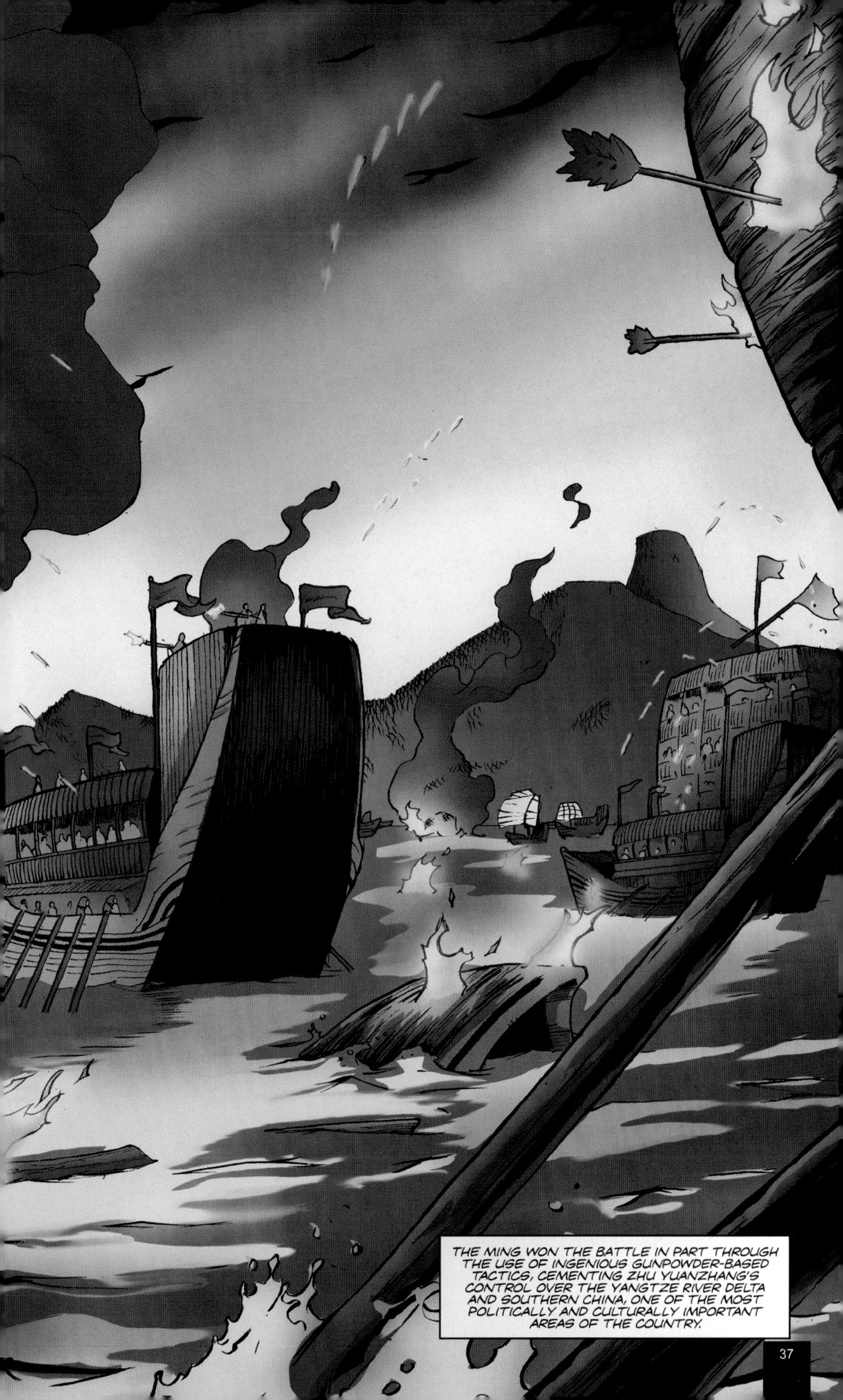
THE MING WON THE BATTLE IN PART THROUGH THE USE OF INGENIOUS GUNPOWDER-BASED TACTICS, CEMENTING ZHU YUANZHANG'S CONTROL OVER THE YANGTZE RIVER DELTA AND SOUTHERN CHINA, ONE OF THE MOST POLITICALLY AND CULTURALLY IMPORTANT AREAS OF THE COUNTRY.

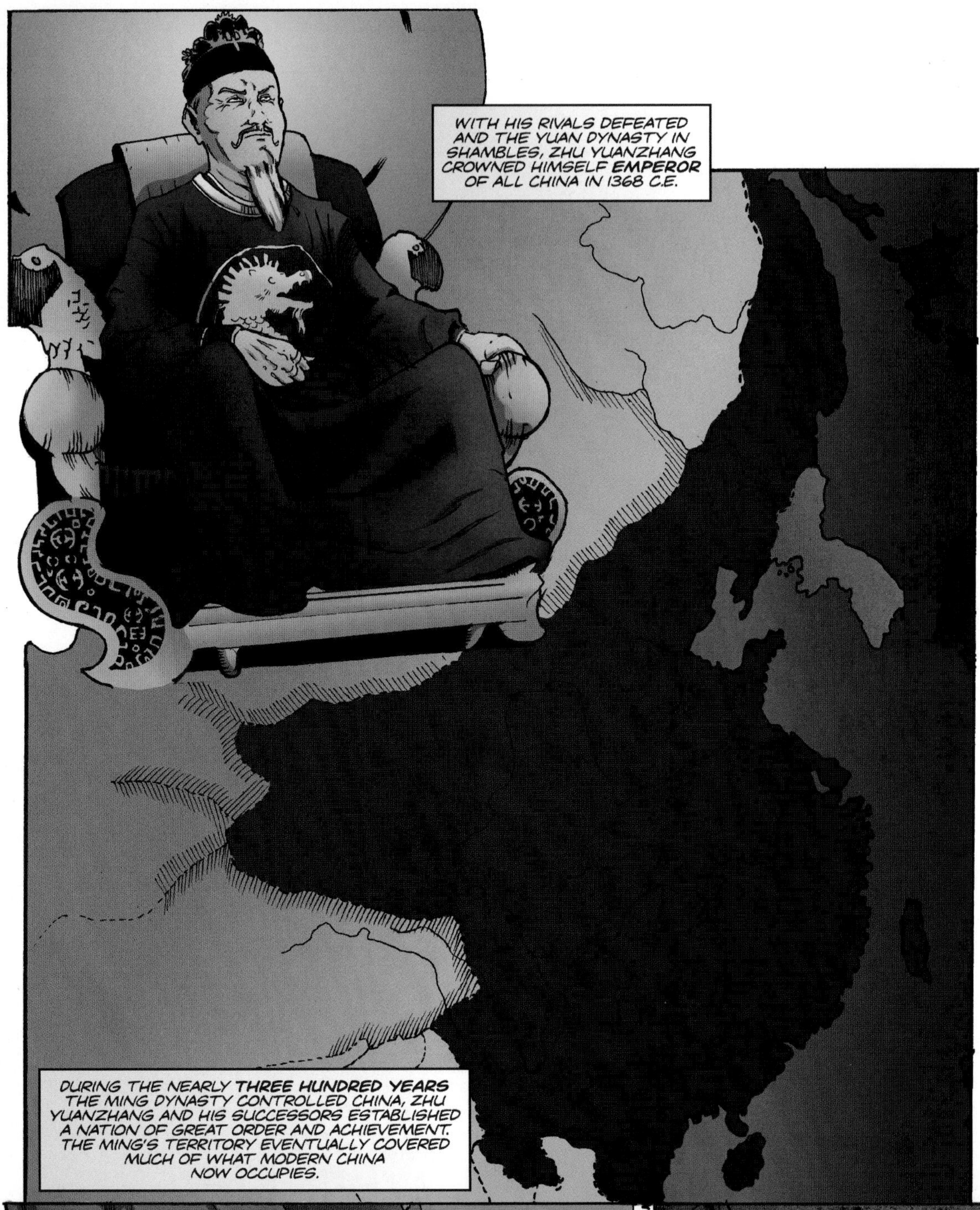
WITH HIS RIVALS DEFEATED AND THE YUAN DYNASTY IN SHAMBLES, ZHU YUANZHANG CROWNED HIMSELF **EMPEROR** OF ALL CHINA IN 1368 C.E.
DURING THE NEARLY **THREE HUNDRED YEARS** THE MING DYNASTY CONTROLLED CHINA, ZHU YUANZHANG AND HIS SUCCESSORS ESTABLISHED A NATION OF GREAT ORDER AND ACHIEVEMENT. THE MING'S TERRITORY EVENTUALLY COVERED MUCH OF WHAT MODERN CHINA NOW OCCUPIES.

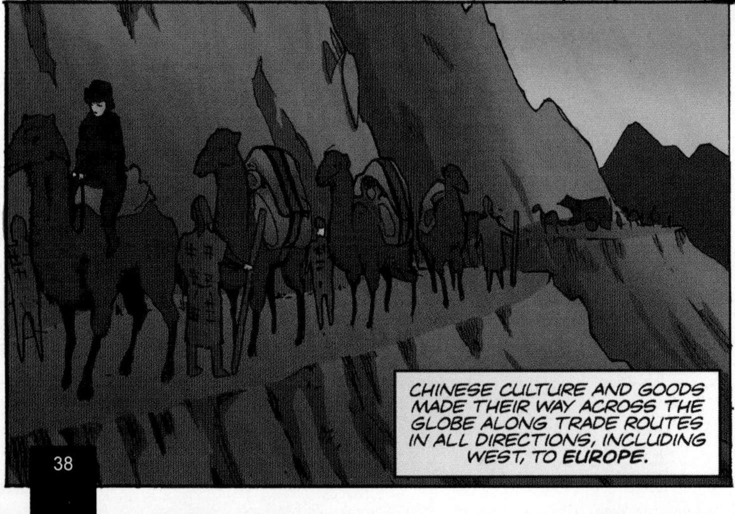
CHINESE CULTURE AND GOODS MADE THEIR WAY ACROSS THE GLOBE ALONG TRADE ROUTES IN ALL DIRECTIONS, INCLUDING WEST, TO **EUROPE**.

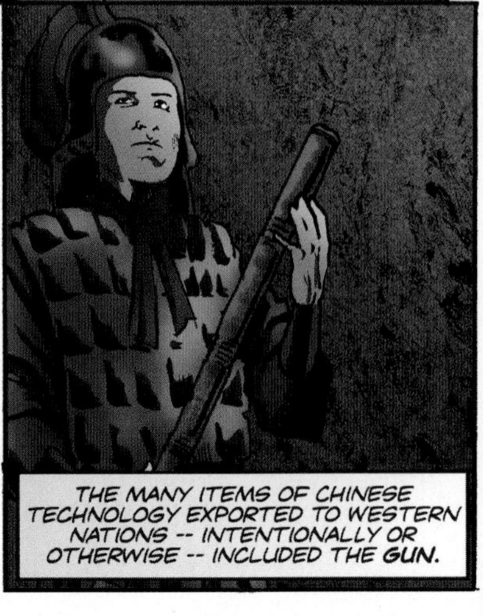
THE MANY ITEMS OF CHINESE TECHNOLOGY EXPORTED TO WESTERN NATIONS -- INTENTIONALLY OR OTHERWISE -- INCLUDED THE **GUN**.

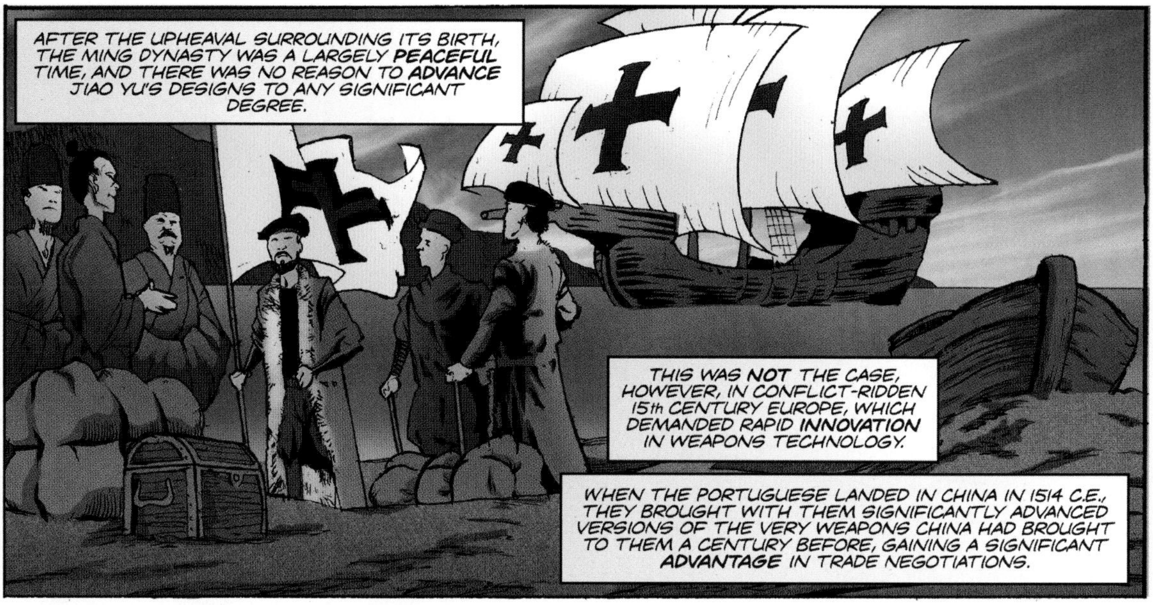
AFTER THE UPHEAVAL SURROUNDING ITS BIRTH, THE MING DYNASTY WAS A LARGELY PEACEFUL TIME, AND THERE WAS NO REASON TO ADVANCE JIAO YU'S DESIGNS TO ANY SIGNIFICANT DEGREE.
THIS WAS NOT THE CASE, HOWEVER, IN CONFLICT-RIDDEN 15th CENTURY EUROPE, WHICH DEMANDED RAPID INNOVATION IN WEAPONS TECHNOLOGY.
WHEN THE PORTUGUESE LANDED IN CHINA IN 1514 C.E., THEY BROUGHT WITH THEM SIGNIFICANTLY ADVANCED VERSIONS OF THE VERY WEAPONS CHINA HAD BROUGHT TO THEM A CENTURY BEFORE, GAINING A SIGNIFICANT ADVANTAGE IN TRADE NEGOTIATIONS.

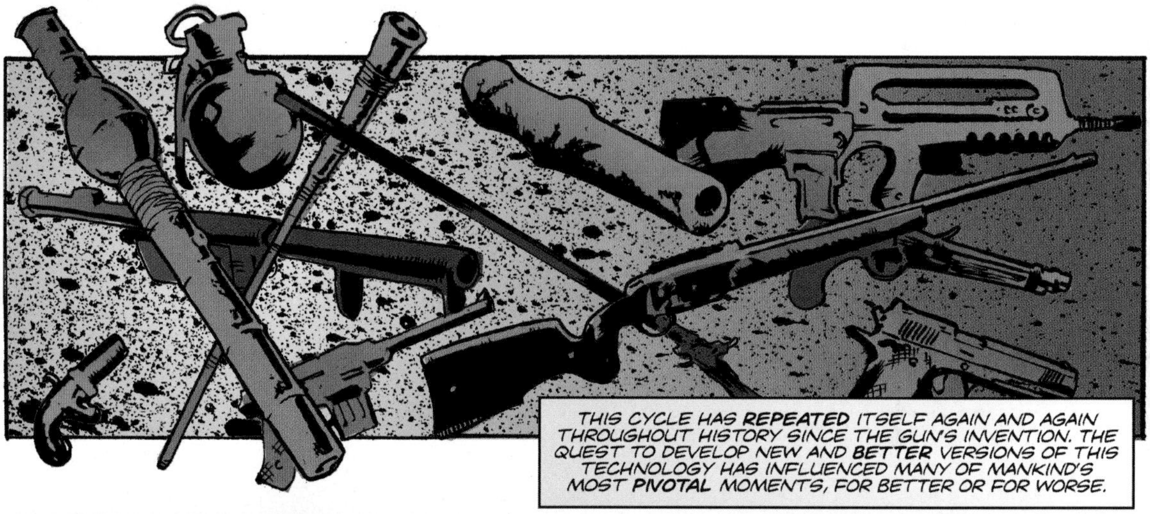
THIS CYCLE HAS REPEATED ITSELF AGAIN AND AGAIN THROUGHOUT HISTORY SINCE THE GUN'S INVENTION. THE QUEST TO DEVELOP NEW AND BETTER VERSIONS OF THIS TECHNOLOGY HAS INFLUENCED MANY OF MANKIND'S MOST PIVOTAL MOMENTS, FOR BETTER OR FOR WORSE.

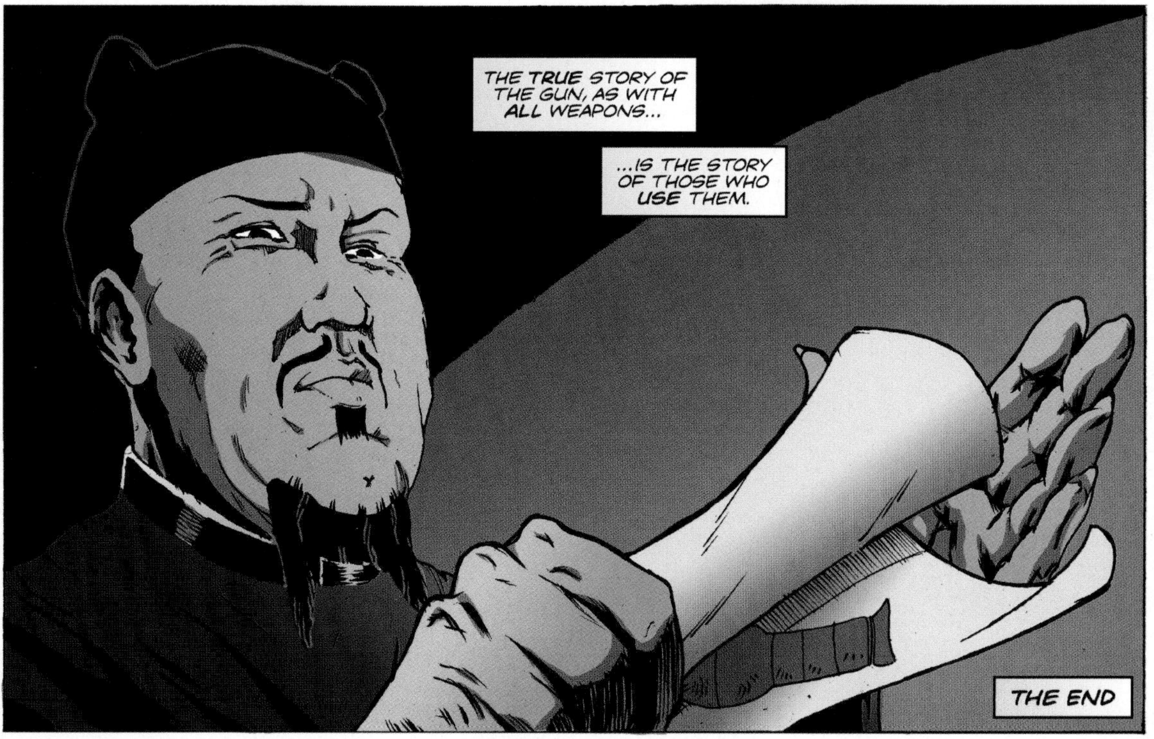
THE TRUE STORY OF THE GUN, AS WITH ALL WEAPONS...
...IS THE STORY OF THOSE WHO USE THEM.
THE END

MANKIND
DECODED

In both *The Mongol World* and *The Gun*, some of the contributions and achievements of ancient China are depicted.

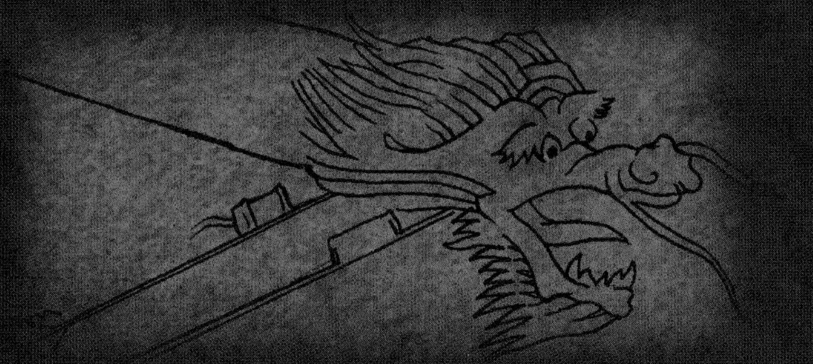

By revolutionizing ***warfare,*** we see the innovation of adding the foot stirrup to the horse saddle as well as the invention of ***gunpowder*** (which quickly spawned guns, hand grenades, and land mines). But there are literally hundreds of other inventions and innovations that also come from ancient China, including:

The Magnetic Compass: incorporating ***iron***, it makes use of the earth's magnetic field, as opposed to earlier compasses that relied on the position of the sun.

Paper: thin, ***wood pulp***- based sheets that replace clay tablets, silk strips, bamboo scrolls, and other materials. For the first time in history, money was more than just metal coins.

Movable Type Printing: a necessary precursor to the ***printing press*** developed by Johannes Gutenberg three centuries later.

The Modern Calendar: showing 365.25 days in the year, several centries before the Julian Calendar is developed in Rome.

Chemical Warfare: smoke from burnt mustard plants and powdered lime directed at enemies.

Fishing Reel: small pulley system attached to a wooden rod used to control the line.

The Fork: a multi-pronged instrument made of bone used for eating prepared food.

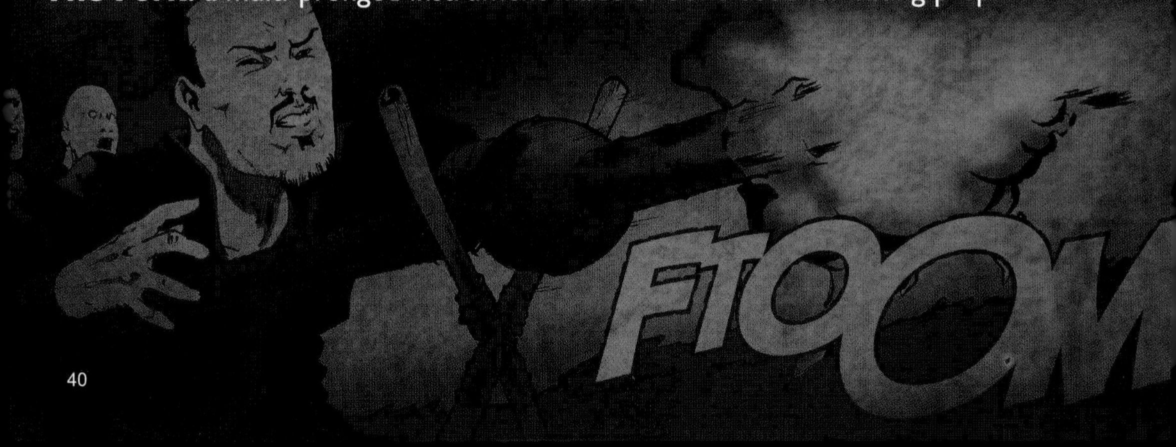
FTOOM

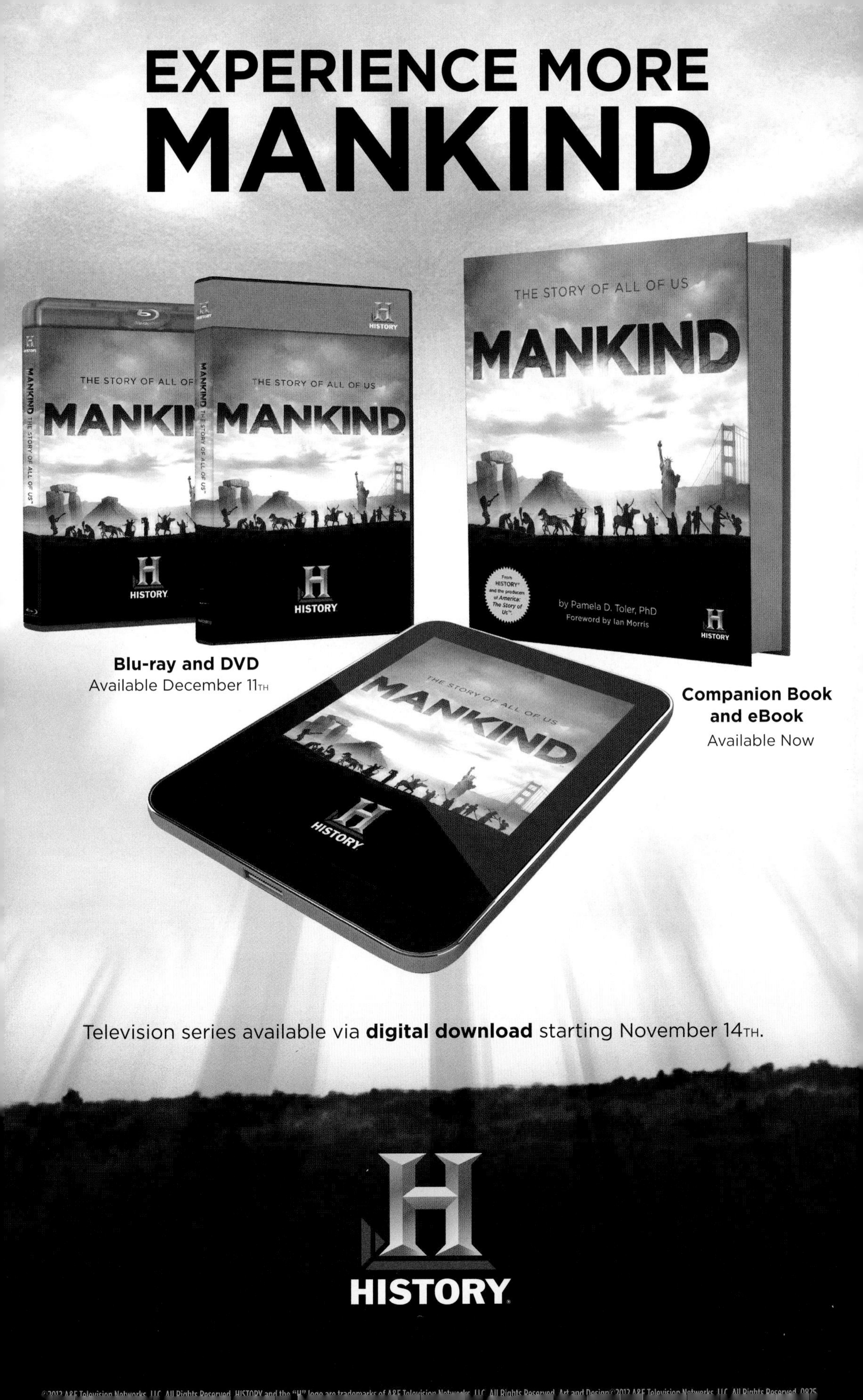
EXPERIENCE MORE
MANKIND
THE STORY OF ALL OF US
MANKIND
by Pamela D. Toler, PhD
Foreword by Ian Morris
HISTORY
Blu-ray and DVD
Available December 11TH
Companion Book and eBook
Available Now
Television series available via digital download starting November 14TH.
HISTORY
©2012 A&E Television Networks, LLC. All Rights Reserved. HISTORY and the "H" logo are trademarks of A&E Television Networks, LLC. All Rights Reserved. Art and Design©2012 A&E Television Networks, LLC. All Rights Reserved. 0825

PLAGUE AND NEW OPPORTUNITY

WRITTEN BY
KEVIN BAKER

ART BY
JAVIER ARANDA

COLORS BY
IAN HERRING

LETTERS BY
JIM CAMPBELL

AS THE BLACK DEATH CONTINUES TO SPREAD, A YOUNG ITALIAN
TRADER PURSUES NEW OPPORTUNITIES ON
THE AFRICAN HORIZON.

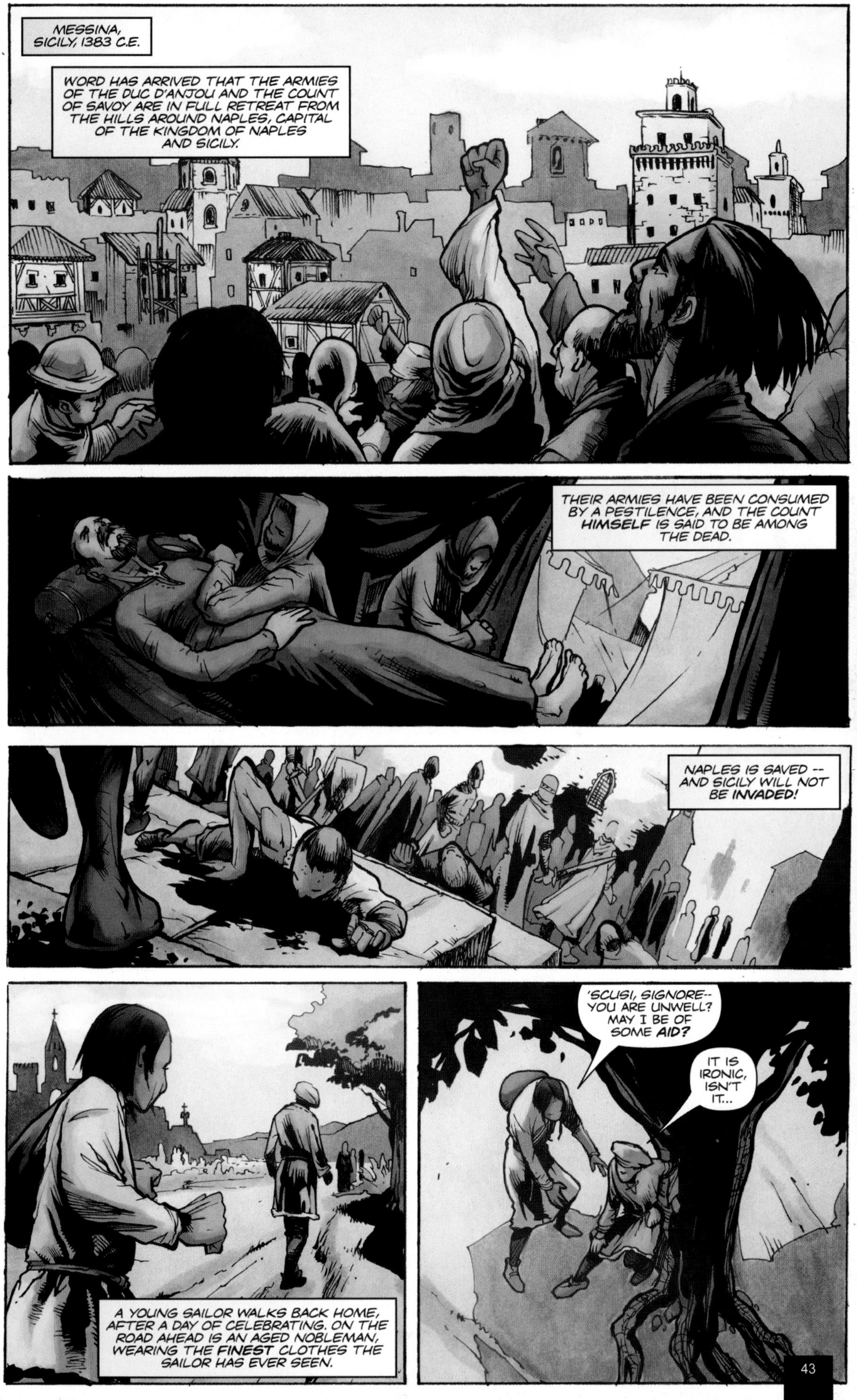
MESSINA, SICILY, 1383 C.E.
WORD HAS ARRIVED THAT THE ARMIES OF THE DUC D'ANJOU AND THE COUNT OF SAVOY ARE IN FULL RETREAT FROM THE HILLS AROUND NAPLES, CAPITAL OF THE KINGDOM OF NAPLES AND SICILY.
THEIR ARMIES HAVE BEEN CONSUMED BY A PESTILENCE, AND THE COUNT **HIMSELF** IS SAID TO BE AMONG THE DEAD.
NAPLES IS SAVED -- AND SICILY WILL NOT BE **INVADED!**
A YOUNG SAILOR WALKS BACK HOME, AFTER A DAY OF CELEBRATING. ON THE ROAD AHEAD IS AN AGED NOBLEMAN, WEARING THE **FINEST** CLOTHES THE SAILOR HAS EVER SEEN.
'SCUSI, SIGNORE-- YOU ARE UNWELL? MAY I BE OF SOME **AID?**
IT IS IRONIC, ISN'T IT...

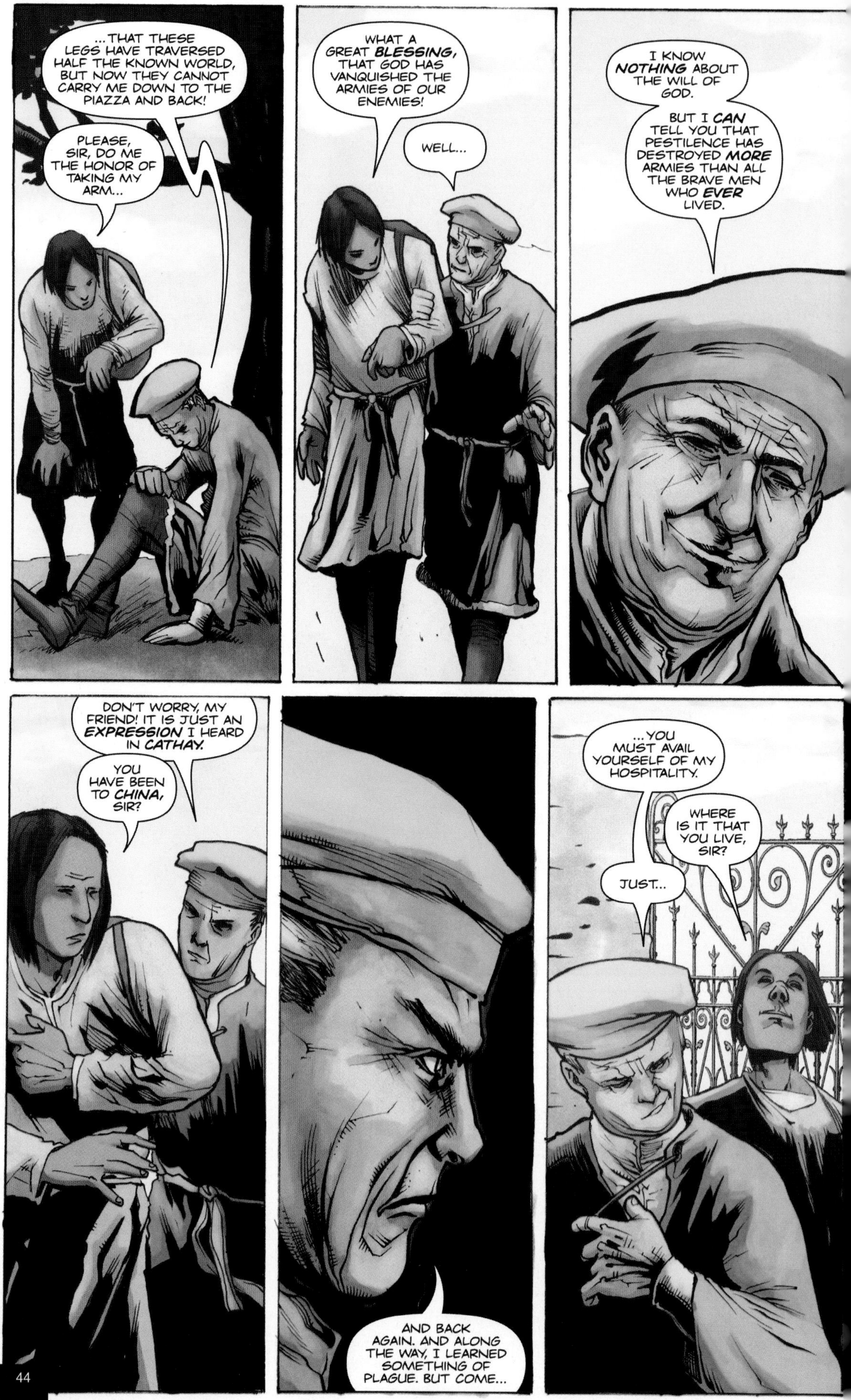
...THAT THESE LEGS HAVE TRAVERSED HALF THE KNOWN WORLD, BUT NOW THEY CANNOT CARRY ME DOWN TO THE PIAZZA AND BACK!
PLEASE, SIR, DO ME THE HONOR OF TAKING MY ARM...
WHAT A GREAT BLESSING, THAT GOD HAS VANQUISHED THE ARMIES OF OUR ENEMIES!
WELL...
I KNOW NOTHING ABOUT THE WILL OF GOD.
BUT I CAN TELL YOU THAT PESTILENCE HAS DESTROYED MORE ARMIES THAN ALL THE BRAVE MEN WHO EVER LIVED.
DON'T WORRY, MY FRIEND! IT IS JUST AN EXPRESSION I HEARD IN CATHAY.
YOU HAVE BEEN TO CHINA, SIR?
AND BACK AGAIN. AND ALONG THE WAY, I LEARNED SOMETHING OF PLAGUE. BUT COME...
...YOU MUST AVAIL YOURSELF OF MY HOSPITALITY.
WHERE IS IT THAT YOU LIVE, SIR?
JUST...

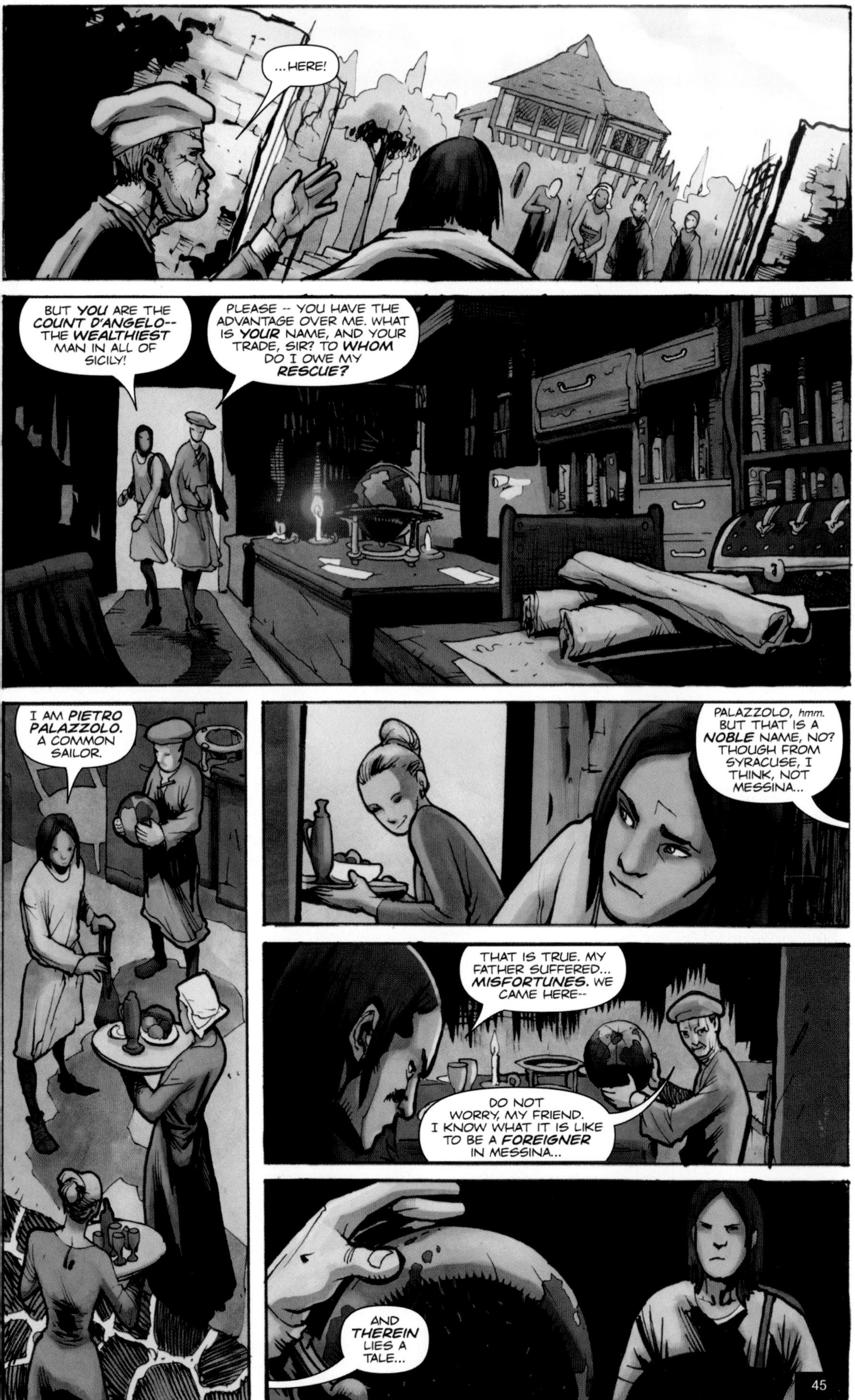

...HERE!
BUT YOU ARE THE COUNT D'ANGELO-- THE WEALTHIEST MAN IN ALL OF SICILY!
PLEASE -- YOU HAVE THE ADVANTAGE OVER ME. WHAT IS YOUR NAME, AND YOUR TRADE, SIR? TO WHOM DO I OWE MY RESCUE?
I AM PIETRO PALAZZOLO. A COMMON SAILOR.
PALAZZOLO, hmm. BUT THAT IS A NOBLE NAME, NO? THOUGH FROM SYRACUSE, I THINK, NOT MESSINA...
THAT IS TRUE. MY FATHER SUFFERED... MISFORTUNES. WE CAME HERE--
DO NOT WORRY, MY FRIEND. I KNOW WHAT IT IS LIKE TO BE A FOREIGNER IN MESSINA...
AND THEREIN LIES A TALE...

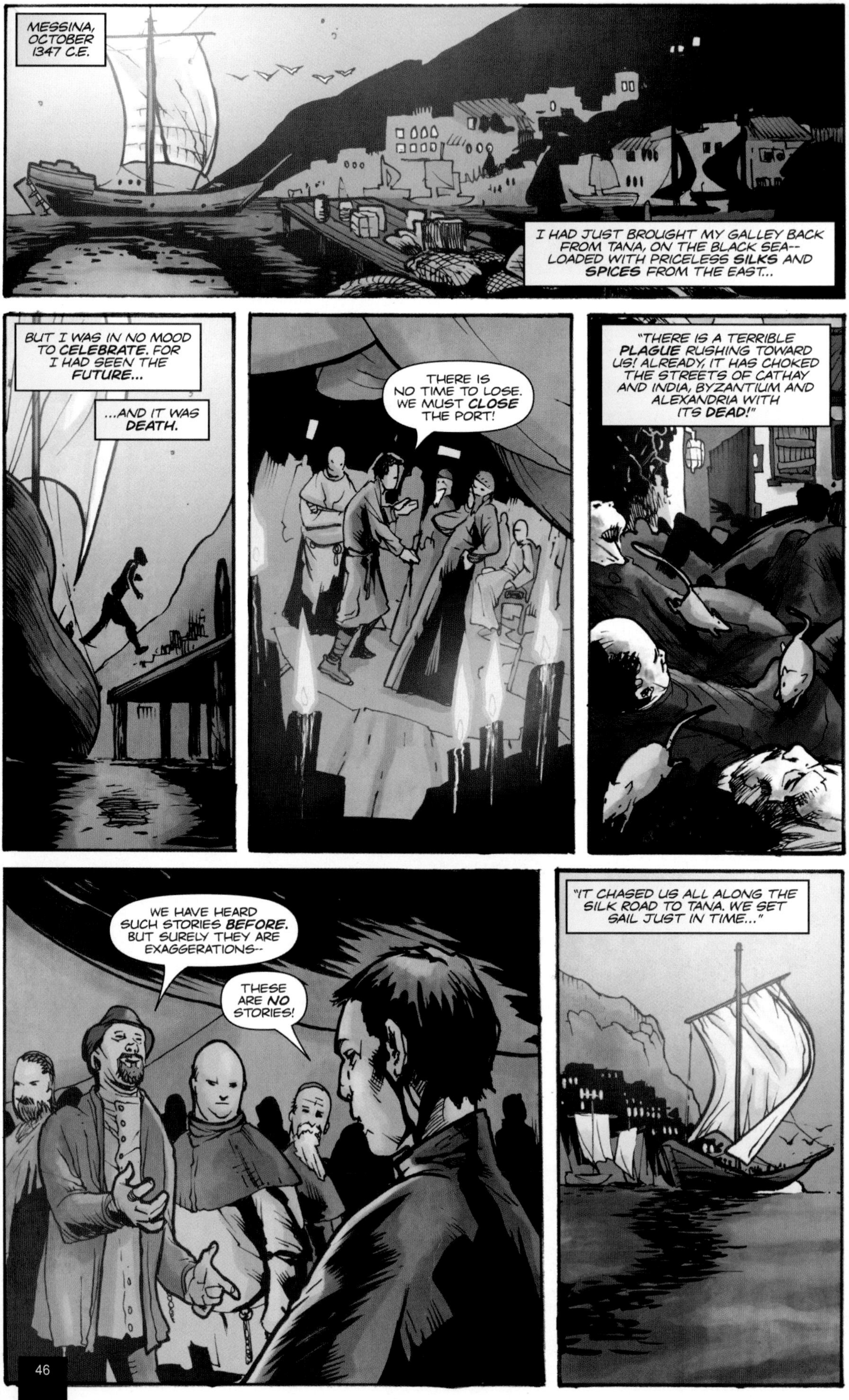
MESSINA, OCTOBER 1347 C.E.
I HAD JUST BROUGHT MY GALLEY BACK FROM TANA, ON THE BLACK SEA-- LOADED WITH PRICELESS SILKS AND SPICES FROM THE EAST...
BUT I WAS IN NO MOOD TO CELEBRATE. FOR I HAD SEEN THE FUTURE...
...AND IT WAS DEATH.
THERE IS NO TIME TO LOSE. WE MUST CLOSE THE PORT!
"THERE IS A TERRIBLE PLAGUE RUSHING TOWARD US! ALREADY, IT HAS CHOKED THE STREETS OF CATHAY AND INDIA, BYZANTIUM AND ALEXANDRIA WITH ITS DEAD!"
WE HAVE HEARD SUCH STORIES BEFORE. BUT SURELY THEY ARE EXAGGERATIONS--
THESE ARE NO STORIES!
"IT CHASED US ALL ALONG THE SILK ROAD TO TANA. WE SET SAIL JUST IN TIME..."

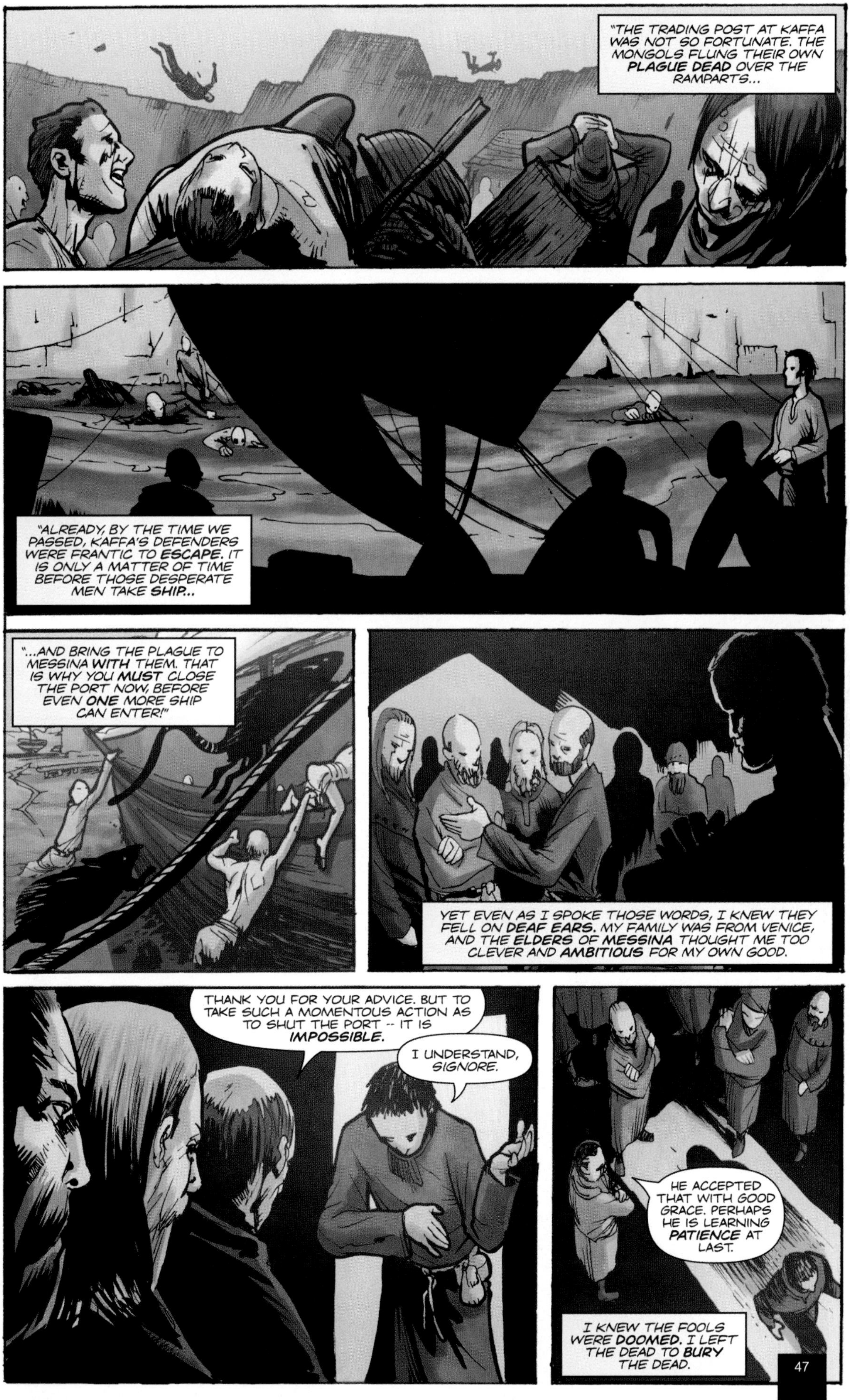
"THE TRADING POST AT KAFFA WAS NOT SO FORTUNATE. THE MONGOLS FLUNG THEIR OWN PLAGUE DEAD OVER THE RAMPARTS...
"ALREADY, BY THE TIME WE PASSED, KAFFA'S DEFENDERS WERE FRANTIC TO ESCAPE. IT IS ONLY A MATTER OF TIME BEFORE THOSE DESPERATE MEN TAKE SHIP...
"...AND BRING THE PLAGUE TO MESSINA WITH THEM. THAT IS WHY YOU MUST CLOSE THE PORT NOW, BEFORE EVEN ONE MORE SHIP CAN ENTER!"
YET EVEN AS I SPOKE THOSE WORDS, I KNEW THEY FELL ON DEAF EARS. MY FAMILY WAS FROM VENICE, AND THE ELDERS OF MESSINA THOUGHT ME TOO CLEVER AND AMBITIOUS FOR MY OWN GOOD.
THANK YOU FOR YOUR ADVICE. BUT TO TAKE SUCH A MOMENTOUS ACTION AS TO SHUT THE PORT -- IT IS IMPOSSIBLE.
I UNDERSTAND, SIGNORE.
HE ACCEPTED THAT WITH GOOD GRACE. PERHAPS HE IS LEARNING PATIENCE AT LAST.
I KNEW THE FOOLS WERE DOOMED. I LEFT THE DEAD TO BURY THE DEAD.

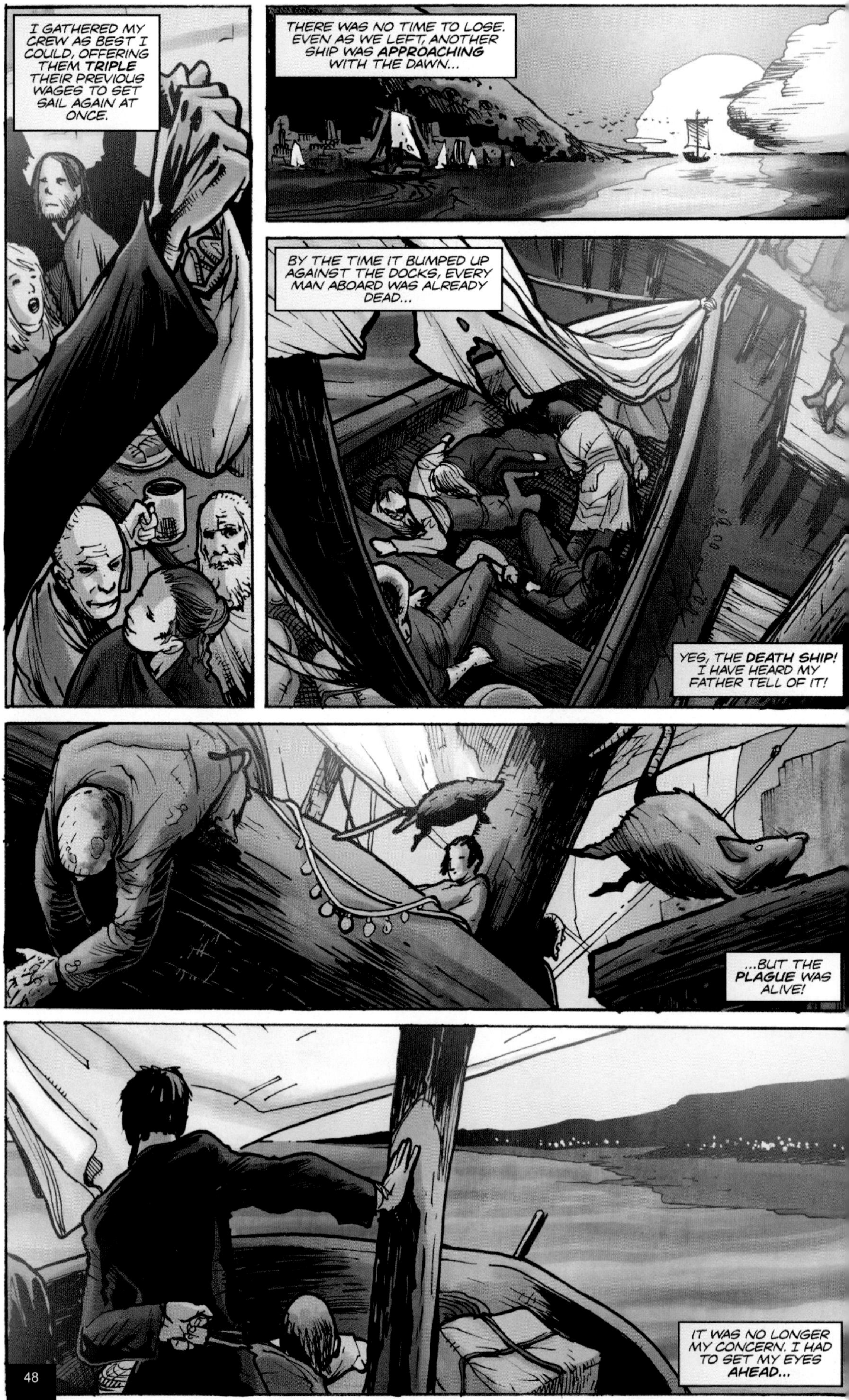

I GATHERED MY CREW AS BEST I COULD, OFFERING THEM **TRIPLE** THEIR PREVIOUS WAGES TO SET SAIL AGAIN AT ONCE.
THERE WAS NO TIME TO LOSE. EVEN AS WE LEFT, ANOTHER SHIP WAS **APPROACHING** WITH THE DAWN...
BY THE TIME IT BUMPED UP AGAINST THE DOCKS, EVERY MAN ABOARD WAS ALREADY DEAD...
YES, THE **DEATH SHIP!** I HAVE HEARD MY FATHER TELL OF IT!
...BUT THE **PLAGUE** WAS ALIVE!
IT WAS NO LONGER MY CONCERN. I HAD TO SET MY EYES **AHEAD...**

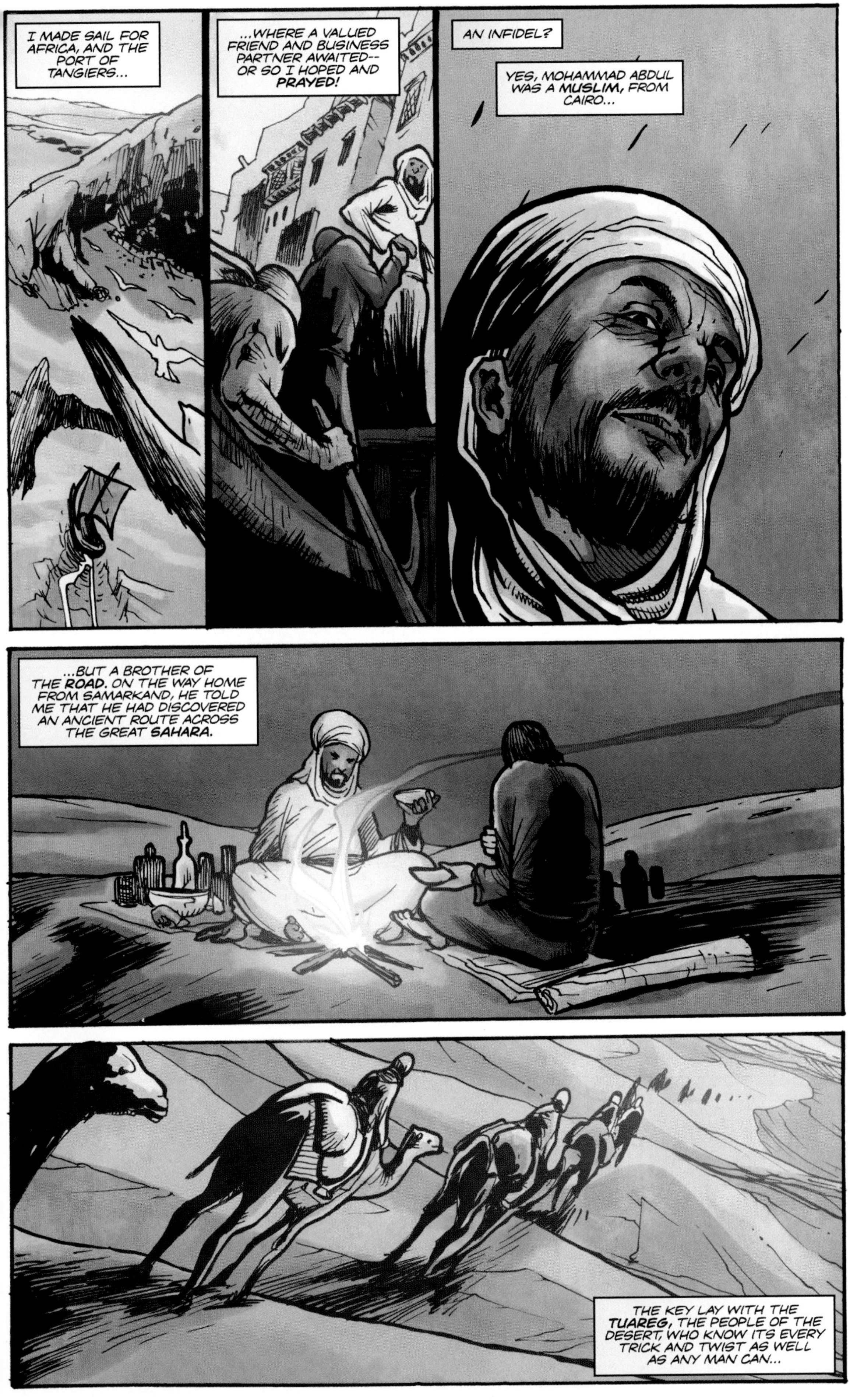

I MADE SAIL FOR AFRICA, AND THE PORT OF TANGIERS...
...WHERE A VALUED FRIEND AND BUSINESS PARTNER AWAITED-- OR SO I HOPED AND **PRAYED!**
AN INFIDEL?
YES, MOHAMMAD ABDUL WAS A **MUSLIM**, FROM CAIRO...
...BUT A BROTHER OF THE **ROAD**. ON THE WAY HOME FROM SAMARKAND, HE TOLD ME THAT HE HAD DISCOVERED AN ANCIENT ROUTE ACROSS THE GREAT **SAHARA**.
THE KEY LAY WITH THE **TUAREG**, THE PEOPLE OF THE DESERT, WHO KNOW ITS EVERY TRICK AND TWIST AS WELL AS ANY MAN CAN...

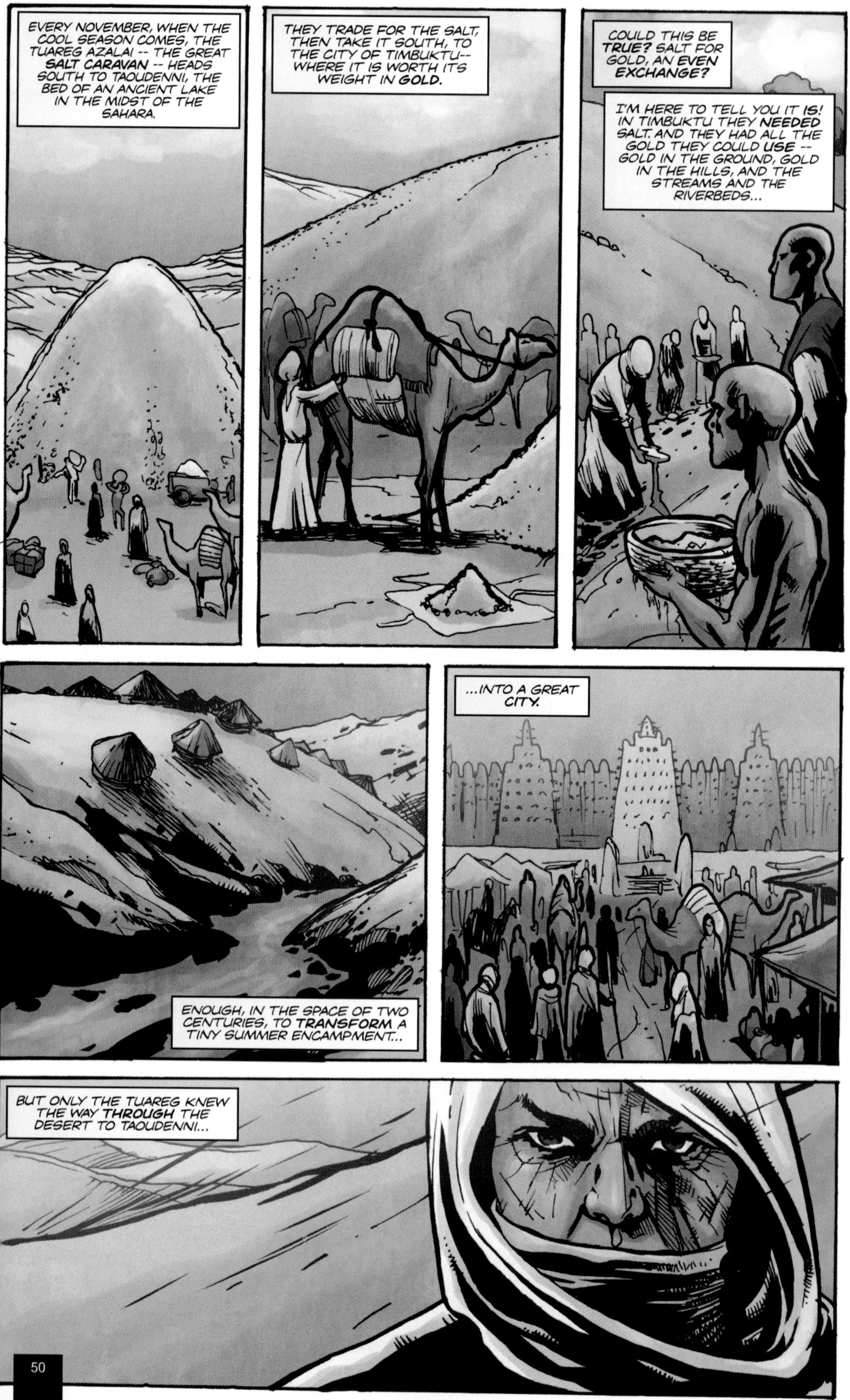
EVERY NOVEMBER, WHEN THE COOL SEASON COMES, THE TUAREG AZALAI -- THE GREAT SALT CARAVAN -- HEADS SOUTH TO TAOUDENNI, THE BED OF AN ANCIENT LAKE IN THE MIDST OF THE SAHARA.
THEY TRADE FOR THE SALT, THEN TAKE IT SOUTH, TO THE CITY OF TIMBUKTU-- WHERE IT IS WORTH ITS WEIGHT IN GOLD.
COULD THIS BE TRUE? SALT FOR GOLD, AN EVEN EXCHANGE?
I'M HERE TO TELL YOU IT IS! IN TIMBUKTU THEY NEEDED SALT. AND THEY HAD ALL THE GOLD THEY COULD USE -- GOLD IN THE GROUND, GOLD IN THE HILLS, AND THE STREAMS AND THE RIVERBEDS...
ENOUGH, IN THE SPACE OF TWO CENTURIES, TO TRANSFORM A TINY SUMMER ENCAMPMENT...
...INTO A GREAT CITY.
BUT ONLY THE TUAREG KNEW THE WAY THROUGH THE DESERT TO TAOUDENNI...

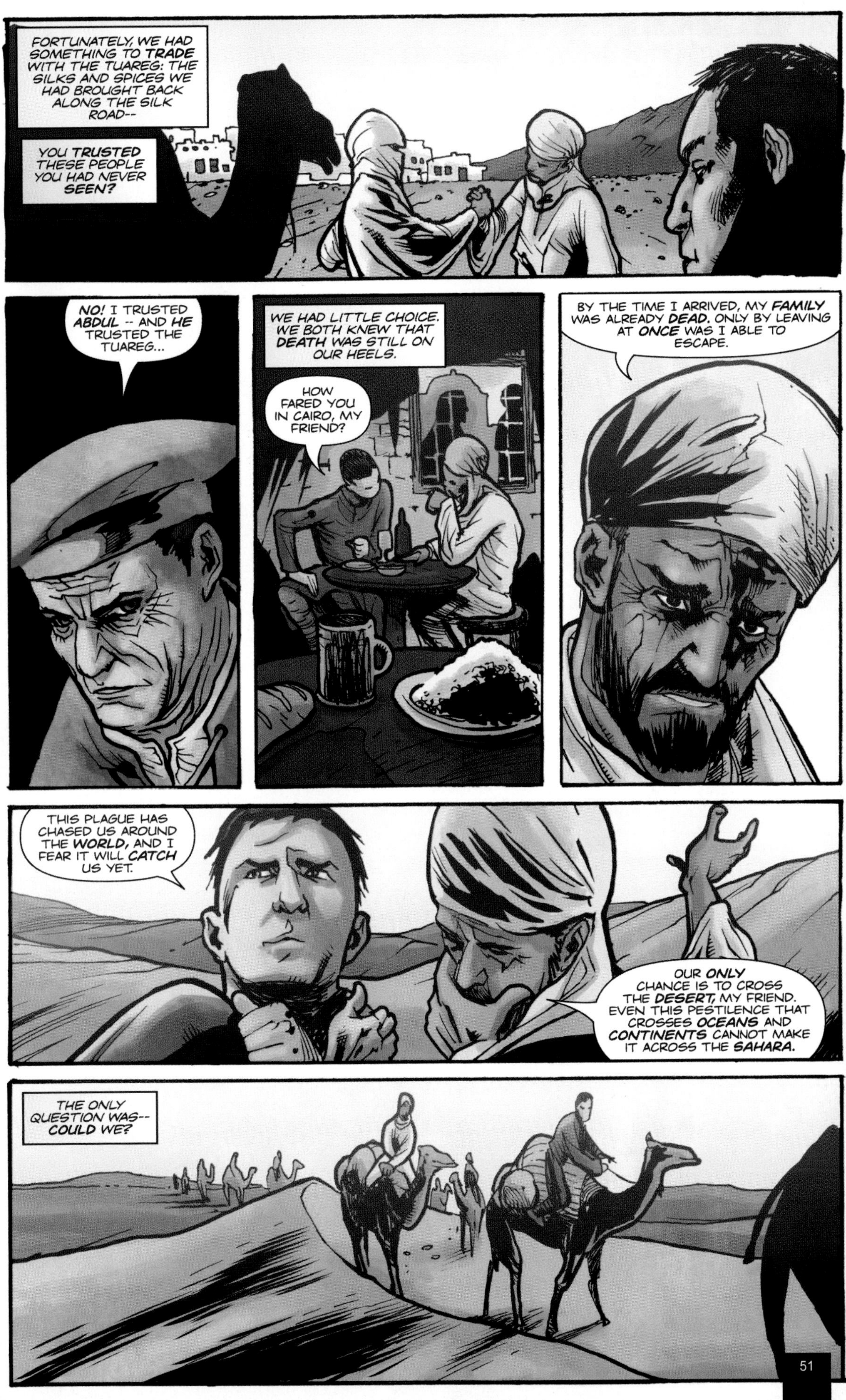

FORTUNATELY, WE HAD SOMETHING TO TRADE WITH THE TUAREG: THE SILKS AND SPICES WE HAD BROUGHT BACK ALONG THE SILK ROAD--
YOU TRUSTED THESE PEOPLE YOU HAD NEVER SEEN?
NO! I TRUSTED ABDUL -- AND HE TRUSTED THE TUAREG...
WE HAD LITTLE CHOICE. WE BOTH KNEW THAT DEATH WAS STILL ON OUR HEELS.
HOW FARED YOU IN CAIRO, MY FRIEND?
BY THE TIME I ARRIVED, MY FAMILY WAS ALREADY DEAD. ONLY BY LEAVING AT ONCE WAS I ABLE TO ESCAPE.
THIS PLAGUE HAS CHASED US AROUND THE WORLD, AND I FEAR IT WILL CATCH US YET.
OUR ONLY CHANCE IS TO CROSS THE DESERT, MY FRIEND. EVEN THIS PESTILENCE THAT CROSSES OCEANS AND CONTINENTS CANNOT MAKE IT ACROSS THE SAHARA.
THE ONLY QUESTION WAS-- COULD WE?

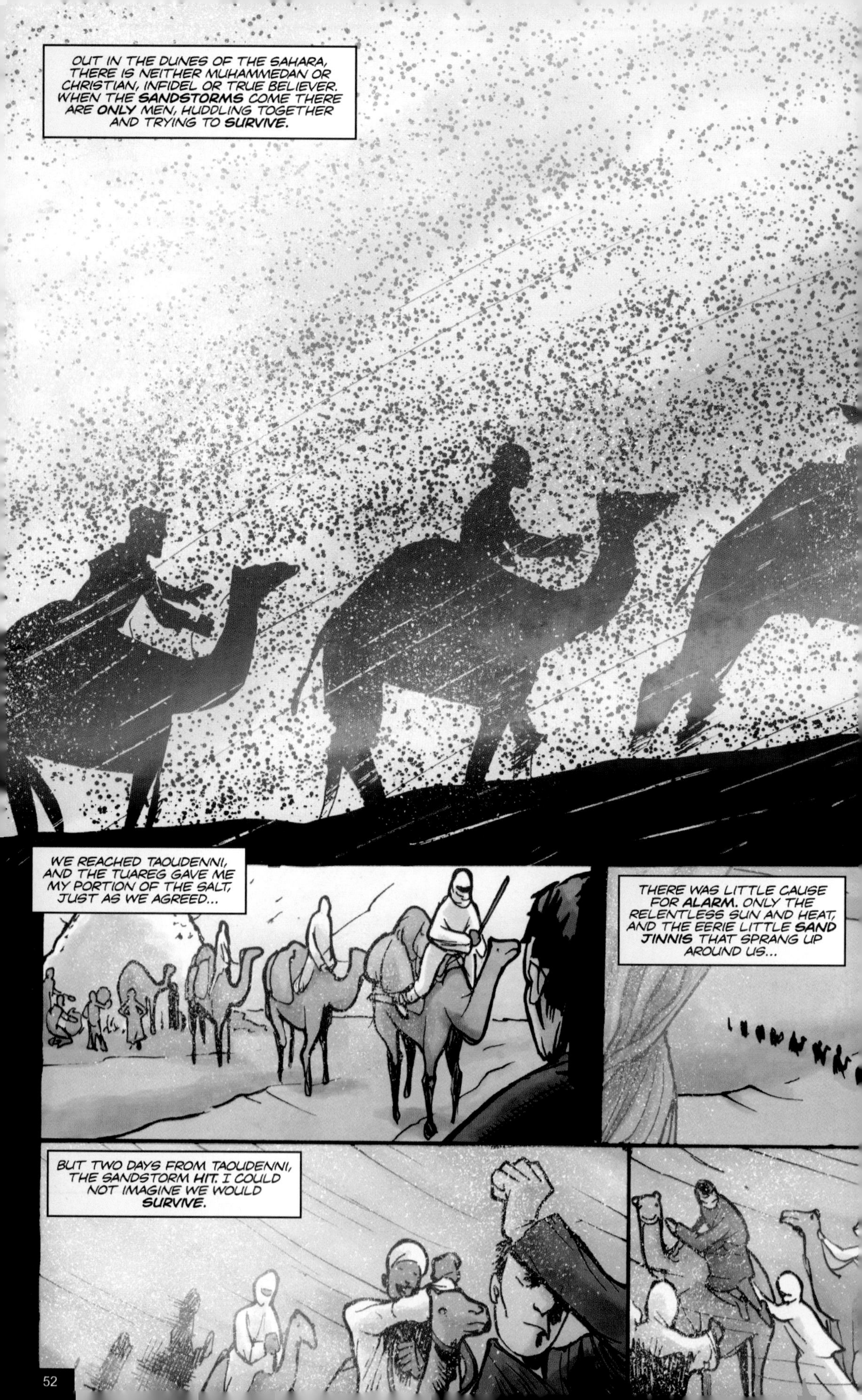

OUT IN THE DUNES OF THE SAHARA, THERE IS NEITHER MUHAMMEDAN OR CHRISTIAN, INFIDEL OR TRUE BELIEVER. WHEN THE SANDSTORMS COME THERE ARE ONLY MEN, HUDDLING TOGETHER AND TRYING TO SURVIVE.
WE REACHED TAOUDENNI, AND THE TUAREG GAVE ME MY PORTION OF THE SALT, JUST AS WE AGREED...
THERE WAS LITTLE CAUSE FOR ALARM. ONLY THE RELENTLESS SUN AND HEAT, AND THE EERIE LITTLE SAND JINNIS THAT SPRANG UP AROUND US...
BUT TWO DAYS FROM TAOUDENNI, THE SANDSTORM HIT. I COULD NOT IMAGINE WE WOULD SURVIVE.

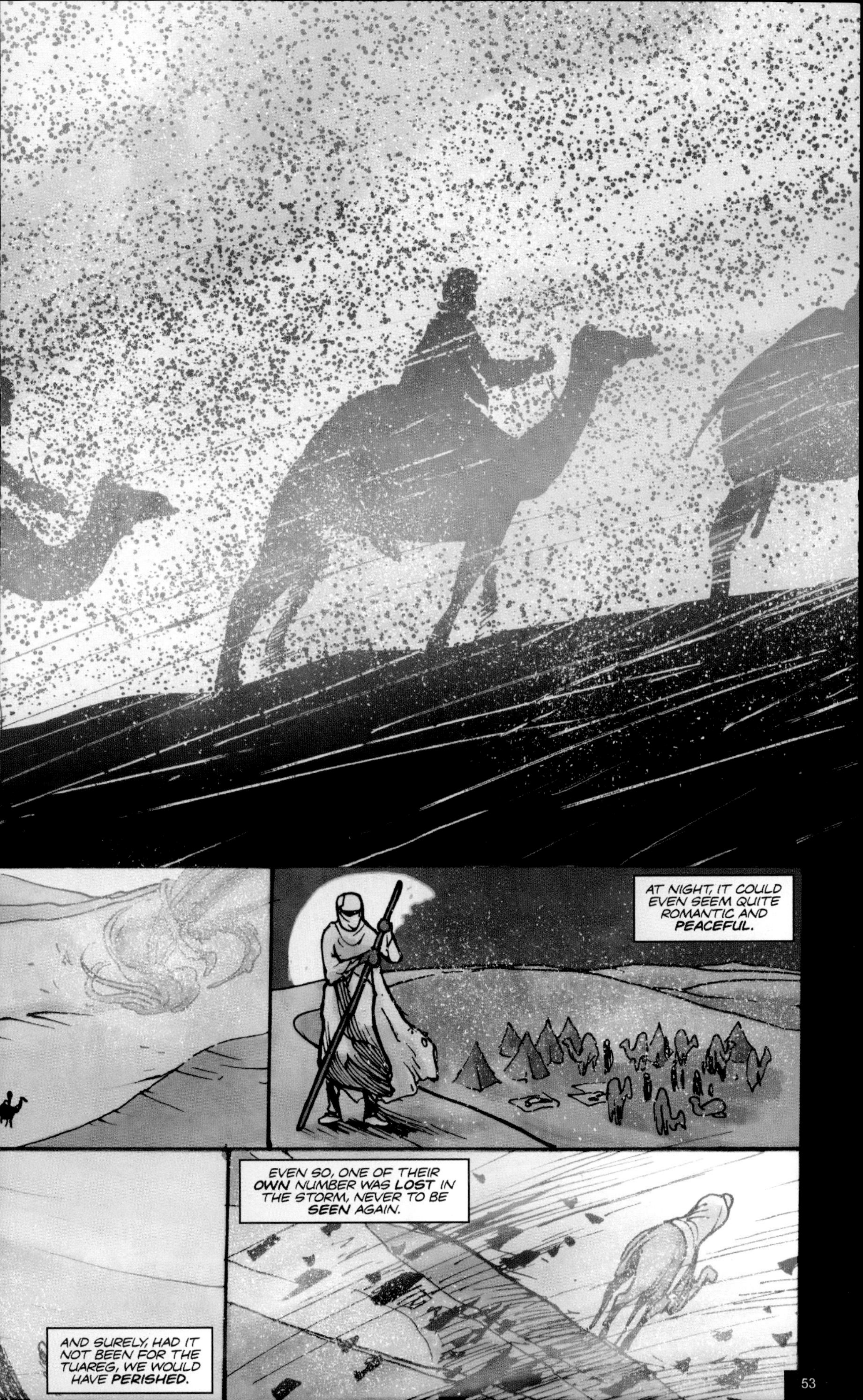
AT NIGHT, IT COULD EVEN SEEM QUITE ROMANTIC AND PEACEFUL.
EVEN SO, ONE OF THEIR OWN NUMBER WAS LOST IN THE STORM, NEVER TO BE SEEN AGAIN.
AND SURELY, HAD IT NOT BEEN FOR THE TUAREG, WE WOULD HAVE PERISHED.

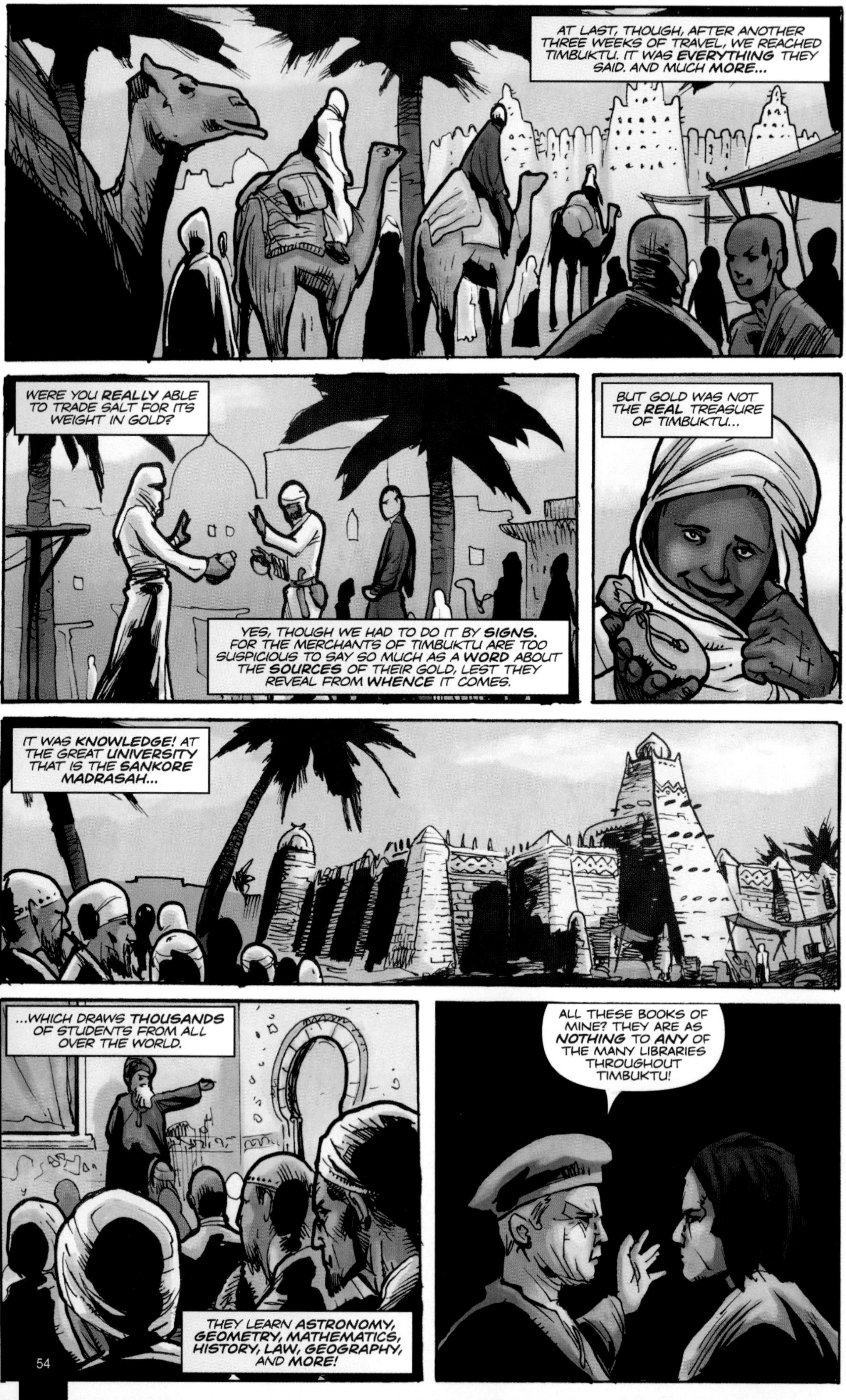
AT LAST, THOUGH, AFTER ANOTHER THREE WEEKS OF TRAVEL, WE REACHED TIMBUKTU. IT WAS EVERYTHING THEY SAID. AND MUCH MORE...
WERE YOU REALLY ABLE TO TRADE SALT FOR ITS WEIGHT IN GOLD?
YES, THOUGH WE HAD TO DO IT BY SIGNS. FOR THE MERCHANTS OF TIMBUKTU ARE TOO SUSPICIOUS TO SAY SO MUCH AS A WORD ABOUT THE SOURCES OF THEIR GOLD, LEST THEY REVEAL FROM WHENCE IT COMES.
BUT GOLD WAS NOT THE REAL TREASURE OF TIMBUKTU...
IT WAS KNOWLEDGE! AT THE GREAT UNIVERSITY THAT IS THE SANKORE MADRASAH...
...WHICH DRAWS THOUSANDS OF STUDENTS FROM ALL OVER THE WORLD.
THEY LEARN ASTRONOMY, GEOMETRY, MATHEMATICS, HISTORY, LAW, GEOGRAPHY, AND MORE!
ALL THESE BOOKS OF MINE? THEY ARE AS NOTHING TO ANY OF THE MANY LIBRARIES THROUGHOUT TIMBUKTU!

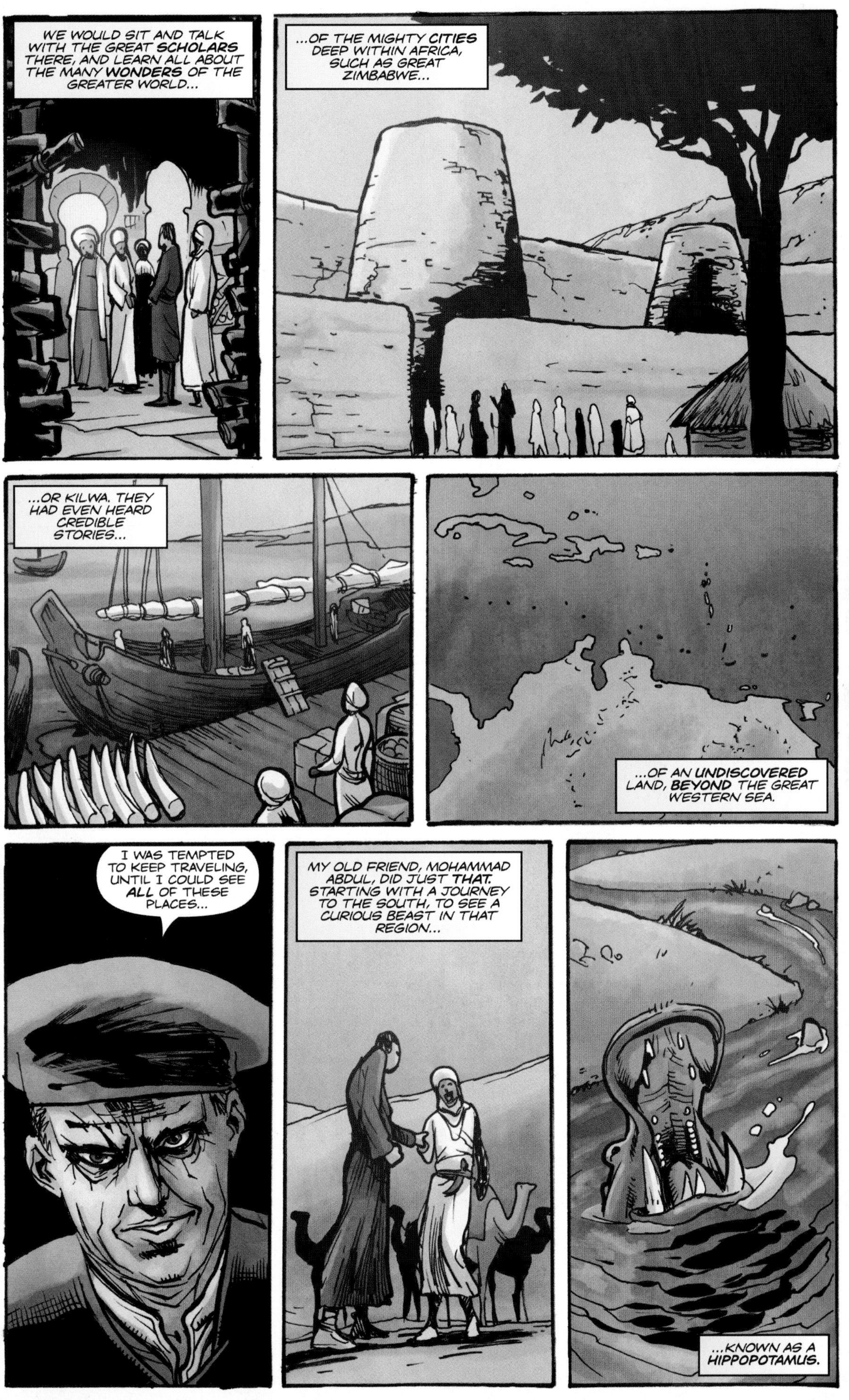
WE WOULD SIT AND TALK WITH THE GREAT SCHOLARS THERE, AND LEARN ALL ABOUT THE MANY WONDERS OF THE GREATER WORLD...
...OF THE MIGHTY CITIES DEEP WITHIN AFRICA, SUCH AS GREAT ZIMBABWE...
...OR KILWA. THEY HAD EVEN HEARD CREDIBLE STORIES...
...OF AN UNDISCOVERED LAND, BEYOND THE GREAT WESTERN SEA.
I WAS TEMPTED TO KEEP TRAVELING, UNTIL I COULD SEE ALL OF THESE PLACES...
MY OLD FRIEND, MOHAMMAD ABDUL, DID JUST THAT. STARTING WITH A JOURNEY TO THE SOUTH, TO SEE A CURIOUS BEAST IN THAT REGION...
...KNOWN AS A HIPPOPOTAMUS.

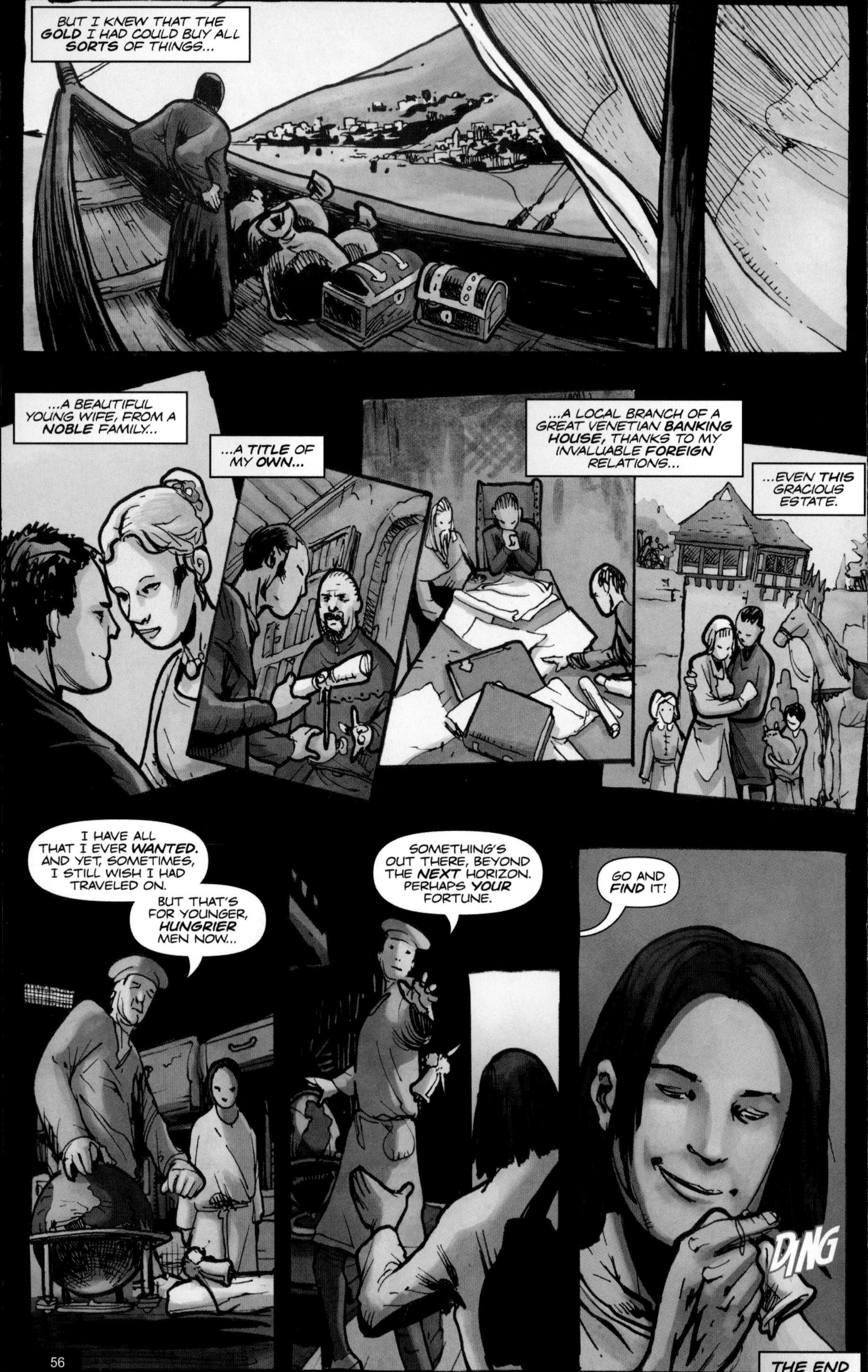
BUT I KNEW THAT THE GOLD I HAD COULD BUY ALL SORTS OF THINGS...
...A BEAUTIFUL YOUNG WIFE, FROM A NOBLE FAMILY...
...A TITLE OF MY OWN...
...A LOCAL BRANCH OF A GREAT VENETIAN BANKING HOUSE, THANKS TO MY INVALUABLE FOREIGN RELATIONS...
...EVEN THIS GRACIOUS ESTATE.
I HAVE ALL THAT I EVER WANTED. AND YET, SOMETIMES, I STILL WISH I HAD TRAVELED ON.
BUT THAT'S FOR YOUNGER, HUNGRIER MEN NOW...
SOMETHING'S OUT THERE, BEYOND THE NEXT HORIZON. PERHAPS YOUR FORTUNE.
GO AND FIND IT!
DING
THE END

MANKIND
DECODED

In *Plague and New Opportunity*, a young Italian trader risks his life in the pursuit of wealth and luxury. The desire for luxury goods has long been a driving force in mankind's exploration and innovation, as the demand for luxury items grew stronger and stronger.

The **Silk Road** was actually a 4,000+ mile network of interlinking routes that connected Asia to Africa, the Mediterranean, and Europe. Although silk was the major commodity traded, many other goods were also traded across these routes; including **spices, salt, gold,** fabric, and other luxury items. It also helped to spread culture, innovation, and inventions across the continents.

Salt has more than 14,000 different uses; including as a flavor additive to food, as a preserver of meat, and as a cleaning agent. At one time, salt was so valuable that it was traded pound-for-pound with gold.

When Christopher Columbus arrived in the Americas, he was actually looking for a shorter trading route to China in order to obtain **pepper** and other luxury spices.

The fast-growing demand for animal fur in Europe helped to spur the continued exploration of North America. It also provided strong incentive for early explorers to forge relations with native peoples in order to trade with them.

VINLAND CONQUEST

WRITTEN BY
WILLIAM MESSNER-LOEBS

ART BY
NACHO TENORIO

COLORS BY
MARLON ILAGAN

LETTERS BY
JIM CAMPBELL

A FIRST ENCOUNTER IN THE NEW WORLD BECOMES A TEST OF
DIPLOMACY FOR A NATIVE AND A MARAUDER

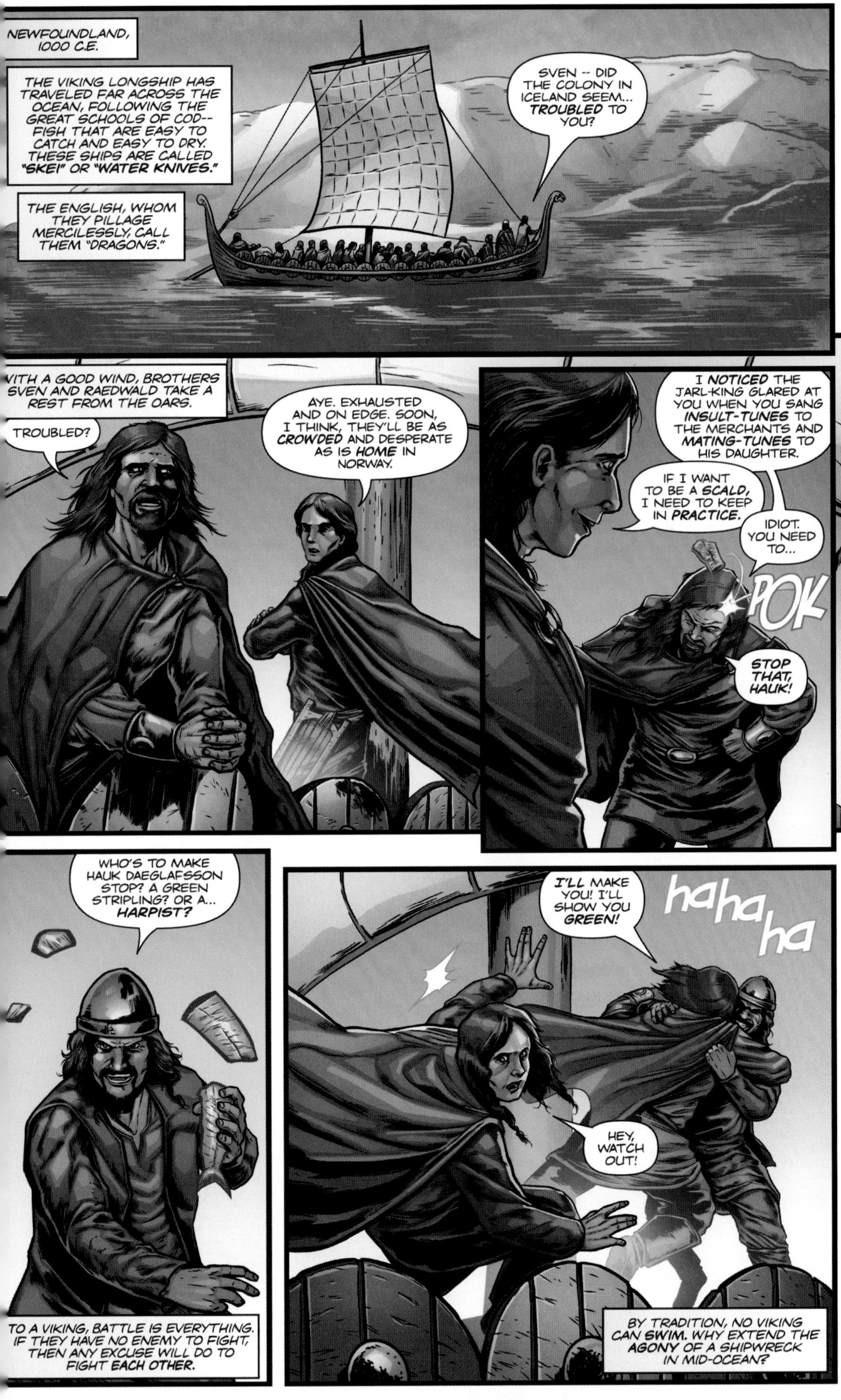
NEWFOUNDLAND, 1000 C.E.
THE VIKING LONGSHIP HAS TRAVELED FAR ACROSS THE OCEAN, FOLLOWING THE GREAT SCHOOLS OF COD--FISH THAT ARE EASY TO CATCH AND EASY TO DRY. THESE SHIPS ARE CALLED "SKEI" OR "WATER KNIVES."
THE ENGLISH, WHOM THEY PILLAGE MERCILESSLY, CALL THEM "DRAGONS."
SVEN -- DID THE COLONY IN ICELAND SEEM... TROUBLED TO YOU?
VITH A GOOD WIND, BROTHERS SVEN AND RAEDWALD TAKE A REST FROM THE OARS.
TROUBLED?
AYE. EXHAUSTED AND ON EDGE. SOON, I THINK, THEY'LL BE AS CROWDED AND DESPERATE AS IS HOME IN NORWAY.
I NOTICED THE JARL-KING GLARED AT YOU WHEN YOU SANG INSULT-TUNES TO THE MERCHANTS AND MATING-TUNES TO HIS DAUGHTER.
IF I WANT TO BE A SCALD, I NEED TO KEEP IN PRACTICE.
IDIOT. YOU NEED TO...
POK
STOP THAT, HAUK!
WHO'S TO MAKE HAUK DAEGLAFSSON STOP? A GREEN STRIPLING? OR A... HARPIST?
TO A VIKING, BATTLE IS EVERYTHING. IF THEY HAVE NO ENEMY TO FIGHT, THEN ANY EXCUSE WILL DO TO FIGHT EACH OTHER.
I'LL MAKE YOU! I'LL SHOW YOU GREEN!
hahaha
HEY, WATCH OUT!
BY TRADITION, NO VIKING CAN SWIM. WHY EXTEND THE AGONY OF A SHIPWRECK IN MID-OCEAN?

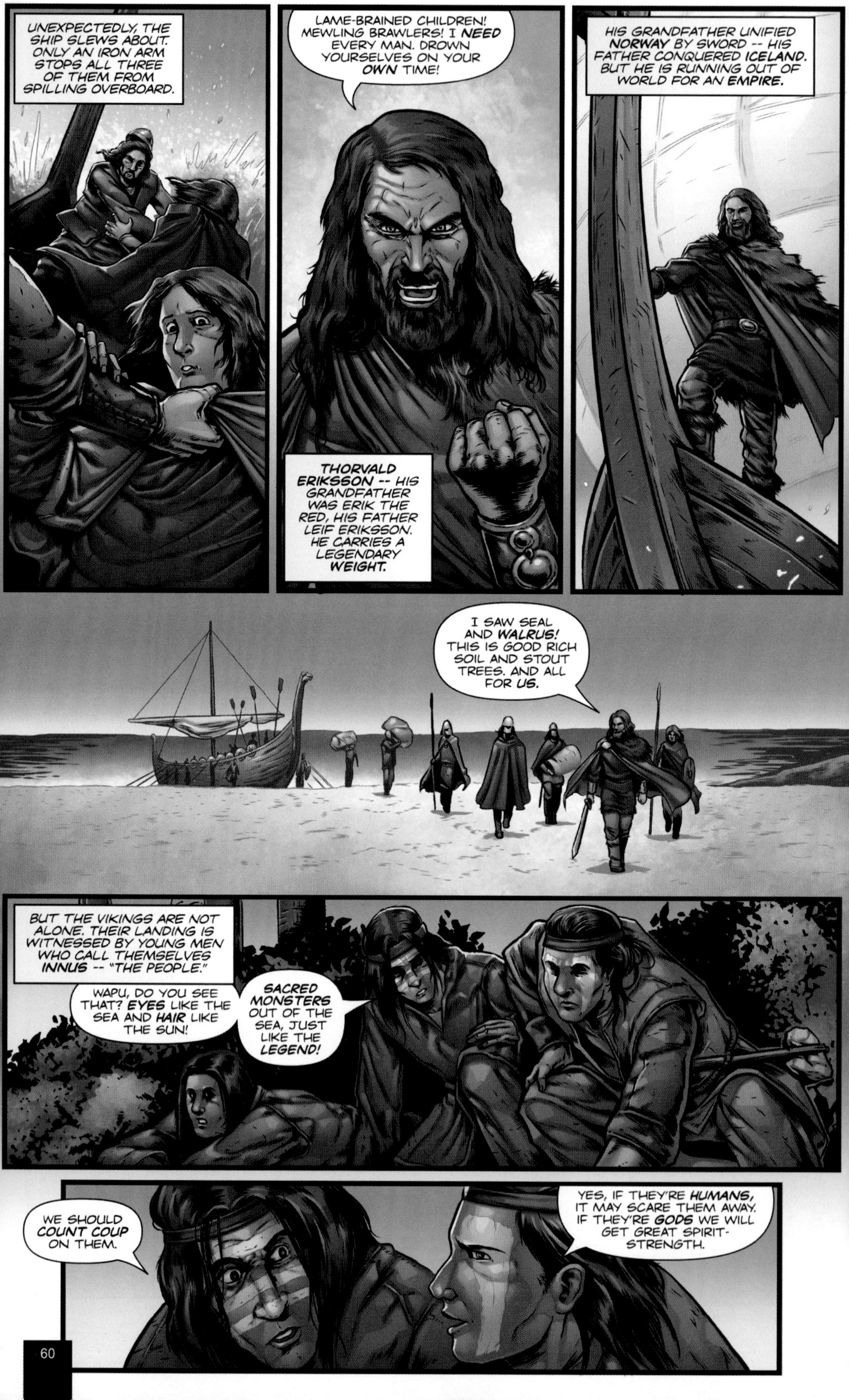
UNEXPECTEDLY, THE SHIP SLEWS ABOUT. ONLY AN IRON ARM STOPS ALL THREE OF THEM FROM SPILLING OVERBOARD.
LAME-BRAINED CHILDREN! MEWLING BRAWLERS! I NEED EVERY MAN. DROWN YOURSELVES ON YOUR OWN TIME!
THORVALD ERIKSSON -- HIS GRANDFATHER WAS ERIK THE RED, HIS FATHER LEIF ERIKSSON. HE CARRIES A LEGENDARY WEIGHT.
HIS GRANDFATHER UNIFIED NORWAY BY SWORD -- HIS FATHER CONQUERED ICELAND. BUT HE IS RUNNING OUT OF WORLD FOR AN EMPIRE.
I SAW SEAL AND WALRUS! THIS IS GOOD RICH SOIL AND STOUT TREES. AND ALL FOR US.
BUT THE VIKINGS ARE NOT ALONE. THEIR LANDING IS WITNESSED BY YOUNG MEN WHO CALL THEMSELVES INNUS -- "THE PEOPLE."
WAPU, DO YOU SEE THAT? EYES LIKE THE SEA AND HAIR LIKE THE SUN!
SACRED MONSTERS OUT OF THE SEA, JUST LIKE THE LEGEND!
WE SHOULD COUNT COUP ON THEM.
YES, IF THEY'RE HUMANS, IT MAY SCARE THEM AWAY. IF THEY'RE GODS WE WILL GET GREAT SPIRIT-STRENGTH.

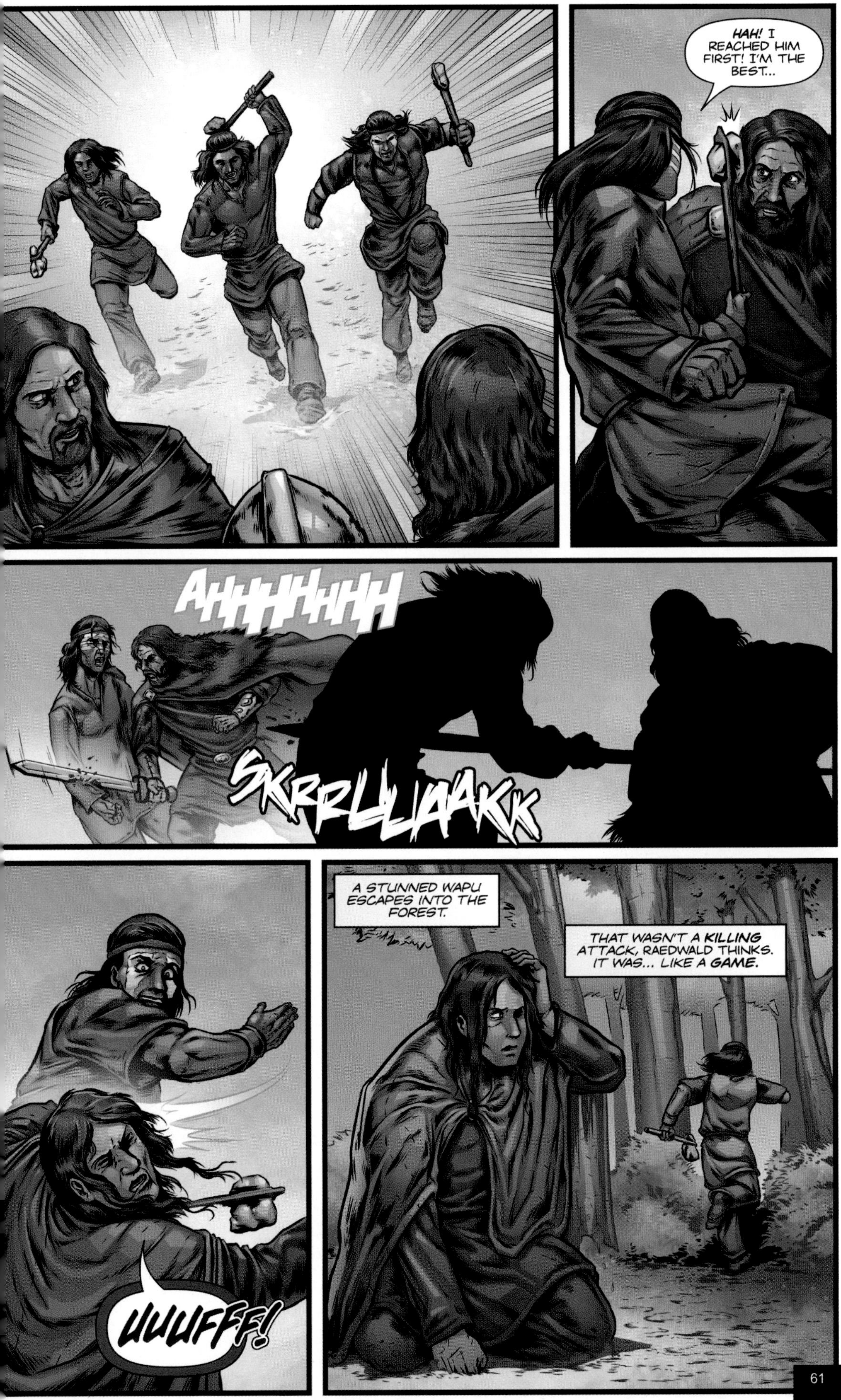

HAH! I REACHED HIM FIRST! I'M THE BEST...
AHHHHHHH
SKRRLLLAAKK
UUUFFF!
A STUNNED WAPU ESCAPES INTO THE FOREST.
THAT WASN'T A KILLING ATTACK, RAEDWALD THINKS. IT WAS... LIKE A GAME.

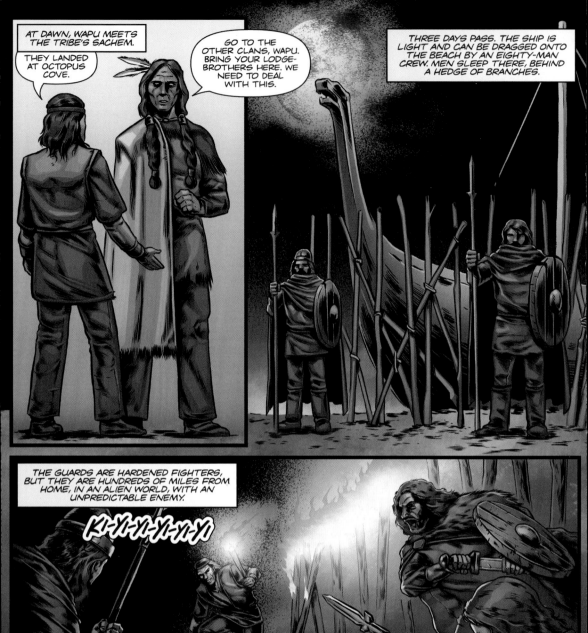

AT DAWN, WAPU MEETS THE TRIBE'S SACHEM.

THEY LANDED AT OCTOPUS COVE.

GO TO THE OTHER CLANS, WAPU. BRING YOUR LODGE-BROTHERS HERE. WE NEED TO DEAL WITH THIS.

THREE DAYS PASS. THE SHIP IS LIGHT AND CAN BE DRAGGED ONTO THE BEACH BY AN EIGHTY-MAN CREW. MEN SLEEP THERE, BEHIND A HEDGE OF BRANCHES.

THE GUARDS ARE HARDENED FIGHTERS, BUT THEY ARE HUNDREDS OF MILES FROM HOME, IN AN ALIEN WORLD, WITH AN UNPREDICTABLE ENEMY.

KI-YI-YI-YI-YI-YI

VIKINGS ARE ANGRY AND CONFIDENT, AND ALSO PROUD OF THEIR WEAPONS AND NERVE. THEY SEE THEMSELVES AS WOLVES AFTER A RABBIT...

...THEY ARE WRONG.

RAZOR-SHARP FLINT ARROWS DRIVEN BY FIVE-FOOT BOWS CAN GO THROUGH OAKEN SHIELDS, STIFFENED LEATHER ARMOR...

SSSSFFFFtt

SSSSFFFFtt

...EVEN THE LINKS OF CHAIN MAIL...

...WITH THE WEIGHT OF A LEGEND.

THUNKKT

THUNKKT

THUNKKT

MOST OF THE VIKINGS MAKE THE SAFETY OF THE SHIP, AND ELECT HAUK DAEGLAFSSON AS THE NEW LEADER.

WE'LL REINFORCE OUR SHIELDS AGAINST THESE ANIMALS, THESE SKRAELINGAR...

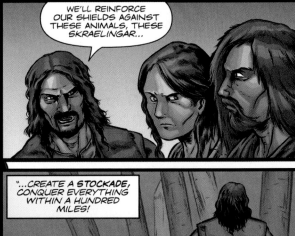

"...CREATE A STOCKADE, CONQUER EVERYTHING WITHIN A HUNDRED MILES!

"I BET THERE'S GOLD SOMEWHERE..."

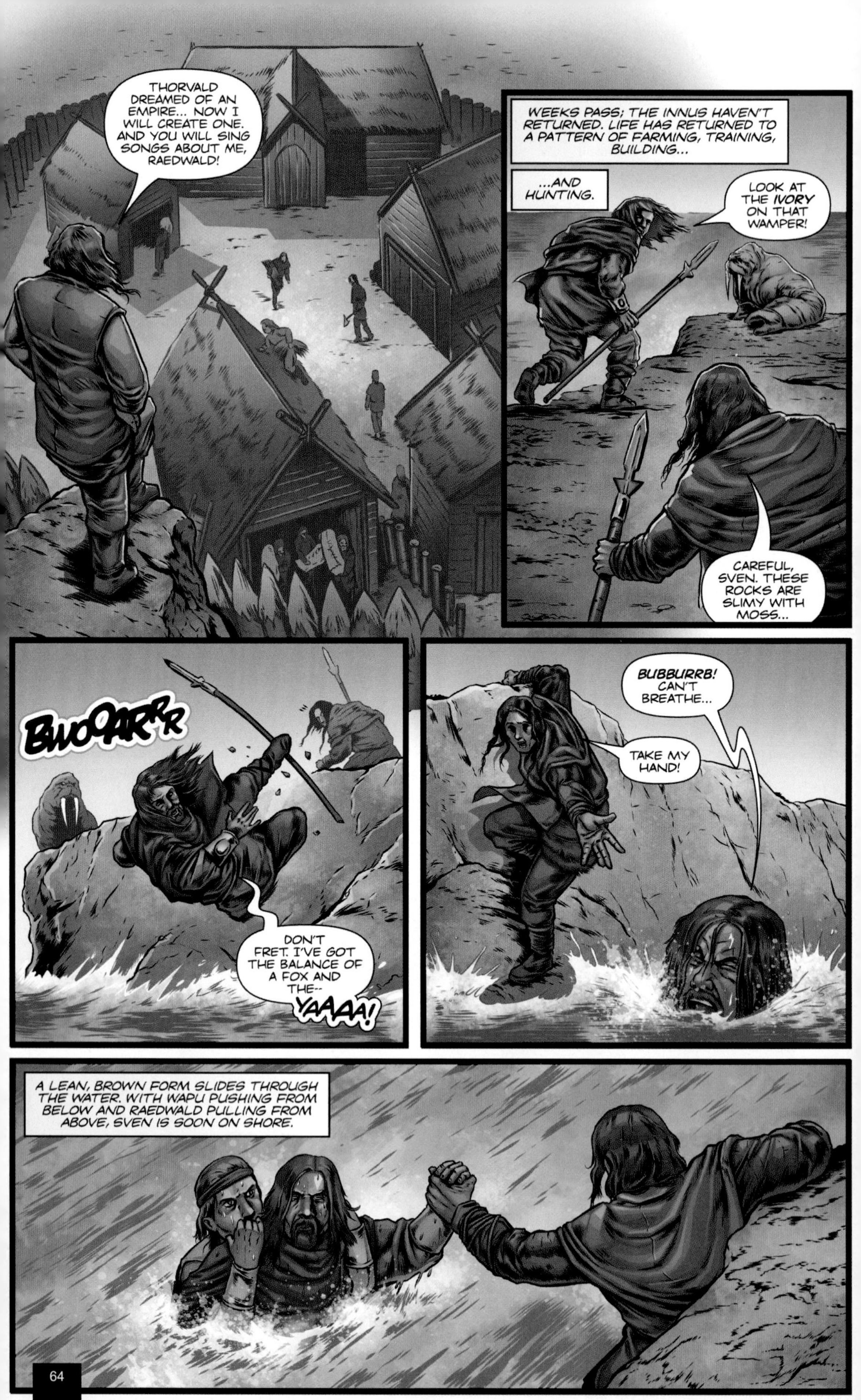
THORVALD DREAMED OF AN EMPIRE... NOW I WILL CREATE ONE. AND YOU WILL SING SONGS ABOUT ME, RAEDWALD!
WEEKS PASS; THE INNUS HAVEN'T RETURNED. LIFE HAS RETURNED TO A PATTERN OF FARMING, TRAINING, BUILDING...
...AND HUNTING.
LOOK AT THE IVORY ON THAT WAMPER!
CAREFUL, SVEN. THESE ROCKS ARE SLIMY WITH MOSS...
BWOOARRR
DON'T FRET. I'VE GOT THE BALANCE OF A FOX AND THE--
YAAAA!
BUBBURRB! CAN'T BREATHE...
TAKE MY HAND!
A LEAN, BROWN FORM SLIDES THROUGH THE WATER. WITH WAPU PUSHING FROM BELOW AND RAEDWALD PULLING FROM ABOVE, SVEN IS SOON ON SHORE.

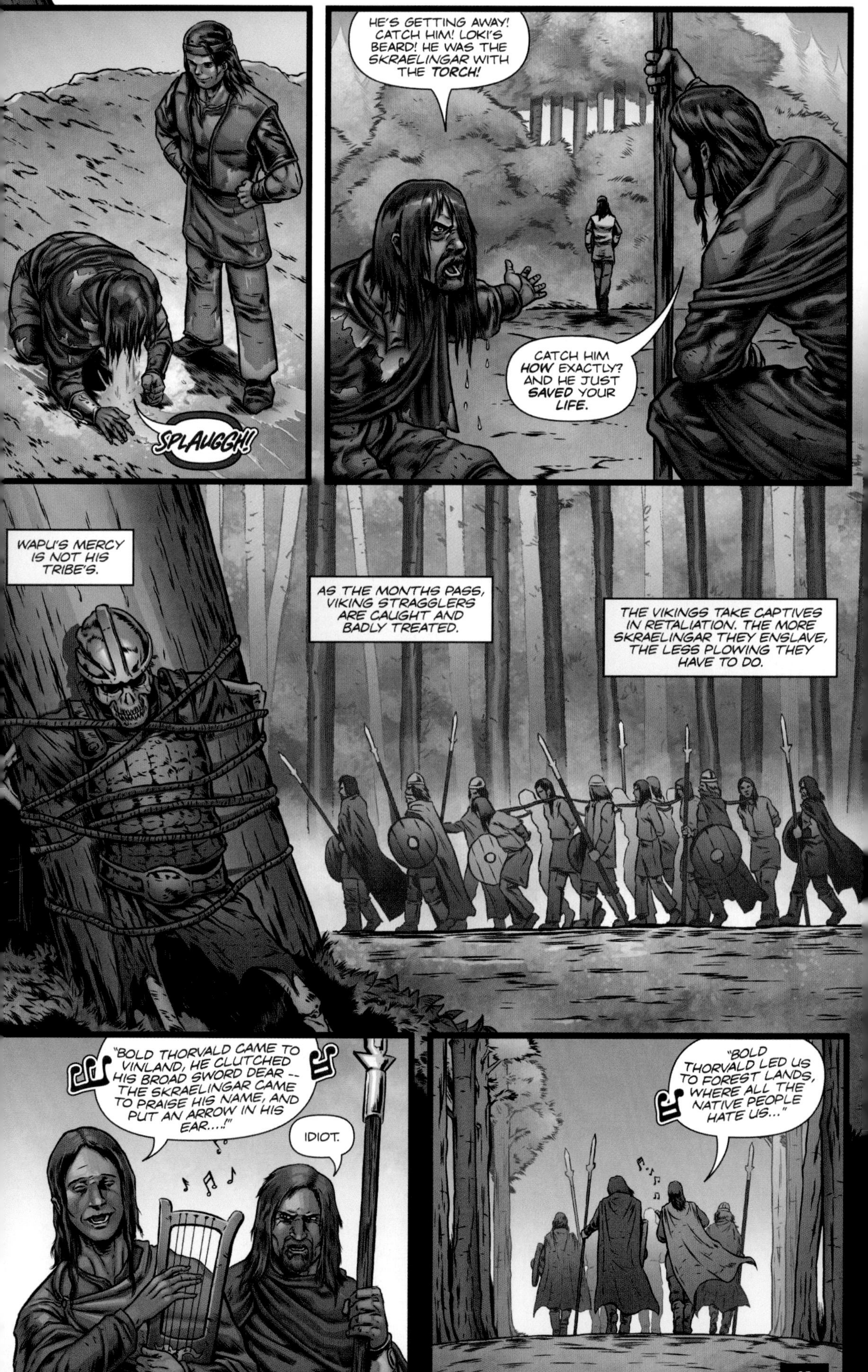
SPLAUGGH!!
HE'S GETTING AWAY! CATCH HIM! LOKI'S BEARD! HE WAS THE SKRAELINGAR WITH THE TORCH!
CATCH HIM HOW EXACTLY? AND HE JUST SAVED YOUR LIFE.
WAPU'S MERCY IS NOT HIS TRIBE'S.
AS THE MONTHS PASS, VIKING STRAGGLERS ARE CAUGHT AND BADLY TREATED.
THE VIKINGS TAKE CAPTIVES IN RETALIATION. THE MORE SKRAELINGAR THEY ENSLAVE, THE LESS PLOWING THEY HAVE TO DO.
"BOLD THORVALD CAME TO VINLAND, HE CLUTCHED HIS BROAD SWORD DEAR -- THE SKRAELINGAR CAME TO PRAISE HIS NAME, AND PUT AN ARROW IN HIS EAR...."
IDIOT.
"BOLD THORVALD LED US TO FOREST LANDS, WHERE ALL THE NATIVE PEOPLE HATE US..."

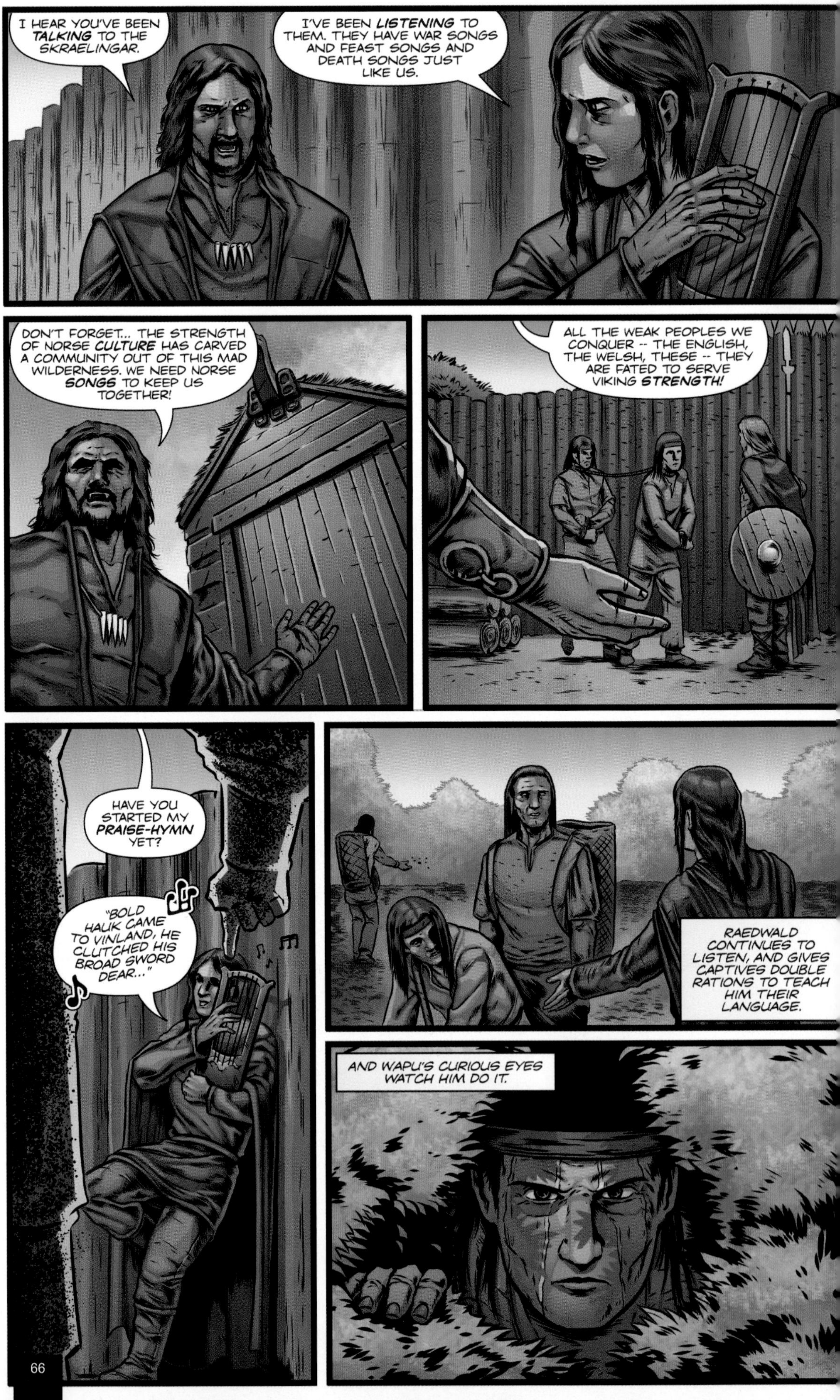

I HEAR YOU'VE BEEN TALKING TO THE SKRAELINGAR.
I'VE BEEN LISTENING TO THEM. THEY HAVE WAR SONGS AND FEAST SONGS AND DEATH SONGS JUST LIKE US.
DON'T FORGET... THE STRENGTH OF NORSE CULTURE HAS CARVED A COMMUNITY OUT OF THIS MAD WILDERNESS. WE NEED NORSE SONGS TO KEEP US TOGETHER!
ALL THE WEAK PEOPLES WE CONQUER -- THE ENGLISH, THE WELSH, THESE -- THEY ARE FATED TO SERVE VIKING STRENGTH!
HAVE YOU STARTED MY PRAISE-HYMN YET?
"BOLD HAUK CAME TO VINLAND, HE CLUTCHED HIS BROAD SWORD DEAR..."
RAEDWALD CONTINUES TO LISTEN, AND GIVES CAPTIVES DOUBLE RATIONS TO TEACH HIM THEIR LANGUAGE.
AND WAPU'S CURIOUS EYES WATCH HIM DO IT.

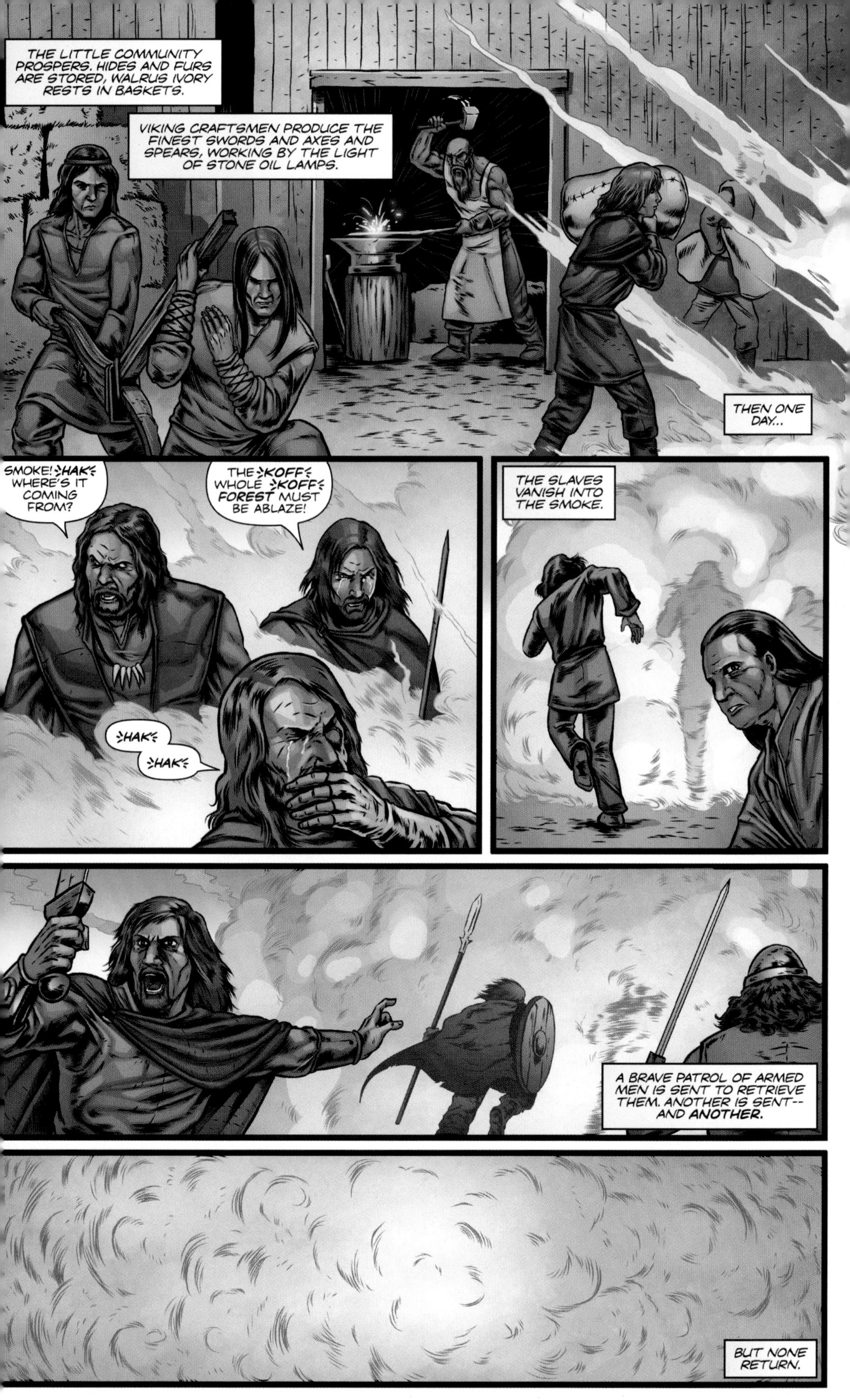
THE LITTLE COMMUNITY PROSPERS. HIDES AND FURS ARE STORED, WALRUS IVORY RESTS IN BASKETS.
VIKING CRAFTSMEN PRODUCE THE FINEST SWORDS AND AXES AND SPEARS, WORKING BY THE LIGHT OF STONE OIL LAMPS.
THEN ONE DAY...
SMOKE! *HAK* WHERE'S IT COMING FROM?
THE *KOFF* WHOLE *KOFF* FOREST MUST BE ABLAZE!
HAK
HAK
THE SLAVES VANISH INTO THE SMOKE.
A BRAVE PATROL OF ARMED MEN IS SENT TO RETRIEVE THEM. ANOTHER IS SENT-- AND ANOTHER.
BUT NONE RETURN.

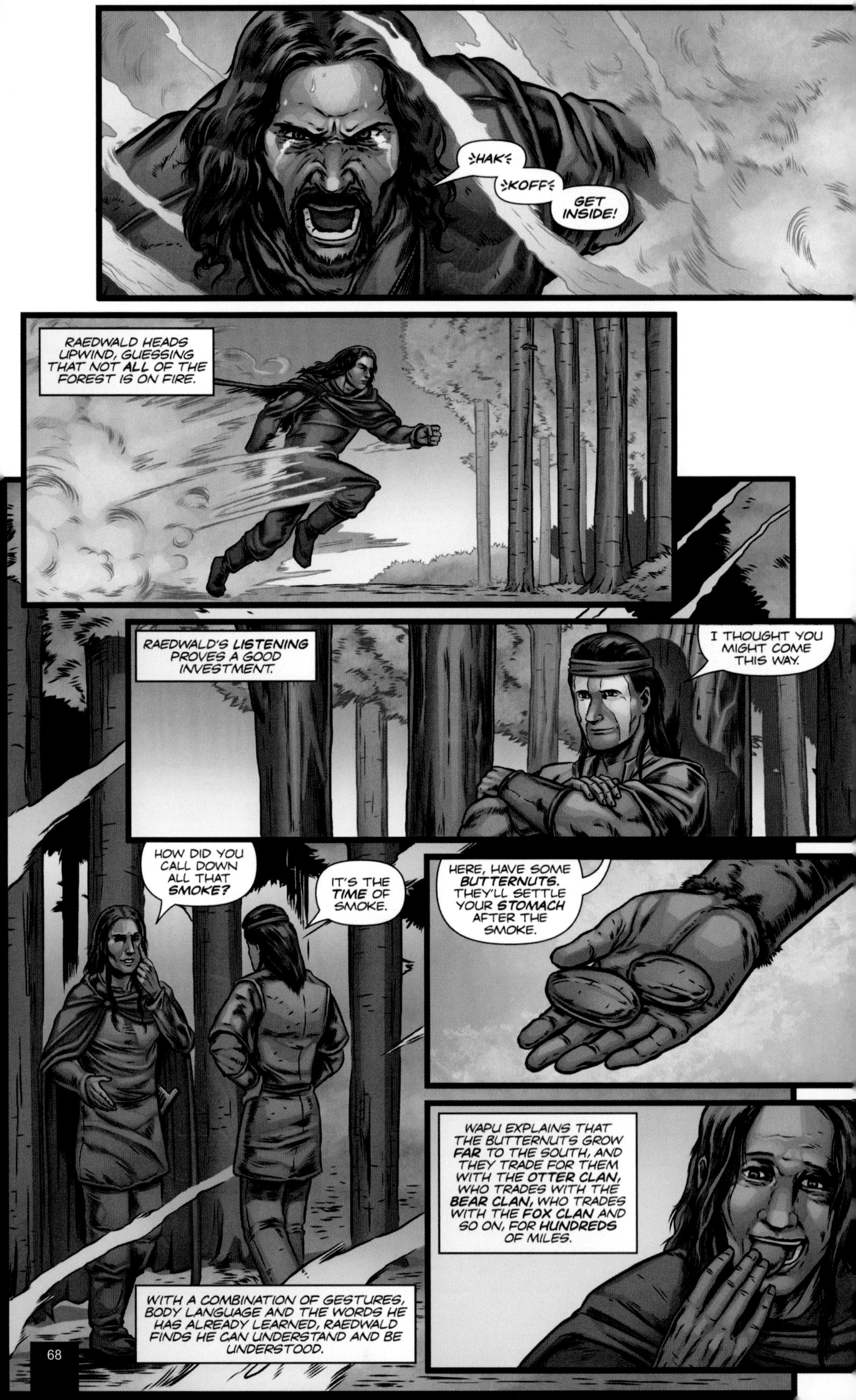
HAK
KOFF
GET INSIDE!
RAEDWALD HEADS UPWIND, GUESSING THAT NOT ALL OF THE FOREST IS ON FIRE.
RAEDWALD'S LISTENING PROVES A GOOD INVESTMENT.
I THOUGHT YOU MIGHT COME THIS WAY.
HOW DID YOU CALL DOWN ALL THAT SMOKE?
IT'S THE TIME OF SMOKE.
WITH A COMBINATION OF GESTURES, BODY LANGUAGE AND THE WORDS HE HAS ALREADY LEARNED, RAEDWALD FINDS HE CAN UNDERSTAND AND BE UNDERSTOOD.
HERE, HAVE SOME BUTTERNUTS. THEY'LL SETTLE YOUR STOMACH AFTER THE SMOKE.
WAPU EXPLAINS THAT THE BUTTERNUTS GROW FAR TO THE SOUTH, AND THEY TRADE FOR THEM WITH THE OTTER CLAN, WHO TRADES WITH THE BEAR CLAN, WHO TRADES WITH THE FOX CLAN AND SO ON, FOR HUNDREDS OF MILES.

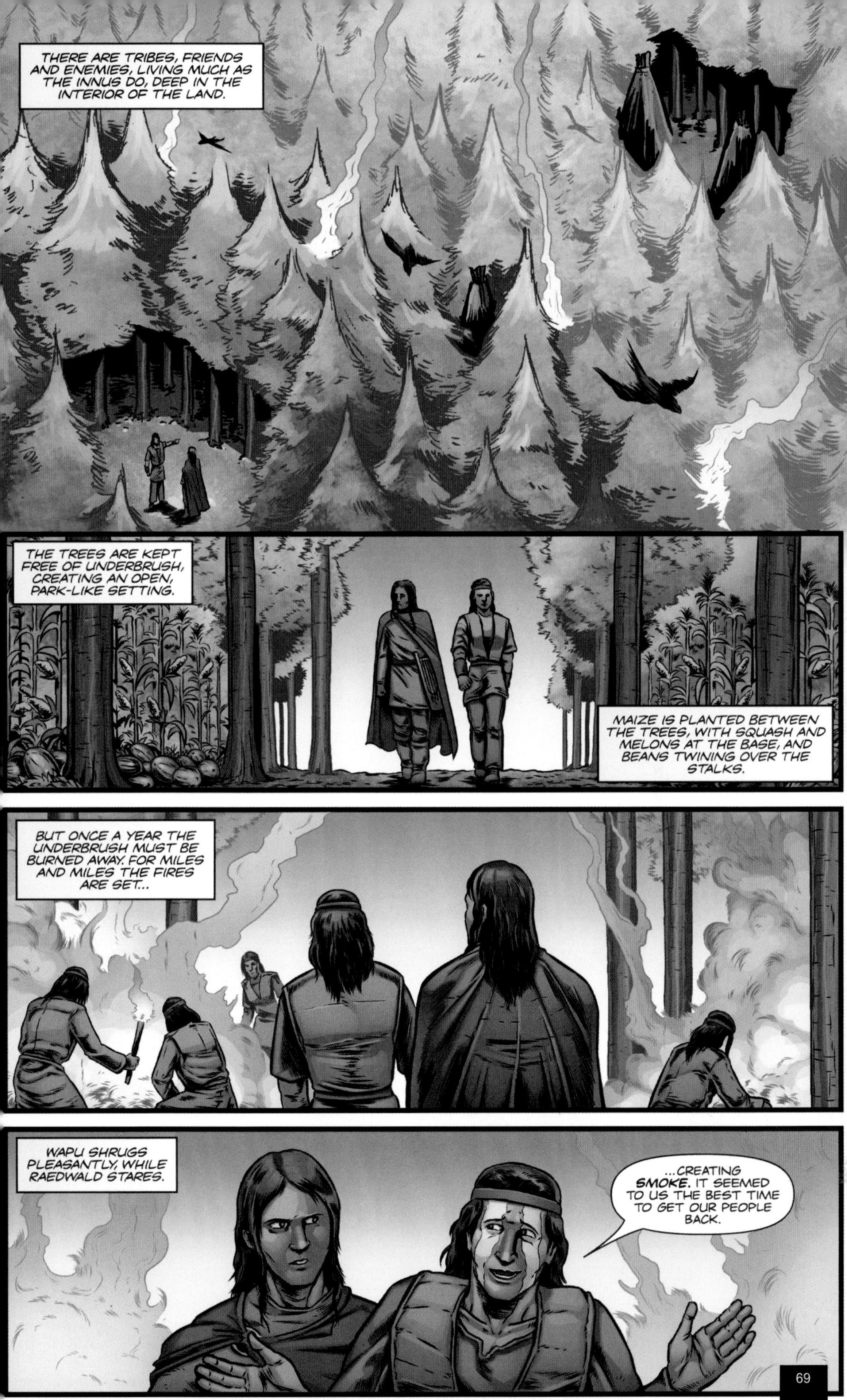
THERE ARE TRIBES, FRIENDS AND ENEMIES, LIVING MUCH AS THE INNUS DO, DEEP IN THE INTERIOR OF THE LAND.
THE TREES ARE KEPT FREE OF UNDERBRUSH, CREATING AN OPEN, PARK-LIKE SETTING.
MAIZE IS PLANTED BETWEEN THE TREES, WITH SQUASH AND MELONS AT THE BASE, AND BEANS TWINING OVER THE STALKS.
BUT ONCE A YEAR THE UNDERBRUSH MUST BE BURNED AWAY. FOR MILES AND MILES THE FIRES ARE SET...
WAPU SHRUGS PLEASANTLY, WHILE RAEDWALD STARES.
...CREATING **SMOKE.** IT SEEMED TO US THE BEST TIME TO GET OUR PEOPLE BACK.

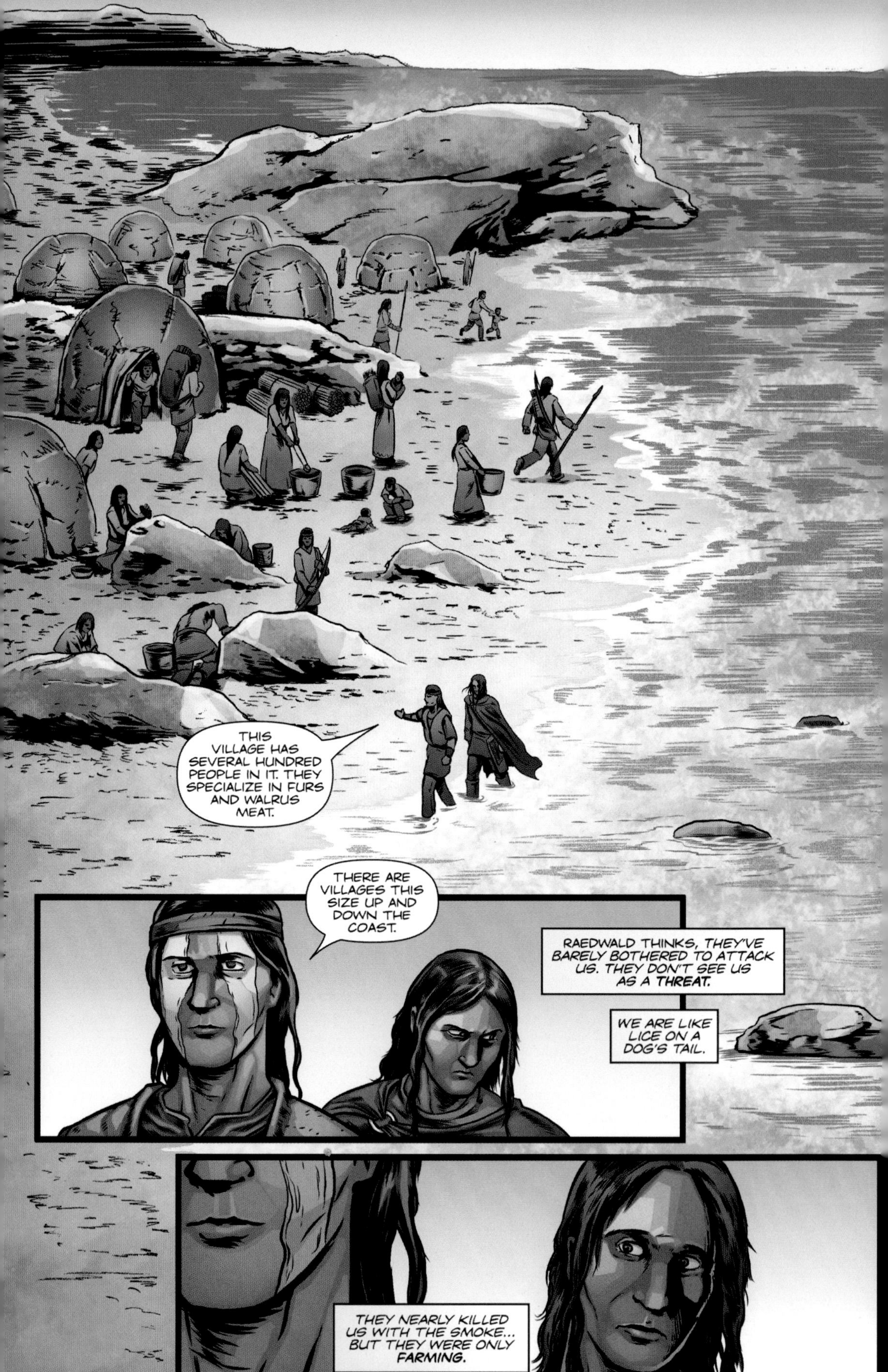
THIS VILLAGE HAS SEVERAL HUNDRED PEOPLE IN IT. THEY SPECIALIZE IN FURS AND WALRUS MEAT.
THERE ARE VILLAGES THIS SIZE UP AND DOWN THE COAST.
RAEDWALD THINKS, THEY'VE BARELY BOTHERED TO ATTACK US. THEY DON'T SEE US AS A THREAT.
WE ARE LIKE LICE ON A DOG'S TAIL.
THEY NEARLY KILLED US WITH THE SMOKE... BUT THEY WERE ONLY FARMING.

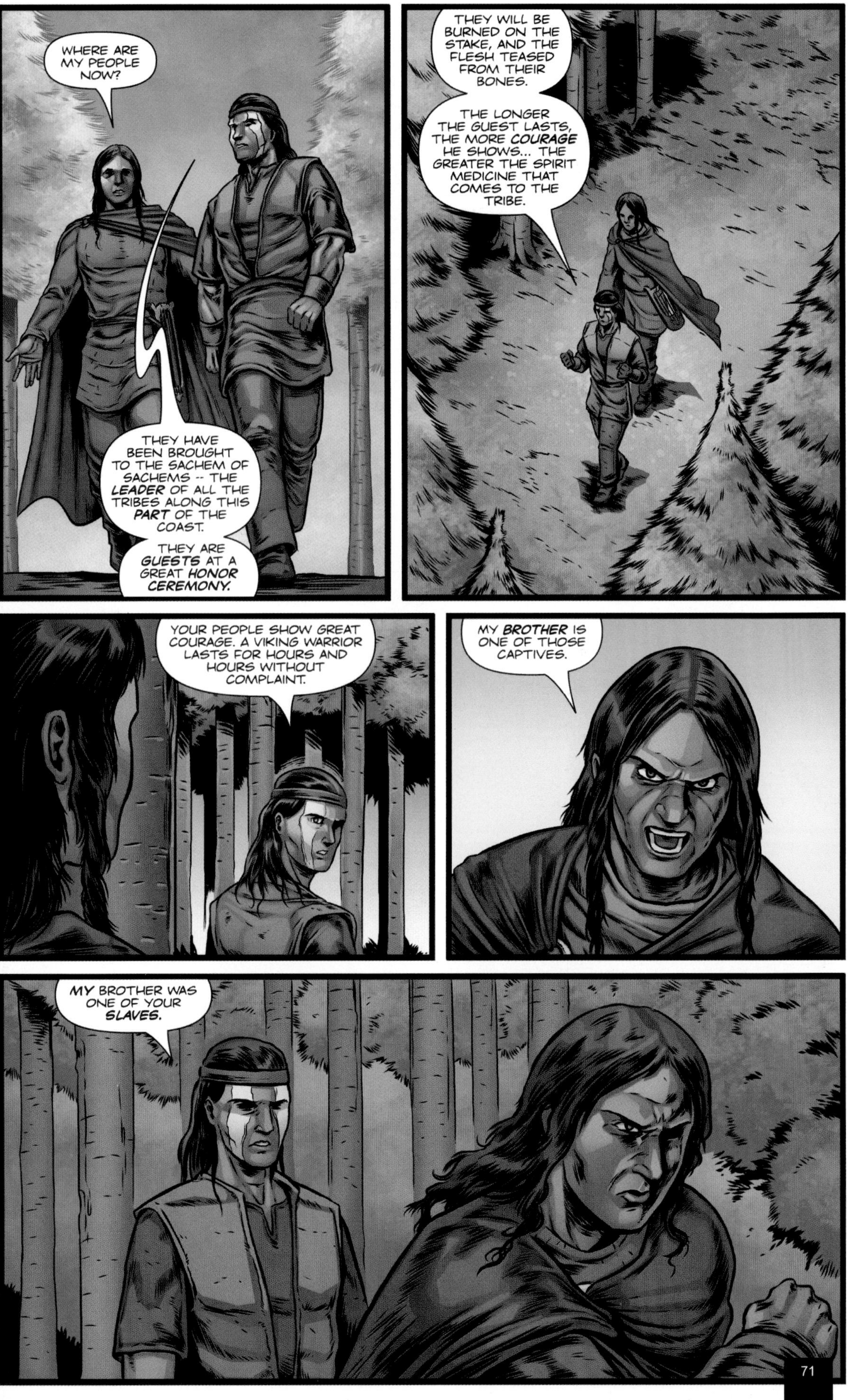
WHERE ARE MY PEOPLE NOW?
THEY HAVE BEEN BROUGHT TO THE SACHEM OF SACHEMS -- THE LEADER OF ALL THE TRIBES ALONG THIS PART OF THE COAST.
THEY ARE GUESTS AT A GREAT HONOR CEREMONY.
THEY WILL BE BURNED ON THE STAKE, AND THE FLESH TEASED FROM THEIR BONES.
THE LONGER THE GUEST LASTS, THE MORE COURAGE HE SHOWS... THE GREATER THE SPIRIT MEDICINE THAT COMES TO THE TRIBE.
YOUR PEOPLE SHOW GREAT COURAGE. A VIKING WARRIOR LASTS FOR HOURS AND HOURS WITHOUT COMPLAINT.
MY BROTHER IS ONE OF THOSE CAPTIVES.
MY BROTHER WAS ONE OF YOUR SLAVES.

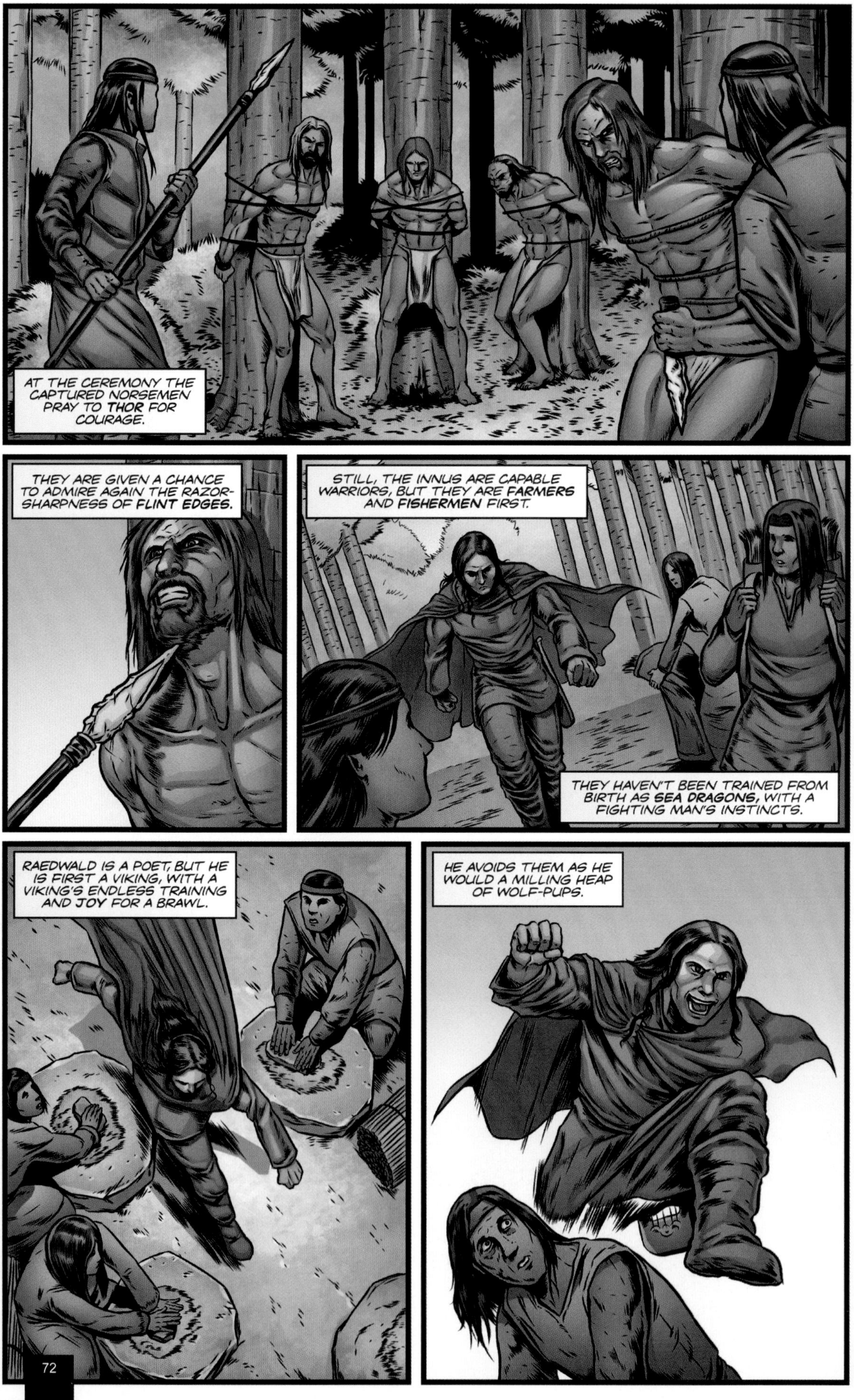
AT THE CEREMONY THE CAPTURED NORSEMEN PRAY TO **THOR** FOR COURAGE.
THEY ARE GIVEN A CHANCE TO ADMIRE AGAIN THE RAZOR-SHARPNESS OF **FLINT EDGES.**
STILL, THE INNUS ARE CAPABLE WARRIORS, BUT THEY ARE **FARMERS** AND **FISHERMEN** FIRST.
THEY HAVEN'T BEEN TRAINED FROM BIRTH AS **SEA DRAGONS,** WITH A FIGHTING MAN'S INSTINCTS.
RAEDWALD IS A POET, BUT HE IS FIRST A VIKING, WITH A VIKING'S ENDLESS TRAINING AND **JOY** FOR A BRAWL.
HE AVOIDS THEM AS HE WOULD A MILLING HEAP OF WOLF-PUPS.

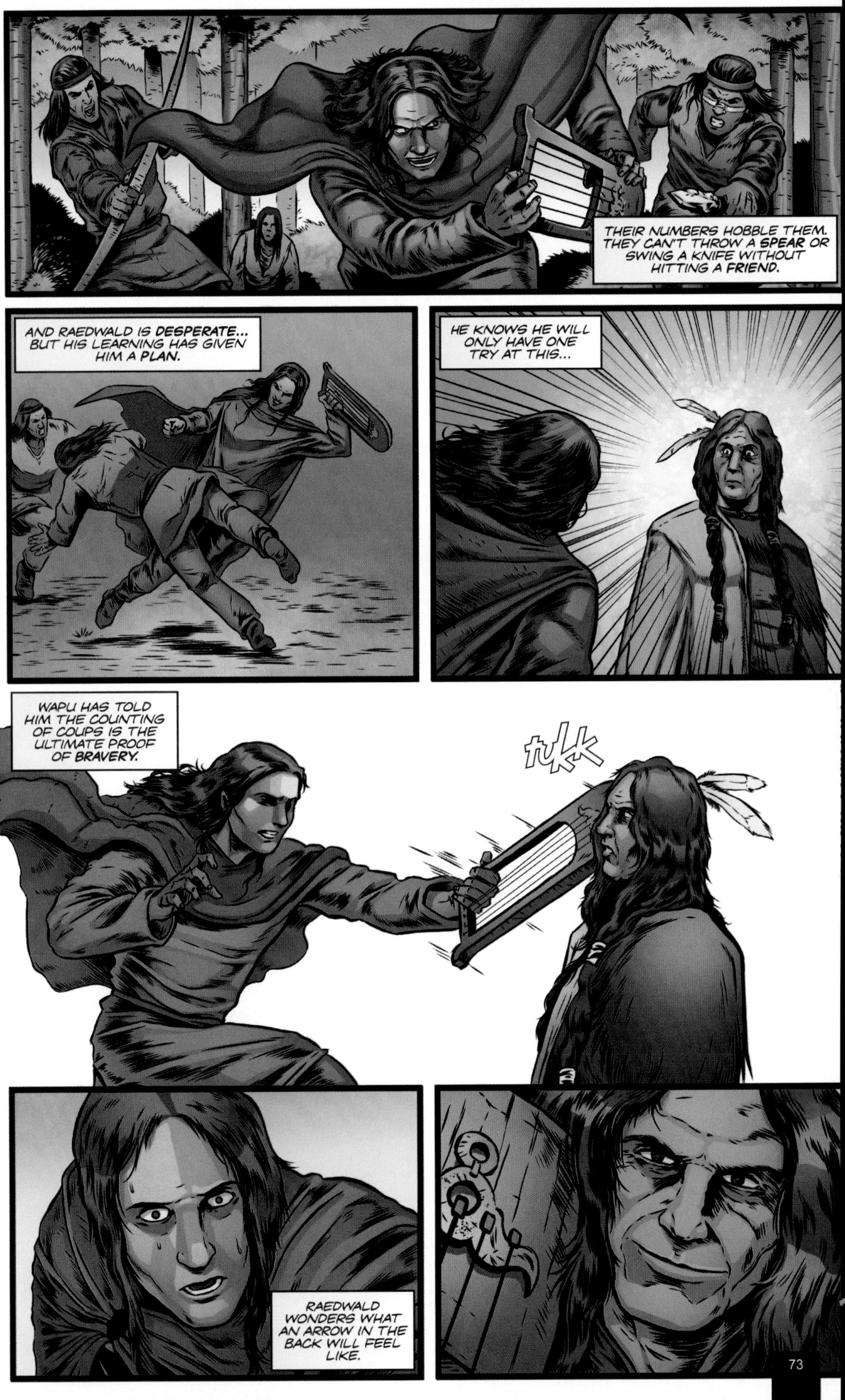
THEIR NUMBERS HOBBLE THEM. THEY CAN'T THROW A SPEAR OR SWING A KNIFE WITHOUT HITTING A FRIEND.
AND RAEDWALD IS DESPERATE... BUT HIS LEARNING HAS GIVEN HIM A PLAN.
HE KNOWS HE WILL ONLY HAVE ONE TRY AT THIS...
WAPU HAS TOLD HIM THE COUNTING OF COUPS IS THE ULTIMATE PROOF OF BRAVERY.
tukk
RAEDWALD WONDERS WHAT AN ARROW IN THE BACK WILL FEEL LIKE.

FIVE YEARS PASS; THE STOCKADE HAS BECOME A TRADING POST, THE MASSIVE **THOR'S HAMMER** IN THE BAY A SYMBOL OF **TRUST** AND **TRADE**.

THREE LONGSHIPS WILL RETURN, LADEN WITH FURS AND IVORY AND BUTTERNUTS.

THE MEN WHO STAY HAVE INNU WIVES.

WILL YOU RETURN?

I'LL TRY, BY BALDUR'S BEARD. NORWAY NEEDS TO BE REMINDED I AM JARL OF THIS COLONY.

BRING MORE **IRON SPEAR POINTS** AND THAT **WOVEN** STUFF. THE WOMEN LIKE IT.

TAKE CARE.

IT'S ALL IN FRIGGA'S HANDS.

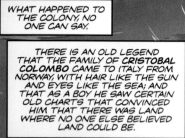

WHAT HAPPENED TO THE COLONY, NO ONE CAN SAY.

THERE IS AN OLD LEGEND THAT THE FAMILY OF **CRISTOBAL COLOMBO** CAME TO ITALY FROM NORWAY, WITH HAIR LIKE THE SUN AND EYES LIKE THE SEA; AND THAT AS A BOY HE SAW CERTAIN OLD CHARTS THAT CONVINCED HIM THAT THERE WAS LAND WHERE NO ONE ELSE BELIEVED LAND COULD BE.

IS IT TRUE? IT **COULD** BE.

THAT'S WHAT MAKES IT A **LEGEND**.

THE END

Vinland Conquest illustrates the exploits of the Vikings in North America.

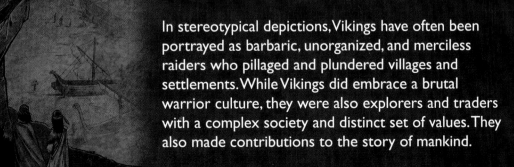

In stereotypical depictions, Vikings have often been portrayed as barbaric, unorganized, and merciless raiders who pillaged and plundered villages and settlements. While Vikings did embrace a brutal warrior culture, they were also explorers and traders with a complex society and distinct set of values. They also made contributions to the story of mankind.

With their innovation of the *longboat*— a sleeker, narrower, more agile ship that combined oar and sail power— the Vikings were able to navigate the ocean independent of wind and attack fast, even in shallow water.

They established independent colonies and settlements throughout Europe, and explored areas as far away as North America and Baghdad. Vikings also made class distinctions that ranged from slave to aristocrat.

Viking colonies often created their own currency; many rulers issued silver coins with their names or symbols on them.

Although the foundation of Viking religion was rooted in Norse Mythology, many Vikings were also Christians.

Vikings buried their dead in their finest clothes, and often with their most valuable possessions— their weapons and tools of their trade. Unlike many other societies, this reverence was extended to common Vikings, not just the nobility or ruling class.

AZTEC RISE AND FALL

WRITTEN BY
JUSTIN PENISTON

ART BY
JORGE PACHECO

COLORS BY
MARLON ILAGAN

LETTERS BY
JIM CAMPBELL

A YOUNG AZTEC FARMER STRIVES TO SHARE HIS BROTHER'S LUCK
AND WINDS UP WITH A FRONT SEAT TO THE DOWNFALL
OF A CIVILIZATION.

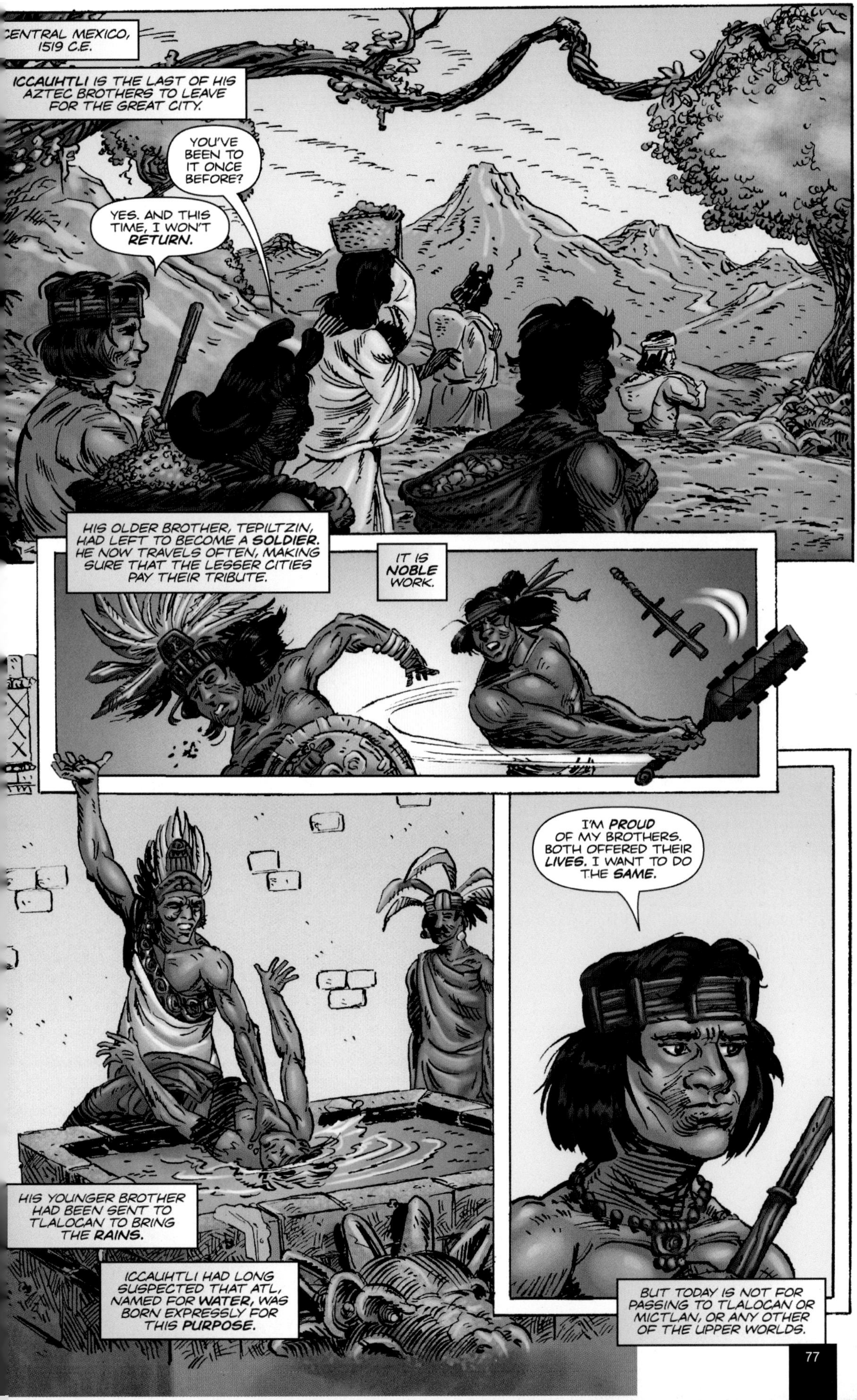
CENTRAL MEXICO, 1519 C.E.
ICCAUHTLI IS THE LAST OF HIS AZTEC BROTHERS TO LEAVE FOR THE GREAT CITY.
YOU'VE BEEN TO IT ONCE BEFORE?
YES. AND THIS TIME, I WON'T RETURN.
HIS OLDER BROTHER, TEPILTZIN, HAD LEFT TO BECOME A SOLDIER. HE NOW TRAVELS OFTEN, MAKING SURE THAT THE LESSER CITIES PAY THEIR TRIBUTE.
IT IS NOBLE WORK.
HIS YOUNGER BROTHER HAD BEEN SENT TO TLALOCAN TO BRING THE RAINS.
ICCAUHTLI HAD LONG SUSPECTED THAT ATL, NAMED FOR WATER, WAS BORN EXPRESSLY FOR THIS PURPOSE.
I'M PROUD OF MY BROTHERS. BOTH OFFERED THEIR LIVES. I WANT TO DO THE SAME.
BUT TODAY IS NOT FOR PASSING TO TLALOCAN OR MICTLAN, OR ANY OTHER OF THE UPPER WORLDS.

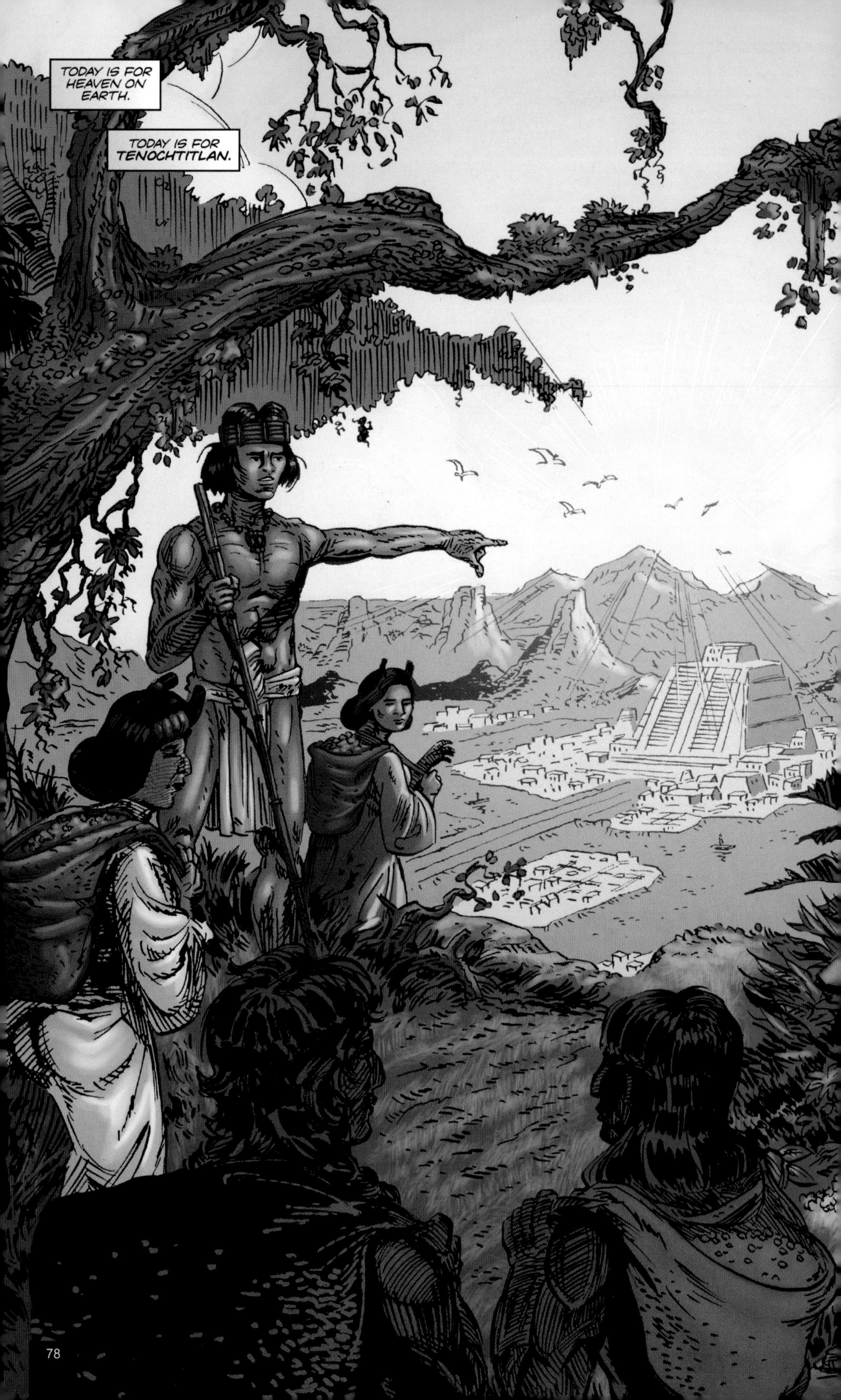
TODAY IS FOR HEAVEN ON EARTH.
TODAY IS FOR TENOCHTITLAN.

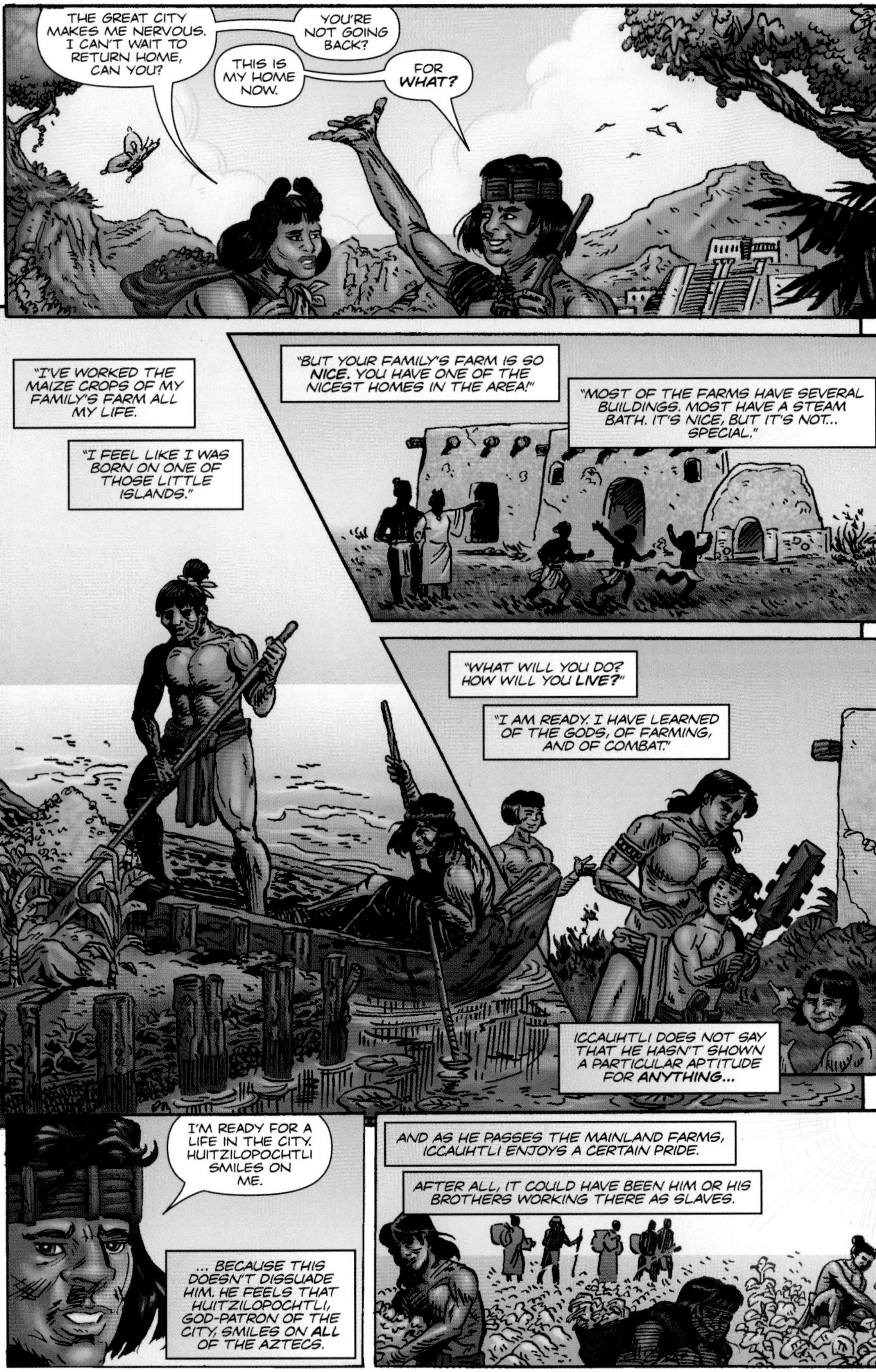

THE GREAT CITY MAKES ME NERVOUS. I CAN'T WAIT TO RETURN HOME, CAN YOU?
THIS IS MY HOME NOW.
YOU'RE NOT GOING BACK?
FOR WHAT?
"I'VE WORKED THE MAIZE CROPS OF MY FAMILY'S FARM ALL MY LIFE.
"I FEEL LIKE I WAS BORN ON ONE OF THOSE LITTLE ISLANDS."
"BUT YOUR FAMILY'S FARM IS SO NICE. YOU HAVE ONE OF THE NICEST HOMES IN THE AREA!"
"MOST OF THE FARMS HAVE SEVERAL BUILDINGS. MOST HAVE A STEAM BATH. IT'S NICE, BUT IT'S NOT... SPECIAL."
"WHAT WILL YOU DO? HOW WILL YOU LIVE?"
"I AM READY. I HAVE LEARNED OF THE GODS, OF FARMING, AND OF COMBAT."
ICCAUHTLI DOES NOT SAY THAT HE HASN'T SHOWN A PARTICULAR APTITUDE FOR ANYTHING...
I'M READY FOR A LIFE IN THE CITY. HUITZILOPOCHTLI SMILES ON ME.
... BECAUSE THIS DOESN'T DISSUADE HIM. HE FEELS THAT HUITZILOPOCHTLI, GOD-PATRON OF THE CITY, SMILES ON ALL OF THE AZTECS.
AND AS HE PASSES THE MAINLAND FARMS, ICCAUHTLI ENJOYS A CERTAIN PRIDE.
AFTER ALL, IT COULD HAVE BEEN HIM OR HIS BROTHERS WORKING THERE AS SLAVES.

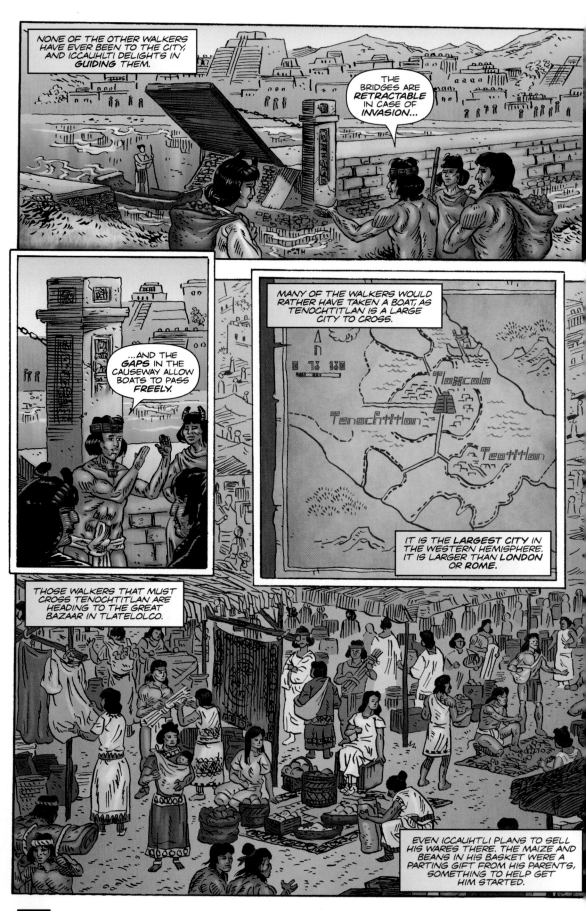

NONE OF THE OTHER WALKERS HAVE EVER BEEN TO THE CITY, AND ICCAUHTLI DELIGHTS IN *GUIDING* THEM.

THE BRIDGES ARE *RETRACTABLE* IN CASE OF *INVASION*...

...AND THE *GAPS* IN THE CAUSEWAY ALLOW BOATS TO PASS *FREELY*.

MANY OF THE WALKERS WOULD RATHER HAVE TAKEN A BOAT, AS TENOCHTITLAN IS A LARGE CITY TO CROSS.

Tlaxcala

Tenochtitlan

Teotitlan

IT IS THE *LARGEST* CITY IN THE WESTERN HEMISPHERE. IT IS LARGER THAN *LONDON* OR *ROME*.

THOSE WALKERS THAT MUST CROSS TENOCHTITLAN ARE HEADING TO THE GREAT BAZAAR IN TLATELOLCO.

EVEN ICCAUHTLI PLANS TO SELL HIS WARES THERE. THE MAIZE AND BEANS IN HIS BASKET WERE A PARTING GIFT FROM HIS PARENTS, SOMETHING TO HELP GET HIM STARTED.

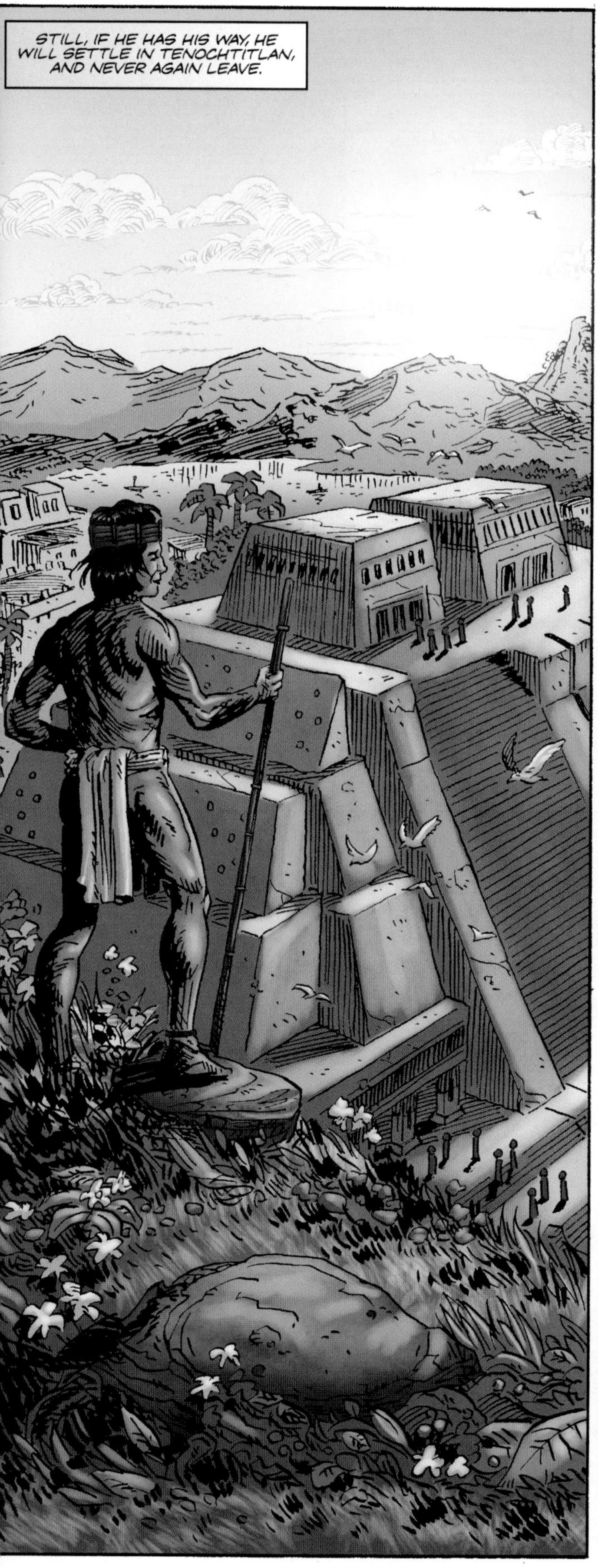
STILL, IF HE HAS HIS WAY, HE WILL SETTLE IN TENOCHTITLAN, AND NEVER AGAIN LEAVE.

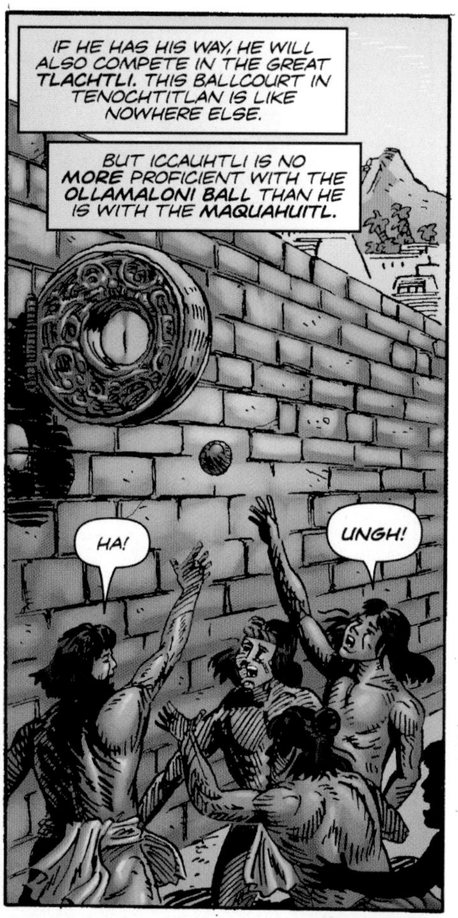
IF HE HAS HIS WAY, HE WILL ALSO COMPETE IN THE GREAT TLACHTLI. THIS BALLCOURT IN TENOCHTITLAN IS LIKE NOWHERE ELSE.
BUT ICCAUHTLI IS NO MORE PROFICIENT WITH THE OLLAMALONI BALL THAN HE IS WITH THE MAQUAHUITL.
HA!
UNGH!

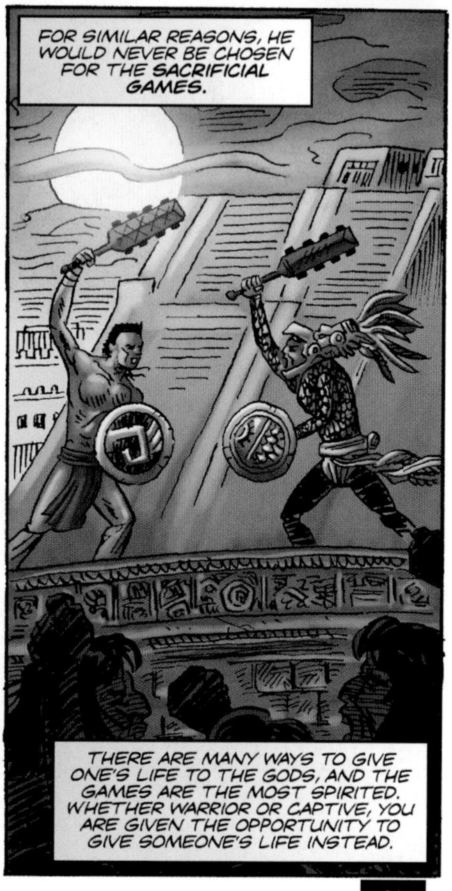
FOR SIMILAR REASONS, HE WOULD NEVER BE CHOSEN FOR THE SACRIFICIAL GAMES.
THERE ARE MANY WAYS TO GIVE ONE'S LIFE TO THE GODS, AND THE GAMES ARE THE MOST SPIRITED. WHETHER WARRIOR OR CAPTIVE, YOU ARE GIVEN THE OPPORTUNITY TO GIVE SOMEONE'S LIFE INSTEAD.

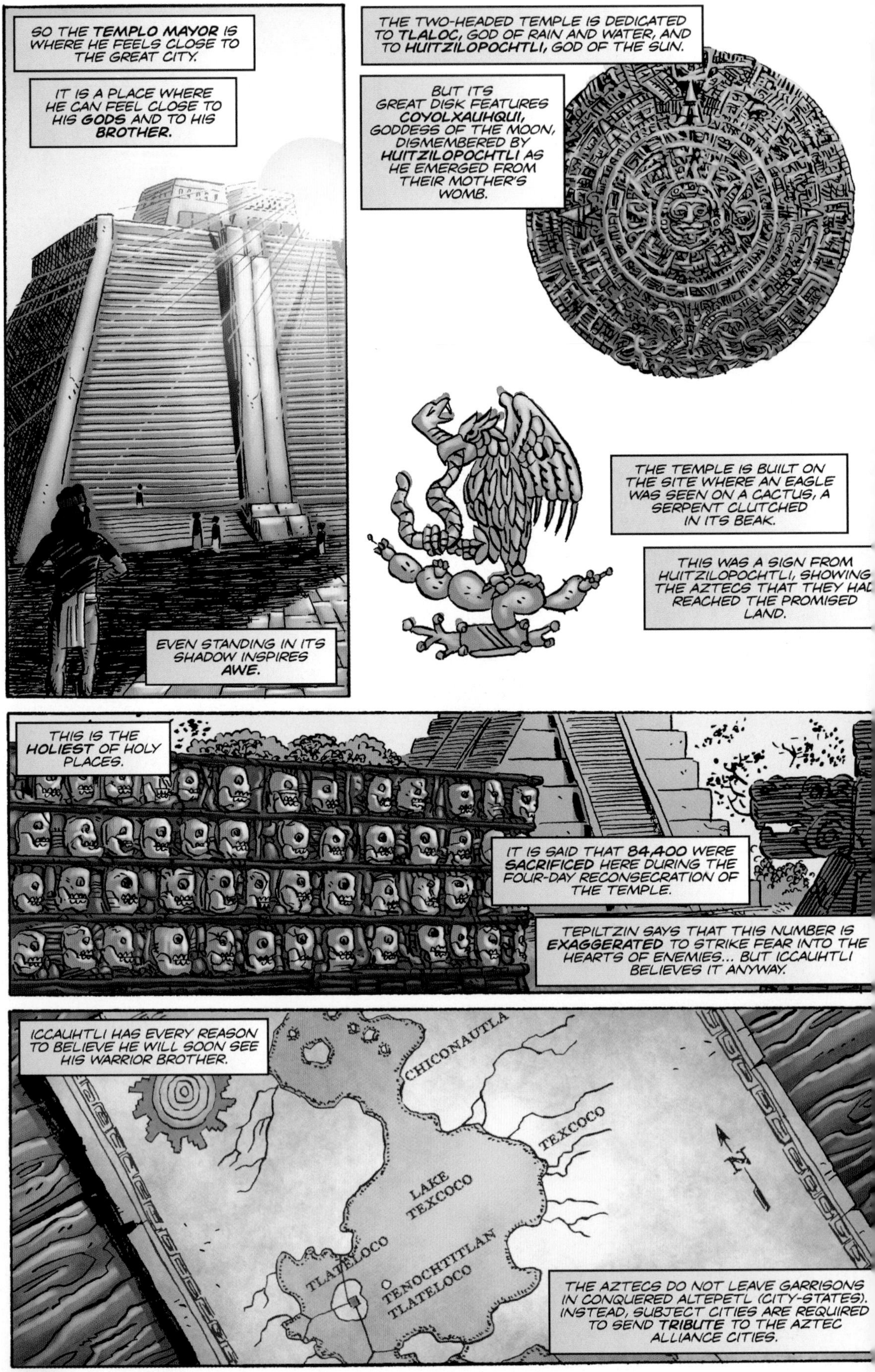
SO THE **TEMPLO MAYOR** IS WHERE HE FEELS CLOSE TO THE GREAT CITY.
IT IS A PLACE WHERE HE CAN FEEL CLOSE TO HIS **GODS** AND TO HIS **BROTHER**.
EVEN STANDING IN ITS SHADOW INSPIRES **AWE**.
THE TWO-HEADED TEMPLE IS DEDICATED TO **TLALOC**, GOD OF RAIN AND WATER, AND TO **HUITZILOPOCHTLI**, GOD OF THE SUN.
BUT ITS GREAT DISK FEATURES **COYOLXAUHQUI**, GODDESS OF THE MOON, DISMEMBERED BY **HUITZILOPOCHTLI** AS HE EMERGED FROM THEIR MOTHER'S WOMB.
THE TEMPLE IS BUILT ON THE SITE WHERE AN EAGLE WAS SEEN ON A CACTUS, A SERPENT CLUTCHED IN ITS BEAK.
THIS WAS A SIGN FROM HUITZILOPOCHTLI, SHOWING THE AZTECS THAT THEY HAD REACHED THE PROMISED LAND.
THIS IS THE **HOLIEST** OF HOLY PLACES.
IT IS SAID THAT **84,400** WERE **SACRIFICED** HERE DURING THE FOUR-DAY RECONSECRATION OF THE TEMPLE.
TEPILTZIN SAYS THAT THIS NUMBER IS **EXAGGERATED** TO STRIKE FEAR INTO THE HEARTS OF ENEMIES... BUT ICCAUHTLI BELIEVES IT ANYWAY.
ICCAUHTLI HAS EVERY REASON TO BELIEVE HE WILL SOON SEE HIS WARRIOR BROTHER.
CHICONAUTLA
TEXCOCO
LAKE TEXCOCO
TLATELOCO
TLATELOCO
TENOCHTITLAN TLATELOCO
N
THE AZTECS DO NOT LEAVE GARRISONS IN CONQUERED ALTEPETL (CITY-STATES). INSTEAD, SUBJECT CITIES ARE REQUIRED TO SEND **TRIBUTE** TO THE AZTEC ALLIANCE CITIES.

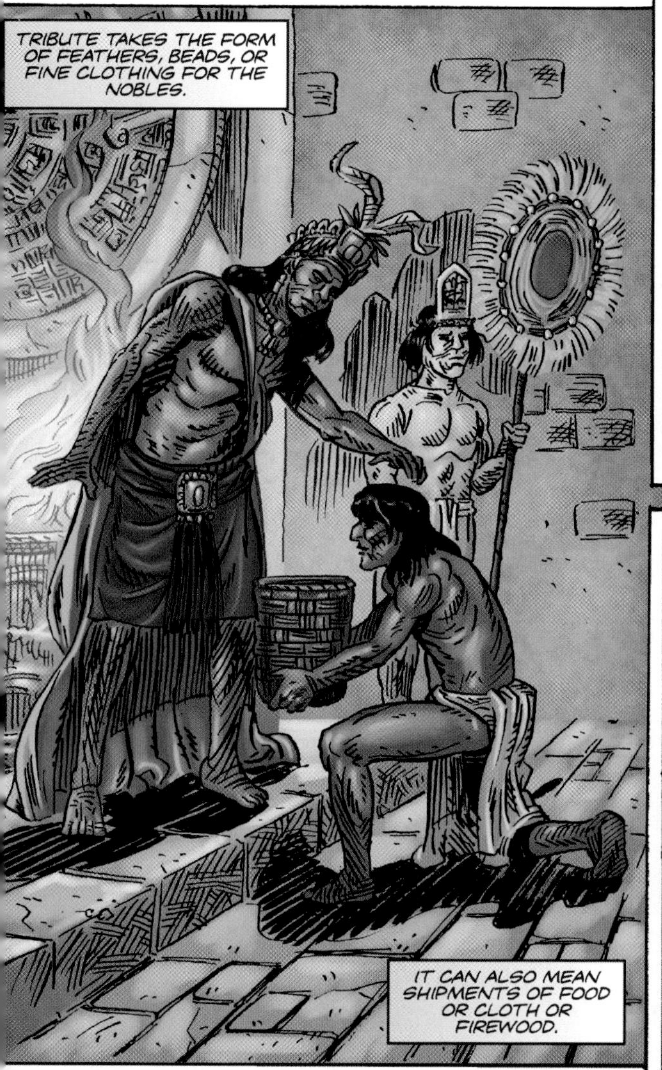
TRIBUTE TAKES THE FORM OF FEATHERS, BEADS, OR FINE CLOTHING FOR THE NOBLES.
IT CAN ALSO MEAN SHIPMENTS OF FOOD OR CLOTH OR FIREWOOD.

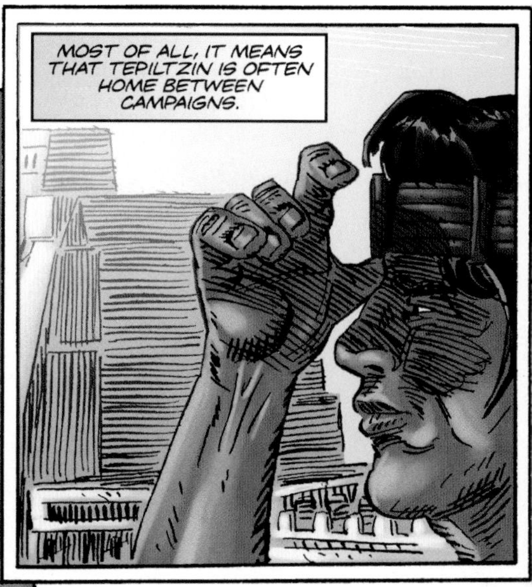
MOST OF ALL, IT MEANS THAT TEPILTZIN IS OFTEN HOME BETWEEN CAMPAIGNS.

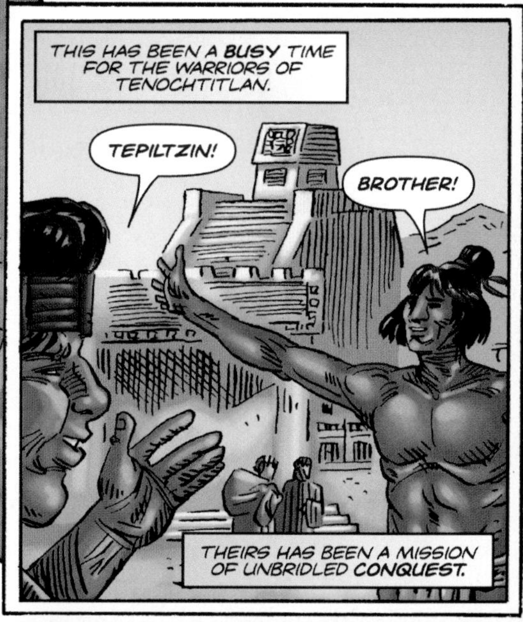
THIS HAS BEEN A **BUSY** TIME FOR THE WARRIORS OF TENOCHTITLAN.
TEPILTZIN!
BROTHER!
THEIRS HAS BEEN A MISSION OF UNBRIDLED **CONQUEST.**

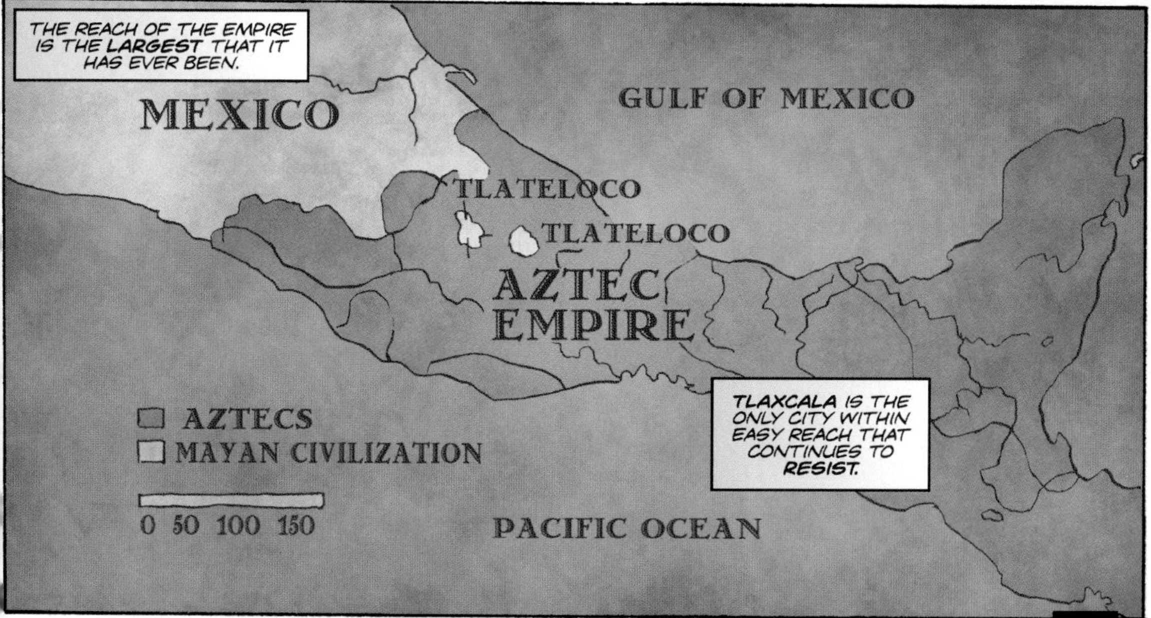
THE REACH OF THE EMPIRE IS THE **LARGEST** THAT IT HAS EVER BEEN.
MEXICO
GULF OF MEXICO
TLATELOCO
TLATELOCO
AZTEC EMPIRE
AZTECS
MAYAN CIVILIZATION
0 50 100 150
PACIFIC OCEAN
TLAXCALA IS THE ONLY CITY WITHIN EASY REACH THAT CONTINUES TO **RESIST.**

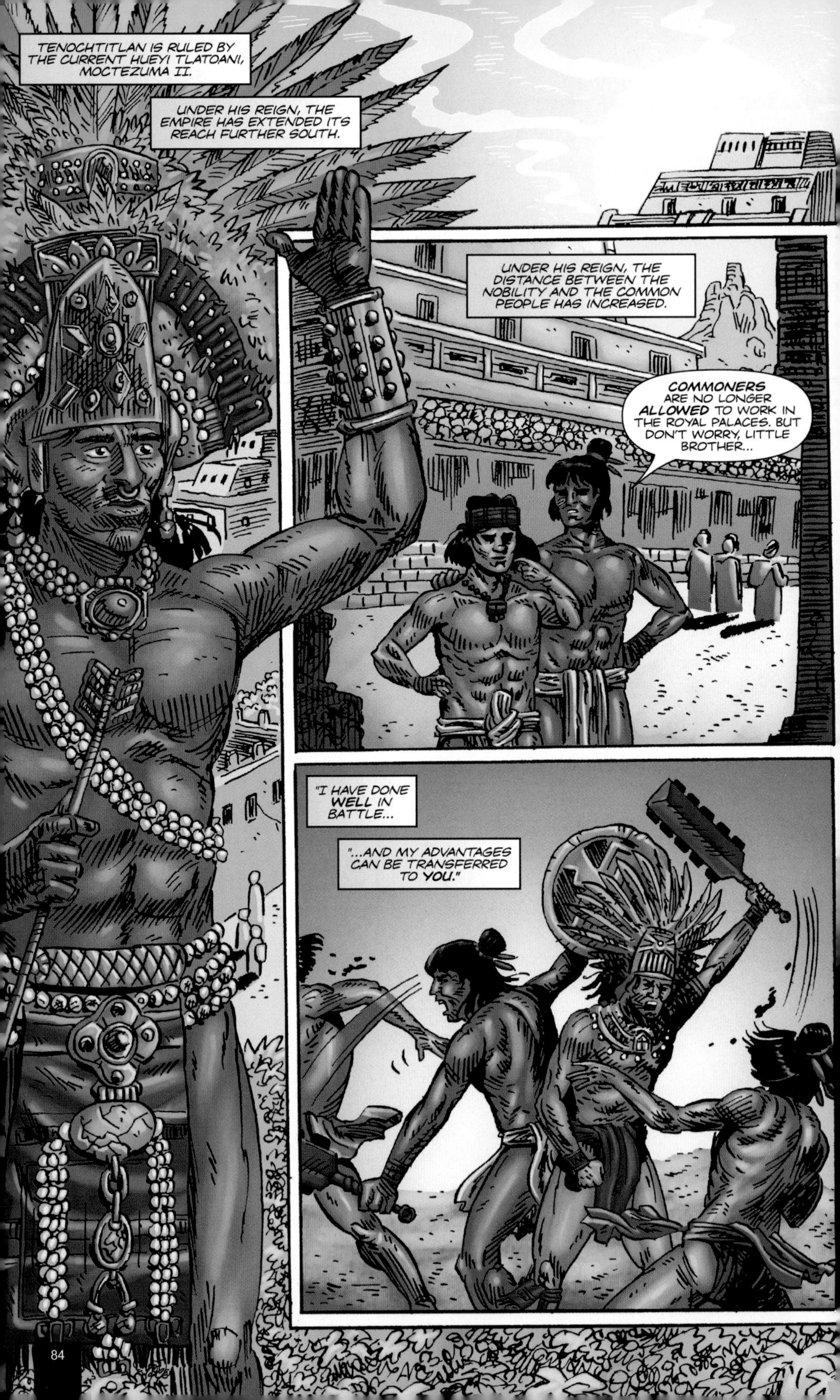

TENOCHTITLAN IS RULED BY THE CURRENT HUEYI TLATOANI, MOCTEZUMA II.
UNDER HIS REIGN, THE EMPIRE HAS EXTENDED ITS REACH FURTHER SOUTH.
UNDER HIS REIGN, THE DISTANCE BETWEEN THE NOBILITY AND THE COMMON PEOPLE HAS INCREASED.
COMMONERS ARE NO LONGER ALLOWED TO WORK IN THE ROYAL PALACES. BUT DON'T WORRY, LITTLE BROTHER...
"I HAVE DONE WELL IN BATTLE...
"...AND MY ADVANTAGES CAN BE TRANSFERRED TO YOU."

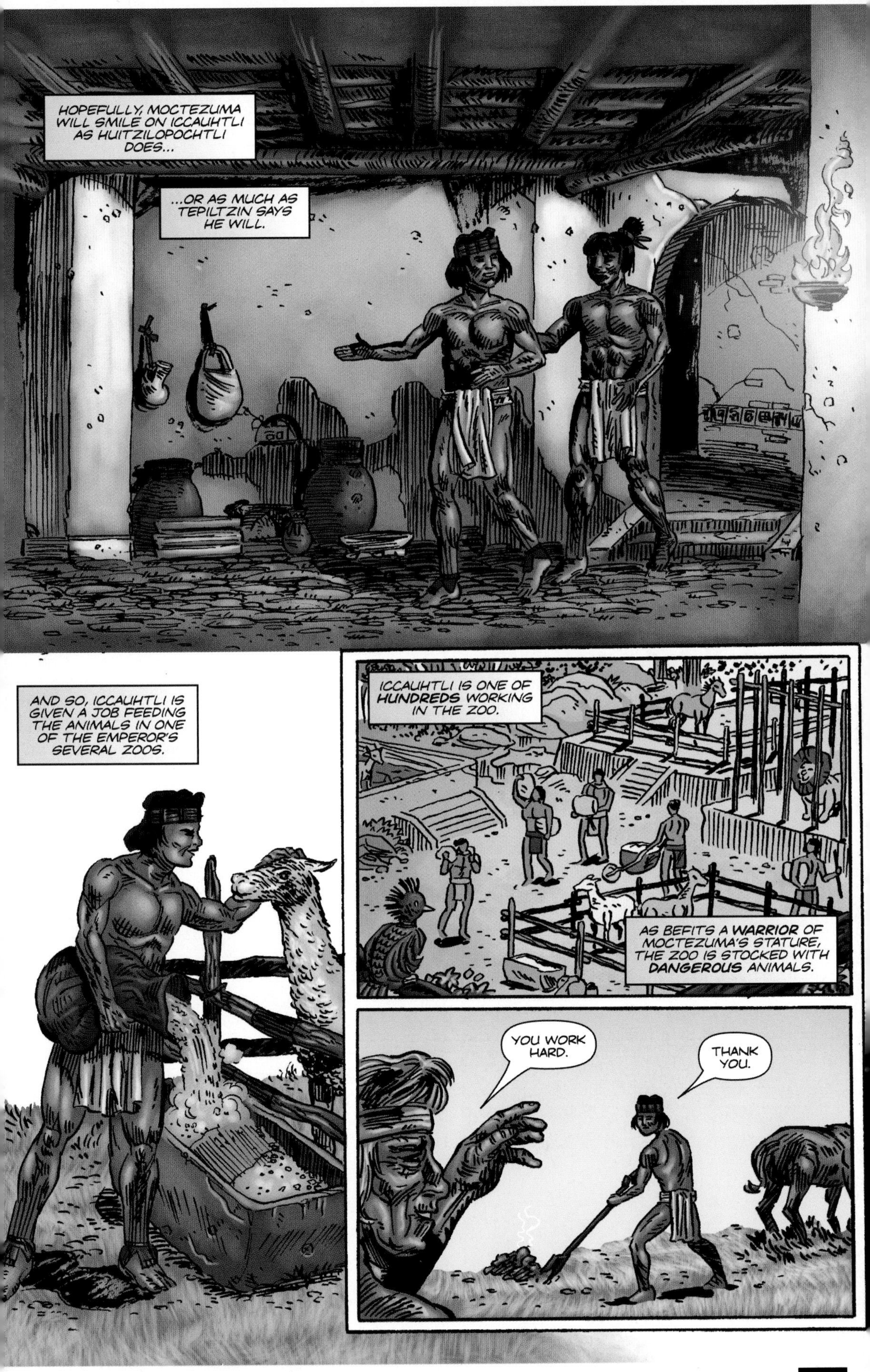

HOPEFULLY, MOCTEZUMA WILL SMILE ON ICCAUHTLI AS HUITZILOPOCHTLI DOES...
...OR AS MUCH AS TEPILTZIN SAYS HE WILL.
AND SO, ICCAUHTLI IS GIVEN A JOB FEEDING THE ANIMALS IN ONE OF THE EMPEROR'S SEVERAL ZOOS.
ICCAUHTLI IS ONE OF **HUNDREDS** WORKING IN THE ZOO.
AS BEFITS A **WARRIOR** OF MOCTEZUMA'S STATURE, THE ZOO IS STOCKED WITH **DANGEROUS** ANIMALS.
YOU WORK HARD.
THANK YOU.

ICCAUHTLI IS OVERJOYED BY HIS GOOD FORTUNE, AND OFFERS HIS THANKS TO THE GODS.

NOT ALL BLOOD OFFERINGS ARE A SACRIFICE OF LIFE.

BUT SHORTLY, ICCAUHTLI HEARS RUMORS.

QUETZALCOATL HAS COME! HE IS IN THE LANDS OF THE TLAXCALA!

THE GODS WOULD NOT GO FIRST TO TENOCHTITLAN'S ENEMY!

IT ISN'T LONG BEFORE SERVANTS OF THE SO-CALLED QUETZALCOATL APPEAR BEFORE THE EMPEROR.

ICCAUHTLI THINKS THAT THEY ARE SIMPLY STRANGE FOREIGNERS...

...BUT HE DOESN'T FIND THIS FAR MORE PLAUSIBLE SCENARIO AT ALL COMFORTING.

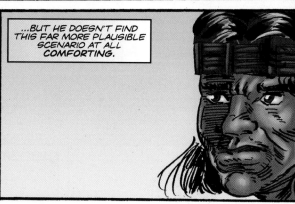

THE RUMORS CHANGE AS SOON AS THE AZTECS LAY EYES ON THE MEN OF HERNAN CORTES.

CORTES' FIRST LANDING BROUGHT HIM INTO CONFLICT WITH THE MAYA.

HE DESTROYED THE AZTEC CITY OF CHOLOLLAN, WHETHER IN RETALIATION, OR SIMPLY TO IMPRESS MOCTEZUMA, IS UNCLEAR.

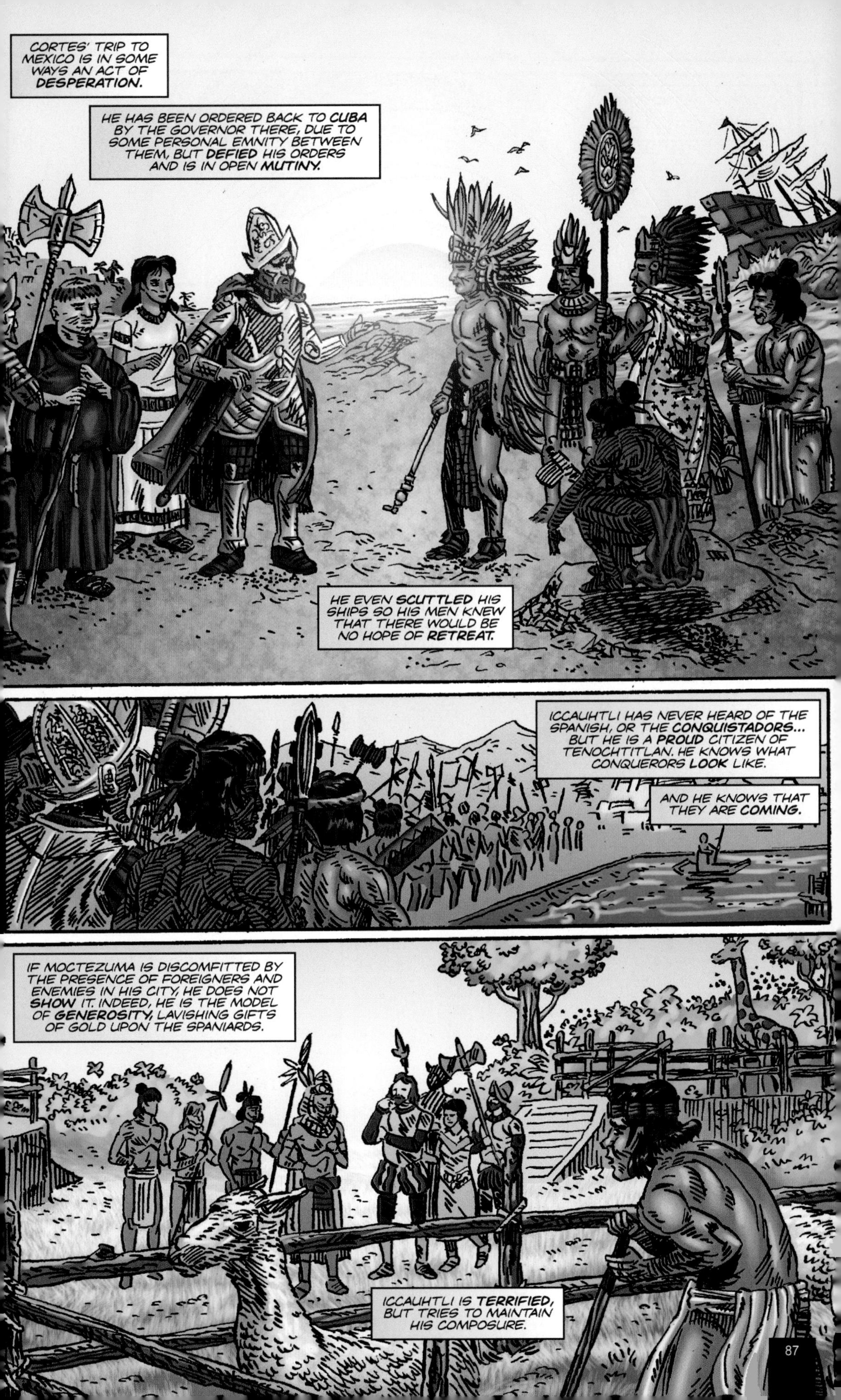
CORTES' TRIP TO MEXICO IS IN SOME WAYS AN ACT OF **DESPERATION.**
HE HAS BEEN ORDERED BACK TO **CUBA** BY THE GOVERNOR THERE, DUE TO SOME PERSONAL EMNITY BETWEEN THEM, BUT **DEFIED** HIS ORDERS AND IS IN OPEN **MUTINY.**
HE EVEN **SCUTTLED** HIS SHIPS SO HIS MEN KNEW THAT THERE WOULD BE NO HOPE OF **RETREAT.**
ICCAUHTLI HAS NEVER HEARD OF THE SPANISH, OR THE **CONQUISTADORS...** BUT HE IS A **PROUD** CITIZEN OF TENOCHTITLAN. HE KNOWS WHAT CONQUERORS **LOOK** LIKE.
AND HE KNOWS THAT THEY ARE **COMING.**
IF MOCTEZUMA IS DISCOMFITTED BY THE PRESENCE OF FOREIGNERS AND ENEMIES IN HIS CITY, HE DOES NOT **SHOW** IT. INDEED, HE IS THE MODEL OF **GENEROSITY,** LAVISHING GIFTS OF GOLD UPON THE SPANIARDS.
ICCAUHTLI IS **TERRIFIED,** BUT TRIES TO MAINTAIN HIS COMPOSURE.

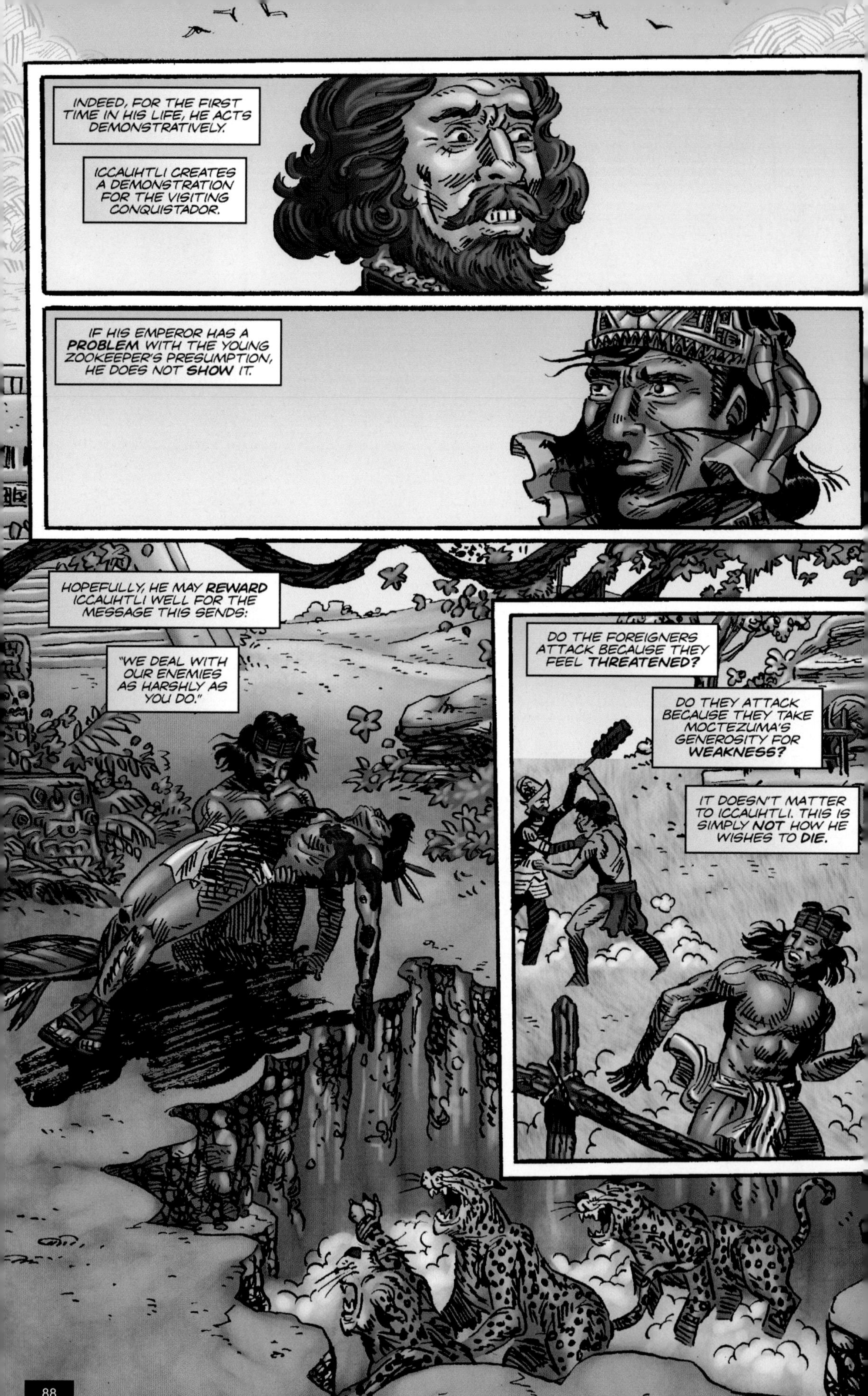

INDEED, FOR THE FIRST TIME IN HIS LIFE, HE ACTS DEMONSTRATIVELY.
ICCAUHTLI CREATES A DEMONSTRATION FOR THE VISITING CONQUISTADOR.
IF HIS EMPEROR HAS A PROBLEM WITH THE YOUNG ZOOKEEPER'S PRESUMPTION, HE DOES NOT SHOW IT.
HOPEFULLY, HE MAY REWARD ICCAUHTLI WELL FOR THE MESSAGE THIS SENDS:
"WE DEAL WITH OUR ENEMIES AS HARSHLY AS YOU DO."
DO THE FOREIGNERS ATTACK BECAUSE THEY FEEL THREATENED?
DO THEY ATTACK BECAUSE THEY TAKE MOCTEZUMA'S GENEROSITY FOR WEAKNESS?
IT DOESN'T MATTER TO ICCAUHTLI. THIS IS SIMPLY NOT HOW HE WISHES TO DIE.

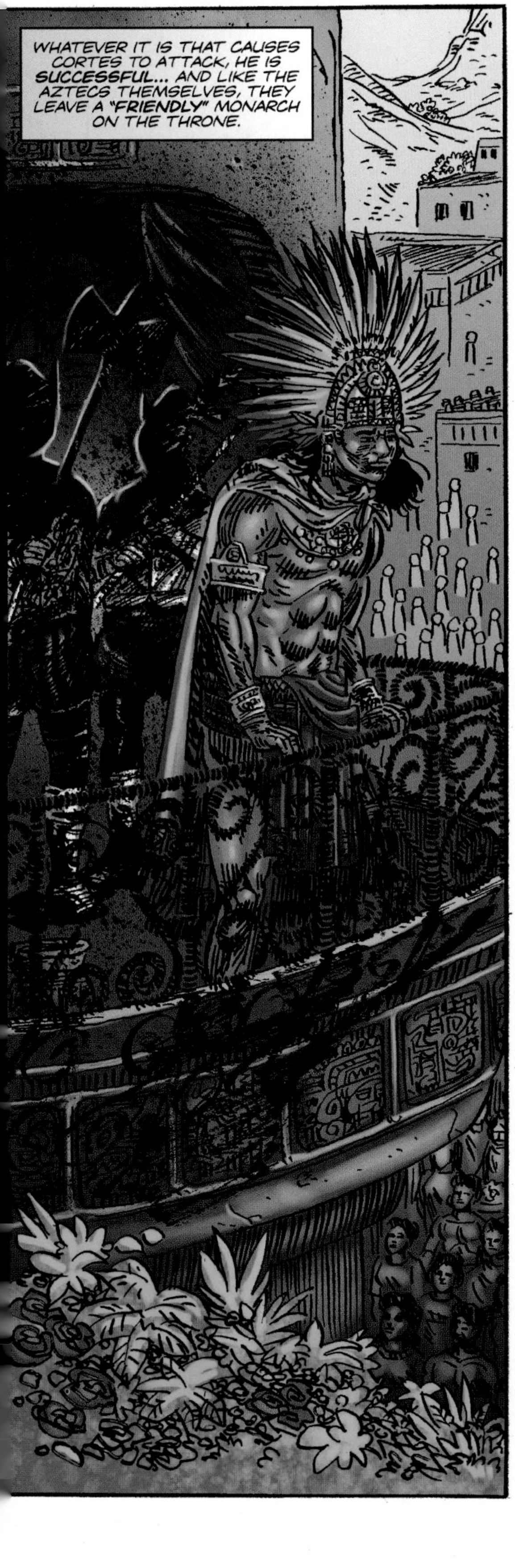
WHATEVER IT IS THAT CAUSES CORTES TO ATTACK, HE IS **SUCCESSFUL...** AND LIKE THE AZTECS THEMSELVES, THEY LEAVE A **"FRIENDLY"** MONARCH ON THE THRONE.

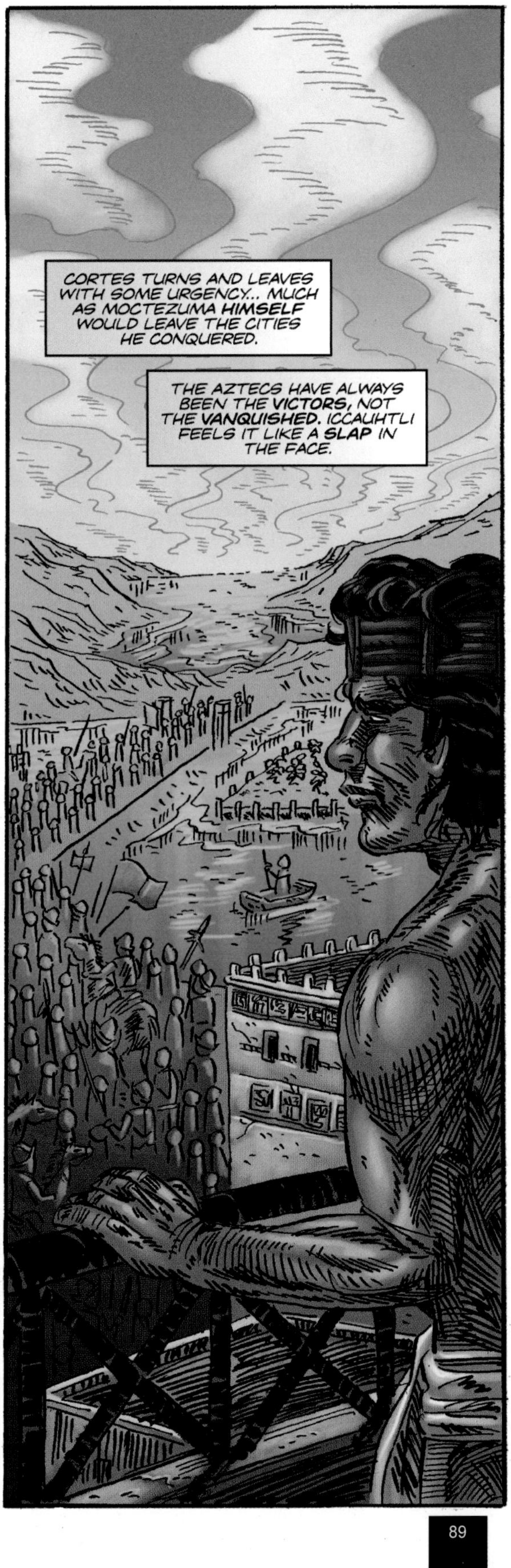
CORTES TURNS AND LEAVES WITH SOME URGENCY... MUCH AS MOCTEZUMA **HIMSELF** WOULD LEAVE THE CITIES HE CONQUERED.
THE AZTECS HAVE ALWAYS BEEN THE **VICTORS,** NOT THE **VANQUISHED.** ICCAUHTLI FEELS IT LIKE A **SLAP** IN THE FACE.

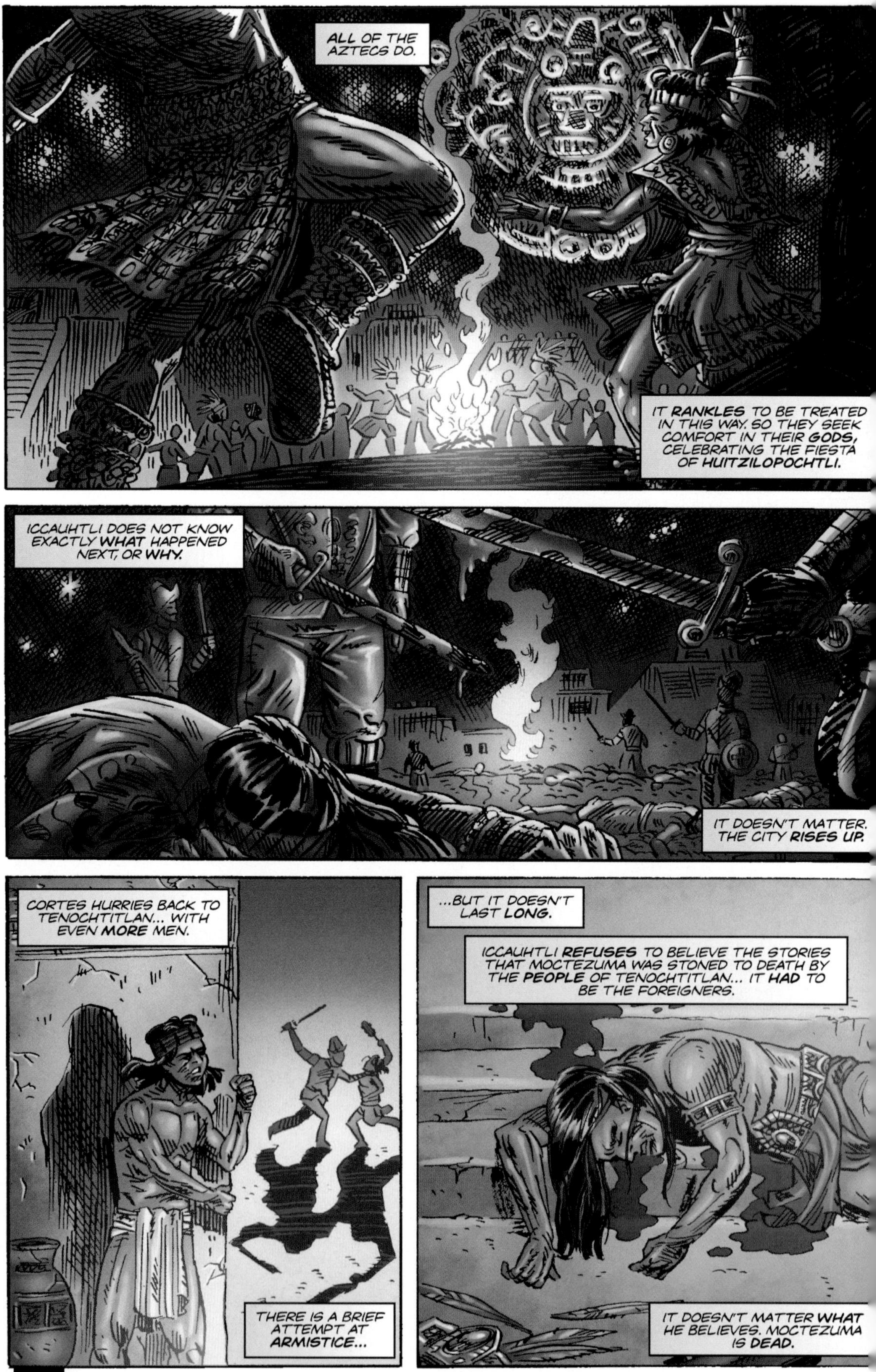
ALL OF THE AZTECS DO.
IT RANKLES TO BE TREATED IN THIS WAY. SO THEY SEEK COMFORT IN THEIR GODS, CELEBRATING THE FIESTA OF HUITZILOPOCHTLI.
ICCAUHTLI DOES NOT KNOW EXACTLY WHAT HAPPENED NEXT, OR WHY.
IT DOESN'T MATTER. THE CITY RISES UP.
CORTES HURRIES BACK TO TENOCHTITLAN... WITH EVEN MORE MEN.
THERE IS A BRIEF ATTEMPT AT ARMISTICE...
...BUT IT DOESN'T LAST LONG.
ICCAUHTLI REFUSES TO BELIEVE THE STORIES THAT MOCTEZUMA WAS STONED TO DEATH BY THE PEOPLE OF TENOCHTITLAN... IT HAD TO BE THE FOREIGNERS.
IT DOESN'T MATTER WHAT HE BELIEVES. MOCTEZUMA IS DEAD.

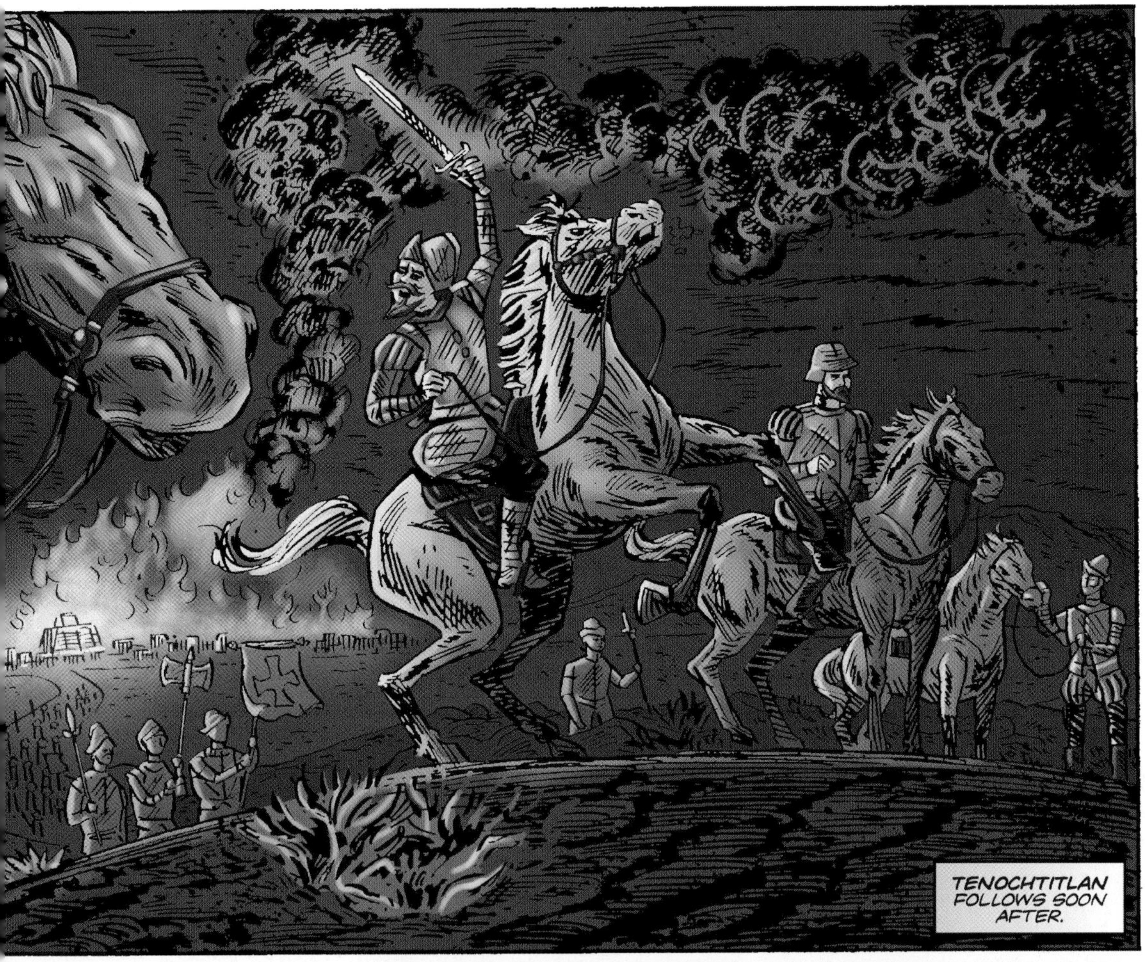
TENOCHTITLAN FOLLOWS SOON AFTER.

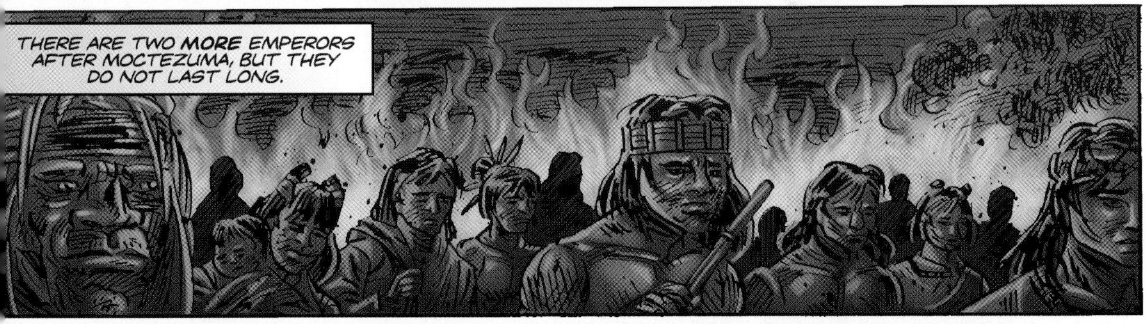
THERE ARE TWO MORE EMPERORS AFTER MOCTEZUMA, BUT THEY DO NOT LAST LONG.

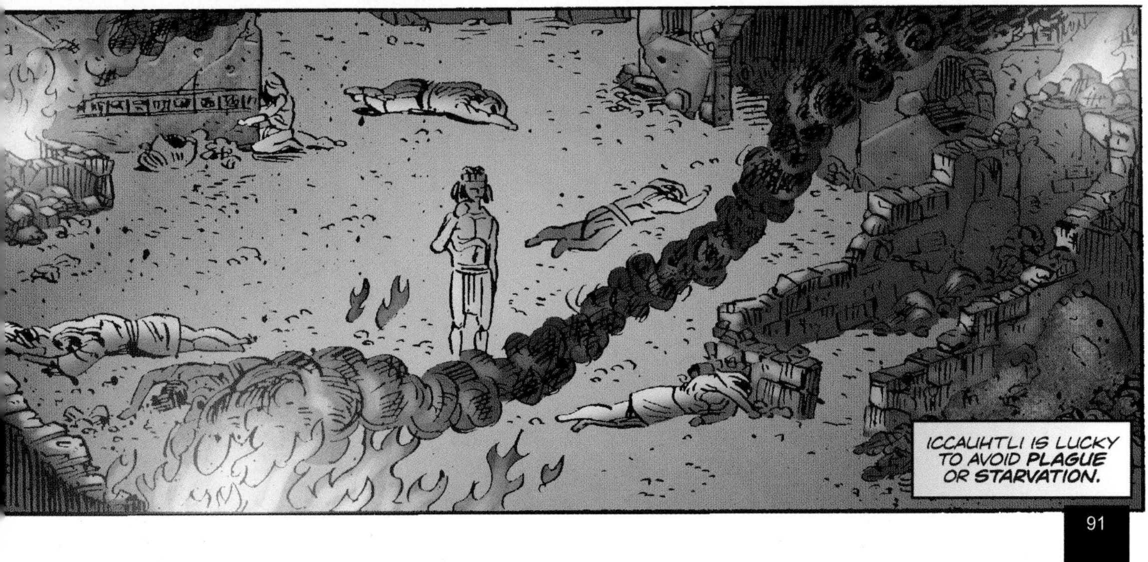
ICCAUHTLI IS LUCKY TO AVOID PLAGUE OR STARVATION.

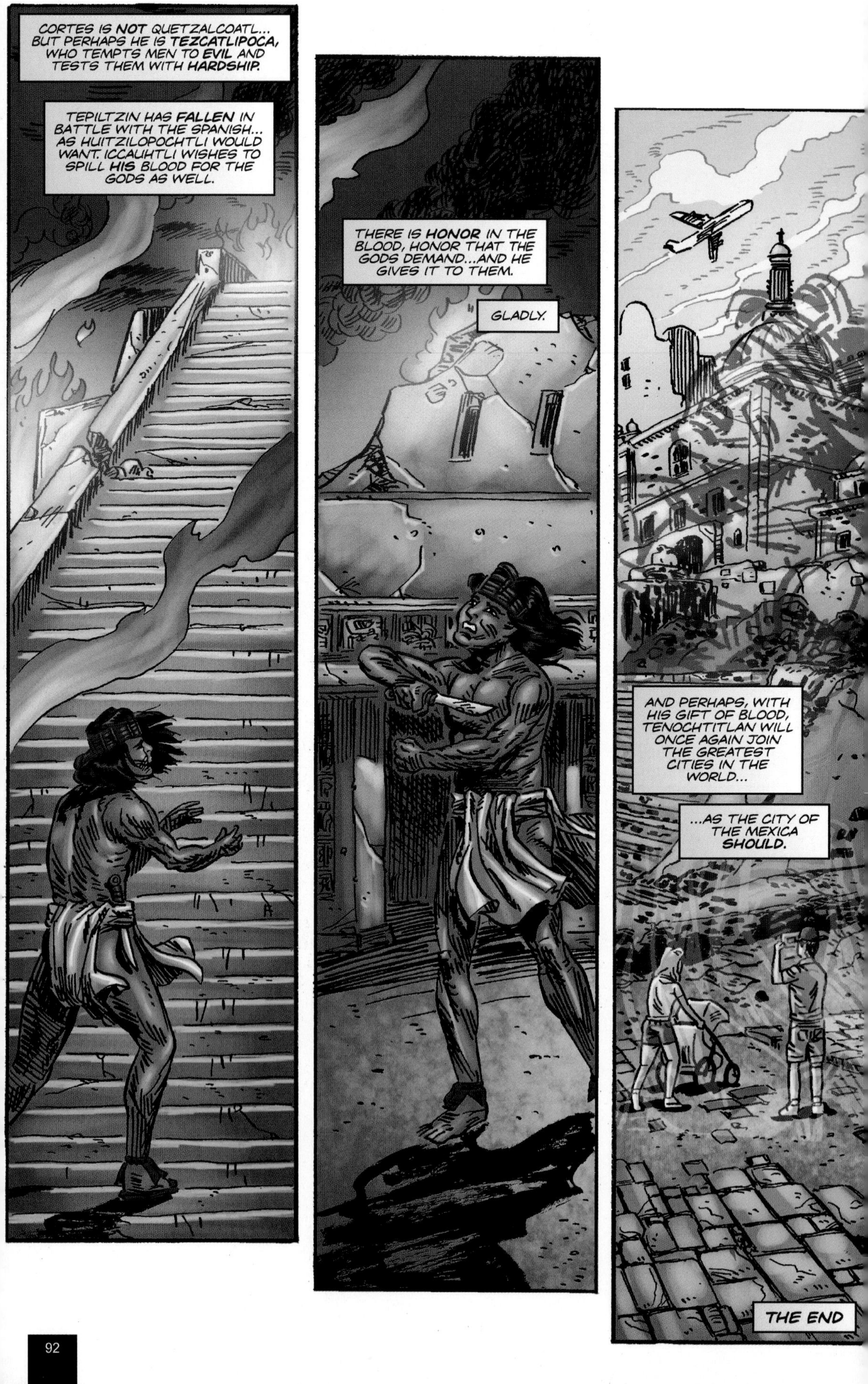
CORTES IS NOT QUETZALCOATL... BUT PERHAPS HE IS TEZCATLIPOCA, WHO TEMPTS MEN TO EVIL AND TESTS THEM WITH HARDSHIP.
TEPILTZIN HAS FALLEN IN BATTLE WITH THE SPANISH... AS HUITZILOPOCHTLI WOULD WANT. ICCAUHTLI WISHES TO SPILL HIS BLOOD FOR THE GODS AS WELL.
THERE IS HONOR IN THE BLOOD, HONOR THAT THE GODS DEMAND...AND HE GIVES IT TO THEM.
GLADLY.
AND PERHAPS, WITH HIS GIFT OF BLOOD, TENOCHTITLAN WILL ONCE AGAIN JOIN THE GREATEST CITIES IN THE WORLD...
...AS THE CITY OF THE MEXICA SHOULD.
THE END

MANKIND
DECODED

**In *Rise and Fall*, Aztecs grow and harvest maize—
known more commonly today as corn.**

Of all the crops they grew, maize was the most important as it
was the centerpiece of the Aztec diet. Unlike other crops, maize
was cultivated and grown in every region of the Aztec Empire.
Even today, corn remains a key staple of modern life:

- The corn we eat does not grow
  naturally - our ancient ancestors
  had to engineer and cultivate
  it from a slender grass called
  teosinte.

- Mankind has been growing corn for more than 7,000 years. Today, corn is
  grown on every continent in the world except Antarctica.

- In the United States, corn production is double that of any other crop.

- Corn is a key ingredient in many of the foods we eat daily: breakfast cereals,
  peanut butter, potato chips, soft drinks, and much more.

THE STORY OF THE OCEAN

WRITTEN BY
ARIE KAPLAN

ART BY
MICHAEL WATKINS & BOB PETRECCA

COLORS BY
MICHAEL WATKINS, JOHN ANDERSON & MARLON ILAGAN

LETTERS BY
JIM CAMPBELL

AS MAN LEARNS TO HARNESS THE WIND AND MASTER THE WAVES, HE NAVIGATES EARTH'S DOMINATING SEAS TO EXPLORE THE WORLD AND DISCOVER NEW RICHES.

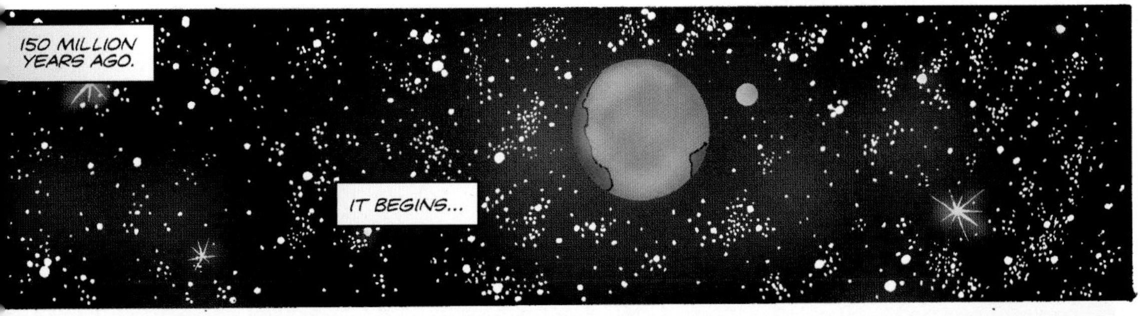
150 MILLION YEARS AGO.
IT BEGINS...

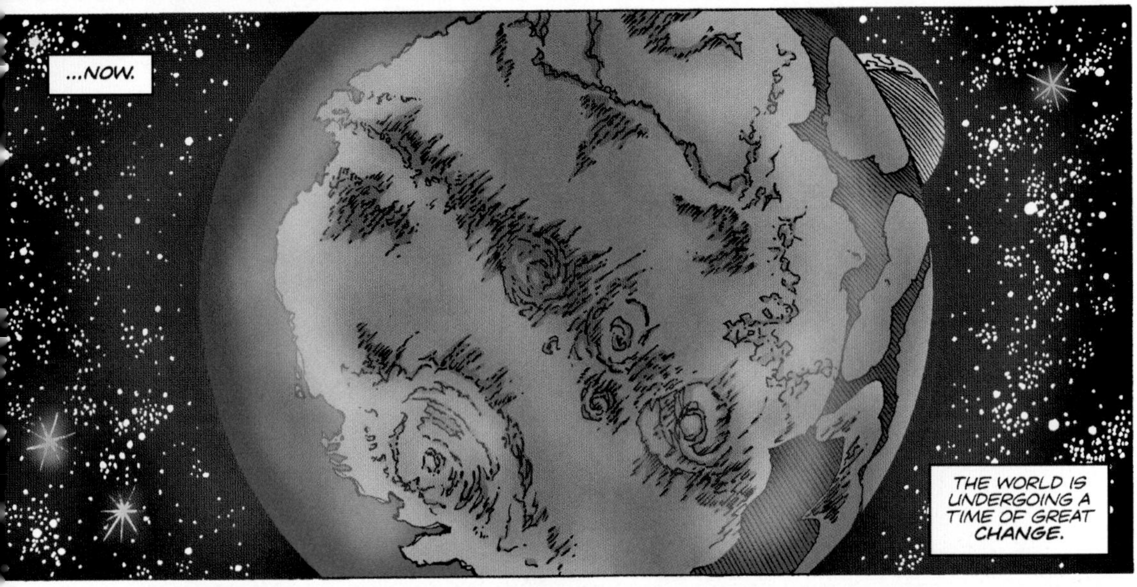
...NOW.
THE WORLD IS UNDERGOING A TIME OF GREAT CHANGE.

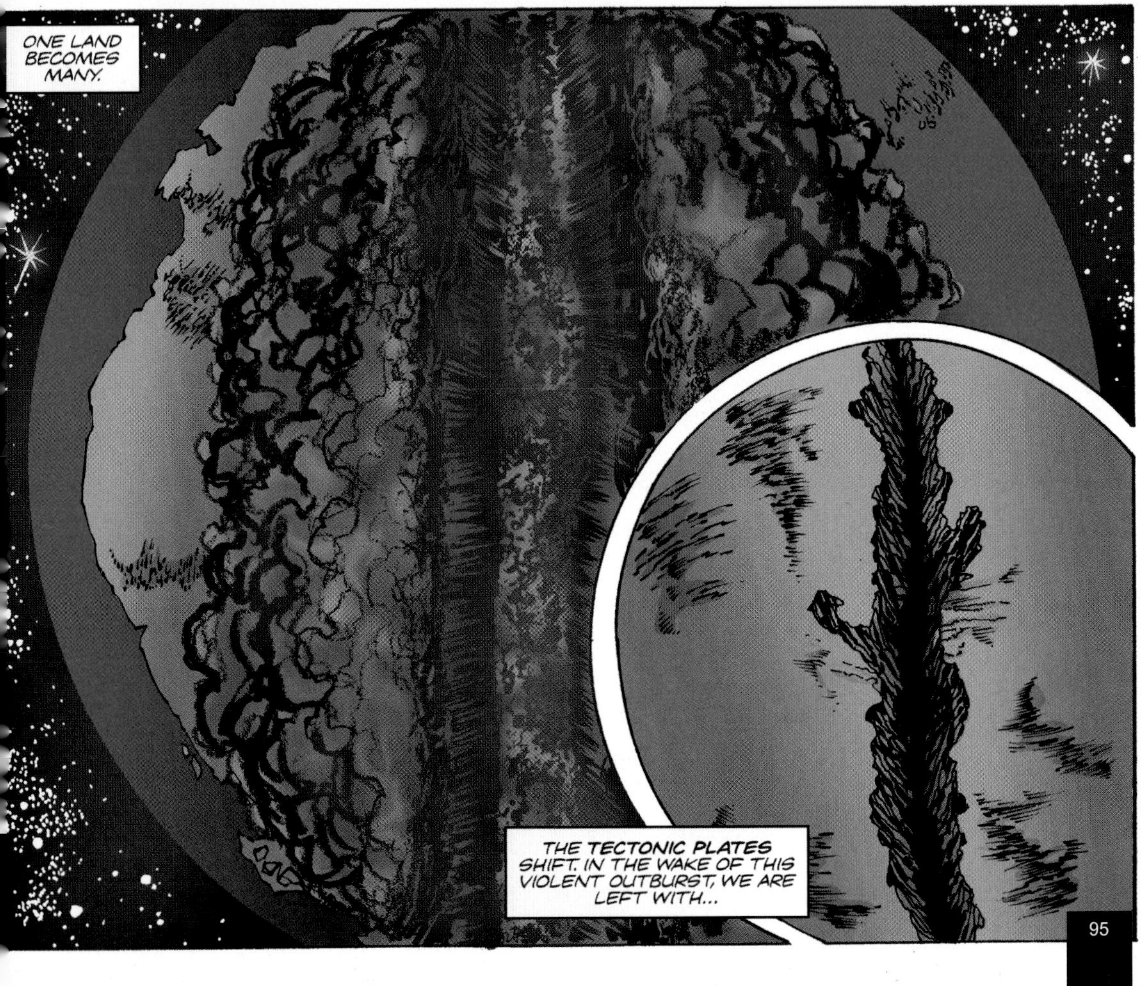
ONE LAND BECOMES MANY.
THE TECTONIC PLATES SHIFT. IN THE WAKE OF THIS VIOLENT OUTBURST, WE ARE LEFT WITH...

...CONTINENTS. **MANY** CONTINENTS.

IN TIME, THESE CONTINENTS WILL HAVE **NAMES.** NORTH AMERICA. SOUTH AMERICA. EUROPE. AFRICA.

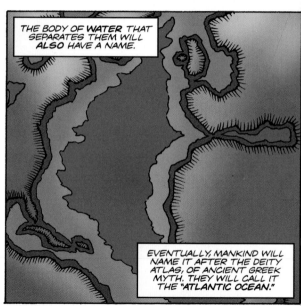

THE BODY OF **WATER** THAT SEPARATES THEM WILL **ALSO** HAVE A NAME.

EVENTUALLY, MANKIND WILL NAME IT AFTER THE DEITY ATLAS, OF ANCIENT GREEK MYTH. THEY WILL CALL IT THE "**ATLANTIC OCEAN.**"

IT IS THE WORLD'S **YOUNGEST** OCEAN. THE SECOND **LARGEST** OCEAN.

AND, RIGHT NOW, THIS OCEAN IS THE **ONE** THING ALL THESE CONTINENTS HAVE IN COMMON.

IN ITS OWN WAY, THIS OCEAN LINKS HUMANITY TOGETHER. THE SAME WATER THAT SURGES FORWARD THROUGH THE ATLANTIC OCEAN...

...PUSHES THROUGH THE **STRAIT OF GIBRALTAR**...

...RIPPLES OUTWARD INTO THE **MEDITERRANEAN SEA**...

...AND EMPTIES OUT INTO THE NILE RIVER.

1900 B.C.E.

BY THIS TIME, SOME CIVILIZATIONS HAVE LEARNED THAT THE OCEAN CAN BE MADE TO DO MANKIND'S BIDDING. GREAT BOATS CAN BE BUILT TO SHIP GOODS FROM ONE COUNTRY TO ANOTHER. MUCH **WEALTH** CAN BE ACHIEVED IN THIS WAY.

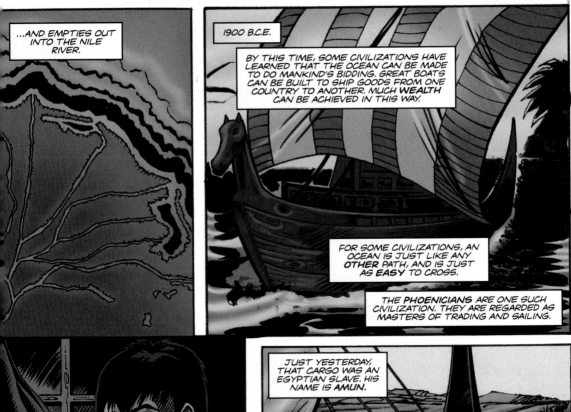

FOR SOME CIVILIZATIONS, AN OCEAN IS JUST LIKE ANY **OTHER** PATH, AND IS JUST AS **EASY** TO CROSS.

THE **PHOENICIANS** ARE ONE SUCH CIVILIZATION. THEY ARE REGARDED AS MASTERS OF TRADING AND SAILING.

JUST YESTERDAY, THAT CARGO WAS AN EGYPTIAN SLAVE. HIS NAME IS **AMUN**.

WHEN IT COMES TO SHIPBUILDING AND SAILING, AMUN IS A **NATURAL**.

BUT THE SAILORS ON THIS PARTICULAR SHIP DON'T REALIZE THAT THEY'RE CARRYING A BIT OF **EXTRA** CARGO.

THE OTHER SLAVES...

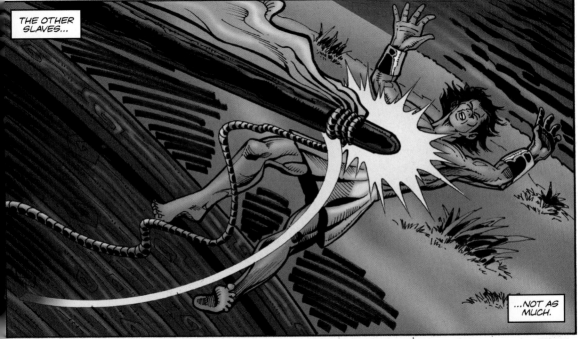

...NOT AS MUCH.

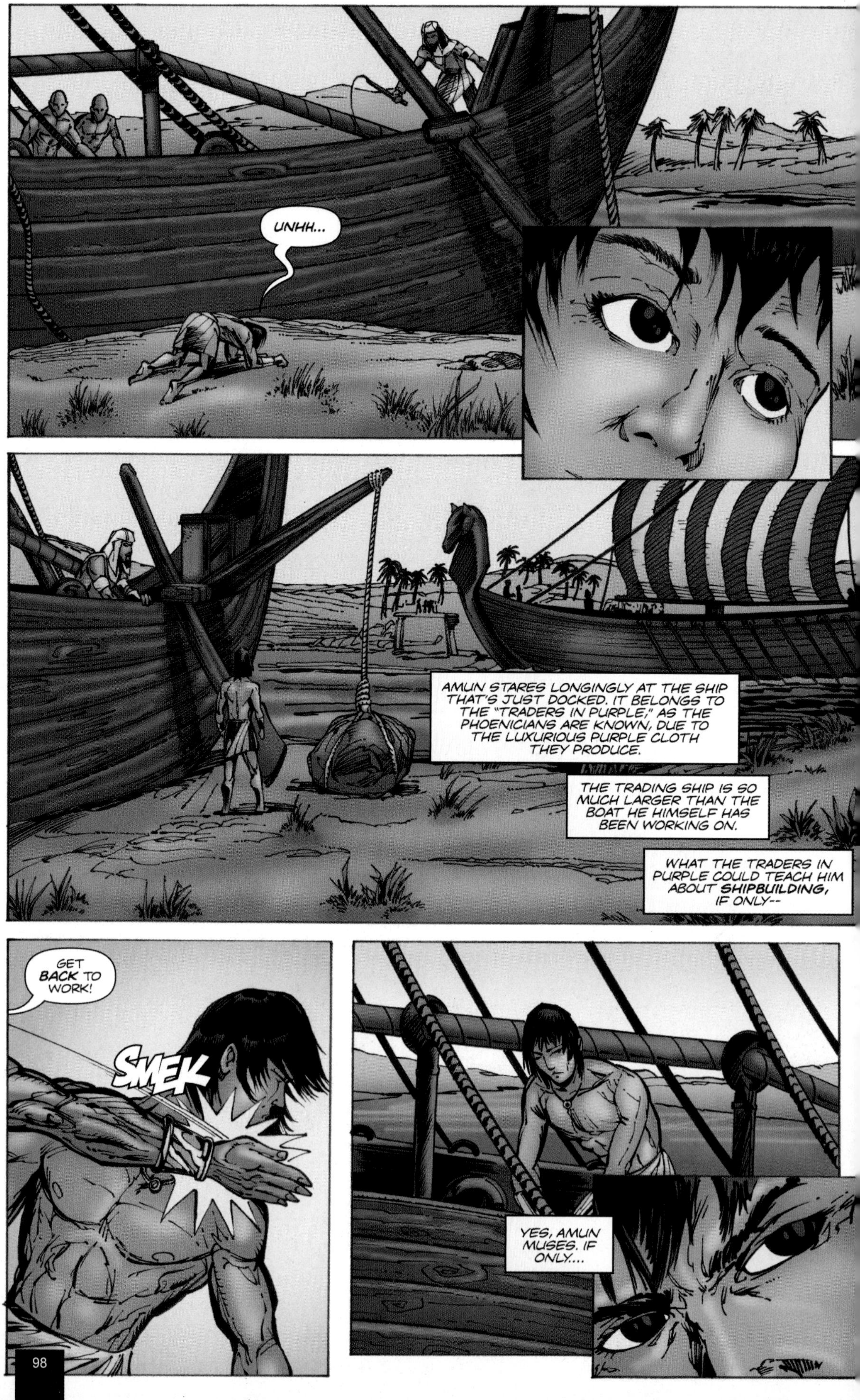
UNHH...
AMUN STARES LONGINGLY AT THE SHIP THAT'S JUST DOCKED. IT BELONGS TO THE "TRADERS IN PURPLE," AS THE PHOENICIANS ARE KNOWN, DUE TO THE LUXURIOUS PURPLE CLOTH THEY PRODUCE.
THE TRADING SHIP IS SO MUCH LARGER THAN THE BOAT HE HIMSELF HAS BEEN WORKING ON.
WHAT THE TRADERS IN PURPLE COULD TEACH HIM ABOUT **SHIPBUILDING,** IF ONLY--
GET **BACK** TO WORK!
SMEK
YES, AMUN MUSES. IF ONLY....

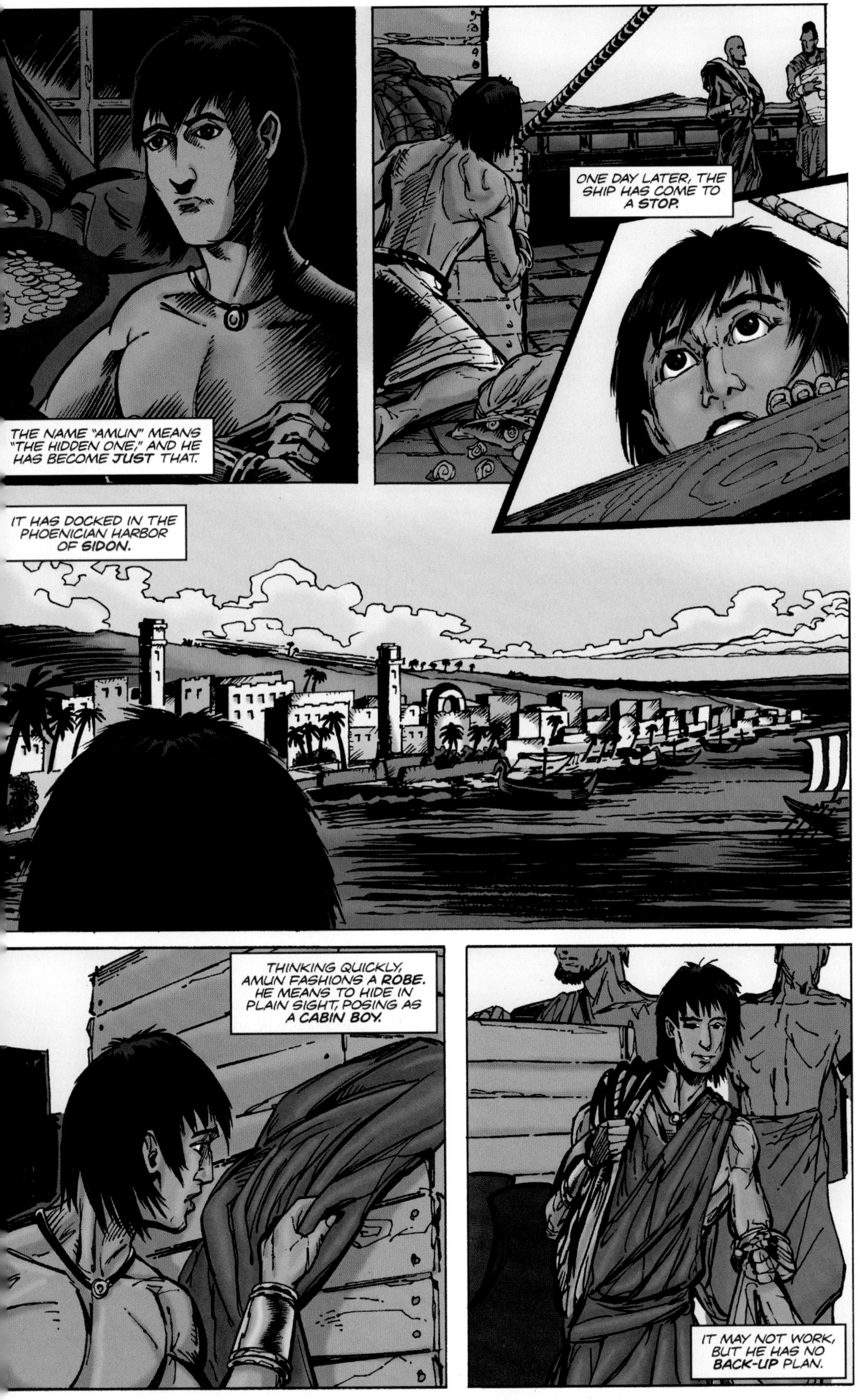

THE NAME "AMUN" MEANS "THE HIDDEN ONE," AND HE HAS BECOME JUST THAT.
ONE DAY LATER, THE SHIP HAS COME TO A STOP.
IT HAS DOCKED IN THE PHOENICIAN HARBOR OF SIDON.
THINKING QUICKLY, AMUN FASHIONS A ROBE. HE MEANS TO HIDE IN PLAIN SIGHT, POSING AS A CABIN BOY.
IT MAY NOT WORK, BUT HE HAS NO BACK-UP PLAN.

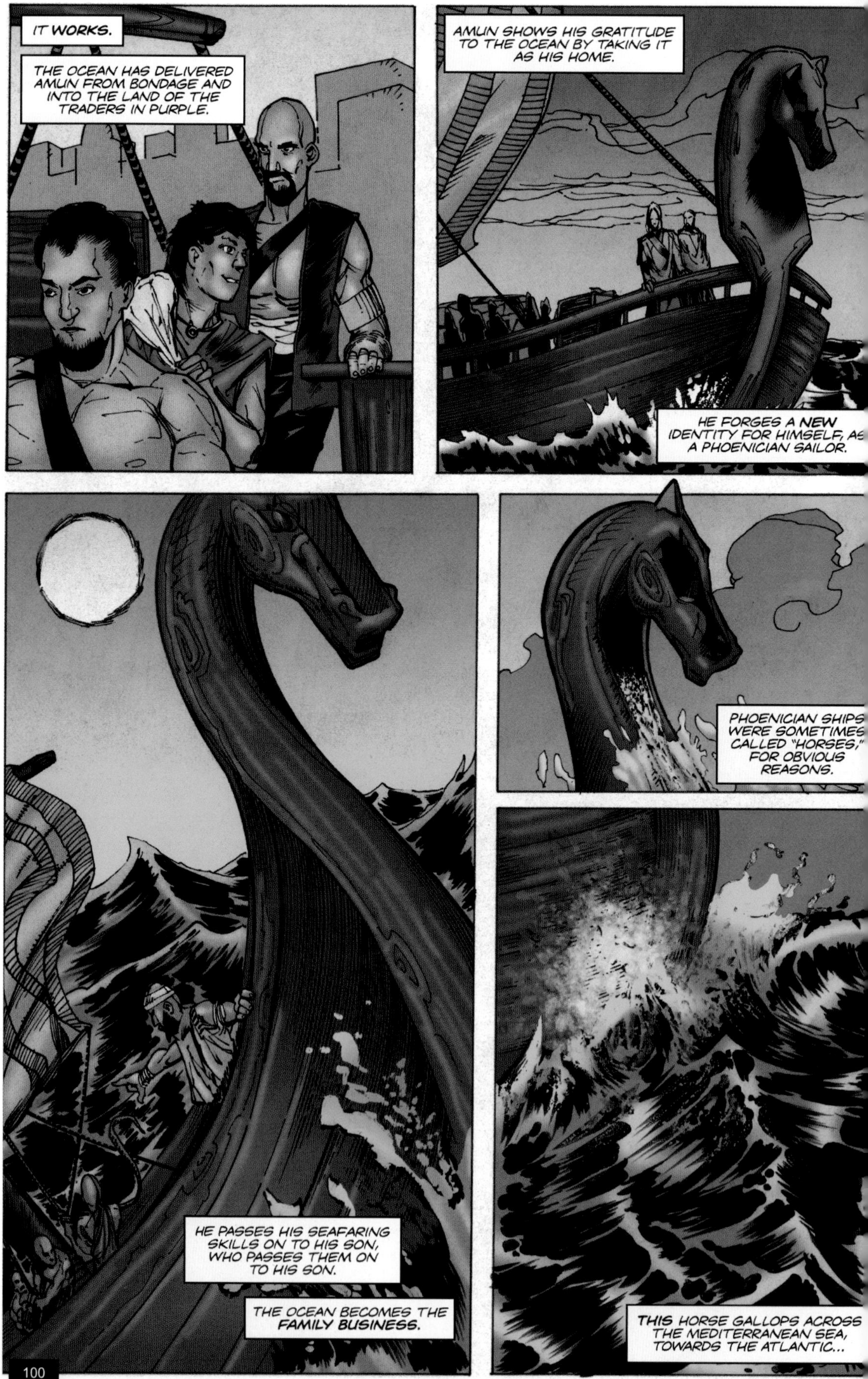
IT WORKS.
THE OCEAN HAS DELIVERED AMUN FROM BONDAGE AND INTO THE LAND OF THE TRADERS IN PURPLE.
AMUN SHOWS HIS GRATITUDE TO THE OCEAN BY TAKING IT AS HIS HOME.
HE FORGES A NEW IDENTITY FOR HIMSELF, AS A PHOENICIAN SAILOR.
HE PASSES HIS SEAFARING SKILLS ON TO HIS SON, WHO PASSES THEM ON TO HIS SON.
THE OCEAN BECOMES THE FAMILY BUSINESS.
PHOENICIAN SHIPS WERE SOMETIMES CALLED "HORSES," FOR OBVIOUS REASONS.
THIS HORSE GALLOPS ACROSS THE MEDITERRANEAN SEA, TOWARDS THE ATLANTIC...

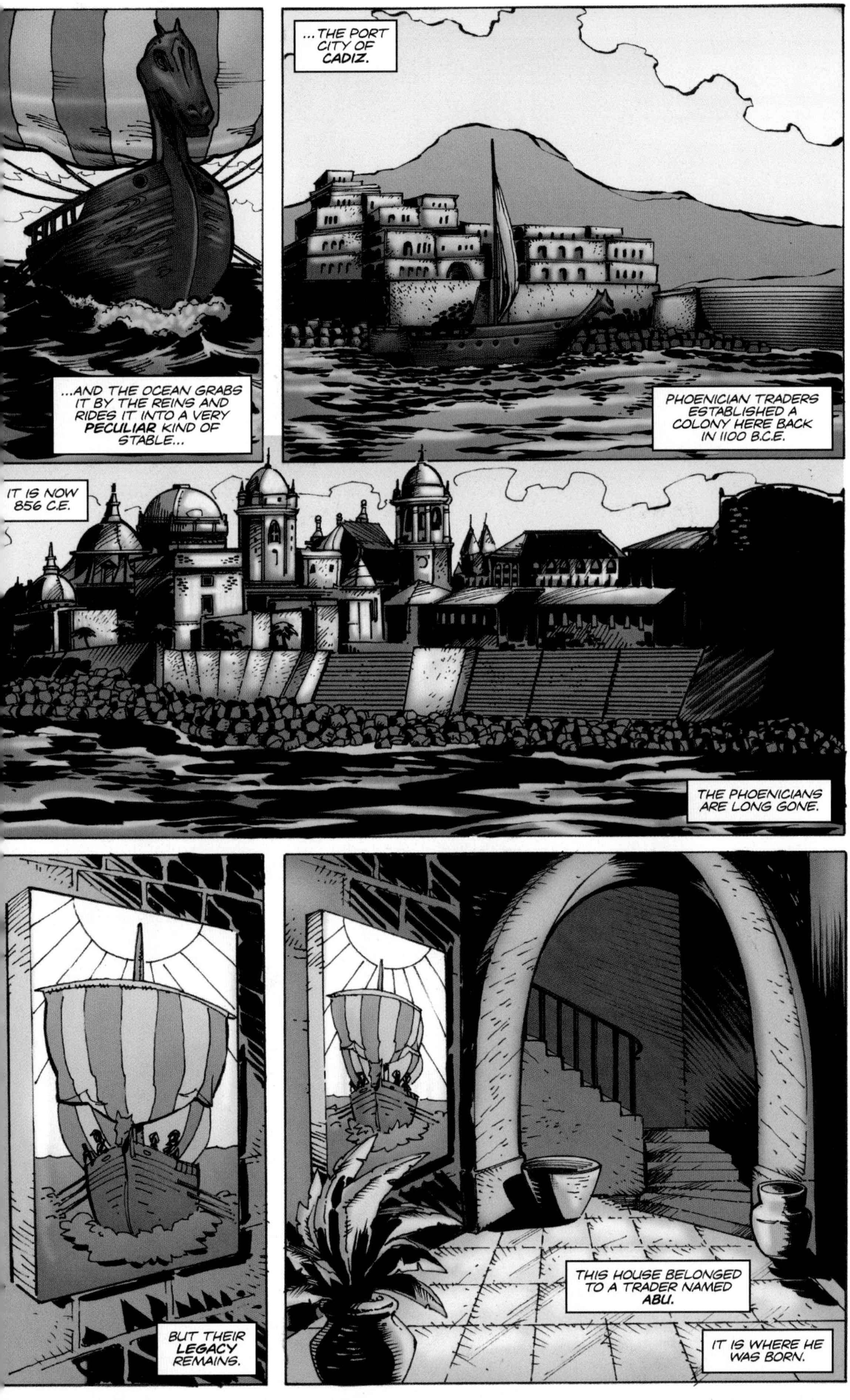
...AND THE OCEAN GRABS IT BY THE REINS AND RIDES IT INTO A VERY PECULIAR KIND OF STABLE...
...THE PORT CITY OF CADIZ.
PHOENICIAN TRADERS ESTABLISHED A COLONY HERE BACK IN 1100 B.C.E.
IT IS NOW 856 C.E.
THE PHOENICIANS ARE LONG GONE.
BUT THEIR LEGACY REMAINS.
THIS HOUSE BELONGED TO A TRADER NAMED ABU.
IT IS WHERE HE WAS BORN.

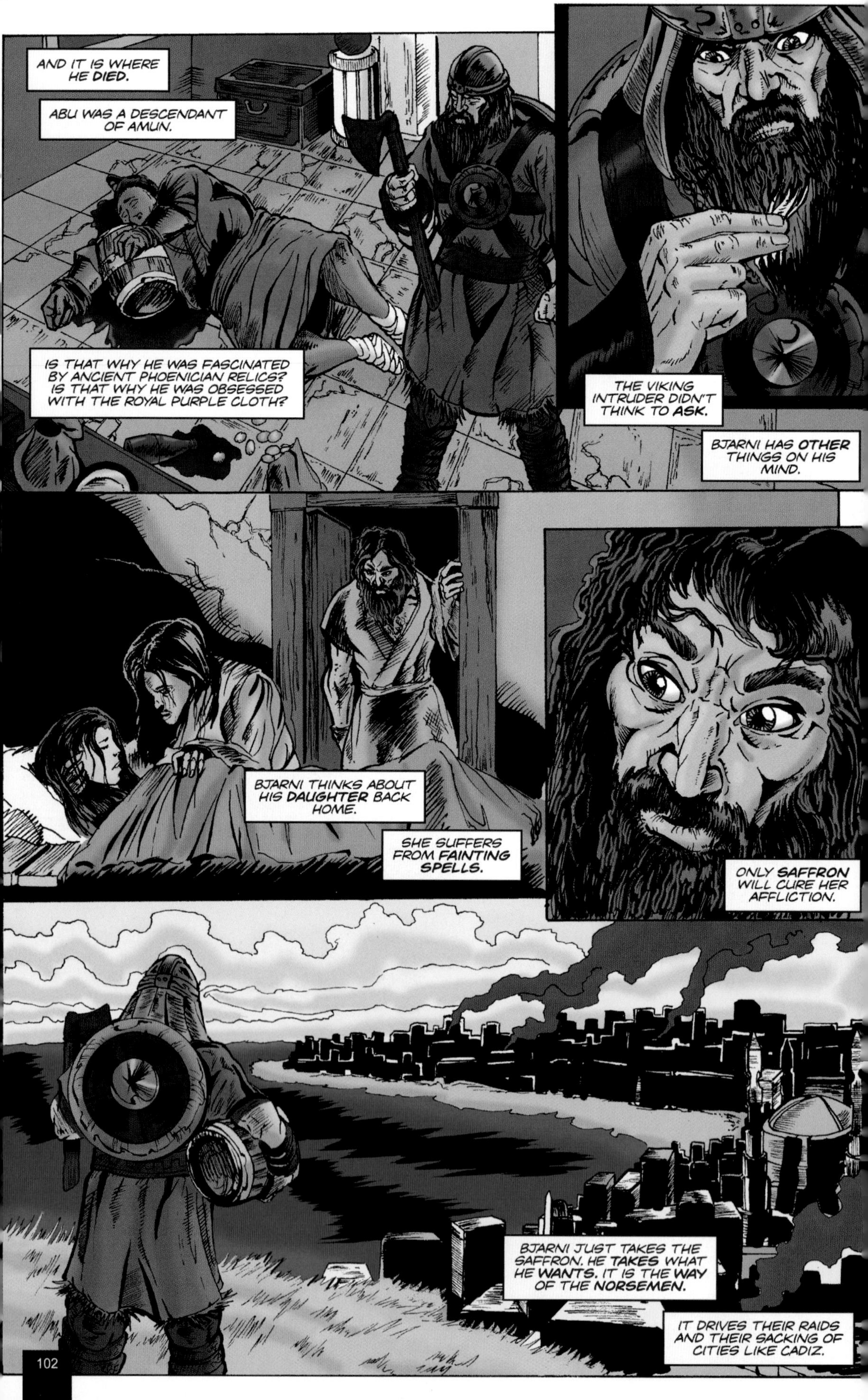

AND IT IS WHERE HE DIED.
ABU WAS A DESCENDANT OF AMUN.
IS THAT WHY HE WAS FASCINATED BY ANCIENT PHOENICIAN RELICS? IS THAT WHY HE WAS OBSESSED WITH THE ROYAL PURPLE CLOTH?
THE VIKING INTRUDER DIDN'T THINK TO ASK.
BJARNI HAS OTHER THINGS ON HIS MIND.
BJARNI THINKS ABOUT HIS DAUGHTER BACK HOME.
SHE SUFFERS FROM FAINTING SPELLS.
ONLY SAFFRON WILL CURE HER AFFLICTION.
BJARNI JUST TAKES THE SAFFRON. HE TAKES WHAT HE WANTS. IT IS THE WAY OF THE NORSEMEN.
IT DRIVES THEIR RAIDS AND THEIR SACKING OF CITIES LIKE CADIZ.

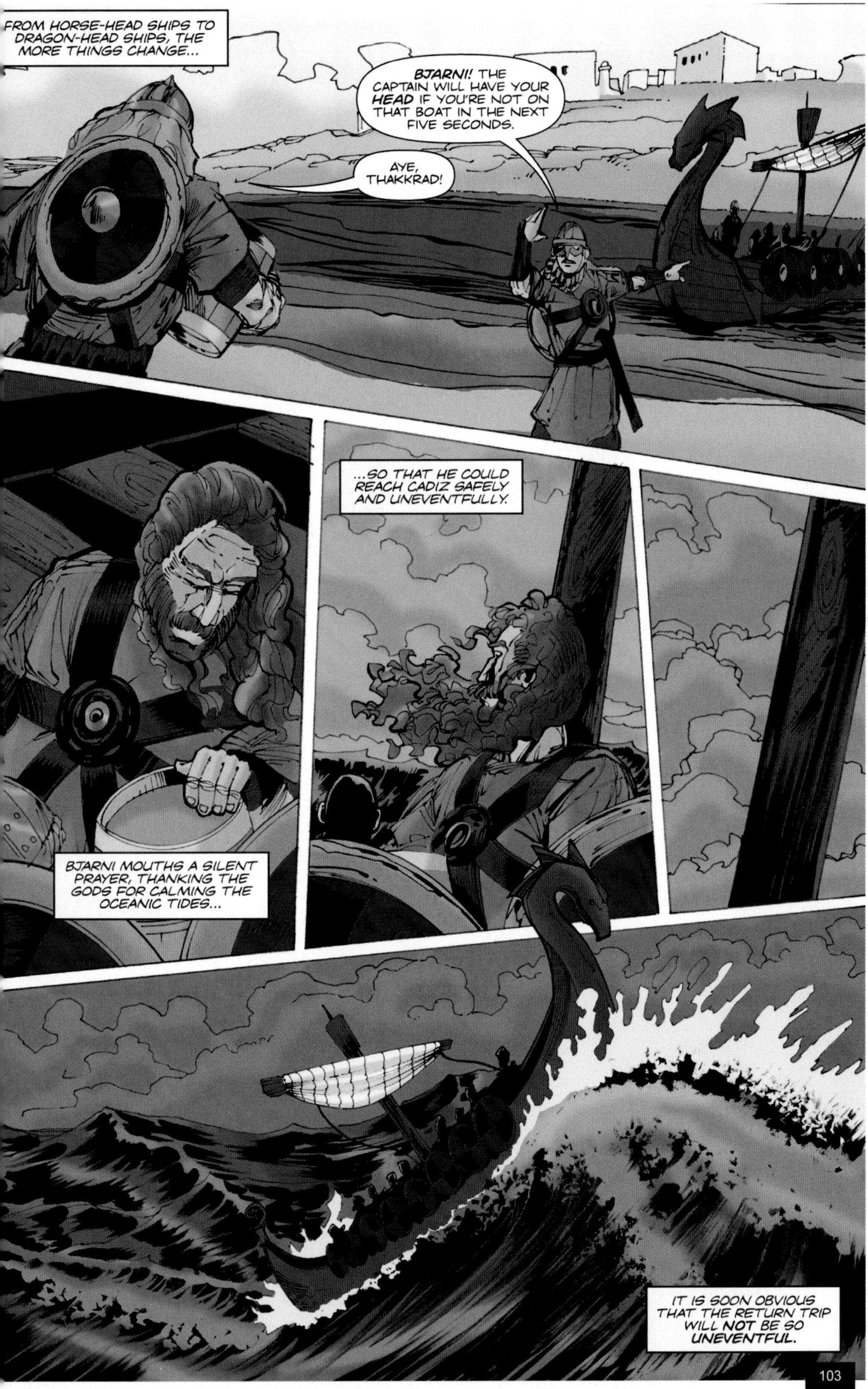
FROM HORSE-HEAD SHIPS TO DRAGON-HEAD SHIPS, THE MORE THINGS CHANGE...
BJARNI! THE CAPTAIN WILL HAVE YOUR HEAD IF YOU'RE NOT ON THAT BOAT IN THE NEXT FIVE SECONDS.
AYE, THAKKRAD!
BJARNI MOUTHS A SILENT PRAYER, THANKING THE GODS FOR CALMING THE OCEANIC TIDES...
...SO THAT HE COULD REACH CADIZ SAFELY AND UNEVENTFULLY.
IT IS SOON OBVIOUS THAT THE RETURN TRIP WILL NOT BE SO UNEVENTFUL.

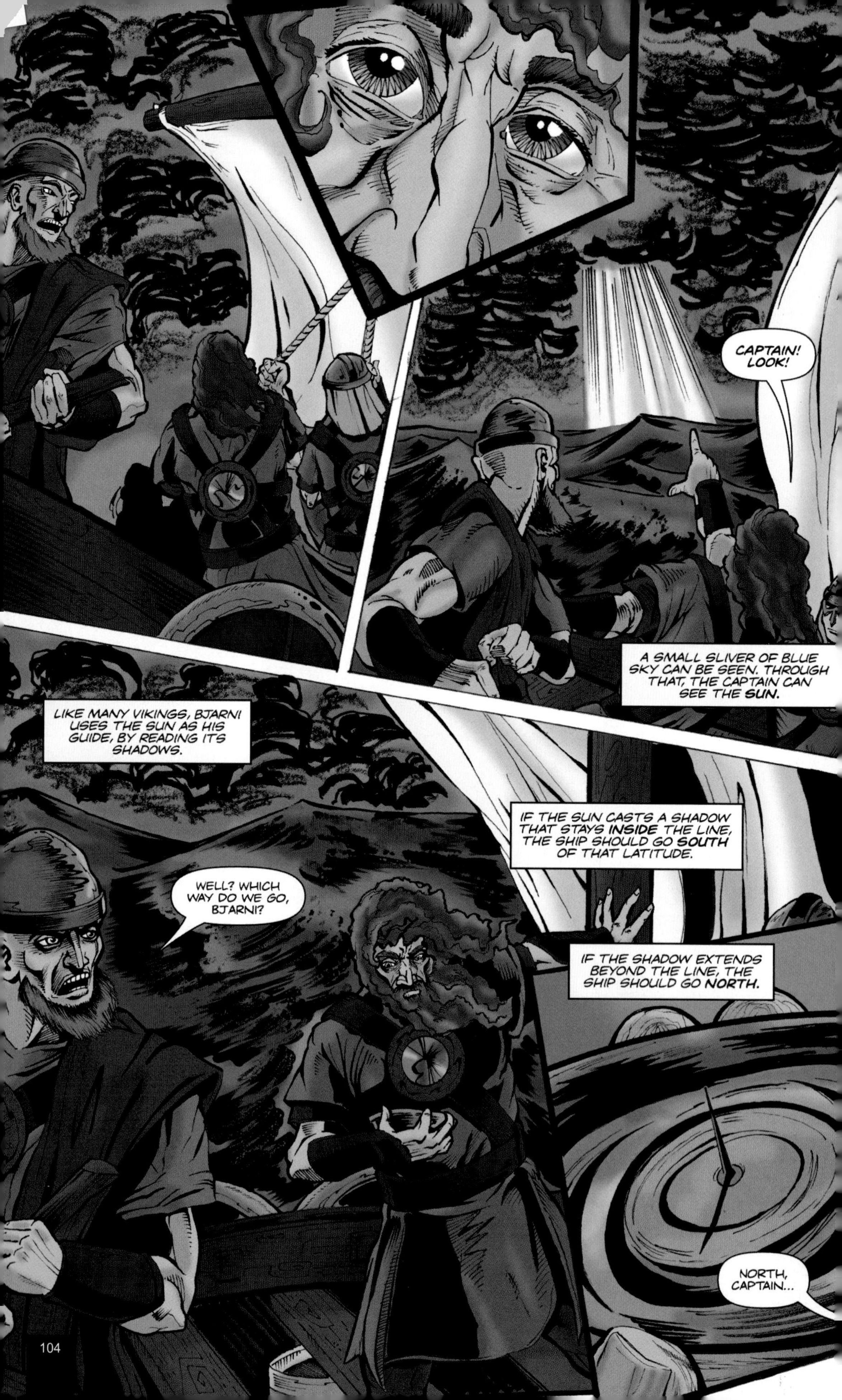
CAPTAIN! LOOK!
A SMALL SLIVER OF BLUE SKY CAN BE SEEN. THROUGH THAT, THE CAPTAIN CAN SEE THE **SUN**.
LIKE MANY VIKINGS, BJARNI USES THE SUN AS HIS GUIDE, BY READING ITS SHADOWS.
IF THE SUN CASTS A SHADOW THAT STAYS **INSIDE** THE LINE, THE SHIP SHOULD GO **SOUTH** OF THAT LATITUDE.
WELL? WHICH WAY DO WE GO, BJARNI?
IF THE SHADOW EXTENDS BEYOND THE LINE, THE SHIP SHOULD GO **NORTH**.
NORTH, CAPTAIN...

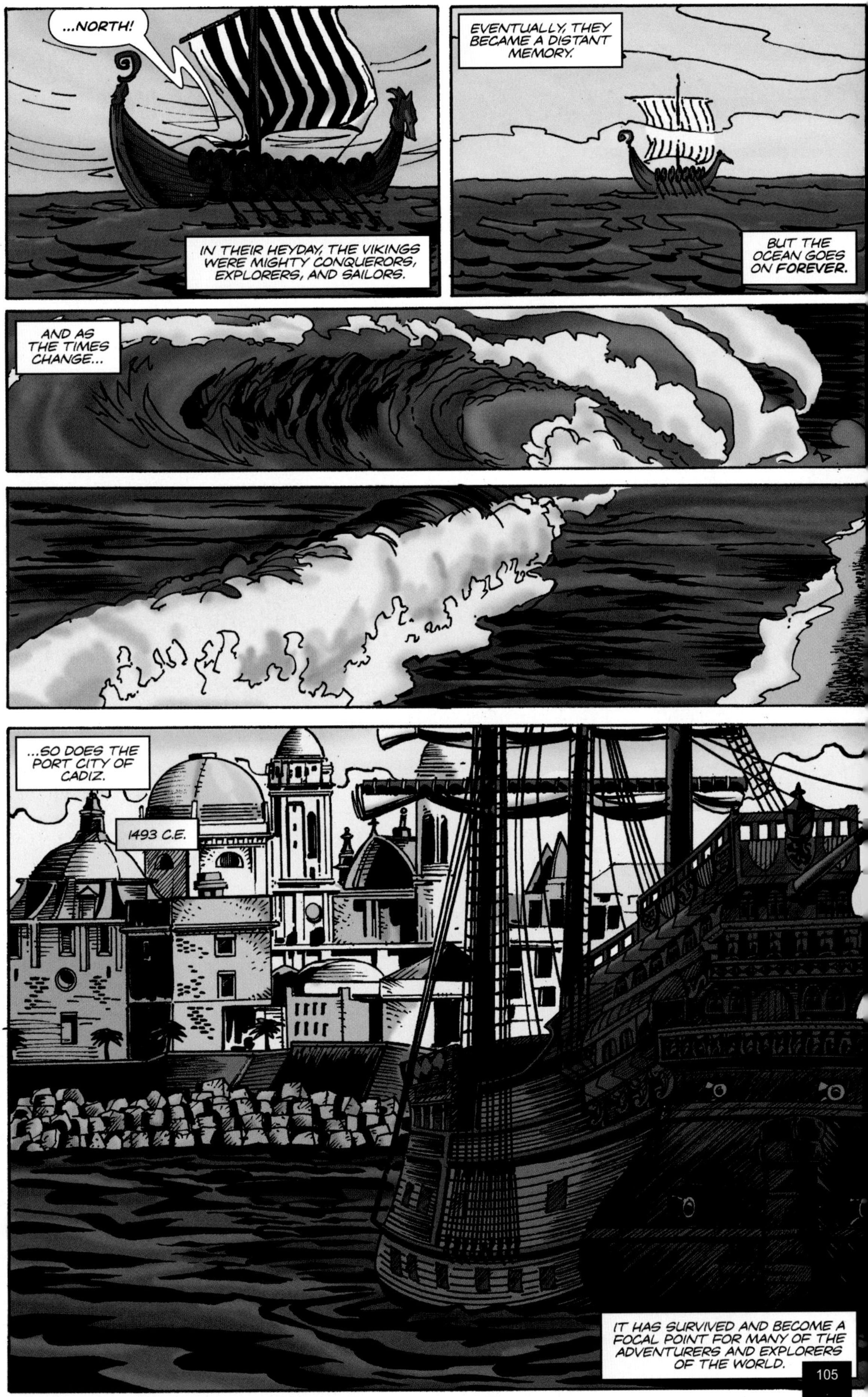
...NORTH!
IN THEIR HEYDAY, THE VIKINGS WERE MIGHTY CONQUERORS, EXPLORERS, AND SAILORS.
EVENTUALLY, THEY BECAME A DISTANT MEMORY.
BUT THE OCEAN GOES ON FOREVER.
AND AS THE TIMES CHANGE...
...SO DOES THE PORT CITY OF CADIZ.
1493 C.E.
IT HAS SURVIVED AND BECOME A FOCAL POINT FOR MANY OF THE ADVENTURERS AND EXPLORERS OF THE WORLD.

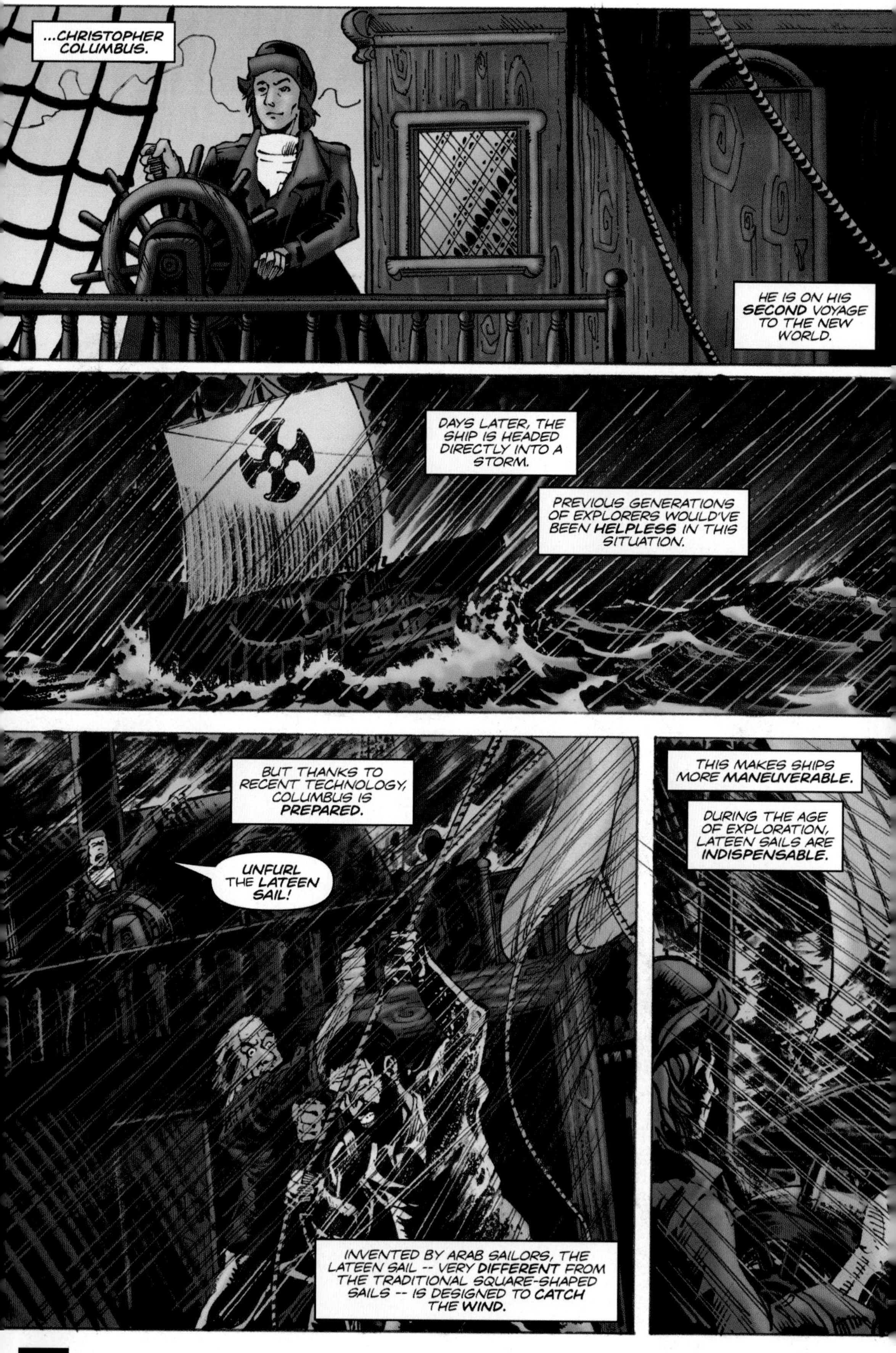
...CHRISTOPHER COLUMBUS.
HE IS ON HIS SECOND VOYAGE TO THE NEW WORLD.
DAYS LATER, THE SHIP IS HEADED DIRECTLY INTO A STORM.
PREVIOUS GENERATIONS OF EXPLORERS WOULD'VE BEEN HELPLESS IN THIS SITUATION.
BUT THANKS TO RECENT TECHNOLOGY, COLUMBUS IS PREPARED.
UNFURL THE LATEEN SAIL!
INVENTED BY ARAB SAILORS, THE LATEEN SAIL -- VERY DIFFERENT FROM THE TRADITIONAL SQUARE-SHAPED SAILS -- IS DESIGNED TO CATCH THE WIND.
THIS MAKES SHIPS MORE MANEUVERABLE.
DURING THE AGE OF EXPLORATION, LATEEN SAILS ARE INDISPENSABLE.

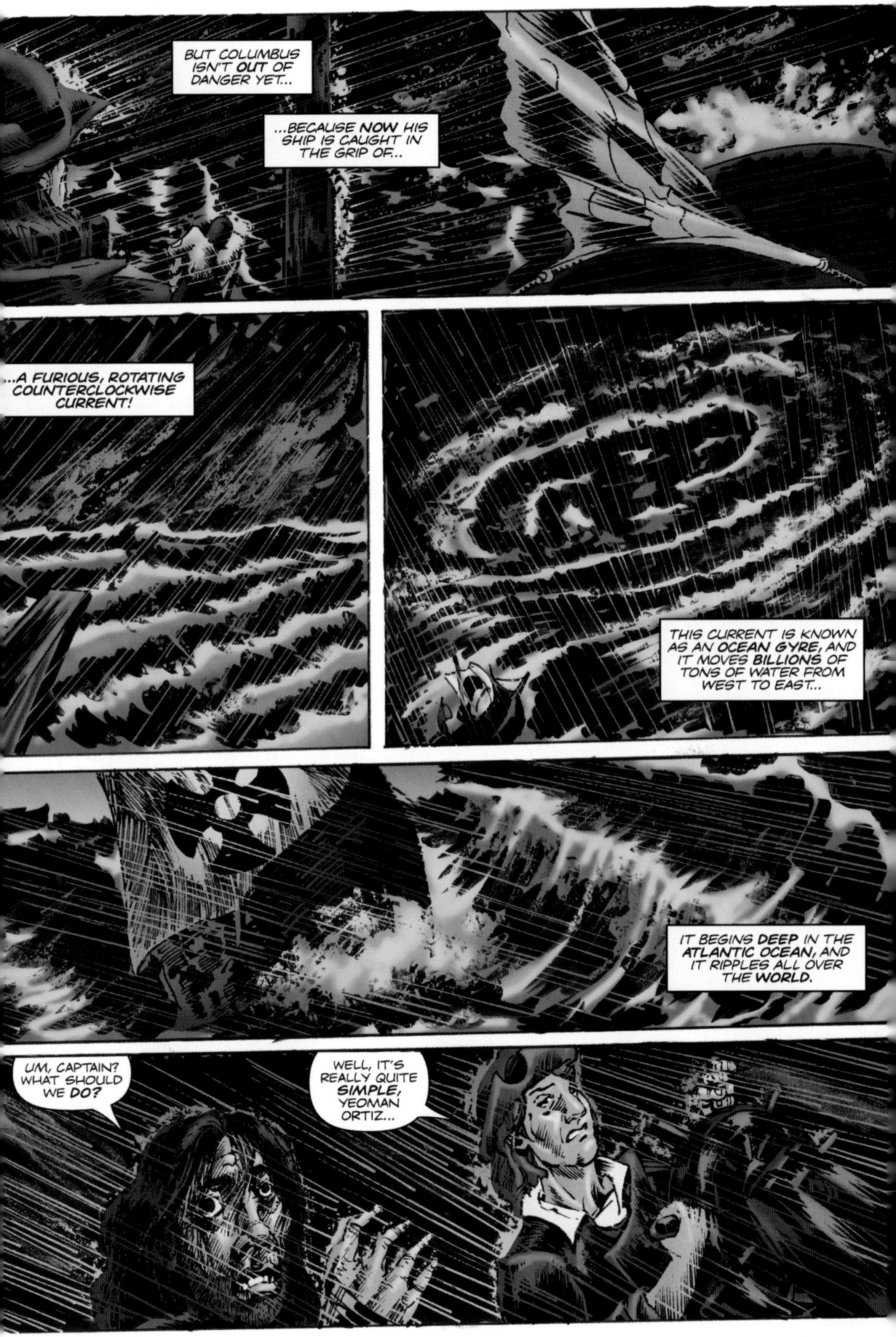

BUT COLUMBUS ISN'T OUT OF DANGER YET...
...BECAUSE NOW HIS SHIP IS CAUGHT IN THE GRIP OF...
...A FURIOUS, ROTATING COUNTERCLOCKWISE CURRENT!
THIS CURRENT IS KNOWN AS AN OCEAN GYRE, AND IT MOVES BILLIONS OF TONS OF WATER FROM WEST TO EAST...
IT BEGINS DEEP IN THE ATLANTIC OCEAN, AND IT RIPPLES ALL OVER THE WORLD.
UM, CAPTAIN? WHAT SHOULD WE DO?
WELL, IT'S REALLY QUITE SIMPLE, YEOMAN ORTIZ...

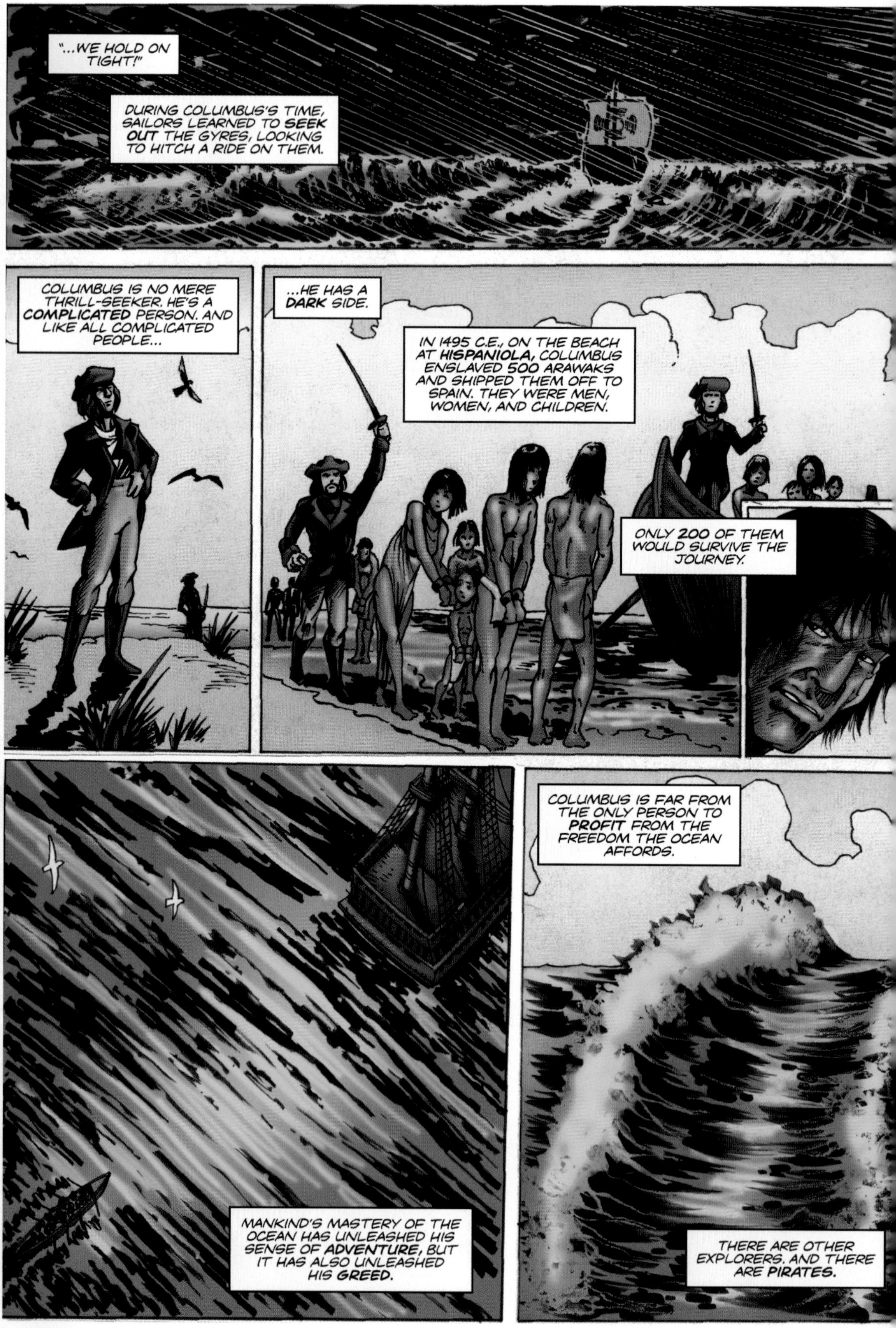
"...WE HOLD ON TIGHT!"
DURING COLUMBUS'S TIME, SAILORS LEARNED TO SEEK OUT THE GYRES, LOOKING TO HITCH A RIDE ON THEM.
COLUMBUS IS NO MERE THRILL-SEEKER. HE'S A COMPLICATED PERSON. AND LIKE ALL COMPLICATED PEOPLE...
...HE HAS A DARK SIDE.
IN 1495 C.E., ON THE BEACH AT HISPANIOLA, COLUMBUS ENSLAVED 500 ARAWAKS AND SHIPPED THEM OFF TO SPAIN. THEY WERE MEN, WOMEN, AND CHILDREN.
ONLY 200 OF THEM WOULD SURVIVE THE JOURNEY.
MANKIND'S MASTERY OF THE OCEAN HAS UNLEASHED HIS SENSE OF ADVENTURE, BUT IT HAS ALSO UNLEASHED HIS GREED.
COLUMBUS IS FAR FROM THE ONLY PERSON TO PROFIT FROM THE FREEDOM THE OCEAN AFFORDS.
THERE ARE OTHER EXPLORERS. AND THERE ARE PIRATES.

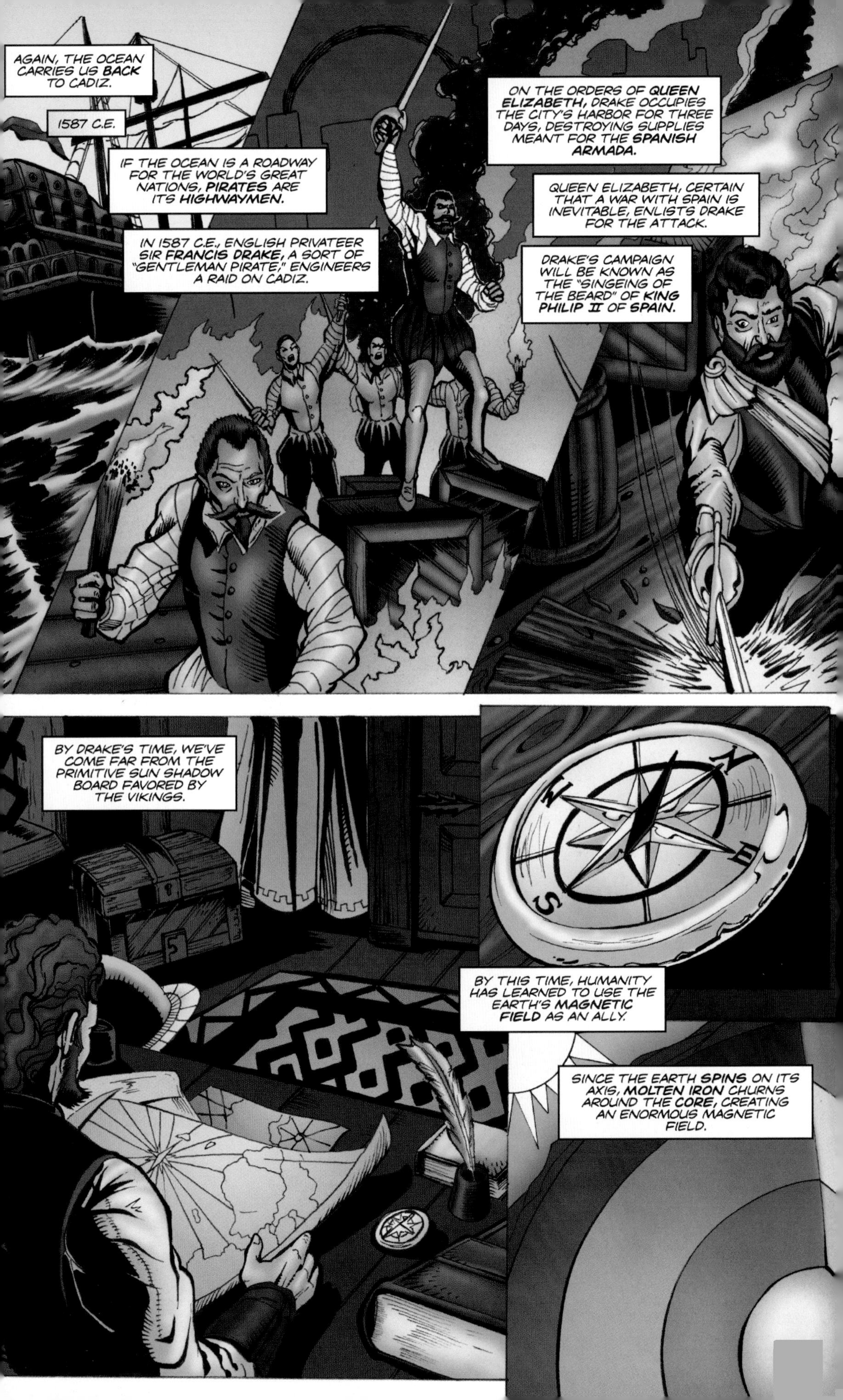
AGAIN, THE OCEAN CARRIES US BACK TO CADIZ.
1587 C.E.
IF THE OCEAN IS A ROADWAY FOR THE WORLD'S GREAT NATIONS, PIRATES ARE ITS HIGHWAYMEN.
IN 1587 C.E., ENGLISH PRIVATEER SIR FRANCIS DRAKE, A SORT OF "GENTLEMAN PIRATE," ENGINEERS A RAID ON CADIZ.
ON THE ORDERS OF QUEEN ELIZABETH, DRAKE OCCUPIES THE CITY'S HARBOR FOR THREE DAYS, DESTROYING SUPPLIES MEANT FOR THE SPANISH ARMADA.
QUEEN ELIZABETH, CERTAIN THAT A WAR WITH SPAIN IS INEVITABLE, ENLISTS DRAKE FOR THE ATTACK.
DRAKE'S CAMPAIGN WILL BE KNOWN AS THE "SINGEING OF THE BEARD" OF KING PHILIP II OF SPAIN.
BY DRAKE'S TIME, WE'VE COME FAR FROM THE PRIMITIVE SUN SHADOW BOARD FAVORED BY THE VIKINGS.
BY THIS TIME, HUMANITY HAS LEARNED TO USE THE EARTH'S MAGNETIC FIELD AS AN ALLY.
SINCE THE EARTH SPINS ON ITS AXIS, MOLTEN IRON CHURNS AROUND THE CORE, CREATING AN ENORMOUS MAGNETIC FIELD.

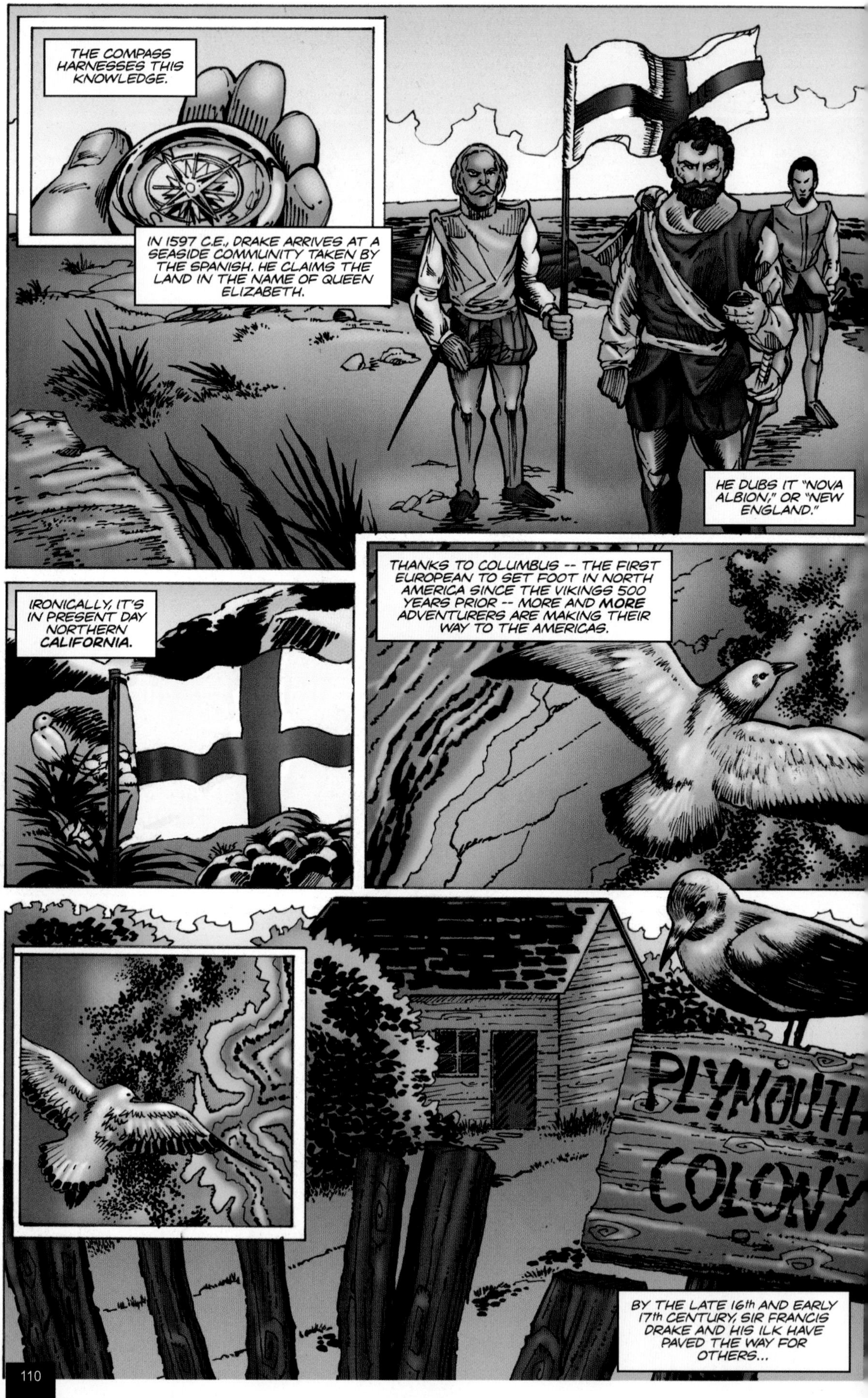
THE COMPASS HARNESSES THIS KNOWLEDGE.
IN 1597 C.E., DRAKE ARRIVES AT A SEASIDE COMMUNITY TAKEN BY THE SPANISH. HE CLAIMS THE LAND IN THE NAME OF QUEEN ELIZABETH.
HE DUBS IT "NOVA ALBION," OR "NEW ENGLAND."
IRONICALLY, IT'S IN PRESENT DAY NORTHERN CALIFORNIA.
THANKS TO COLUMBUS -- THE FIRST EUROPEAN TO SET FOOT IN NORTH AMERICA SINCE THE VIKINGS 500 YEARS PRIOR -- MORE AND MORE ADVENTURERS ARE MAKING THEIR WAY TO THE AMERICAS.
PLYMOUTH COLONY
BY THE LATE 16th AND EARLY 17th CENTURY, SIR FRANCIS DRAKE AND HIS ILK HAVE PAVED THE WAY FOR OTHERS...

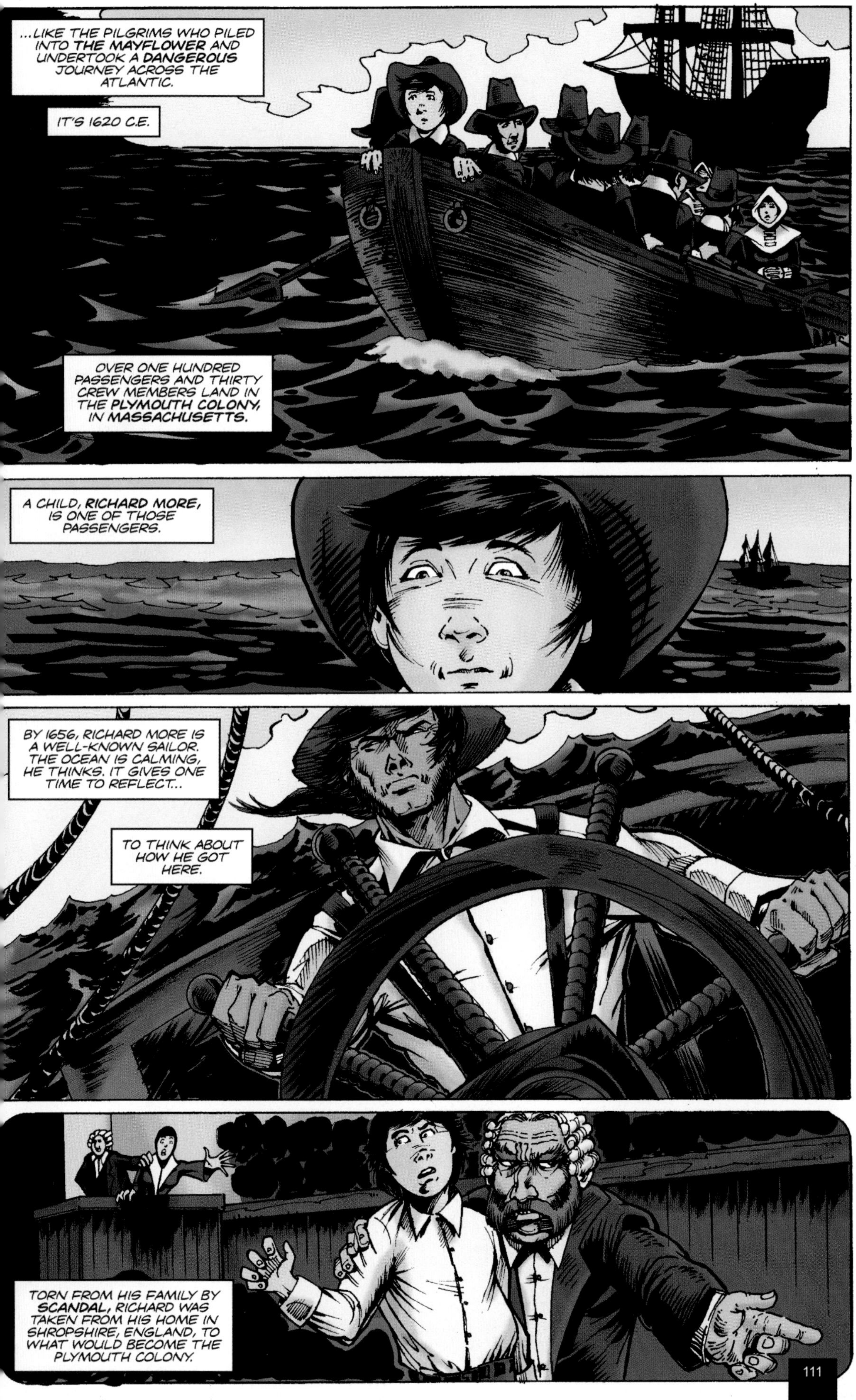
...LIKE THE PILGRIMS WHO PILED INTO **THE MAYFLOWER** AND UNDERTOOK A **DANGEROUS** JOURNEY ACROSS THE ATLANTIC.
IT'S 1620 C.E.
OVER ONE HUNDRED PASSENGERS AND THIRTY CREW MEMBERS LAND IN THE **PLYMOUTH COLONY,** IN **MASSACHUSETTS.**
A CHILD, **RICHARD MORE,** IS ONE OF THOSE PASSENGERS.
BY 1656, RICHARD MORE IS A WELL-KNOWN SAILOR. THE OCEAN IS CALMING, HE THINKS. IT GIVES ONE TIME TO REFLECT...
TO THINK ABOUT HOW HE GOT HERE.
TORN FROM HIS FAMILY BY **SCANDAL,** RICHARD WAS TAKEN FROM HIS HOME IN SHROPSHIRE, ENGLAND, TO WHAT WOULD BECOME THE PLYMOUTH COLONY.

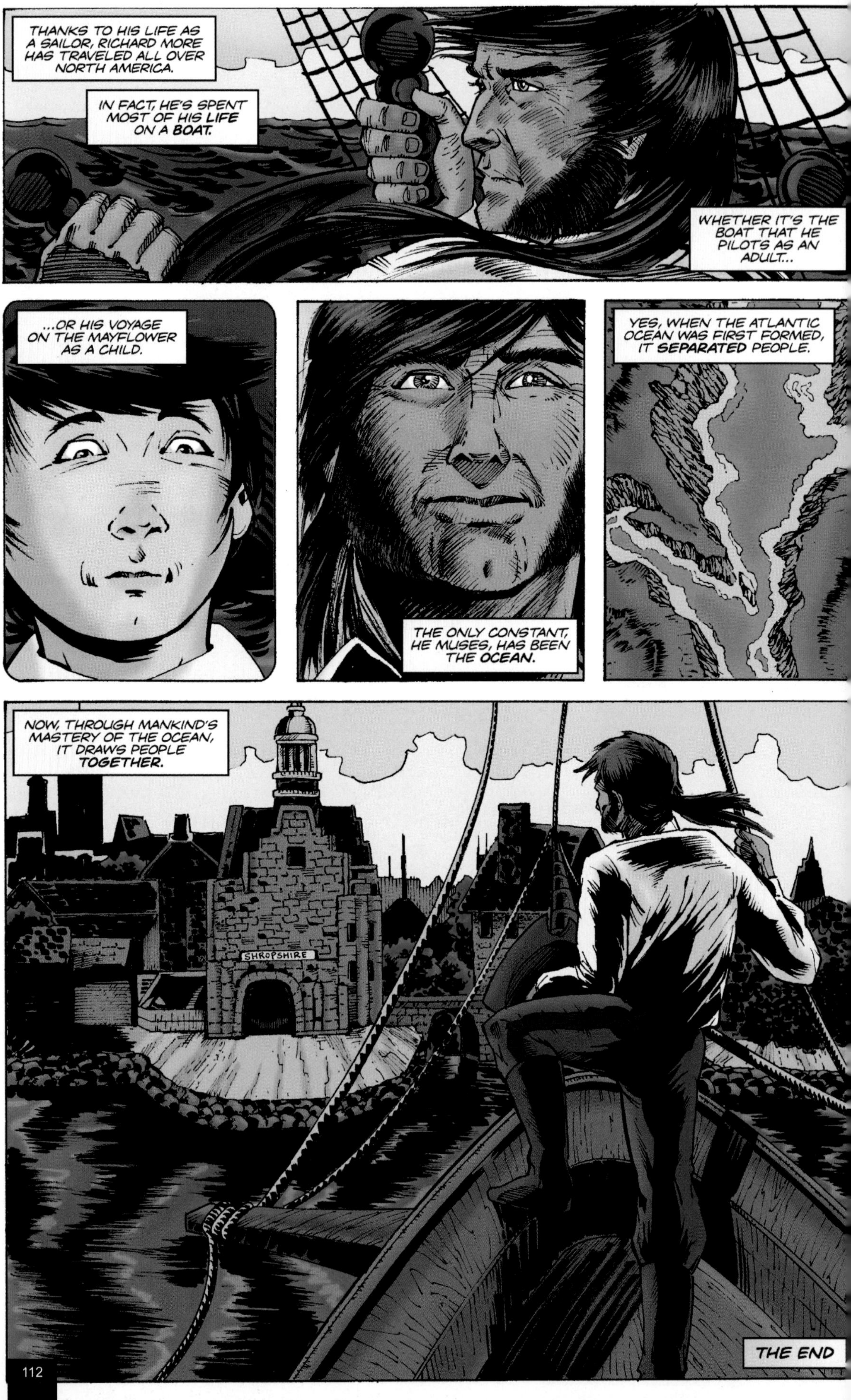
THANKS TO HIS LIFE AS A SAILOR, RICHARD MORE HAS TRAVELED ALL OVER NORTH AMERICA.
IN FACT, HE'S SPENT MOST OF HIS **LIFE** ON A **BOAT**.
WHETHER IT'S THE BOAT THAT HE PILOTS AS AN ADULT...
...OR HIS VOYAGE ON THE MAYFLOWER AS A CHILD.
THE ONLY CONSTANT, HE MUSES, HAS BEEN THE **OCEAN**.
YES, WHEN THE ATLANTIC OCEAN WAS FIRST FORMED, IT **SEPARATED** PEOPLE.
NOW, THROUGH MANKIND'S MASTERY OF THE OCEAN, IT DRAWS PEOPLE **TOGETHER**.
SHROPSHIRE
THE END

THE OFFICIAL ART

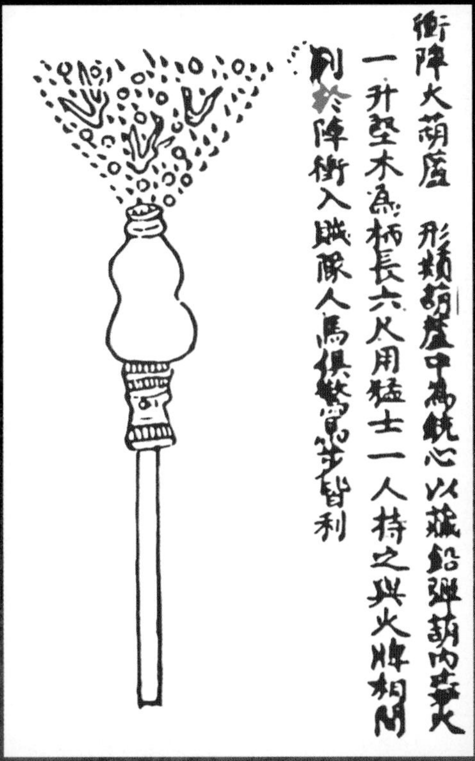
衝陣火葫蘆 形類葫蘆中為銃心以硫鉛彈葫內盛火
一升堅木為柄長六尺用猛士一人持之與火牌相間
則於陣衝入賊隊人馬俱驚當之皆利

HISTORICAL DEPICTION

I'D KNOWN ABOUT THE *HUOLONGJING* - A TREATISE ON EARLY CHINESE GUNPOWDER-BASED WEAPONRY WRITTEN IN THE 14TH CENTURY - FOR YEARS, AND ALWAYS FOUND IT FASCINATING. THE DESCRIPTIONS OF THE WEAPONS WERE INCREDIBLY EVOCATIVE. THE *HUOLONGJING* WOULD NEVER CALL A WEAPON A MERE "LAND MINE." NO, THEY'D USE SOMETHING LIKE "EARTH KING'S FIRE BLOSSOM EGG."

Phalanx-Charging Fire Gourd

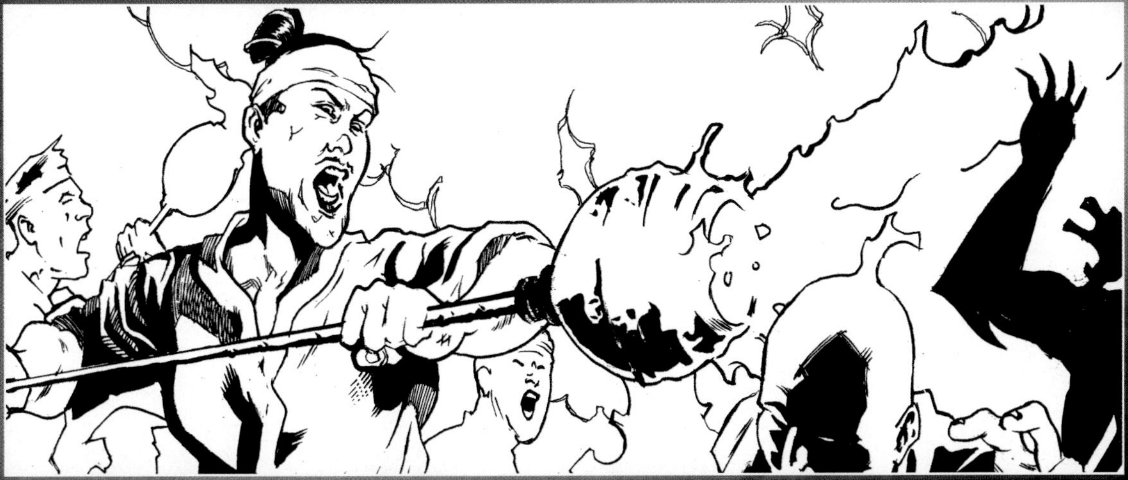

ARTIST RENDERING

Submerged Dragon-King Bomb

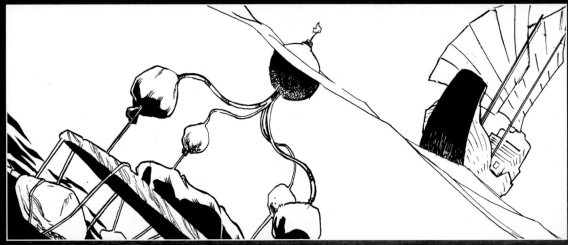

ARTIST RENDERING

HISTORICAL DEPICTION

THERE WAS THEATRICALITY TO THE TEXT AND THE ACCOMPANYING DESIGNS THAT I ALWAYS THOUGHT WAS ABSOLUTELY WONDERFUL. NOW, DON'T GET ME WRONG - I'M AWARE THAT THESE WERE MILITARY TOOLS USED TO GREAT, TERRIBLE EFFECT AGAINST THOUSANDS OF SOLDIERS. STILL, IF YOU ABSOLUTELY MUST BUILD A FLAMETHROWER, CRAFTING IT IN THE SHAPE OF A DRAGON DOES EXHIBIT A CERTAIN FLAIR!

Flying Cloud Thunderclap Eruptor

WHILE THE *HUOLONGJING* WAS AN INTERESTING CURIOSITY, I NEVER THOUGHT IT WAS SOMETHING I'D PUT INTO A COMIC, AT LEAST UNTIL THIS PROJECT CAME ALONG. MY GOAL WITH THIS PAGE WAS TO SHOW THE BOOK'S WEAPONRY IN ACTUAL CONTEXT, AS THE IMAGES IN THE ORIGINAL TREATISE ARE VERY STYLIZED AND ABSTRACT.

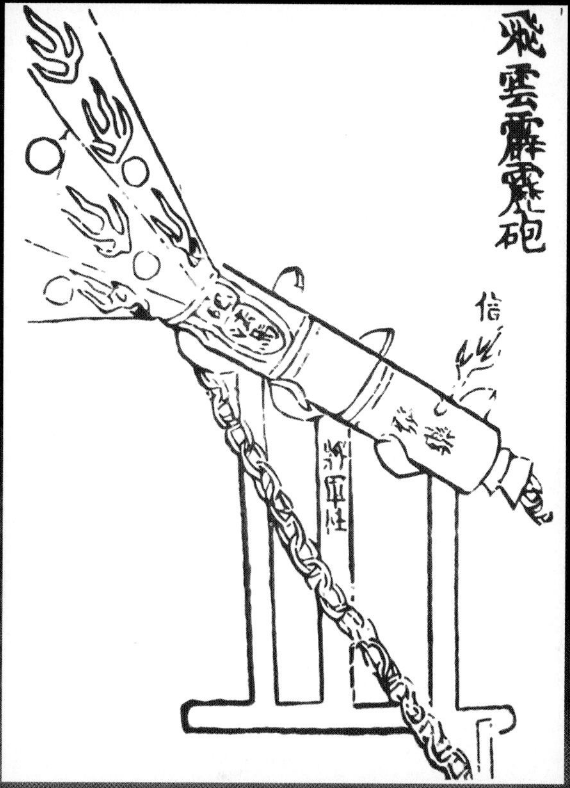
飛雲霹靂砲

HISTORICAL DEPICTION

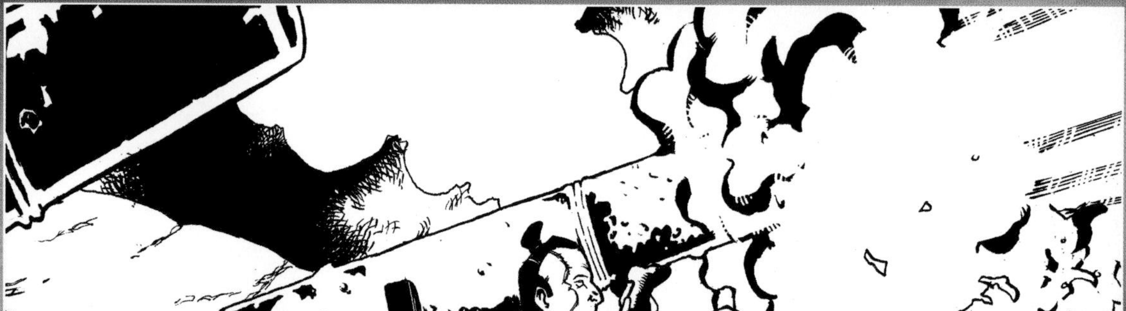

ARTIST RENDERING

Flying Crow with Rocket Bomb

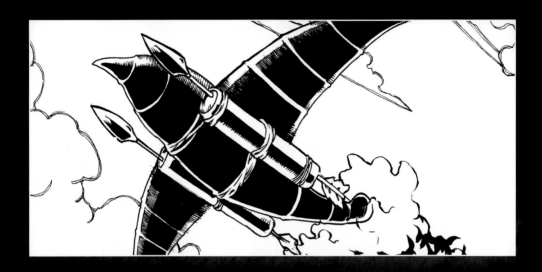

I THOUGHT IT WOULD BE INTERESTING TO SEE HOW THE CHINESE FIREARMS WERE ACTUALLY USED, ESPECIALLY TO ILLUSTRATE THE EFFECT THEY MIGHT HAVE ON ENEMY SOLDIERS. UNAI DID A FANTASTIC ART JOB! I'M SURE IT WASN'T THE EASIEST THING TO RECREATE BIZARRE, CENTURIES-OLD WEAPONS, BUT HE REALLY ROSE TO THE CHALLENGE. AS A WRITER, I COULDN'T BE HAPPIER WITH THE OUTCOME.

-CHARLES SOULE

神火飛鴉

HISTORICAL DEPICTION

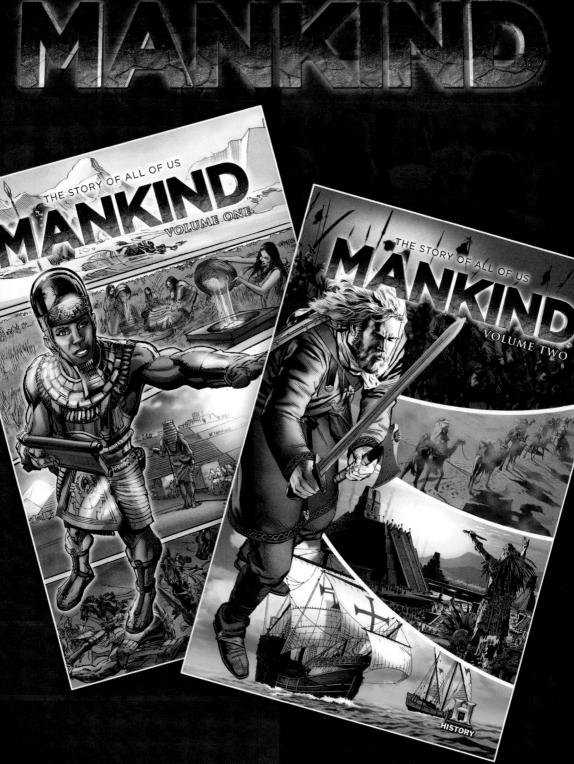

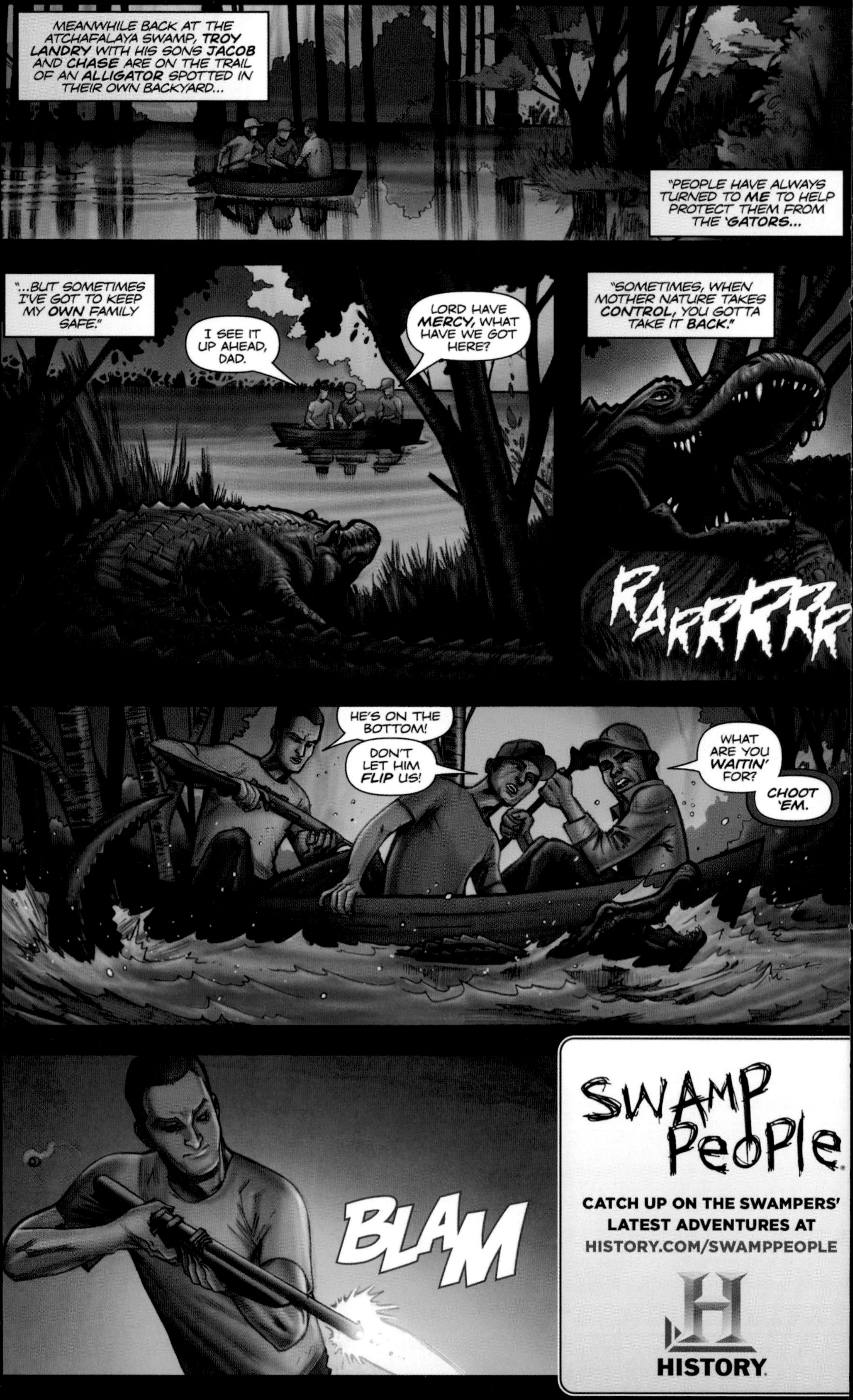
MEANWHILE BACK AT THE ATCHAFALAYA SWAMP, **TROY LANDRY** WITH HIS SONS **JACOB** AND **CHASE** ARE ON THE TRAIL OF AN **ALLIGATOR** SPOTTED IN THEIR OWN BACKYARD...
"PEOPLE HAVE ALWAYS TURNED TO **ME** TO HELP PROTECT THEM FROM THE 'GATORS...
"...BUT SOMETIMES I'VE GOT TO KEEP MY **OWN** FAMILY SAFE."
I SEE IT UP AHEAD, DAD.
LORD HAVE **MERCY,** WHAT HAVE WE GOT HERE?
"SOMETIMES, WHEN MOTHER NATURE TAKES **CONTROL,** YOU GOTTA TAKE IT **BACK.**"
RARRRRR
HE'S ON THE BOTTOM!
DON'T LET HIM **FLIP** US!
WHAT ARE YOU **WAITIN'** FOR?
CHOOT 'EM.
BLAM
SWAMP PEOPLE
CATCH UP ON THE SWAMPERS' LATEST ADVENTURES AT HISTORY.COM/SWAMPPEOPLE
HISTORY

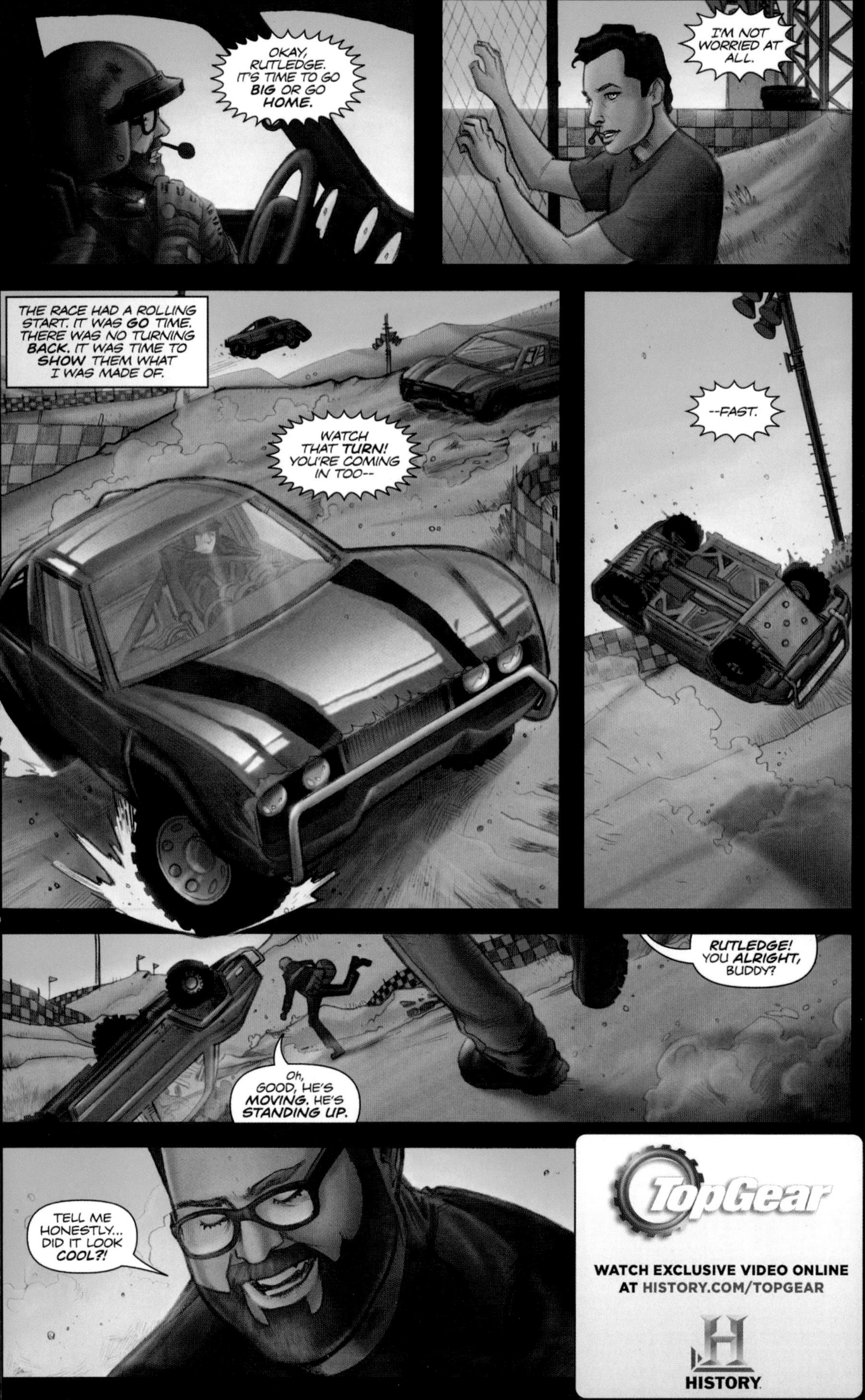
OKAY, RUTLEDGE. IT'S TIME TO GO BIG OR GO HOME.
I'M NOT WORRIED AT ALL.
THE RACE HAD A ROLLING START. IT WAS GO TIME. THERE WAS NO TURNING BACK. IT WAS TIME TO SHOW THEM WHAT I WAS MADE OF.
WATCH THAT TURN! YOU'RE COMING IN TOO--
--FAST.
RUTLEDGE! YOU ALRIGHT, BUDDY?
Oh, GOOD, HE'S MOVING. HE'S STANDING UP.
TELL ME HONESTLY... DID IT LOOK COOL?!

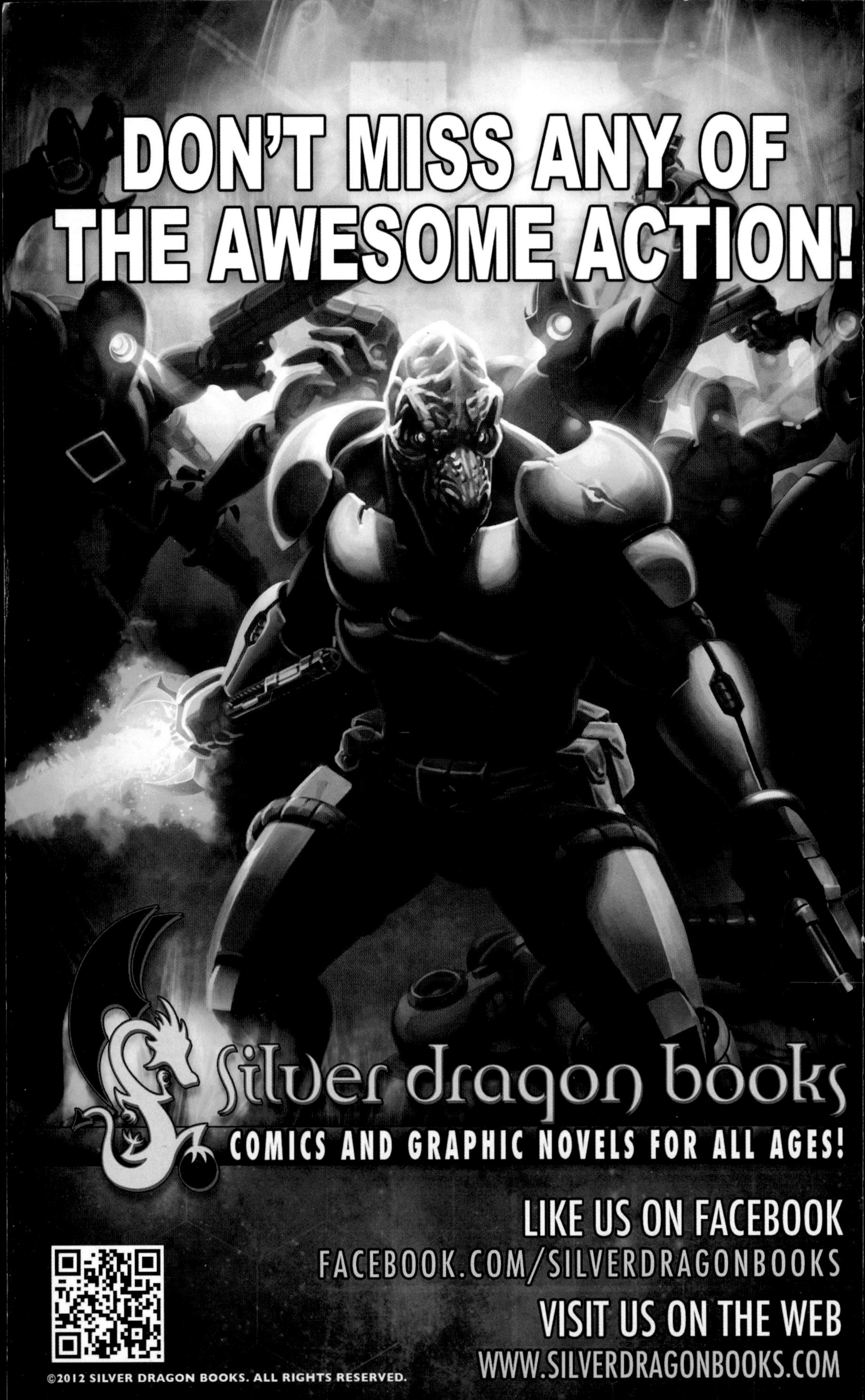
DON'T MISS ANY OF
THE AWESOME ACTION!
silver dragon books
COMICS AND GRAPHIC NOVELS FOR ALL AGES!
LIKE US ON FACEBOOK
FACEBOOK.COM/SILVERDRAGONBOOKS
VISIT US ON THE WEB
WWW.SILVERDRAGONBOOKS.COM